THE SUN

Frank F. Weber

THE SUN
Copyright © 2025 Frank F. Weber

Front and back cover photos:
Trisha Spencer of Xsperience Photography

Cover Art Graphics: Jill Kurtz Libby

All Rights Reserved
ISBN: 979-8-89660-801-1
EISBN: 979-8-89660-798-4

Published in partnership with BookBaby
7905 N. Crescent Blvd.
Pennsauken, NJ 08110
And

The Story Laboratory www.writeeditdesignlab.com
Published by Moon Finder Press
500 Park Avenue
P.O. Box 496, Pierz, MN 56364

THE SUN

This book is dedicated to my oldest son, Shane Weber. Brenda and I have known your incredible problem-solving abilities and tender-hearted empathy since you were young. You've turned out to be a compassionate yet strong man, loving husband, and great father—one of the most impressive people on earth!

I am so grateful for the opportunity to work with editor Emily Piller again. Emily understands and guides my work in a manner that challenges me to take my writing to another level. Thank you, Emily!

Thank you, Jennifer Brenny Lezer, for your cover model work. Jenny is so helpful to work with. Jon Frederick mystery buffs may remember Jenny from the cover of *Murder Book*. You were exactly the person needed to make this cover work: a tough, former Buckman gal who could handle the frigid Minnesota weather.

Trisha Spencer, Xperience Photography, once again, for your amazing photography work on another cover.

Chris Marcotte, thank you for the peer review and well-thought-out feedback on my work.

I want to give a special thanks to the Honorable Judge Jeffery Thompson for his work in the justice system and his insightful contributions to this novel.

This story was inspired by a true crime case.

Frank F. Weber, True Crime mysteries
(Jon Frederick series) include:

Murder Book (2017)

The I-94 Murders (2018)

Last Call (2019)

Lying Close (2020)

Burning Bridges (2021)

Black and Blue (2022)

The Haunted House of Hillman {H_2OH} (2023)

Scandal of Vandals (2024)

The Sun (2025)

Each chapter is written from the perspective
of the person listed at the top.

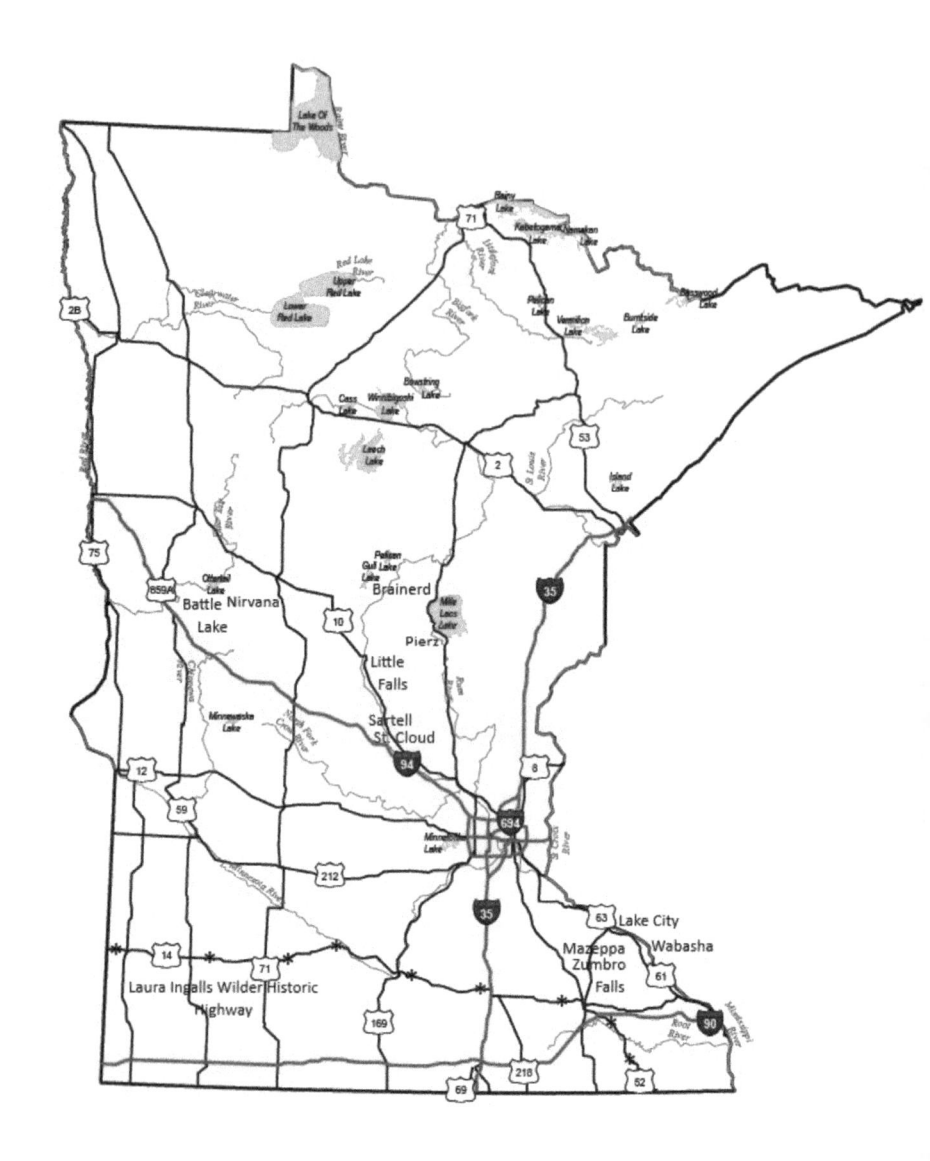

Minnesota Map

- Lake Of The Woods
- Rainy Lake
- Kabetogama Lake
- Namakan Lake
- Red Lake River
- Upper Red Lake
- Lower Red Lake
- Pelican Lake
- Vermilion Lake
- Burntside Lake
- Basswood Lake
- Bigfork River
- Bowstring Lake
- Cass Lake
- Winnibigoshish Lake
- Leech Lake
- St. Louis River
- Island Lake
- Pelican Lake
- Gull Lake
- Brainerd
- Otter Tail Lake
- Battle Nirvana Lake
- Mille Lacs Lake
- Pierz
- Little Falls
- Minnewaska Lake
- Sartell
- St. Cloud
- Minnetonka Lake
- Lake City
- Mazeppa
- Wabasha
- Zumbro Falls
- Laura Ingalls Wilder Historic Highway
- Mississippi River

Highways: 2B, 75, 71, 53, 2, 35, 10, 8, 94, 694, 12, 59, 212, 14, 71, 169, 35, 63, 61, 90, 69, 218, 52

MINNESOTA AND THE MINNEAPOLIS METRO AREA

CHARACTERS

Jon Frederick .... Bureau of Criminal Apprehension (BCA) Investigator and Profiler

Serena Frederick .... Private Investigator

Nora and Jackson ... Serena and Jon's children (ages 8 & 5 in 2024)

Taytum Hanson .... Attorney

Tug Grant .... Former Attorney and Convicted Murderer

Roan Caruso .... Entrepreneur, Convicted Murderer, and Spouse of Catania

Catania Turrisi .... Mafia Boss, Restaurateur, and Spouse of Roan

Lorenzo Turrisi Caruso .... Roan and Catania's Son

Eliana Castillo .... Single Mother and Lorenzo Turrisi Caruso's Partner

Heather Hilton .... Attorney

Clay Roberts .... Construction Worker

Agnes Schraut .... Irascible Octogenarian

Zave Williams .... Minneapolis Police Officer and Investigator

Terry Brink .... Concrete Truck Driver and Abstract Philosopher

Dr. Randy Kimball .... Professor of Sociology and Spouse of Juliet

Juliet Kimball .... Head of Security at Hennepin Healthcare and Spouse of Randy

Melanie Pearson ..... Business Analytics at Carlson Tower
Cade Anthony Bennett .... Melanie's first love at age 14
Sebastian .... Melanie's first live-in lover
Darius Country .... Melanie's fiancé

Ricky Day .... Pillsbury Employee and Convicted Killer

Michael Day .... Business Manager and Ricky and Halle's older brother.

Halle Day .... Therapist, Roan's daughter, Ricky and Michael's niece.

Daniel Nelson .... Assistant Dakota County Attorney

Dr. Fleure Duaire ... Professor at the University of Argosy

Enzo Angelini "The Wizard of Odds" .... Mafia

Nico Larmarte .... Mafia

The Assassin .... Mafia

"These violent delights have violent ends."
—WILLIAM SHAKESPEARE, *Romeo and Juliet*

Chapter 1

TUG GRANT

6:00 A.M., TUESDAY, NOVEMBER 15, 2021
MINNESOTA CORRECTIONAL FACILITY – LINO LAKES
7525 4TH AVENUE, LINO LAKES

The cells in each pod at Lino are dull brown concrete with blue metal doors. I shiver as I glance out the thin side window, waiting for the day to start. Everybody wears two layers because there's a chill that runs through this cellblock on a cold night that you can't shake. The common area has blue metal tables and chairs bolted to the floor. It would be impossible to make a seat less comfortable than the flat steel circles mounted too close to our tables.

I'm tempted to call the Innocence Project. Dick Doden murdered my wife, Deb Grant. Doden testified that my friend, Roan Caruso, hired him for the hit. And that's where the evidence ends. How the hell did I get convicted of murder-for-hire? Prosecutor Bridget Bare claimed the circumstantial evidence was overwhelming. But was it? Is taking out an insurance policy on your partner evidence of murder? Ten million dollars might have been a little excessive, but it's not enough to convict a man of murder. I had loaned Roan one hundred thousand dollars before Deb's murder. That loan and the insurance were all they had. It was all circumstantial. Roan never implicated me.

No direct evidence exists. Given the circumstance that I'd taken out an insurance policy on my wife, the inference was made that I was setting her up for murder. This is not a reasonable inference. The jury ignored that I'd loaned money to Roan multiple times, beginning years before Deb's murder, choosing again to infer that this circumstance was evidence of malice aforethought. Once I'm out of here, I'm going to contact the Reparations Board and demand a multimillion-dollar settlement. I will have the last laugh. This isn't about guilt or innocence. The game is played with evidence, and they didn't have enough to convict me. But until then, here I sit. This is my life, day after miserable day at the Minnesota Correctional Facility in Lino Lakes.

> 2:05 A.M. *Count. This means every prisoner must be accounted for, so they shine a light on me, and I always wake up.*
> 5:00 A.M. *Count.*
> 6:30 A.M. *Shift change. I'm awake again as the staff trample in and out.*
> 7:30 A.M. *Breakfast.*
> 8:00 A.M. *Programming. I help imbeciles work toward their GED with the understanding I'll get transferred to the work program.*
> 11:10 A.M. *Back in cell.*
> 11:20 A.M. *Count.*
> 12:30 P.M. *Lunch.*
> 1:00 P.M. *Yard time. Basically, walking in a circle.*
> 2:00 P.M. *Back to helping with classes. There are religious programs and programs for sex offenders, but I don't need that.*
> 2:30 P.M. *Count.*
> 5:30 P.M. *Supper.*
> 9:00 P.M. *Standing count. Everyone stands outside their cell.*
> 10:00 P.M. *Lights out.*
> 11:00 P.M. *Count.*

I need to get out of here. I'll never live through twenty more years of walking in circles and listening to idiots arguing. There's a TV in the general population area, but we never watch an entire show. Somebody always changes the channel right before the end and then taunts the crowd to see if anyone wants to fight him over it. No one wants to do thirty days in segregation, so the behavior goes unchallenged.

The guys here know I was a lawyer, so I'm constantly asked legal questions. I tell them I'll answer—as soon as I see some money deposited in my account. I'm not a fool. I do provide free legal advice for the shot-caller in here. Giving guidance to the most influential prisoner enables me to move about with complete protection.

Since I have a murder conviction, I'm in a "wet cell," meaning the toilet is inside my cell, and I get locked in after the standing count. Half the inmates have dry cells, so they use an out-of-cell restroom. It's a disgusting life, but I'm working on making it tolerable. I have two regular visitors: my son, Lincoln, who thinks I'm guilty, and my attorney/lover, Taytum, who thinks I'm innocent.

7:00 P.M.

TAYTUM SITS ACROSS the table from me, looking like a goddess with sapphire-blue eyes and flowing blond hair. When she opens her blazer, it's clear that she's braless beneath her white dress shirt.

"Thank you for that," I remark.

"The underwire sets off the metal detector. I didn't want to mess around with a search." Her eyes light up as she grins, "but I do put up with the search for my other clients."

"You've got to get me out of here, Taytum. I can't take the monotony. More importantly, it's torture to be without you."

"You need to be patient," she says. "This is a course that has to be carefully charted. We have minimal room for mistakes. We can't afford to waste your appeals on unwinnable arguments."

"What do you have?"

"I have feelers out, and I'm waiting to hear back. The judge followed procedure impeccably in anticipation of an appeal. Nothing tangible yet." Her positive demeanor gave way to concerns that she was a disappointment to me. Taytum offered, "I am spending every free minute on your case. My bed's full of court documents because I fall asleep every night while working on this case. I promise I'll find something." She leaned toward me. "You are mine. That won't change. Time apart from you only makes me want you more."

Her assurance provided some comfort. I needed her to stay strong. "How are you holding up?"

"I miss you. I had a disturbing nightmare last night. I was lying in my casket at my wake, observing people standing over me. Mom was angry at Dad—as if it were his fault. Dad was nonplussed. Jon and Serena Frederick seemed sad. They've always been nice to me. Roan and Catania Turrisi jeered me like maniacal clowns. I never liked them. I still don't know why you insist I defend Roan."

"Defending Roan will pay your bills while you establish a practice." I changed the subject back to her dream. "I assume there were lots of handsome men strolling by your body."

"A few," Taytum smirked, noting my envy. "None of them meant anything to me. What made the dream disturbing was that you weren't there. You'd already left me. When I awoke, I realized I was going to die alone."

"Not if I have any say in it." I don't mind her struggling without me, but I can't have her falling apart. She was a law student studying under me when I became enamored with her, and now I need her in a place of determined strength to take on the county attorney for me. It's in her nature. "Taytum, I'm going to tell you this once, and I need you to remember it. I love you. Not like the love chatter everyone else banters. Our love. Our way. The way we've shared our lives since we first met. Room to breathe. No upper limits. You're a superstar. We deserve each other."

"Thanks, Tug," she murmured. "I needed that." Then Taytum got down to business. She opened a binder with various sections tagged for easy information retrieval and began sharing her strategy.

My beautiful, blond Taytum remains loyal. If I ever get out of here, I should marry her. I won't, but I should. I had to meet with a psychologist, Katie Kissner, to get approved for the work crew. She believes I have a "Madonna-whore complex." While I want to be seen with a woman people put on a pedestal, I desire a sexual partner who has been degraded. The theory originated with Sigmund Freud, who wrote, "Where such men love, they have no desire, and where they desire, they cannot love." It's all bullshit.

In the end, everybody hates their lover, for your lover eventually has expectations that weren't in the initial agreement. I told Deb before we were married my goal was to be the greatest attorney ever. After we were married, she had suggestions for me every year. Being the greatest wasn't enough. When Taytum finally says, "I love you," I'll know we're at the beginning of the end. At that point, she becomes a disposable product. Lovers think that because they would do anything for you, you should do anything for them. When you think about it, it's quite self-centered. I don't fall into the trap. Sure, I'll say, "I love you." That doesn't cost me anything. Other than that, I remain vague, and they work their ass off trying to please me. I do need Taytum—for now.

(1 year later)
10:00 A.M., THURSDAY, DECEMBER 1, 2022
MINNESOTA CORRECTIONAL FACILITY – LINO LAKES
7525 4TH AVENUE, LINO LAKES

IT PAYS TO have friends with influence. My old pal Brent Parker and his wife, Blair, shared the story of my frame-up with a sociology professor at Argosy University, Dr. Randy Kimball.

The professor and I have exchanged letters, and Dr. Kimball has offered to write a book about me. Appealing to his work on corruption in bureaucracies, I suggested that my conviction was part of a government conspiracy. Dr. Kimball was now at the prison, waiting to visit me.

After being patted down, I was escorted in my orange jumpsuit through a series of locked doors. The visiting room resembles a school lunchroom, with prisoners on one side of the table talking to guests on the other.

Doc was easy to spot in his outdated tweed suit jacket, light blue shirt, and brown tie. I hoped his writing wasn't as dull as his fashion sense. He was clean-shaven, had thick, home-cut brown hair, and was in good shape. I imagined he jogged every morning and worked out at the gym. Randy reminded me of the uber-Christians I'd see when Deb would drag me to church. Randy and I weren't allowed to shake hands, so we awkwardly nodded and sat across from each other at the cafeteria-style table.

I started the conversation by massaging his ego. "I read your article, 'Government Use of Precarity in Subjugation.' The proposal that politicians take advantage of uncertainty to keep people under their thumb is genius." Honestly, I thought his use of the words *precarity* and *subjugation* were haughty and arrogant, but I needed this guy. I let him preen for a moment, then got down to business. "Okay, here's the deal." I had decided to go all the way with this, but I knew there had to be some truth to the story since Doc would be checking. "Roan Caruso steered government contracts in certain directions for kickbacks. They had Roan dead to rights on the murder of Deondre Johnson, and they had planned on using that conviction to get Roan to give up the names of his inside sources. But I got Roan's charges dropped on a technicality, and they lost their leverage."

"Your conviction was truly an abomination," Dr. Kimball proclaimed. "I didn't believe the Parkers when they first told me about you being railroaded, but everything I've researched supports it. People who saw you on vacation with Debra all say you doted on her. I've read through the court transcripts, and there was no evidence that you hired Roan to kill your wife. None. Your attorney ended the hearing with that very statement."

I love that court transcripts only include what was said. Taytum told me that the tone in which I addressed my former mistress, Melanie Pearson, along with grabbing Taytum's leg and kissing her cheek in court, are what got me convicted. None of that is in the court transcripts. "Doc, I—"

"Call me Randy," he insisted. "I just can't comprehend why you got steamrolled by the Attorney General. Perhaps it would be prudent to start with this. Why did you get Caruso out of a murder charge?"

I looked around the cafeteria as I considered my answer. Pretending I was making sure no one was listening, I quietly said, "Okay—the gun was planted. I believe in justice for all." I hung my head in penitence. "I had been a sinner, engaging in adulterous transgressions, but I had turned over a new leaf and given my life to God. I took Deb on the vacations she deserved and committed to my family. Like a phoenix, I rose from the ashes—strong and virtuous. That changed everything. When I was a sinner, the Feds had fodder for blackmail. After I repented, they had nothing and needed to ice me. I know too much about too many important people. So, that's exactly what they did. With my conviction, no one listens. It's just the rant of a crazy psychopath."

Randy's eyebrows furrowed, and I worried that I had embellished a little too much, so I added, "I had the perfect marriage. The perfect family. I had no motive."

"Ten million dollars," he muttered.

"I respect Ben Franklin, who once said, 'The more a man has, the more he wants. Instead of money filling a void, it makes one.'" I most admired Franklin for dismissing his sentiment and accumulating a great deal of wealth, more than three and a half million in today's dollars. I plan on doing better. In addition, the man was notoriously unfaithful yet highly respected—a man to emulate. There were dead bodies discovered in Franklin's basement, which people assume were cadavers he purchased illegally to study anatomy.

After considering my professed indifference to money, the Doc said reverently, "'All of the things that make us happy—money, health, love—are finite.' Immanuel Kant." The Doc rambled on, "Jesus was crucified. Muhammad died from being poisoned. If Minnesota had a death penalty, they would have put you to death. Instead, they gave you life."

"I can't think of a more perfect analogy," I acknowledged. "If you could post something about my wrongful conviction online, someone would eventually come forward with evidence." If I had to pay someone to make a statement, I would. "You must have students interested in justice. Perhaps they could help get the word out."

"Absolutely. I will address this with my classes."

I grinned at my successful manipulation. The internet is perfect for creating a groundswell of support for my release, and Dr. Randy Kimball will serve as my frontman. After Doc makes a post, people will chat about it, and within a week, my innocence will be accepted as fact. I'll have Taytum create a site where people can donate to my defense. The first step to my release is completed. When it's all said and done, I'll sue the State for false imprisonment.

(5 weeks later)
8:00 A.M.
WEDNESDAY, JANUARY 4, 2023

DR. RANDY KIMBALL is off and running, preaching the conspiracy of my conviction online. My wisdom has enabled me to develop a profitable gig here. The Institution Community Work

Crew program (ICWC) is understaffed, so I offered to take on the scheduling. They eagerly handed over the task, and after we lost a guard to an injury, I was placed in charge of a crew in the community. For the first time, the facility had no complaints of the crew sneaking in contraband or being underpaid, and it didn't cost the prison a cent.

In appreciation, the Department of Corrections allowed me to select a new roommate. I got rid of the angry guy who beat his wife half to death and replaced him with Dr. Ashton Heaps. I'm not sure that Heaps is any better, as he obsessively talks about his former medical practice. Dr. Heaps is serving four years for sexually abusing a client under anesthesia.

Heaps paced in front of me while I lay on the top bunk, considering his request to join my work crew. His thin face looked like it had been squished in a book. I finally interrupted him. "How many times did you get away with it before you were caught?"

"Why would you ask that?" he smirked.

"Buddy, if you want on my crew, you've got to give me the story. It's boring as hell in here."

Heaps looked out the cell door to ensure no one was listening, then turned back. "Only a couple of times at work. Did it to women on dates four times. I found the perfect anesthetic, used only rarely in surgeries. It knocks the person out for about an hour, but during this time, the doctor can ask the patient to engage in physical movement and they comply. And the patient has no memory of it."

"How did you get caught?" I wondered.

"I took some home, and a nurse noticed the missing doses. She walked in on me at work, snapped a photo on her phone, and called the police." He shrugged. "Okay, I told you, now do I get on the crew?"

"No." I sat up. "I want the drug."

"You can't sneak that drug in as contraband. If we're caught, we'd both be looking at another twenty years." Heaps's beady eyes studied me. "I've heard about the hustle you're running. I want to be a customer. I've got money."

"I'm not using the drug in here," I laughed.

"I'll give you the name of it if you get me on your crew," Heaps offered.

"Not good enough. The name's worthless if I have no access to it." I scratched my chin. "I want the drug."

"What makes you think I still have some?"

"I know what people are saying based on what they're *not* saying. You didn't say, 'I'm out.' You said you wouldn't sneak it in here." I smiled.

"I have four doses left," Heaps admitted. "But how does that help you? You're stuck here for decades."

"I have an appeal pending that my attorney says I'm going to win. If you get me those doses, I'll get you on the work crew today."

"You can pick them up today, but you have to agree that this covers my first payment for being on the crew," Heaps's grin now covered the width of his face. "They're hidden in the back of a vintage Hamm's beer sign in my ex-wife's basement. I'll call her and tell her I sold it to you. Here's a tip: Put Valium in the woman's purse. The anesthetic isn't Valium, but it looks like it on the drug tests. If she makes an accusation, it gives you an out."

1:30 P.M.

I DIDN'T ANTICIPATE needing the drug, but I could see its potential. I've had sleepless nights agonizing over my former lover, Melanie Pearson, testifying against me. I will humiliate that bitch once I'm released, even if I have to drug her to do so. After Heaps and I made our phone calls, Taytum was on her way to pick up a Hamm's beer sign for me. Life was starting to look up. I've proven to be a responsible supervisor, and I even have an office now. It's a crappy cement room in the basement of the Plymouth Ice Arena with no windows, but an office, nonetheless. I let the guard who comes with us sleep in it while I take care of business. When he does his rounds, I bring the crew in half at a time to enjoy a hooch toast.

As I prepared for another day's work, an officer entered our cell and fitted us both with ankle monitors. None of us can leave the Ice Center without setting off the monitor. This is fine. I have no intention of running. Escapees never get far, and they get another decade added to their sentence.

2:15 P.M.,

PLYMOUTH ICE CENTER,

3650 PLYMOUTH BOULEVARD, PLYMOUTH

ONCE MY OVERINFLATED guard was comfortable sitting back in my office chair, he told me, "I don't know what you've done to get this crew calmed down, but it's nice that they show up on time without bitching now. And everyone's in a good mood when they go home."

"Just got to treat people with respect."

"Yeah, I doubt it," he scoffed. "Maybe I don't want to know. Wake me in an hour."

Because of staff shortages, the guards were working extra shifts. It was a dangerous job, and he appreciated that I gave him the opportunity for a safe catnap. I headed upstairs to the women's restroom.

I stepped inside the cement-floored room and glanced under the stalls. I smiled when I observed a pair of shapely legs in a green work uniform. "Porsha, this is Cottontop."

The stall door opened, and inside, a pale, bony woman slipped out of the forest-green uniform she had used to enter the building. She tossed her matching green baseball cap to the floor and let her tucked-up pink hair fall. Her caked-on makeup probably covered meth sores, but as a result of her artistry, I didn't have to think about it. She stripped down to black lingerie. It was time to wear that painted glossy red lipstick off her collagen-inflated lips. This girl had no idea what was coming down the pike, but for now, she was exactly what I needed.

"Lose the bra," I directed. I joined her in the stall and let my navy jumpsuit drop over my shoulders. I slid it down to my ankles and said, "Get on your knees and get to work."

It was almost worth coming to prison to pull off this gig. Porsha enters the ice arena with a vendor's card and heads to a restroom no one uses. She services me for free since I am the puppet master, and then she services my cleaning crew one by one. She's paid ahead of time by contacts the men have on the outside, so no money is exchanged here. The money has already been mailed to Taytum. I've told Taytum that people are donating to my defense fund, which, in a way, is true.

Porscha bit her bottom lip and, trying to be cute, asked, "Do you want me to talk dirty?"

"If I was interested in what you had to say, do you think you'd be in this position?" I grabbed Porsha by the hair and worked her head like I was shaking a tambourine. As my breathing became shallow, I said, "Just do what you're good at, hon."

Chapter 2

JON FREDERICK

1:15 P.M., WEDNESDAY, JANUARY 4, 2023
1430 MARYLAND AVENUE EAST, ST. PAUL

Bureau of Criminal Apprehension Investigator Paula Fineday asked to meet at the BCA headquarters in St. Paul. Paula was a strong, solid woman with dark hair and Native American features who had worked the Last Call case with me. Paula glanced at me and commented, "Still lean and clean, huh? I can't do it. Too much stress-snacking."

Maintaining healthy strength was essential when my investigative work put my life on the line. I obsessively maintained a routine of working out three days a week before my family was awake so I wouldn't lose time with Serena and the kids.

Paula escorted me to the conference room and sat in front of a pile of file folders that were so disorganized that it would be difficult to say where they started or ended. Paula pushed the top of the pile aside and laughed at the look I gave her mess. "Say what you're thinking, Jon Frederick."

"You carried in a large pile of cases looking for a connection. After not finding a link in the first few, you started randomly pulling cases, and eventually, it turned into this." I gestured at the folders.

"This is why I want you to work the case with me." She placed her hand on the small mountain. "It's files of missing Indigenous women. It would be easier if it were one killer. It's disturbing to consider that so many different people hurt these women. What does that say about our society? I shudder at the generational impact Native American federal boarding schools still have on our people."

"We have to create programs that effectively help the poor and not just throw money at communities and schools. I want accountability. No taxation without representation."

"Are you going to start throwing tea into Lake Mille Lacs?" Paula teased.

"It would have to be double matcha green tea. That's Serena's 'cup of tea,' so it's all we have at home."

"I know you like working rural Minnesota, but I've got an investigation in the metro you're going to want in on."

"You have my curiosity." I fought the urge to straighten the avalanche of files in front of me.

"I picked up Steel Nickaboine on the rez for a drug violation last week." Paula continued, "I asked him to give me a reason to send him to treatment instead of prison. Steel was on Tug Grant's cellblock in Lino. Steel reported that Tug is running a prostitution ring through the prison work crew. Steel couldn't afford to participate, but he knew guys who did. Tug and the crew are at the Ice Center today. Any desire to pay him a visit?"

I stood. "Let's go."

2:30 P.M.

PLYMOUTH ICE CENTER, 3650 PLYMOUTH BOULEVARD, PLYMOUTH

AFTER WE WERE informed Tug had been given an office at the Plymouth Ice Center, I got the key from the arena manager and asked him to find Tug on the security cameras. He agreed to call as soon as he had Tug's location. Paula and I rushed to the basement. I put the key in Tug's office door. Paula and I nodded in unison, and we swung it open.

An overweight corrections officer slumbered, head down on the desk. I slapped the door to wake him, and he stumbled to his feet. Paula flashed her shield and commanded, "Please step outside while we have a look."

"I need to go check on the crew," he said.

"Not just yet. Wait outside," Paula instructed.

A box of 32-ounce bottles of Scope mouthwash was sitting in the corner. It rested on a box of 32-ounce bottles of Ocean Spray grapefruit juice. I opened one of the bottles and told Paula, "They're sealed. Want a taste? I'm betting this is food-colored alcohol. Look at the bottles. They're close to Scope green, but none are exactly the same shade."

Paula opened a bottle and took a sip. "Vodka. How did they get them all sealed?"

"Have you been to a taproom?"

"Hair dryers and plastic seals." Paula nodded. She pointed to the pink Ocean Spray bottles. "Your turn. I hope it's one of those puke-bait super sweet drinks like a Cosmo or Sex on the Beach."

I opened one Ocean Spray bottle. The factory seal appeared intact, so I thought I'd chance it. I sniffed and took a sip. "Grapefruit juice." Tug had the mixings for a Greyhound, one of the most popular vodka drinks.

"Imagine what that dyed green vodka looks like mixed with pink juice," Paula commented.

"It's still a big improvement over the hooch they make out of ketchup and barbecue packets." Everything's relative.

Paula searched the room while I knelt and looked at the underside of the desk. The night before Tug's conviction, a laptop was found in a compartment beneath the middle drawer of his desk. People repeat patterns of hiding places. *And there it was.* This time, instead of a laptop, a Beretta Pico handgun was taped under his desk. I stood up and said, "Look at this." I emptied bullets from the gun. The Beretta Pico was less than an inch in width and was considered one of the easiest handguns to conceal.

When we left the office, Paula told the guard, "You need to take a breathalyzer for me."

Insulted, the guard said, "I don't drink on the job."

"Then the test is to your advantage," Paula assured him. "Did you know those bottles of Scope are full of vodka?"

"That son of a bitch," he swore.

"There was a loaded gun hidden in the office," I added.

"I had nothin' to do with any of that." He threw his hands in the air. "I just bring the crew over to clean and bring them back. I've never brought anything in."

I believed him. I could see Tug having all this delivered. I needed to find him. I called the arena manager. "Where's Tug Grant?"

"He's cleaning the women's bathroom on the second floor. Do you want me to get him?"

"No, I'd like to pay him a surprise visit." I quickly raced up the steps.

A yellow plastic stand that read "Closed for Cleaning" stood in the women's bathroom entry.

I stepped around the sign to see Tug pulling his jumpsuit on. A pale white woman with pink hair was bare-chested and on her knees in front of him in the open stall.

Surprised, Tug glared at me. "I found her in here when I came to clean. I told her she needed to get out of here; we've got a crew coming through."

"Step outside. Your community release days are over." As the informant suggested, Tug was bringing in sex workers, and I had just caught him with his pants down.

"I didn't do anything wrong. Think about it. I'm standing in a bathroom stall, like men do." Once he realized I wasn't going to waste my breath arguing with him, Tug challenged me, "Don't think this is over. My stay here is only temporary."

"That's true for everyone on earth," I gibed. I had no desire to argue with him.

"It's a bullshit conviction!" Tug continued, "They had nothing tying me to the murder."

"Then you must not be much of an attorney."

"Fucking ass!" Tug responded.

"Not true. I guess it's a matter of preference."

Paula entered the bathroom and, having heard my remark, laughed. She asked, "Do you want me to take Tug?"

"Please do," I said.

Tug was marched away, face red with fury.

The sex worker dressed.

I told her, "If you cooperate, you might walk out of here without charges. I need to know how the whole scheme works."

Chapter 3

JON FREDERICK

6:30 P.M., MONDAY, FEBRUARY 6, 2023
CIAO THYME 113 1ST STREET SOUTHEAST, LITTLE FALLS

Taytum Hanson called me to meet her at Ciao Thyme in Little Falls. This restaurant features the talents of chef extraordinaire Scotty Stocco and is one of my favorite places to eat. I ordered the Lenten special, which was three pounds of crab, and Taytum went with the Mushroom and Fennel Pappardelle—fresh mushrooms over pasta in a light cream sauce.

Taytum was Tug Grant's former legal assistant and was now his attorney. Tug was convicted only four years ago, but Taytum appeared to have matured a decade. Gone were the pulled-back hair and feigned coquettishness. She had let her blond hair grow out and was wearing faded jeans, presenting with casual confidence. Taytum was no longer Tug's sidekick; she was a force to be reckoned with. Tug Grant had been the head of the State Bar Association when he had been convicted of hiring a hitman to kill his wife. Taytum, his faithful mistress, was searching for grounds to appeal his case. There was no evidence presented in the original hearing that directly connected Tug to the murder. I not only believed Taytum *could* get his conviction overturned, but I believed she eventually would. We hear about innocent people who have been convicted but never see stories about the guilty people who got away with murder. Every experienced investigator and law enforcement officer has a tale.

In an open black leather blazer, partially covering a black V-neck T, Taytum leaned slightly forward and said, "Tug wanted you to be the first to know that we've got a prosecutorial error that will get him a retrial. You suggested that with Tug and Prosecutor Bridget Bare's hostile relationship, it wouldn't surprise you if the prosecutor held back evidence. It turned out she did." Sitting with perfect posture, Taytum said with satisfaction, "Dick Doden recanted his statement after Roan Caruso had him beat down in jail. The prosecutor convinced Doden to go back to his original story, and he did. Failure to disclose that Doden recanted was a clear Brady violation, which will warrant a new trial. This is a winnable case. Tug will be smart enough to stay off the stand this time. His ego was what got him convicted. I love Tug, but we both know how he gets." Bothered by her declaration, she added, "I'm smart enough never to tell Tug I love him. That would be a victory for Tug, and when he wins, it's on to the next game."

Instead of frantically using up Tug's appeals, Taytum wisely avoided asking for the review until she had a winnable argument.

Taytum continued in a matter-of-fact tone, "Tug wanted me to tell you that he walked on the prostitution charges. He hadn't paid her any money."

I inwardly smiled at Tug's narcissism. While I had moved on and worked the Haunted House of Hillman case, Tug was convinced I was sitting back and gloating about his conviction. He didn't quite get it: Tug wasn't that important to me. There's always another slimeball to investigate. I was more interested in the arrival of my meal. My mushroom soup had the savory flavor of beef stroganoff, and my pile of crab presented a wonderful challenge.

"Tug was just being Tug." Taytum smiled. "We both know what was going on. Tug's too smart to leave a money trail, so there isn't a way to prosecute him. If it's any consolation, he was sent to segregation for the possession of alcohol and a gun, although he never admitted either was his. He lost the privilege to leave the prison, which is driving him crazy."

"Well, at least I accomplished that." I felt the need to warn her, "Getting him released may be the death of you. Tug always seems to be destroying a lover. Do you really want to be next?"

Taytum leaned uncomfortably close and seductively said, "Jon Frederick is worried about me."

"Tug is dangerous. He had Deb murdered."

"I know that's what you and his son believe." Taytum retreated from my personal space as she continued, "Lincoln told me, 'Don't put anything in your name that Tug can cash in on.' But honestly, I don't believe Tug killed Deb, even if he told Serena he did. You know how Tug is. If you accuse him of something absurd enough, he will eventually start saying, 'Yeah, I did it.'"

"Serena believes Tug works the word 'okay' into the sentence when he's lying."

Taytum reflected and said in disbelief, "At the moment, I'm drawing a blank. I remember the gist of our conversations but not the words. I have to believe Tug would be smarter than that."

"It's not intentional. It's a tell." I switched topics. "Did Brent Parker ever find Liam Davis?" Tug claimed that a prisoner named Liam Davis would prove his innocence, and Tug's friend Brent had taken on the mission of finding the prisoner.

"No. Brent even flew to the ADX Florence federal prison in Colorado to see if Liam Davis was there."

Colorado is home to the "supermax" United States Penitentiary, Administrative Maximum Facility, otherwise known as USP Florence ADMAX. It is the largest federal prison in the US.

Taytum continued, "ADMAX claimed they never had a Liam Davis. Brent told me this is exactly what they would say if this were all a big cover-up."

"It's also exactly what they would say if there was no Liam Davis and the whole thing was just a bullshit story Tug made up," I pointed out.

"I never put too much stock in that story. The first I heard of it was when Tug proposed it to you in the courtroom." Taytum flashed her perfect teeth as she grinned. "Give me a taste of your profiling talents. Who is your run-of-the-mill mentally ill person most likely to kill?"

"I don't know that there is a run-of-the-mill mental illness. I would want to know as much as I could about the person. I can tell you that a schizophrenic man is most likely to kill his mother because she is the one who stays close no matter how bad it gets. Bipolar individuals are most likely to kill their parents because they set limits. A depressed and suicidal mother is most likely to murder her children, as she worries about their well-being and feels they are better off with her in death. Being both mentally ill and a substance abuser increases the risk of violence ten times. Did you have a specific mental illness in mind?"

"No. I'm impressed. You know your stuff." Taytum gave me a once-over and shifted gears. "So, what drives Jon Frederick?"

"I enjoy the challenge of an investigation, but Serena and the kids give my life the greatest satisfaction. Simple man, simple dreams."

"We're not that different. I love the challenge of the law, but I also enjoy showcasing
my cleverness to Tug. There's an element of impressing Serena that drives you, too."

"A better question is, why does a young, successful woman wait around for a philandering man who's been convicted of murder?" I asked.

"I'm well aware of my assets and the potential benefits. It's why I take care of my mind and body. When I was a child, I'd drag my mattress into the closet to sleep, hoping a stranger wouldn't find me. Dad was always working late, and Mom dumped her anxiety on me. I finally got tired of being scared and said, 'Enough.' I told my parents, 'Deal with your shit, and I'll make my own life.' Now, I aggressively go after what I want and live without regrets."

"Now you're the one breaking into homes," I remarked.

"Cheap shot," she said with a devilish smirk. "When a successful man bestows his mistress with lavish gifts, who's the fool? Tug never hungered for conversation with Deb or Melanie as he did with me. Deb was his housemaid, and conversations with Melanie had as much significance as the clang of a cowbell. I was never envious of either of them. I never wanted to be the car he drove to work every day. I was the one he cherished and took out on special occasions."

My profiling brain went to work. "As a child, you admired a parent who was both successful and unfaithful."

"You're good." Taytum grinned. "Dad was a plastic surgeon. He was the very best, but he had lovers. Quid pro quo was alive and well in his circle. Mom suffered from his infidelity but stayed because she loved the money. If a man gets on my nerves, I walk. I make no commitments. I'm not responsible for the morality of the men who pursue me."

I accepted her explanation to a degree.

Sensing my doubt, she said, "Honestly, I've become more attracted to Tug than I ever planned. He's my guilty pleasure." Taytum pointed to a statue called Crouching Venus across the street in the window at The Shoppes of Little Falls.

The original Crouching Venus statue was completed two hundred years before the birth of Jesus by a Greek artist named Daedalsas. It depicts a naked and surprised Aphrodite, after leaving the bath, covering her body and looking back at an intruder.

Taytum continued, "Aphrodite was sculpted as a normally proportioned naked woman, and nobody thinks of it as pornography. You type in nudity now, and all you see is pervs displaying porn of women with silicone-inflated boobs engaging in demeaning behavior."

"And we've responded by creating unrealistic body images of men, too. That is why superheroes need body suits that portray unrealistic abs and pecs now, right?"

"And we call that progress," Taytum laughed. "I understand men. When you see Serena lying naked, what do you think?"

Feeling the question was too personal, I didn't respond. Instead, I cracked crab legs and ate.

She laughed and answered her own question. "You're thinking, 'I just won the lottery,' She's thinking, 'My legs are too fat.' People might think I'm the problem, but I'm the solution. Be comfortable with yourself." She leaned back. "I'm not hitting on you, Jon. I would never want to interfere with that quirky roleplay thing you and Serena have going. If the stories are true, it's too entertaining to obstruct. I'd love to be there sometime to witness it. You're a good investigator. Fair and not judgmental. I'm just delivering Tug's message. I know he doesn't want to work with you again, but I want you to know you're good with me."

"Thank you."

"Prosecutor Bridget's going to want to deal because Tug will be acquitted," Taytum revealed. "It's my preference to take it to trial and let Tug start over with a clean slate."

8:00 P.M.

PIERZ

HEAVY FOG HAD saturated the winter darkness, so I leaned forward and gripped the steering wheel tight as I drove home. The tension in my eyes was finally relieved when I found my driveway and approached the warm lighting of my rural home. A powerful storm was moving in tomorrow, starting with freezing rain and ending with drifting snow. Honestly, I didn't mind the storm now that I was home. I looked forward to hunkering down with Serena and our kids, Nora and Jackson, for a couple of days.

An orange glow from the fireplace lit the living room. Shadows from the flames danced on the ceiling, and the house was eerily quiet. Our five-year-old, Jackson, was constructing a tower of blocks on the kitchen floor. I kissed Jackson on the top of the head. "Great work, my man."

"Thump-thump. Thump-thump, Thump-thump," reverberated from the basement.

Serena was standing at the counter in her cream-colored night shirt, cutting up apples for a bedtime snack. Her long brunette curls hung over her shoulders, and she smiled as she said, "Now that you're home, I can finally relax."

Noticing white gauze wrapped around her hand, I asked, "Are you okay?"

"Yeah, just tired and got a little careless." She stepped into me and kissed me. The warmth of her full lips was inviting, and her emerald-green eyes allowed me to abandon all thoughts of work.

""Thump-thump. Thump-thump, Thump-thump," continued. "What is that?"

"Not sure." Serena shrugged. "Would you mind checking? Nora's down there."

My brain went to the worst-case scenario. Fearing Nora was trapped under something, I raced downstairs. I found our eight-year-old daughter throwing a tennis ball into the corner, ricocheting it directly back to herself. Nora casually told me, "It's too cold to throw outside." She wanted to be the next Pierz girls' softball star, following in the footsteps of talented athletes such as Britney Schommer, Maddie Gaffke, Lizzie Gross, and the Sadlovsky sisters.

"This is math." I sat by her, "You figured out the perfect angle to bring the ball back to you. Let's see if you can angle it to me."

It took several tries but soon we were bouncing the ball back and forth. It wasn't long before Jackson joined us.

When I brought the kids upstairs, Serena had their snack waiting. Now relaxed, I took in her beauty. Her shapely body, comfortably covered with a nightshirt, was alluring. She teased, "Barefoot in the kitchen. Not pregnant but injured."

"Walking in this door is the highlight of my day. Time for

you to grab a glass of wine and chill." Serena kissed me and dug out a bottle of cabernet from the kitchen cupboard.

Not wanting her to experience any further pain in her injured hand, I uncorked the bottle for her. She snuggled into me, and we embraced. We fit together so perfectly. At that moment, my life couldn't have been any better.

AFTER OUR DYNAMIC duo was tucked into bed, I came downstairs in a T-shirt and boxers to find Serena sitting on the living room floor, paging through old yearbooks. She turned to me. "I'm going to find her." Serena was a private investigator and helped me with my investigations. We finished our work on the Haunted House of Hillman case last May, and she was having a hard time letting go of the fact that there was one unidentified victim. The rapist kept jewelry as trophies, so we knew this victim wore a gold necklace with a sideways cross on it. It was a common way many women in the Pierz area wore the cross, and most of the names in the file were women who lived in the area. The necklace wasn't in a sealed container, so there was no usable DNA on it. The rapist had recently hinted to a corrections officer that the unidentified victim's name was in the case file.

"You're solving this tonight?" I wondered. I wasn't in the mood for any more work. But Serena's desire for adventure is no less than mine. *Why should she be denied the opportunity to investigate?* I added, "If you do, it's okay. I'm opening an ice-cold Jack Pine Cream Ale and relaxing in front of the fire." I called Serena twenty minutes ago and had her put the lager in the freezer for me.

"I'll be joining you in a second," she said. "Names keep running through my head. Lauren Harold helped me interview people, so she's in the Haunted case file. I hope it isn't her." As Serena turned pages, she casually said, "It bothers me when you have dinner with a woman like Taytum."

"No worries. I love you. You're stuck with me."

"No worries about your spending time with a buxom blonde model who had an affair with a married man? Love is all about worry."

"I don't think about any woman but you. I agree that love involves worrying about someone, but I can't say all worry is productive. I worry that work takes me away from you so often. I never want to lose you."

She paused and studied me. "You don't act jealous."

"That doesn't mean I'm not. I try to act like the man I want to be. I can only control the choices I make, so I try to behave like a decent person. It doesn't mean I always think like one. Why do you think I rub your feet at night?"

"Because you're a kind, loving, amazing man."

"Let's go with that."

"I will." She picked up her glass of wine and joined me on the couch. With the back of her hand, she lovingly brushed my cheek. "Tell me."

"How often does rubbing your feet lead to sex?"

"Almost never," she responded curiously. "If that's your goal, it's the wrong thing. Getting my legs rubbed doesn't arouse me; it completely relaxes me."

"My intent is to relax you. I want you to be able to trust your body with me. I will do what you desire, with no ulterior motive, because I love you. Physical contact with you brings me peace."

"Do you think we'd have sex as often if you didn't rub my feet?" Serena asked.

"I don't. It's a way for me to express my love for you. I'm not as good with words as you are."

"I don't know if that's true." She grinned.

My inability to come up with a response supported my theory. Feeling a need to say something, I shared what came to mind. "In physics, I participated in competitions involving non-destructive testing of model bridges. Weights were placed on the bridges to see how much they could hold before breaking. Once it broke, I adjusted the structure so it would never have the same weakness again. Every new bridge was stronger."

"Did you ever have one that didn't break?"

"This marriage." I grinned.

Serena's soft lips kissed me once again. "I think there should be a reward for your commitment to working close to home as often as possible."

"You are rather behavioral." As the words left my mouth, I wanted to pull them back. I was offered passionate bliss, but instead, I extended the conversation.

"What's that supposed to mean?"

"Remember when you were getting on me for having too many empty hangers in my section of the closet? You said, 'New rule. If there are more than eight empty hangers in the closet, we're not having sex.'"

"Did I ever follow through with that?" She blushed.

"There haven't been eight empty hangers in the closet since."

"Okay, maybe that was a little operant," Serena laughed.

A little? This time, I wisely kept my mouth shut. That thought was soon a wisp of air that vanished in the cold winter morning while her warmth exuded gratifying pleasure.

"Sorry," she offered.

Her simple response got me thinking about my mother, Camille. Mom died of a massive stroke four years ago. As incredibly kind as she was, I don't remember her ever apologizing. She was very much into living in the moment and letting go of the past.

"So, what's the next step with Tug Grant?"

"I'll call the prosecutor and ask her to retry Tug. I'm not sure I'll have any success. She's been all about settling cases recently."

"Bridget's got a lot on her plate with the surge in shootings and carjackings in Minneapolis," Serena suggested. "Settling cases saves her time."

"It irritates me that Tug got by with running a sex trafficking scheme in prison. I picture that pale woman I saw him with and am pained knowing Tug made money by having her raped by eight inmates."

"And beat up by a pimp if she didn't comply," Serena added. "Probably still beat up, even if she did. What happened to her?"

"I had her placed in detox. I'm not sure what became of her. The Office of Special Investigations stepped in since they investigate prison crimes, even though the Hennepin County Attorney argued they should have jurisdiction since the crime occurred in the community. I moved on to the Hillman case and lost track. I never had her real name, so there's no way for me even to check. Enough about work." I leaned back. "I was also thinking, I wish I would have thanked Mom more."

"She knew you loved her. You used to tell her she was your hero. I'd love to hear one of our kids say that to me someday. But I can be satisfied just *not* being told I ruined their life. I remember you sharing that you and Camille used to sit up late on Friday nights watching old movies together. I picture you as a little boy snuggled up to her."

"Wrong picture. There was no snuggling. Remember, we didn't hug until you became part of our family. We would each sit at our end of the couch. Mom would tell me if I started to nod off, 'Sit on a hard chair. That will keep you awake.'"

"Because it feels so much better to be uncomfortable and dead tired than to sleep," Serena laughed.

"The movies were Mom's escape, and she didn't want me to be denied the entire story. It was all right. Not as good as lying with you and watching a show, but her heart was in the right place."

"And this is why you always fall asleep with me. You can finally relax. Where was the rest of the family on those Friday nights?"

"Dad was in either the house or the barn fixing something. Theresa was somewhere she wasn't supposed to be, and Vic was in the woods, skipping the light fandango."

"Light fandango?"

"Spanish phrase for carefree dancing."

"Well, Camille was proud of the man, husband, and father you've become. Your mom and I were so different; I'm surprised you fell for me."

"I'm not a fan of Freud's Oedipus theory. I never wanted to be with someone like Mom. There are a hundred different kinds of wonderful. Mom was one kind, and you're another. You're the kind I'm attracted to, but I can appreciate Mom."

"I think we need a short vacation. Just the two of us," Serena suggested.

"Saint Urho's Day celebration is coming up in March in Menahga," I teased. Saint Urho is the fictional saint of Finnish Vineland workers who, as the story goes, chased grasshoppers from the grape fields with a Trident.

"Urho does mean hero in Finland," Serena remarked. "Isn't that the celebration where people take off their clothes, put them on a pile, and then grab what they can and redress?"

"It's how Saint Urho would want to be remembered—in somebody else's clothes," I remarked.

"I'd have to make sure I'm standing next to someone larger than me. I don't want to have to try to get into a ninety-pounder's clothing. With my luck, a petite little pixie like Heather Hilton would stand by me, and her jeans would just cover my knees." She pursed her lips. "Why do you think Heather turned from being my friend to reveling in my misery?"

"Heather was infatuated with Clay, and Clay had a crush on you. That's hard to accept." Serena didn't appear satisfied with my answer. Still puzzled, she asked, "Why do you have two bottles of shampoo in our shower?"

I love Serena, but she is quick to notice when I have something out of order in the house. For example, she can have four feet of countertop covered with her paperwork, but if I leave my keys on the counter, she glances at them and gives me a look. I had anticipated she'd notice the second bottle, so I responded, "Do you realize you have a dozen woman cleaners in our stall?"

"I doubt it," she rolled her eyes.

"Would you like to bet on it? I could be wrong."

Serena studied me and laughed. "I know you too well. I would bet I have exactly twelve beauty products. There are hair treatments, and I use different shampoos and conditioners for distinct occasions. I have soaps for my body, for my face, and, of course, exfoliators."

"Of course."

"It's complicated being a woman—why am I even explaining this? Okay, smarty, you have two bottles of the same shampoo. None of my twelve are the same."

"One is almost empty. Here's a thought: Did Ivan Pavlov condition his hair?"

Ignoring my attempt at humor, Serena casually responded, "Okay, the second bottle is a replacement." With a loving grin, she asked, "Do you ever think of our nights as teens on the riverbank?"

"Love, whether newly born, or aroused from a deathlike slumber, always creates sunshine, filling the heart so full of radiance, it overflows upon the outward world—from Nathaniel Hawthorne's Scarlet Letter." Feeling we were finally getting back on track, I leaned into her and kissed her luscious lips.

She slowly pulled back and, in a gentle and reserved tone, said, "I love that you read the classics with me. How about if we practice St. Urho's frenzy right here? It's no problem for me. I've slept in your T and boxers before." Serena leaned into me and gave me a warm kiss that drew my body to the heat of hers. She teased, "But I'll warn you that if we start this, you have to take me to the promised land. After all, it is a 'finish' celebration."

Chapter 4

TAYTUM HANSON

10:00 A.M., MONDAY, FEBRUARY 13, 2023
HENNEPIN COUNTY GOVERNMENT CENTER
300 SOUTH 6TH STREET, MINNEAPOLIS

I gave my gunmetal-gray power suit one last glance before I stepped into the courtroom. I was properly caffeinated and amped to go head-to-head with Prosecutor Bridget Bare once again. Roan Caruso's goons almost beat Dick Doden to death when they were incarcerated together in the Hennepin County Jail. For a brief period after, Doden recanted his statement and said Caruso and Tug Grant had nothing to do with Deb Grant's murder. Prosecutor Bare never provided that information to us, which was a huge omission. She had to know this exculpatory evidence was missing. As Tug's defense team, we certainly would have brought it up in court if we'd had it. The recantation would have created the reasonable doubt we needed.

Today's hearing was a bench trial, meaning a judge would hear it with no jury present. I was defending both Roan Caruso and Tug Grant. I was using Roan's case as a trial run so I could be fully prepared for anything the prosecutor would throw out regarding Tug.

In the original hearing, the prosecuting attorney speaks first. However, in appellate cases, the appealing attorney gets the first shot. Once called on by the judge, I stood and explained my brief. "The extent of misconduct involved in Roan Caruso's arrest and conviction is disturbing. First, a 4th Amendment violation occurred on the night Roan was arrested. The police arrested Roan with no probable cause and without a warrant. That night, Roan's daughter-in-law and grandchild were shot to death in his home by Disciples gang members. While Roan was grieving, the police marched in and arrested him. They had no eyewitness testimony, no confession, and most importantly—no warrant. Ultimately, it was determined that Roan was protected by the Castle Doctrine when he returned fire from his home at the gang members who were slaughtering his family with automatic weapons. In State vs. Carothers, the Minnesota State Supreme Court ruled that a person should not be required to retreat from his home. Therefore, no arrest was warranted."

My well-versed argument elicited a glimpse of a smile from the judge. I was proud of having honed my skills since Tug was sentenced. After pausing and allowing my statement to sink in, I continued, "If that wasn't enough, Roan Caruso was convicted of first-degree murder and sentenced to life imprisonment based primarily on the statement made by the actual killer, Dick Doden. There is no question Doden killed Debra Grant. Then Doden turned around and implicated Roan. In a moment of repentance, Dick Doden rescinded his lie and proclaimed Roan Caruso was innocent. But Doden's repudiation was withheld from the defense. Prosecutor Bare is guilty of a Brady disclosure violation by failing to make us aware that Doden recanted his association with Roan. Doden's statement exonerated both Roan Caruso and Tug Grant of this crime. Their murder charges should be dismissed. Even if it should be found that no single error is sufficient to require a new trial, the conspectus of the proceedings warrants a new trial. To summarize, the cumulative effect of the alleged claimed errors, as well as the errors sustained, substantially influenced the defendant's conviction and denied him due process." I paused and finished, "No conviction should be obtained by methods regarded as repugnant to basic values protected by the Constitution." I proudly sat back down.

Prosecutor Bridget Bare's crimped hair was grayer than ever. She ruffled papers as she prepared to present her argument for upholding the conviction. Tug referred to her as "horseface," and he would have loved to see her today in her drab chestnut brown suit. *The old gray mare, she ain't what she used to be.*

In the blink of an eye, Bridget managed to pull it together. She stood and declared confidently, "Dick Doden's repudiation was a fabricated product of coercion." She clicked on the screen, and it displayed pictures of Doden's bruised and cut-up face. One eye was completely swollen shut. "When the defense speaks of justice, she is omitting the justice entitled to victims." Bridget clicked again, and the following screen displayed the medical examiner's photo of Debra Grant's badly beaten and bruised body. "Despite Caruso's obvious guilt, we are mindful that even those guilty of the most heinous offenses are entitled to a fair trial. The defendant is entitled to a fair trial, but not a perfect one. Because of human involvement, no criminal proceeding disposed of by a trial is likely to be completely free of defects, irregularities, or errors. Applying these standards and acknowledging that the defendant's argument is not devoid of merit, we are nevertheless convinced that the cumulative effect of the errors did not substantially influence the defendant's conviction. Apart from the defendant's illegal arrest, no single error was of Constitutional dimension. Despite the State's intransigent position" — Bridget casually glanced my way— "perhaps provoked by our adversary system, the complexity of today's criminal proceedings, and the tactics of defense counsel, errors were committed." She turned back to the judge. "But neither the defendant's illegal arrest nor other errors claimed have been demonstrated to be, in total effect, so contrary to fundamental principles of fairness as to require that the trial proceedings be repeated."

When Bridget had finished, the silver-haired judge asked me, "Do you have any evidence that the omission was intentional?"

Do I believe it was intentional? I have no doubt. Still, proving malice was an argument I didn't need to make and could lose. I was mindful that the judge didn't want to grant my appeal. He was handing me the rope to hang myself. I wasn't accepting it. I calmly responded, "The intentionality of its exclusion is irrelevant. Denying the defense access to this evidence is a colossal omission. Dick Doden was the one who got Tug sent to prison." *Whoops, I meant Roan.* I quickly added, "Doden's testimony got Roan Caruso and Tug Grant convicted. Doden's statement that Roan and Tug had nothing to do with Debra Grant's murder could have been crucial to the defense and certainly would have impacted the jury."

Bare objected, "They tampered with a witness to throw the wheels of justice off track. They are fortunate they didn't receive additional time for it."

"Crystal clear Brady violation!" I retorted.

The judge hammered his gavel, silencing us. "I will review the briefs and render a decision. Prosecutor Bare, that was a well-versed statement. I understand your argument that the recantation was coerced, but shouldn't a jury make that decision? The dilemma is that we don't know if Doden's retraction would have impacted the jury because it wasn't available to them. If you don't want a retrial, I'd strongly encourage you to work out an agreement with Ms. Hanson."

Prosecutor Bare told him, "I will meet with her immediately."

My goal was to retry the case, but Tug would be disappointed in me if I didn't at least try to get an offer. I had to strike while the iron was hot. If word got out that Tug's verdict might be dismissed due to Bridget's errors, she would be reluctant to make a deal.

We met in the Litigant Pro Se support room. The room is set aside for litigants who can't afford an attorney. Pro se means "on one's own behalf." It is a space for people to look over records before stepping into the courtroom to defend themselves. I smiled confidently at Bridget Bare as she sat across from me. I had the upper hand. The judge agreed that failing to disclose that a key witness recanted his statement was a significant blunder.

Bridget studied me with weary eyes over her reading glasses, asking, "How did you discover an error was made in the information we released?"

I inwardly laughed at her careful wording. She wasn't admitting that she deliberately omitted evidence, as I'm sure she did. I had made it known to the staff in the prosecutor's office that I was looking for a loophole in Tug's conviction. The Hennepin County Prosecutor's Office has over five hundred employees. I knew if I was patient, someone would eventually turn on her. The Brady violation was given to me by an assistant in her office as part of a deal on another case. I owed Tug for opening doors for me in the judicial field, and I repaid my debts. I answered, "It doesn't make any difference. What matters is where we go from here."

"I'll retry Tug and get a conviction again," Bridget stated with feigned confidence.

"If we settle this, we can keep your mistakes out of the press," I pointed out.

"I'm not admitting any mistakes."

"Okay. If the offer's good enough, you won't have to admit your office messed up. We'll address it quietly and quickly. It's my preference to retry the case, so you better make it sweet."

"I still have Roan to deal with. You know they call him 'the merchant of death.'"

"I believe that's a moniker you tagged him with during his trial."

"Was I wrong?" Bridget retorted tiredly. "Of all the crap Roan's pulled over the years, Dick Doden is the only one who testified against him. And Roan had him bludgeoned to the verge of death for doing so. The only reason Roan didn't have him killed was because he needed Dick to recant."

"I don't care about Roan." As far as I'm concerned, Roan's a thug. I'm in this, with all my heart, for Tug.

"Well, you should care about Roan. He's dangerous, and as soon as he feels working with you isn't in his best interest, your life is in danger. If I cut a deal with Tug, I'll have to make the same agreement with Roan," Bridget reflected. "Otherwise, I'm still dealing with the same bad publicity. You can't honestly believe freeing the merchant of death is in your best interest? I swear it's going to come back and bite you in the ass."

"I can accept whatever needs to happen to free Tug. He used to say, it's better for ten guilty men to escape justice than to have one innocent person suffer."

"He stole that from Ben Franklin. There are no innocent men here, Taytum." Bridget blew out a long, frustrated breath. "So, Tug only does four years for having Deb beaten to death. That hardly seems fair." She shook her head regretfully. "This is the best I can do. Tug accepts the guilty plea, with credit for time served. He can no longer go after the ten million dollars in insurance money, he can't sue the county for false imprisonment, and he remains disbarred."

"And he is released immediately?" I questioned. I inwardly celebrated. I was going to get the chance to showcase my talents in court. Tug would never agree to this deal if it meant he'd have to give up ten million dollars.

"And it stands that I got Tug convicted," Bridget gloated. "I'm not going to make him admit I won. Just having him know it is good enough for me." A grin crept across her face. "He can be released immediately, provided his internet platform is shut down."

"What makes you think Tug had anything to do with that?"

"It reeks of his narcissism. Even you must be uncomfortable with the suggestion that Tug is a martyr. His conspiracy theory mercenaries have made threats to my life. They're educated enough to block us from tracing the sources."

"Shutting the site down is doable, but I don't know that Tug will accept this. You sure you can't do better?" I leaned back and reminded her, "We both know a new trial would acquit Tug. All I need to do is keep Tug off the stand so you can't rake him over the coals like you did last time."

Bridget considered my proposition before saying, "I'm only offering this deal in the interest of saving the county money. This takes Tug's ability to get a settlement for false imprisonment off the table. He gets no money for having Deb killed. His internet platform must be shut down, and there will be no press conference about his release. That's the offer."

"I'll see what he says." Bridget must believe she's going to lose to make this offer.

"It's a sweetheart deal, so you have until the end of Valentine's Day to accept it."

10:30 A.M., TUESDAY, FEBRUARY 14, 2023
MINNESOTA CORRECTIONAL FACILITY – LINO LAKES
7525 4TH AVENUE,
LINO LAKES

TUG AND I sat in a gray cement visiting room, discussing his pending release. A guard stood in the same room, out of hearing range, watching us. Tug was five and a half feet tall and kept himself fit. His thick hair, short and blond, was starting to gray, and I wondered if he dyed his hair regularly before he was incarcerated. Still, it looked classy. I was doing my best to discourage him from accepting the offer. "We can win this if you agree to avoid taking the stand."

"I've learned my lesson." He stared directly into my eyes and said softly, "I need to get out of here. I'm serious. I'll accept a guilty plea if they release me immediately." Tug was as humble as I've ever seen him. He looked afraid.

"Has someone threatened you?"

"I exchanged some words with a couple of Disciples gang members. I need to watch my back for a bit."

"Should I request a transfer to PC?" PC refers to protective custody. It's essentially solitary confinement, but at least he'd be safe. If Tug hadn't had enemies when he was first sent, I imagine he does now. He has a strong personality and isn't the kind of man who backs down in an argument.

"In here, PC is referred to as Punk City. No way."

"Do you realize what you're giving up by accepting Bridget's offer? You're disbarred. If we win this case at trial, you can go back to being an attorney. You can go after the ten million in insurance they owe you."

"The money is gone," he said morosely. "It vanished the moment I was convicted."

"What makes you say that?" This wasn't like Tug.

"Do you honestly think the insurance companies will give me ten million if I'm found not guilty now? What they'll do is take me to civil court, where the burden of proof is lower, and they'll use circumstantial evidence to withhold the money. In civil court they don't need to prove me guilty beyond a reasonable doubt; they only need a preponderance of evidence to win."

Tug was a genius. To win a civil case, they would only need to show that it was more likely than not that Tug was involved in Deb's death. He was right. He would never be awarded ten million dollars. I asked, "Are you willing to quit being an attorney?"

"Horseface has no say in whether I get reinstated as an attorney. I'll get reinstated." Tug gave me a sly grin. "You can do just about anything but steal your client's money and still be an attorney. If we lose, I spend the rest of my life in this cage. I can't take that chance. I can't risk it. I'll get rich again. If we don't win a retrial, my life is over."

"We will win. They have nothing. No one has directly connected you to Deb's murder."

"Her parents have turned my kids against me. Lincoln still visits, but he treats me like I'm guilty. If the prosecutor gets Lincoln to make a statement against me, that will be enough to sway the jury. Taytum, make the deal." The day-to-day grind in prison was wearing him down.

"Okay. But I can win this," I said, disappointed.

Tug reached over and took my hand.

The guard standing by the door stepped closer. "No physical contact!"

Tug pulled his hand back and said softly, "I miss you."

It bothered me to see him so beat down. I wanted to give him hope. "I'll talk to the county attorney. Once you're out, get a physical to certify that you have no sexually transmitted diseases. We'll talk then. But no more sex workers—okay?"

"Absolutely." With a glimmer, Tug added, "I only let her blow me."

"Do you think I'm foolish enough to believe this happened just the one time you were caught? Don't insult me."

"You're right. But I only let them blow me, and it was always before they were with anyone else."

"Anyone else *at the prison*. It's disgusting. I get it; in prison, a hooker probably looks pretty good. But if I get you out, you live like a man with class. You walk away from insults—and you stay away from trash."

"All right. I'm not arguing with you. Just get me out."

"There is one more thing. What's the story with you and Professor Kimball? You've got money coming in, and I've heard he plans on writing some tale that you're the second coming—comparing you to Jesus and Muhammed."

"Just having a little fun with the guy." Tug laughed. "It gets pretty damned boring in here."

"I want no part of slandering religious groups. You ruffle the wrong feathers, and they'll slam your cell door shut tight. Bridget Bare insisted that you shut down the internet site before she agrees to a deal."

"Okay, I'll tell Doc I've been muzzled. He's a do-gooder. He'll shut it down if he thinks it could impact my release. I'll tell him his social justice movement was successful. Maybe I'll even let him write a book about me. But I'll have the website taken down today."

"Speaking of your do-gooder friends, did you hear Brent Parker died? Had a heart attack on the golf course."

"I did. I've written to his widow, Blair. They were two friends who never wavered in their belief in my innocence."

Chapter 5

TUG GRANT

3:30 P.M., FRIDAY, MARCH 3, 2023
WINDY HILL COURT, SUNFISH LAKE

Freedom is exhilarating! I rolled out of bed and nudged Taytum. "You need to get dressed. Lincoln's visiting after school today." I grabbed my slacks off the floor and slid them on.

"Boo." She jokingly pulled the satin sheet over her head for a second before pulling it back down. "Kidding. I like your son. I have work I need to get to anyway."

I pulled the sheet away, admiring her shapely naked body. "You really could have been a model."

Taytum made no effort to cover herself. I respected her comfort with nakedness. Ignoring my compliment, she rolled to her side and teased, "How's therapy going?"

"I'm seeing Roan's daughter, Halle. I thought she'd just sign off for me, but she's making me do the work. It's the usual—mother issues rhetoric."

"Well, your mother did leave your family to be with the father of a kid who bullied you daily."

"That was a long time ago. I don't think about the whore anymore."

Realizing I wasn't in the mood to discuss this, she took a deep breath and asked, "When does Blair get home?"

"Not until six. She's at Taste of the Twin Cities, celebrating women who've risen."

"While I'm here celebrating men who've fallen," Taytum remarked.

"Someday, Taytum, you'll laugh about gripping Blair's gaudy headboard in ecstasy."

Her devilish smile suggested she was already.

The doorbell rang, and I slipped on my white dress shirt. Anxious to see my son, I rushed to the door.

Lincoln stood five feet eight inches tall. I pulled him into an embrace and said, "I can't believe how tall you are. Seventeen years old and bigger than your old man."

He looked down at my bare belly and said, "Dad, button your shirt."

I put on a little bit of a potbelly in prison, but I survived. That's all that matters.

Lincoln admired the vaulted ceiling in the entry. He sat on the cushioned bench, removed his shoes, and said, "How can you afford this house? This place is a mansion."

"You can't keep a good man down. I told you I'd bounce back. You'll love this place."

Taytum casually approached us, still buttoning her blouse. She gave me a peck on the cheek and said, "Another time." She turned to Lincoln, "Haven't seen you since court. You're looking good. I hope the two of you have a great time. You'll have to check out the billiard room."

Lincoln nodded as she exited.

I picked up his duffle bag and carried it up the wide cherry staircase. "Let's toss this in your room. You've got your own master bath."

Bewildered, Lincoln followed me upstairs and gazed at the pond outside his bedroom window. "How can you afford this? You just got out."

"I married—again." It was a lot for a boy to take in. Trying to calm him, I sat on the edge of the bed. "It was a small wedding, just me and her family. I didn't want to bring all the drama from our family into it. You know your Grandma Greta would have insisted on being there with the kids, and she would have made a big scene. I didn't think it was fair to do that to my new bride. I know she'll never be your mom, but I need somebody."

"Taytum seems nice enough, but I can't call her 'Mom.'" Lincoln added with sadness, "She's only about a decade older than I am." He paced around the room. "I guess I never expected you'd be alone. It just seems a little quick."

"I didn't marry Taytum."

"You just slept with Taytum."

"It's complicated." I would always sleep with Taytum. Anyone in their right mind would sleep with Taytum at every available opportunity.

"Who did you marry?"

"I married Blair Parker. We fell in love over our shared grief for her husband's death. This is her house. I let her keep the Parker last name. Blair and Brent were married for twenty-five years, so that's how everybody knows her."

"How old is she?"

"She's older than me, and her health isn't great, but she's kind. You'll like her."

"Why did you marry Blair instead of Taytum?"

"I didn't have money. Now I do." I couldn't hold back my grin. "I'm a multi-millionaire. Set for the rest of my life. We're going to have some fun."

Lincoln looked at me in disbelief. "I have to go to the bathroom."

I grabbed the clipboard I had set on his dresser. It held a form that required his signature. When he returned, I opened it to the last page and handed him a pen. "It's just a formality. I highlighted the area in yellow where you need to sign."

He paged back to the very beginning and read through it. Finally, he turned to me and said, "You're trying to circumvent the Son of Sam law."

"You've done your homework." I smiled with pride. David Berkowitz, the Son of Sam killer, attempted to sell his story after killing six people. The New York legislature stepped in and passed a law reallocating the money made from Berkowitz's story to the victims' families. Minnesota has also passed this law. In Deb's murder, Lincoln and his sisters were the surviving victims. I needed them to relinquish their rights to the proceeds of any story I told about the murder. This could be a Netflix movie, and I could make a fortune. I had the form postdated to Lincoln's 18th birthday. I told him, "It's bad enough I lost four years of my life in prison. Does anyone else deserve rights to the story I tell?"

With an eerie calm, he said, "I hate you," and tore up the form. "No way. You killed Mom for money. How could you think I'd be okay with this? I called for Grandpa to pick me up when I was in the bathroom. I'll wait for him outside." Lincoln grabbed his duffle bag and left.

Chapter 6

ROAN CARUSO

8:30 P.M., SATURDAY, MARCH 4, 2023
THE PANTOWN BREWING COMPANY, 408 37TH AVENUE NORTH, ST. CLOUD

I've never been wild about Taytum Hanson, but the blond bambina bella got me out of the clink, so I'm good with the little goomah for the moment. She thinks she's Ms. Liberated when the truth is her commitment to Tug makes her the devil's right hand. I paid her a small fortune for her work, and she still expects a thank you for my release. It's not happening. The truth is, I was the one who got Doden to recant. Taytum simply brought it to light, and it took her four years to do so. As far as I'm concerned, Tug had one great woman in his life: his wife, Deb. Taytum was just another one of Tug's playthings. My complicity in Deb's murder is my greatest shame. People think the devil tempts a person to hell. The reality is you buy a ticket, and you have a dozen opportunities to head in another direction before that ticket's punched, but you don't. And once it's punched, anything goes.

Tug called and asked me to meet him in Pantown this afternoon. Samuel Pandolfo started a company called Pan Auto a little over a century ago that produced cars in St. Cloud from 1917 to 1922. Pandolfo built houses for his workers and six blocks of tunnels that connected them. It allowed homeowners to visit without having to walk outside in the winter. My wife, Cat, had a great-uncle who told stories about escaping from the cops in the tunnels during prohibition when they partied in St. Cloud.

I was reluctant to meet with Tug. Cat hated him. My life would be fine if I never spoke to him again, but I did have a bone to pick, so I agreed.

Tug entered, wearing a colorful designer shirt and designer jeans. He was always dressed to pick up a lover and was more successful than one might imagine.

I stood up and shook his hand. "Nice incognito outfit. I thought we were done talkin'."

"We're good." Tug glanced around. "We can't be charged again anyway. It would constitute double jeopardy." We both appreciated the value of our time, so it didn't surprise me when Tug immediately asked, "Why did you hire that imbecile Doden for the job? I asked you to make it as painless as possible, and it ended up just the opposite."

I'd never wanted Deb murdered. Tug said someone was going to kill her, regardless of whether I helped, so I brokered the deal, thinking a failed effort would prevent future efforts. I hired a guy I thought would never pull it off and gave him a gun that didn't fire. I insisted he take no other weapons into her home. He pistol-whipped her when the gun didn't fire and then stabbed her to death with one of her kitchen knives. I'd even given Deb a firearm, but Tug removed it before he left that morning. I pointed out, "The beating I had put on Doden is the reason we're free. If I would have killed Deb, as you requested, you'd be doin' life. I didn't say a word, and they still convicted you."

"*You* would have made it look like an accident, and I wouldn't have had to do four years in prison."

"If you think I owe you something, you're wrong." My blood started to boil. I stepped into him. "You mentioned you're seeing my daughter for therapy. That chaps my ass. When we said we'd stay away from each other, that should have included family."

"Chill, I'm not upset with you." Tug waved his hand. "There's no game with Halle. Just therapy. And she's good. She demands accountability but is still understanding. Like the mom I should have had."

I considered the fact that Halle isn't recorded as my daughter in any official documents. I'm also court-ordered into therapy as part of my release. I *could* go visit my daughter.

"I have a favor to ask." Tug interrupted my train of thought.

I looked around to make sure no one was in earshot. "For God's sake, Tug, I'm not killing Blair Parker."

"I'm not having Blair killed." Tug laughed, "I need to keep her alive as long as possible. As long as she's alive, I have complete control of her money, so I'm quietly moving it out of sight. Once she dies, her kids will step in and battle me for it."

Becoming impatient, I demanded, "What do you want?"

"You're going to love this job. I want you to torment Melanie Pearson. It infuriates me that she testified for the prosecution. I loved that woman. I was going to leave Deb for her. It's one thing to break up with me but then try to send me to prison the rest of my life—I've been thinking of ways to get back at her since they slammed my cell door shut."

"We're both on probation," I warned. He'd piqued my curiosity, but I wasn't going back to prison for him.

"This isn't the kind of stuff people get locked up for. I still have keys to her apartment and a set of keys to her car." Tug was giggling like a small child. "Let's start with this: I want you to find a cat that looks exactly like hers and switch it. Make her wonder what's going on with that stupid feline she always had on her lap."

"What?"

"Then, we mess with her clothes. I want you to replace everything in her closet with exact replicas of progressively larger sizes. Make her think she's shrinking. When she starts feeling good about herself, we'll take it the other way and size down until she feels she's becoming super fat."

Now I was laughing.

"In all your mob games, you must have used a seamstress. Have the seamstress change the tags." Tug continued, "I'll buy all the clothes and pay for everything. I've come into some money."

It was too good to walk away from. "Okay, but I want $100,000, and you pay all the expenses."

Chapter 7

RICKY DAY

9:00 P.M., MONDAY, MARCH 13, 2023
CARAWAY WEST APARTMENTS,
BLACKSTONE, ST. LOUIS PARK

Melanie asked me to meet her at her St. Louis Park apartment. I'm not exactly sure what melancholy means, but it might be the long version of her name. She sounded sad, and I wasn't sure what to expect. I don't know how to love her. I don't really know how to love anyone. When I express appreciation for her caring soul, she pulls away. And then she tells me stories of how she worked her ass off trying to please guys who treated her like crap. Sometimes, I feel like she's trying to turn me into a man I don't want to be. I remind myself, *Be kind.* Melanie appreciates all things red, so I bought her a box of Hot Tamales candy.

She answered my knock and smiled at her gift. Oversized clothes draped her body. I wasn't sure what that was about. Melanie took my hand and walked me to the couch. She forced out, "I'm sorry, Ricky. But I'm breaking up with you."

"Why? What did I do?" My heart hurt. I loved Melanie. I looked forward to every second with her.

"Darius wants to give us another chance. I feel like I owe it to him. Imagine the humiliation he felt while I testified that I allowed Tug to use me as his plaything for a weekend during our engagement. I still feel so guilty about it. Honestly, Ricky, you're the one who should be walking away from me."

"We can both be so much more than what we were, Melanie." I wanted to say, "If you push me out the door, I'll never speak to you again." I had a feeling that if I said it, she would beg me to stay. Instead, I reminded myself to live as a Christian. *John 15:12 Love one another as I have loved you.* I said, "I will leave, but if you need me, I will never turn my back on you." I felt a flood of emotions with hurt and anger on the forefront, but I told myself, *shut up, shut up, shut up.* I could handle this if I could just not say anything for a bit. I reminded myself that I survived prison. I wanted to beg, but I wouldn't. I understood. *Who wants to be with a man who killed his family?* Tamping down my self-hate, I said, "Okay. If there's something I should fix, please tell me."

"You were perfect." Melanie teared up as she squeezed my bicep. Not helpful. "You told your family about me."

"I did." She teared up. "My dad. My mom's dead."

"I'm sorry."

"Me too. Dad said he would never speak to me again if I dated you. Honestly, he doesn't speak to me much anyway." She ran both hands through her hair and then yanked her hair in frustration. "You can imagine how my court testimony embarrassed my dad—and Darius. Trying to justify being with you is too much for me right now."

"My life never got better from acting out of shame. It always seemed to end with me getting beat up." I had to fight back my anger and forced myself to recall Ephesians 4:2: *Be completely humble and gentle, be patient, bearing with one another in love. Make every effort to keep the unity of the Spirit through the bond of peace.*

Melanie was distraught and wasn't going to be dissuaded.

"I'm okay." I closed my eyes for a couple of seconds and reminded myself, *ease her mind.* I was lucky she even cared. "I will quietly walk away. You will never have to worry about me again." I deserved to suffer. I took her hand. "But I'd like to share a thought: I've come to realize my crazy behavior at sixteen was out of fear I'd never get to love someone. I thought I loved this girl, but any time Dad got wind of me having a date, he'd always create work and make me cancel. But that was puppy love, not like my love for you. Right now, it hurts like hell. You made me feel in ways I haven't felt before." I searched my brain for the words to express my appreciation for her empathy. "Happiness is hard to find, Mel, and in the short time we've been together, you've given me more than I deserve. Thank you." I forced myself to my feet.

    Melanie quickly stood, and we embraced.

    With no more said, I departed. Love sucks.

Chapter 8

JON FREDERICK

6:00 P.M., TUESDAY, MARCH 14, 2023
CAFÉ ENA, 4601 GRAND AVENUE SOUTH, TANGLETOWN,
MINNEAPOLIS

Ricky Day called and asked to speak to me. I checked in with my supervisor, Sean Reynolds, and he suggested I meet with Day, so I picked Ricky up at home. Since serving his prison time, Ricky has been sober, works full-time, and has no violations. Twice a week, he makes meals for people without homes and hands them out on the streets of the Twin Cities.

Ricky wore a faded blue button-down flannel with a white thermal undershirt and jeans. "Where we headed?" he asked.

"I'll buy lunch at Café Ena. It's Latin Fusion, and the chef uses a French technique to perfect it. I love the ceviche here. The seafood is marinated in lime juice overnight, and the limes' acid cooks it."

"They don't cook it at all?"

"They blanch it for food safety."

"After twenty years of prison food, everything tastes fricken' amazing. But you don't have to buy."

"I think God would kick my ass if I passed up the opportunity to buy lunch for someone who feeds the homeless."

After we were seated at our mahogany table and had placed our orders, Ricky said, "I need some advice about a woman."

"I'm no expert on women," I laughed. "You should have asked your niece, Halle. Her therapist's advice would be far better than mine."

"It's a little weird for me to ask for help from Halle. I went to prison for trying to kill her, and now she's supposed to fix me? I can't."

"Okay, I get that."

"Do you and Serena ever have problems?" Ricky asked.

"All couples do. Are you a Taco John's or a Taco Bell guy?"

"They're both great," Ricky responded, "but I don't eat out much."

"I like Taco John's. Taco Bell puts sugar in their guacamole. I don't like sugar added to everything I eat. But here's my point. Where would you stop if you had a friend who worked at Taco Bell, but you like Taco John's better?"

"Taco John's—better tacos."

"Serena would go to Taco Bell, and if I were with her, I would too. Every enduring relationship involves compromises. I love Serena. When we sit down to watch a movie, she talks through for the first half hour and then says, 'I can't figure out what's happening in this show.' I could say something that would hurt her feelings, but knowing she'd rather be talking to me than watching the movie is a compliment. Being on good terms is more important than any movie." Ricky looked troubled and certainly didn't call me to hear about my marriage. "Tell me about the woman you're interested in."

"Melanie Pearson. Beautiful ginger hair. Sweet as honey. I can't get her out of my head." I could see a wave of sadness wash over him as he continued. "The last few years have been hard on her. First, Mel was committed to Sebastian, but he left her for someone else. Then there was Tug, who strung her along and used her. She had a rebound affair with Darius, a control freak who treated her like a sidekick rather than an equal. But Melanie's returning to him anyway. I don't get it. I need some guidance here." Ricky scratched his head and said with frustration, "I know

I could make her happy. Melanie asked me to leave, so I walked. But I miss her like crazy."

"You need someone who loves you the same as you love her. If she's asking you to walk, that's a solid signal."

"Can you at least give me your thoughts about her? You're a profiler."

"Okay, here's my two cents' worth. Some people are like a ping-pong ball bouncing on a marble floor. They bounce from person to person. Melanie is more like wet clay dropped on a marble floor. She's in it for the duration. Melanie's not leaving until her partner pries her away. Your problem is Darius hasn't done that yet."

"Why do you think she cheated on Darius?"

"Because she was still in love with Tug. Emotionally, she hadn't left Tug."

"Do you think she still feels that way?" he asked.

"No. Tug severed those ties with his brutality toward her in court."

"So, what should I do?"

"Either move on or wait to hear back. When I was told by a woman I loved that she needed space, I did the same damn thing—looked for opportunities to talk to her. All I accomplished was annoying the hell out of her. So, I switched gears and gave her the space she desired. I lived as if she didn't exist. Every day, from morning until night, I focused on tasks that would make me a better man. I worked out, studied, stayed sober, focused on spirituality, and tried to sleep. I was still miserable, but now I had a purpose. Eventually, I attracted someone better." It was still Serena, but a healthier version of her, and she got a stronger version of me. She benefited from taking care of herself, and I profited from proving I could survive without her.

"I used to bring her something red. She loves red. Maybe I should send her a shirt."

"Terrible idea. You don't buy a woman clothing until your relationship is solid enough to be forgiven."

"Why?" Ricky asked.

"Think about it. That shirt might look good to us, but what if it doesn't fit right? What if the material is itchy and uncomfortable? That will be the association she will always have with you. Wait until you hear from her, and then give her something she can throw away without guilt. Nothing threatening. Something positive. And no creepy notes. Just write something like *Wishing you the best.* Heartache is part of the path, Ricky. We all experience it at some point and tell ourselves, 'No one has felt pain like I have.' But it eventually ends, and life goes on." I thought about sitting around the fire as a teen with Serena and said, "Charles Dickens wrote, "I have been bent and broken, but—I hope—into a better shape."

"I'll need to think about that. What was the name of the book?"

"*Great Expectations.*"

"If it were written about me, it would have been titled, 'No Expectations,'" Ricky reflected despondently.

I held a napkin so Ricky couldn't see I was writing the word *Tomorrow* on it. I asked, "What did I write?"

"No idea." Ricky shrugged.

"True." I opened the napkin and showed him the word. "There will be another lover. You can't see tomorrow's pleasures today. You just have to tough it out."

7:15 P.M.
OAKLAND AVENUE, PHILLIPS, MINNEAPOLIS

NOT LONG AFTER dropping Ricky off, my phone buzzed with a call from Melanie.

"Can I ask you a question?" Melanie asked.

"Yes." She didn't seem to be in crisis, so I teased, "Did you have another question, or was that it?"

"Okay, smarty, two questions. You gave me your card and

said I could call you. I know Ricky thinks highly of you, so I'd like to pick your brain."

"Pick away."

"Do you think I'm a fool to break up with Ricky?"

"I don't know." *How did I suddenly become an expert on relationships?* "I guess it depends on how understanding you can be. If you can accept the man he is now, you could have a great relationship. But a mass killing is hard to get over. I get it. Consider this: People who grew up in that home forgave him. They have an insight that none of us have."

"I feel guilty about not being able to forgive him." Melanie acknowledged, "He is such an incredibly kind and humble man."

"I've never thought forgiving is essential. It implies I have a say in it, but I'm not his judge. I don't know that I can *forgive* him for killing his family. But I am big on moving forward when there's nothing more to do about it. If you can't move forward, you shouldn't be in a relationship with him. Shaming him won't resolve anything; he's not short on shame. You deserve a good life, and so does he, but if you can't see yourself enjoying your life with him, you need to move on."

"If I didn't know his history, loving him would be so easy."

"He's trying to live an honest Christian life. It's stated in Proverbs, 'Whoever conceals their sins does not prosper, but the one who confesses and renounces them finds mercy.' I respect his honesty and humility."

"Am I a terrible person for turning my back on him?"

"Now you're asking me to judge *you*. Melanie, you need to take care of yourself. Let's make it simple. What would make you happy?"

"I turned my back on my best friend a long time ago, and it still haunts me. I don't know what to do. That's the problem."

"You'll know soon enough."

"How?"

"Either you'll be happy, or you won't."

Chapter 9

RICKY DAY

6:30 P.M., THURSDAY, MARCH 16, 2023
KIP'S IRISH PUB & RESTAURANT, 9970 WAYZATA BOULEVARD,
ST. LOUIS PARK

God, I missed Melanie. Our honest conversations have been the best moments of my life. I feel like I don't deserve to love someone, but I love her so completely. I've learned what it's like to be ghosted. Today, I received a text that simply said, "I hope you're okay." I bought a bunch of red Gerbera daisies and planned on giving them to her as a friendship gift.

When I arrived at her apartment complex, she was walking down the sidewalk with a Middle Eastern-looking man her height and age. *That must be Darius.* Melanie looked sad. I know it's not my business anymore, but I don't like to see people hurt, and I worry about Melanie. *Am I a stalker? I don't want to be a stalker.* I know Darius has slapped her in the past, and I can't tolerate the thought of anyone abusing Melanie. My head felt full of tears, and my eyes strained to keep them inside. *Maybe if I can just see her happy, I'll know she's okay, and I'll find a way to move on.* I parked my car, quickly exited, and followed them up the sidewalk. They stepped into Kip's Irish Pub.

I hesitated for a minute. I wasn't going to violate my probation. I took out my phone and looked up the bar. After seeing it served food, I realized I was okay to enter. *What am I doing?* I needed verification that she was safe and happy.

Melanie and the man were sitting at the round bar.

I asked for a menu and sat at a table, unnoticed. Melanie had a plastic cup of water, and the guy was drinking a martini. I couldn't quite hear what was said, but it was clear he was belittling her.

She dabbed away tears as he spoke.

I wanted to tell her, *You're worthy of being loved. You don't deserve that.* As a Christian, I am not without anger. In fact, my anger rages hotter than most, so I can't go there. I tamped it down and didn't interfere.

Finally, Melanie got up and headed to the restroom. On her way back, she noticed me and hesitated for a moment.

Darius made his way to the restroom, and as he crossed Melanie's path, he purposely dipped his shoulder and slammed into her.

She was forced to take a step back to maintain her balance.

I was on my feet and at her side in a fraction of a second. I stepped into his space. "I don't know what the two of you got going, but you don't body slam women."

His dark eyes glared into mine. "Back off, jerk-off! Who are you?"

"Ricky Day." I stood my ground. "Look me up. You don't want to mess with me." As the words left my mouth, I realized I'd committed the sin of false pride. I implied that somehow, I should be respected for what I'd done, or at least feared.

Darius turned to Melanie. "Let's get out of here." He addressed me, "And buddy, you can go to hell."

"I'll be there waiting for you," I responded.

Melanie came to my side and looked Darius in the eye. "I can't do this. I won't be pushed around by anybody. Goodbye, Darius."

"You can have the homely bitch—" he snarled at me.

"Enough." I cut him off.

Darius nodded in disgust and walked away.

I turned to Melanie. "Are you okay?"

"Yeah." Melanie leaned into me. "I can't tell you how much I've missed you."

"What about your dad? I don't want to pull you away from your family."

"He pulled away a long time ago. I don't know that he cares about me. He simply doesn't want me to embarrass him, like Mom did. Ricky, I love that you are always honest about your shame. I've never been honest about mine. And you know what's sad about it? I didn't do anything wrong before I met Tug." She took my arm. "Can we go for a walk?"

"I'd love to."

"I need to get some things off my chest, but I can't walk far." Melanie told me, "None of my shoes fit anymore. I don't know what's going on with my feet."

I took her to her apartment and promised to stay and watch the movie *Are You There God? It's Me, Margaret* with her. Melanie was concerned I wouldn't like it because it was a chick flick based on a Judy Blume book she'd read as a child. I was elated. This was the first time in my life a woman asked me to watch a movie with her. It could have been *Frosty the Snowman,* and I would have enjoyed it.

Before leaving for the evening, I ran back to my car and retrieved the bouquet of red daisies.

Melanie cried, this time with tears of happiness.

Chapter 10

MELANIE PEARSON

5:00 P.M., TUESDAY, MARCH 21, 2023
CARAWAY WEST APARTMENTS, BLACKSTONE, ST. LOUIS PARK

I don't know what's going on with Simba these days. My cat treats me like a stranger. I wonder if she's got some type of virus. I need to make an appointment for her with a veterinarian. I was digging through my closet, trying to find something to wear on my date with Ricky tonight. I must be losing weight. My blouses are enormous. After I finally found a blouse I could make work, I pulled on my jeans. *That's weird.* They're loose and don't feel as worn as I remembered. *Are these the right jeans?* I had an ink stain on the inside of the left pocket. I looked for it, and it was gone. But I only had one pair of these jeans. I searched the closet again. This was the only pair. Maybe the stain washed out. *It's weird.* I never had to wear a belt with these jeans before, but I guess that's all right. I smiled with a sense of satisfaction.

Ricky Day is the anchor in my life who keeps me grounded and pulls me back when I wander too close to the edge. I was leery initially, but he was always incredibly kind and respectful. For the first time in my adult life, I'm with a man who is genuinely caring. When I need space, he backs off, and when I need him, he's there. Ricky appreciates and adores me, in his naïve boyish way, and I love it. I love him.

Finally dressed, I sat on the living room couch to slip my shoes on. *What the hell?* My feet typically sit flat on the floor. My heels don't reach the floor anymore. I swear I'm losing my mind. I'm already running late. I need to get going. I dismiss the thought and head off to see Ricky.

Chapter 11

SERENA FREDERICK

7:15 A.M. WEDNESDAY, MARCH 22, 2023
PIERZ

Jon sat at the counter eating a bowl of cereal loaded with fresh fruit while I finished making his mocha. He wore an untucked button-down forest green shirt and black jeans. I was still in my pajamas. I poured the mocha into his travel tumbler and sprayed whipped cream on top. I couldn't help noticing the grin on his face when I set his mocha next to him. "What?"

"Thanks! I love the way you look in the morning." He stood up and pulled me into a hug and a kiss.

"And then you get home and wonder, 'what happened?'"

"When I get home, you're still beautiful." He looked directly into my eyes. "What's bothering you?"

"Tug got away with murder." I stepped away. "Are people like Deb Grant and I, who stay home with the kids, meaningless?" He squeezed me into a hug.

"You're the most important person on earth. I'm not happy about it, either. It's not justice, but the case is over." Jon returned to his breakfast. "If another crime related to Tug surfaces, I'll investigate. But I've been assigned another case, and I'm happy to be working close to home again. I could take time away from you and the kids to investigate him in my free time, or I could just enjoy our life."

"I want you home." I had stepped around him and smothered him in a hug from behind. "Our life is wonderful. The business with Tug just bothers me. Lily Walker is stopping over tonight." Lily is the daughter of former Deputy Del Walker. Del was killed working the Lying Close case with us, and Lily had struggled with substance abuse after her father's death but is clean now. I was closer to her sister, but I liked Lily, who was the black sheep in her family. But even at her worst, she was likable. She had accepted the position of Tug's secretary after Melanie quit.

7:30 P.M.

LILY WALKER KICKED back in a cushioned lawn chair by our firepit. I had invited her over to see if she had any additional information on Tug that could lead to sending him back to prison. Lily had dark, layered hair that looked undone. She was makeup-free and had a healthy skin tone, suggesting she was maintaining her sobriety. We enjoyed a glass of homemade lemonade while Nora and Jackson jumped on the trampoline. I asked, "How was your visit with Agnes Schraut?" Jon and I had befriended the irascible octogenarian during the Lying Close case. Agnes reveled in her irritability. If you could be thick-skinned around her, she was damn funny.

"I love talking to Agnes," Lily said. "When I talk to her, I'm reminded of the kindness of people in the Twin Cities."

"You know she isn't from the Twin Cities."

"Yes," Lily said with a grin. Her expression saddened as she said, "It was hard getting over Dad being shot. It's worse when it's in the line of duty because he hadn't done anything to deserve it. He hadn't ripped somebody off, and he wasn't sneaking around with some guy's wife. Dad was protecting the community."

"There have been twelve police officers shot in Minnesota this year. There were only two shot last year. It infuriates me. What is wrong with people? People need to stop acting like everybody is a victim." I stopped myself. "I'm sorry. Preaching to the choir, right?"

"I hear you. It helps me to know someone else is angry about it." Lily crossed one leg over the other, scratched her ankle, and said, "Enough about Dad. Here's another ship I've run aground, and I need your feedback. Before Tug, I dated a guy named Bo when I was in treatment. A month into our relationship, he relapsed and overdosed. I wonder sometimes what choice I would have made had I been with Bo that night." She sighed, "We could have had a Romeo and Juliet ending."

"Romeo and Juliet died because of miscommunication, not because it was a great plan."

"Yeah, he didn't get her message."

"She probably told him, and he wasn't listening. Typical guy thing."

"I can't believe you said that." Lily busted out laughing. "Juliet referred to Romeo as 'day in night' and 'whiter than snow upon a raven's back,' as if his presence illuminated the darkness. What did Romeo call Juliet?"

"I don't recall. I used to know."

Lily sighed and said, "I miss Bo, and I miss Dad."

"I'm sorry for your losses." I reached over and squeezed her hand. "I'm damn glad you weren't with Bo that night. You're resilient if you can stay clean through your time with Tug."

"Thank you, Serena."

"I was so stupid to be with Tug," Lily said. "He's a narcissistic psychopath."

"You could have Agnes vet your dates for you," I remarked.

Lily was able to smile for a second. "There's a reason Agnes has always been single."

"Do you think Debra Grant was stupid?"

Lily stared straight ahead.

"Deb was brilliant and kind and loving," I continued. "A woman to emulate. But she was also manipulated by Tug. That's how good he is at it."

"He called me."

"Tug? What did he want?"

"He wanted me to come back and work for him."

"I hope you didn't agree."

"I didn't." Lily took a large swallow of lemonade. "Tug married a widowed millionaire named Blair Parker about five minutes after her husband died. Her son, Elon, did some research and found out I used to be Tug's secretary, and he took me to lunch. Surprise, surprise, things are going awry in paradise."

"What a shocker," I said sarcastically. "She'd be wise to get out while she's still alive."

"Blair discovered Tug's been sleeping with another woman in her bed and filed for divorce. Elon said that since she filed, her money has been disappearing. He offered me money to go back to work for Tug and be his inside source. Money's tight, but I'm not crazy."

"I hope Blair had a prenup. If not, her fortune will be divided equally, not equitably. I know a little about financial laws. Once she filed for divorce, he had to turn over all relevant financial information. Has Tug been deposed?"

"Yes," Lily said. "He claimed under oath he's released everything. And she has a prenup."

I grinned. "If Tug gets caught taking Blair's money, he's not only guilty of a crime, he's also guilty of perjury, and he goes back to prison."

"Elon asked me if I knew of anywhere Tug could be hiding money. Elon contacted the credit reporting agencies, and nothing has been flagged in Blair's accounts."

What is he doing? I needed to think about that. "Are you okay, Lily? I hope you never consider going back to Tug."

"I'm over Tug. I understand Tug's superpower."

"Tug has a superpower?" I laughed.

"He does." Lily leaned forward. "Everyone knows Tug's a liar. But he has an unparalleled ability to convince anyone that *they* are the one person he is completely honest with. Melanie

THE SUN

believed it. I believed it. Even Taytum believes it. She's the one who really surprises me. Taytum's so smart, but she will defend Tug to her death."

"Erotomanic delusional disorder. Sometimes, a relatively normal person can become completely obsessed with one person. When they come across evidence that contradicts their delusion, they defend it more strongly. It used to be called de Clérambault's syndrome and referred to a young woman becoming obsessed with a man of higher social standing."

"Nailed it." Lily teased, "Jon is rubbing off on you."

"I'm the one with the psychology degree. Don't give him credit for my work."

"Message delivered. But I thought your degree was in business management."

"You're right. I don't technically have a psychology degree. I had a minor in psychology—a few credits short of a major. But I attended therapy a couple of years ago, which should count as graduate work in the field." I stopped myself. "Just kidding. I did attend therapy, but I'm not expecting college credit for it."

Surprised, Lily grinned, "I hear you, girl. I learned more in treatment than in college."

I explained, "I thought I'd use psychology in my business work. Instead, I'm doing psychological work and occasionally tying my business knowledge into it. But I've got to admit, both are useful in my marriage."

Lily smiled and coyly said, "I called the office to see who accepted Tug's offer, and you'll never guess who's come back."

"Not Melanie Pearson."

"Yes, the one and only—Melanie! I suggested to Elon that maybe Melanie would be interested, and I imagine he gave her an offer she couldn't refuse. Tug destroyed her in court. If he would have done that to me, I might have accepted just to get back at him, too."

I would find a way to investigate Tug. My first order of business was to check into Melanie's emotional state. I remember the glassy look in Melanie's eyes on the night Jon and I rescued her from Tug's office. It was symptomatic of a dissociation from reality. I pleaded with her to get help. I hope she followed through.

When Lily departed, I called Jon for Melanie's number and then called Melanie. After introductions, I told her, "Melanie, I'm worried about you. Did you ever follow through and see the therapist I suggested?"

"No. I didn't have any time back then, and now I don't have any extra money."

Frustrated, I said, "I know what you're doing."

"What am I doing?" Melanie responded snidely.

"Elon Parker has asked you to gather information on Tug's finances, and you want to get back at him for bullying you. I need to warn you, Melanie, you can't get even with narcissists. Tug will kill you before he'll let you win. The best you can do is walk away and let him find someone else to target."

The line fell silent. Finally, Melanie told me, "He's not done with me, Serena. I know Tug better than anyone. After we made love the last time, Tug told me, 'If you ever betray me, I'll end you.' He wasn't angry. At that moment, we were lying peacefully in bed. It was a matter-of-fact warning. "

"That's creepy. And he accepted your offer to work for him without question?"

"Tug's convinced I will always love him. I told him no sex, but I'd like to help him start over. Unfazed, he said, 'I knew you'd be back.'"

Melanie was right. Tug wasn't done with her.

"That last night when I was in the office with him, I felt his pure evil crawling into my skin. Tug's coming after me for testifying against him. I'd rather know what I'm up against than have him blindside me." Melanie cajoled, "Please help me, Serena. It's scary to do this alone. I need your wisdom, and I know you hate him as much as I do. We both know that he's always doing something illegal. Let's work together and find a way to send him back to prison."

"He's a millionaire now. He doesn't have to do anything illegal to walk away with tons of money. Why would he take that chance?"

"Because he's Tug."

She was right. "Have you had any episodes of losing time? Even just seconds? You looked a little out of it the night before Tug's arrest—at his office." Melanie was handcuffed when Jon broke in and rescued her. She had a blank look and said little when she left with us.

"No, absolutely not!" Melanie sounded insulted. "I'm okay. And according to Elon, Tug is only a millionaire until Blair dies. Then the money goes to the children."

Chapter 12

TUG GRANT

4:00 P.M., MONDAY, MARCH 27, 2023
2442 WEST LAKE OF THE ISLES PARKWAY, KENWOOD, MINNEAPOLIS

My therapist, Halle Day, sat modestly dressed, long, shapely legs crossed, in her stylish office. The maple wood walls, adorned with pictures featuring comforting teal tones, were classy, far above Roan's grade. Her electric blue eyes, highlighted with black, gave her an arousing mysteriousness. She had long blond hair, the natural blend you see from women who come from "old money." But the torture began as soon as she started talking. Deciding to flip the script, I said, "I'm just going to throw this out there. If you're ever interested in sleeping with me, I'd take you on the vacation of a lifetime—perhaps Paris—all expenses paid."

"I will never sleep with you, Tug." She maintained her cool composure in her reply. "Not under any circumstances. Not for any amount of money. Not even if it costs me my life."

She didn't have to be cruel. Halle had a streak of her father, Roan, in her.

Feeling the need to clarify her response further, she said, "Let's start with this: you're married."

"Marrying Blair was a no-brainer. I'm a millionaire, and you could be the benefactor."

"Tug, you went to prison for your involvement in your first wife's death. Now you're not happy with your second wife. You're forcing me to determine whether your history makes this a mandated report."

"I will swear on a Bible that I will bring no harm to Blair. I plan to do everything in my power to keep her alive."

"Moral concern number two: You're still sleeping with Taytum."

"Did I say that? I don't remember saying that." Although, of course, I am sleeping with her. Taytum is a goddess.

"You implied it. Third, you hired Melanie Pearson back, which you wouldn't have done unless you planned on having sex with her. She has to be a mess after you humiliated her in court. I think you see a lot of your mom in Melanie. You got to call Melanie a whore in front of a room full of reporters. I can only imagine the unconscious gratification you felt. It was an opportunity you were denied because of your mom's untimely death. And now Melanie's under your thumb once again."

"My mom was a whore." Before I graduated from high school, she died in an accident, driving home on an icy road. Angry now, I said, "Mommy issues again. You're a stereotype. Do you realize that?" I took a deep breath, just as she had taught, before continuing. "Rumor is the Vikings are going to give up all their draft choices this year for a shot at a quarterback. I'm willing to give up all my women and potential future paramours for a night with you."

"Wow—for one night! Let me get this straight: you're giving up your millionaire wife, your model-like attorney, your faithful secretary, and players to be named later for one night?"

"The truth is that if you could unhook that chastity belt, I'd give you pleasure the likes of which have never been bestowed on you before. There's a reason every single one of my partners has come back for more."

"There is. It's called a 'personality disorder.' I need to stop seeing you, Tug. This isn't a healthy dynamic. And understand that even with terminating therapy, I will never have sex with you under any condition."

"You honestly think you're better than me. I know where you came from. You were rural white trash left for dead in a Godforsaken farmhouse. Now you're in Kenwood, the richest neighborhood in the metro, and you think you've become the supreme deity." I calmly asked, "Did I ever tell you about one of my biggest victories as an attorney?"

"Probably," she remarked curtly.

"I don't think I told you about this one. A man was angry at his babe because she wanted to dump him. Kind of like you're doing to me. He beat her up, stripped her, and tied her to a chair naked. He rubbed the flat part of a Bowie knife all over her body, and I mean *all* over her body." I studied Halle—no reaction. Her silence was disturbing, so I continued, "He then cut lines across her chest while she shamelessly begged for her life. Once he had diminished her to her lowest state of humility, he demonstrated his complete dominance by untying her and making the chastened bitch walk around the outside of his house naked. He didn't have to drag her. She felt so demeaned that she just submitted. When he finally let her back in the house, she raced to the bathroom and cut her wrists."

"Why are you telling me this?" Halle interrupted.

"He called 911, and the medics saved her life."

"He could have killed her."

The story had struck a chord with her. I said, "She charged him with felony assault. As his defense attorney, I suggested to the jury she was into sadomasochism and it was all part of their sexual play. She had the opportunity to run but returned to the house."

"She was so humiliated that she'd rather end her life than spend another second with him."

"The jury found him not guilty." I couldn't conceal my roguish grin. The story pained Halle. Mission accomplished.

"What happened to him after?"

"What difference does it make? The point is, I win against all odds."

"I'd like his name," Halle insisted.

"Not pertinent." He's now locked up in Lino for stabbing a woman, but that was someone else's case. I had nothing to do with it.

After a moment of silent reflection, Halle looked directly at me as she spoke. "I know why you told me this story."

"The moral is simple. I am a great attorney."

"You *were* an attorney. You *were* a family man. You *were* the head of the bar. If I'm going to get you to change, I need you to accept that all of that is lost. We can only go forward from where we are."

She had to rub that in my face.

Halle continued, "You told me this story because I refused your advances. It was your passive-aggressive way of threatening me because I bruised your ego."

"Okay, we're not having sex. Statement accepted. No more threats." I couldn't afford to get kicked out of therapy. It was a condition of my release. "I have to say, Halle, you're impressive. You make me think, and I need that if I'm going to be a better man."

She gave me a dismissive smile.

"What?" I asked.

"You're still trying to sleep with me. Bribing me didn't work. Bullying didn't work. So, you've switched gears. 'How vulnerable is she to flattery?' Being a millionaire seems to have added some hubris."

"Let me just make this point. I'm not an incel guy or a crazy conspiracy theorist. But you need to consider how you benefit from being a beautiful woman. Blair and I were eating at Friend or Pho last week, and the chef was ogling you like you were

Wagyu prime rib. That doesn't happen with me or any other guy when we walk in."

"That chef is my fiancé." Halle held up her left hand, revealing a modest diamond ring.

"If you'd have told me that, I never would have propositioned you. The only married women I've been involved with were my wives. You think I'm some racist misogynist prick. It couldn't be further from the truth."

"Which one of those aren't you?" Halle jibed.

"Let's start with this. I have never hurt a woman of color."

"I think anyone who isn't white, weak, and middle to upper class unnerves you. This is why you're intimidated by Taytum and me. It's why you killed Deb. Alive, she would have ultimately outclassed you. And now that you know my fiancé is Black, talking to me must be terrifying for you." She continued, "But these are things you don't want to know about yourself. Perhaps that's why you started today's session by sabotaging therapy. You knew I'd drop you as a client if you hit on me, and that safeguards you from admitting you're running away in fear."

"Don't flatter yourself." My anger boiled. I needed to control it. *Don't for a second relish the thought that you're superior, and don't you dare reject me.* I countered, "Have you heard of the 'manosphere?'"

"I have. It's a group of misogynist men who feel castrated by strong women. Think about it, Tug. If men feel this way, is it the woman's issue or the man's issue?"

"Why would a heartless shrew like you become a therapist? The only reason anyone listens to you is because you're pretty. I think you never forgave Ricky for shooting you, and you're taking it out on me."

I made her pause. Finally, Halle offered, "I promise to consider what you said. I agree that pretty women get by with untreated mental illness more than they should because people make exceptions for them. Honestly, I am sometimes disrespectful to you, and I apologize if you feel degraded. That isn't my purpose. You need someone who will challenge your thinking."

"Apology accepted." I held back my sense of satisfaction. I could feel her backing down.

"Can't you see it?" Halle leaned forward. "Your manner of thinking resulted in the death of your wife. Deb was the person you loved the most in your life. If you don't change, the result doesn't change. Who's next? I'm trying to save you from heartbreak. Maybe I can't." She sighed and leaned back. "I will keep seeing you if you promise to take a moment and consider how your actions could result in a tragedy for someone you love. Mark my words: if you don't change, someone close to you will be the victim of retaliation when one of your illicit transactions goes bad. This is always how it plays out—not maybe—always. Please consider this before it's too late."

Dodged a bullet. I inwardly smiled with pride. I took a shot and suffered no consequences. Halle agreed to keep seeing me. She will be a project, but a skilled litigator can charm the pants off anyone.

Chapter 13

SERENA FREDERICK

4:15 P.M., MONDAY, MARCH 27, 2023
EAST FRANKLIN AVENUE, VENTURA VILLAGE, MINNEAPOLIS

While Tug was at therapy, Melanie and I had a chance to go through his computer. Before Jon and I became an item, I was employed in billing and finance, so I knew a little about investing. Once Melanie got me into the history on Tug's computer, I found this list of searches: Aardvark, Baalim of Arrows, Caballer, Dagga, and E & OE.

As I went down the list, I considered an animal, a group of archers, a plotter, a South African name for marijuana, and the abbreviation for Errors and Omissions Excepted. I wondered if there was a connection that would give us a larger clue. There were seventy-eight categories.

Melanie peeked at the directory over my shoulder.

"What do they all have in common?" I asked.

"I don't know. Maybe things people consider superfluously important? I do know I filled out a lot of savings account forms last week. Each one with a new bank."

Giving up, I called Jon. "There's a list of words on Tug Grant's computer. Let me give you the first five and see if you have anything: Aardvark, Baalim of Arrows, Caballer, Dagga, and E & OE. They must mean something. Any idea?"

"You're thinking about this wrong."

"How so?"

"The words are meaningless. He's categorizing."

"There are seventy-eight words listed." I looked at the words again—still nothing.

Then Jon shared an insight I could have kicked myself for missing. "They're the first word listed in the dictionary under each letter. Is the twenty-seventh word 'aardwolf?'"

"What in God's name is an aardwolf?"

"It looks like a jackal, but it's a termite-eating hyena in southern Africa. If aardwolf is the twenty-seventh word, and there's a total of seventy-eight, he's been through the dictionary three times."

"It is. Each word started with the next letter of the alphabet. Then he started over. *Why would Tug need all of these categories?* And then it hit me. "He's cuckoo smurfing."

"He's what?" Jon laughed.

"He's smurfing. It's a way of laundering money. If you want to move a large amount of money unnoticed, you create multiple small accounts just below the regulatory threshold to avoid detection. Thank you—love you—call you later. Melanie and I have work to do."

"Glad I could help. Love you, too."

"Cuckoo smurfing?" Melanie asked.

"It's typically called smurfing, but at times, cuckoo smurfing because it's a crazy amount of work if you're trying to hide millions of dollars. Financial institutions are required to send a form to the Internal Revenue Service for each monetary transaction over $10,000. The $10,000 threshold was created as part of the Bank Secrecy Act, passed by Congress in 1970. Smurfing involves hiding money undetected with lots of $10,000 transactions."

Melanie was impressed. "How do you know all this?"

"I was on the dean's list as a business management major at St. Ben's." I grinned. "I don't have many opportunities to show that off anymore."

Melanie pulled a chair over to me. "This is going to be fun. I graduated from my own private school of 'Hack,' and while I wasn't on the Dean's list, I will soon be on Tug's list."

Chapter 14

RICKY DAY

8:15 P.M., TUESDAY, MARCH 28, 2023
CARAWAY WEST APARTMENTS, BLACKSTONE, ST. LOUIS PARK

After a mild winter, the overcast sky dumped on us today. We would have nine inches before it was over. Melanie called me crying. Travel was not advised, but I was so thankful she sought solace with me that I hurried to her apartment. I found the door unlocked.

"Melanie," I called. When she didn't answer, I rushed in. *Please be okay.*

Melanie was sitting on the floor against the wall in her living room in agonizing misery. I hated to see Melanie falling apart. I'd seen it happen many times in prison. The pressure of the day-to-day fear that someone's going to take their life before the next hour passes becomes more than they can bear, and they deteriorate into a mental health mess.

"Thank God you're okay." I knelt by her, and she hugged me tightly.

When I leaned back and studied her dried tears, I noticed her blouse buttons were strained so tightly a button could fly off through a window and kill a bird at any moment.

"I can't go out with you tonight. I put on weight, and none of my clothes fit."

"We shouldn't be driving anywhere tonight anyway." Trying to ease her pain, I suggested, "Put on something comfortable, and we'll order out and watch a bad movie."

"I'm too fat." She dropped her shoulders in frustration. "Are you embarrassed to date a pig who would eat her way out of her clothes?"

"You're beautiful." I gently lifted her chin. "I don't see any difference, and even if there is, you're still beautiful."

Melanie leaned into me for a hug. "All of my food tastes like cinnamon."

"Maybe you used it accidentally instead of salt or pepper."

"I can't stand cinnamon," she explained. "I don't have any in the house."

I squeezed her tight. "It's okay. Let's just sit and talk." I didn't have an explanation to offer.

She pulled away and led me by the hand to the couch.

I sat and then stood up and sat again. "Did you do something to your couch?"

"No." Melanie asked, "Why?"

"No." Melanie asked, "Why?"

"Maybe it's just me, but it seems higher."

"That's what I thought!" Melanie exclaimed.

I hated to feed into her paranoia, but I knelt and tipped the couch up. "Look at this." There was a block attached to each of the couch legs.

Melanie got on the floor and looked at the couch leg. She laughed hysterically. "Son of a bitch." She crawled back to her feet. "That jerk. I don't know how he did it." Melanie marched over to her oversized purse and pulled out a shirt. "I just had a thought." Too bitter and manic to be modest, she tugged off her shirt in the kitchen and quickly slipped on the one from the bag. Melanie gleefully twirled around, "Do you see this? This shirt fits perfectly. Sophie borrowed it from me a month ago and finally returned it to me at work. He switched my shirts."

Melanie went to the kitchen and returned with a bowl of roasted broccoli. "Taste this."

I humored her and took a piece. "It tastes like cinnamon."

"You're not messing with me, are you?"

"No. Honestly, it tastes like cinnamon. Who would know you couldn't stand cinnamon?"

"Anyone I've ever dated." Melanie grabbed her phone off the kitchen counter. She thumbed a number and put her phone on speaker. Melanie shouted into the phone. "Stay away from my apartment, asshole! And return my key."

"Are you going to send one of your killer boyfriends after me?" the caller yelled back.

"That was a cheap shot, Darius. And give me back my cat."

"I threw away the key." He guffawed, "And I hated your damn cat Sambo or whatever his name was."

"You didn't kill him?!" Melanie shrieked.

"No! I don't have your damn cat, you crazy bitch!" He hung up.

Melanie shouted at the phone, "Creep!"

"Isn't your cat still here?" I asked cautiously.

"It doesn't seem like my Simba."

"You spend every day, for sixteen years, fearing for your life in prison, and you get a sense when people are telling the truth. He sounded like he was telling the truth."

"Sophie knows a woman who used to date Darius. She said Darius was all flowers and chocolate at the beginning but became controlling and mean. She dumped him after he bitch-slapped her." There was a sudden sadness in her tone as she finished, "It's got to be Darius. It couldn't be—" she didn't finish.

"Did he ever bitch-slap you?"

"You heard in court what I did." Melanie turned away in shame. "I can't really blame him."

I tamped down my anger at Darius and knelt on the carpet before her. "Slap me."

Melanie's green eyes pled with mine. "Please don't ask me to do that. I can't."

"Why not? I killed innocent people. If you deserved it, I deserve it more."

"Point taken." She pulled me to my feet and hugged me. "You're right. Nobody deserves that."

It was all too weird. *Why would someone do this?* "Do you mind if I call Jon Frederick?"

Chapter 15

ROAN CARUSO

6:00 P.M. WEDNESDAY, MARCH 29, 2023
PIERCE STREET NORTHEAST, BELTRAMI, MINNEAPOLIS

The temperature was back above freezing, and water puddled on the sides of the streets as the snow melted. Catania and I sat at the dinner table, dining on lasagna layered with rich meat sauce and topped with perfectly browned mozzarella. She remarked, "What's eating you?"

"Halle fired me from therapy."

"You just started with her." Beneath her dark brows, Cat's witchy gaze pierced through me. "Now what? Isn't seeing her a condition of your release from prison?"

"Yeah. I need to figure out what I'm going to do with that."

Cat set down her fork. "Fix it. I can't be left alone here again. The last four years have been miserable."

By the time I was released from prison, Catania was fit to be tied. I always liked that saying. I've known more than my share of characters who were "fit to be tied," and many were. The saying comes from the old days when they'd tie mentally ill folks up in straightjackets. It fits Cat perfectly when she goes off the rails.

"Why did Halle dump you as a client?" She asked.

"I've been doing some favors for Tug."

"Are you kidding me?" Her eyes blazed. "I thought you were done working with Tug."

"It's just stupid shit." I chortled to minimize it all. "Tug is paying me to mess with Melanie's head. Move her car to different spots, replace her clothes with different sizes, become a fake friend online. Goofy stuff like that." I thought Halle would get a chuckle out of it. Instead, she was angry and accused me of being a manipulative narcissist with no conscience."

Cat stood up and looked out the kitchen window. "What does Halle charge you for a session?"

"Halle doesn't charge me anything. She says she can't officially count it as therapy, but she signs the form that says we met, and that's all I need." After chewing one more bite of lasagna, I asked, "What are you thinking?"

"Halle's right." She turned back to me. "Are you out of your mind?"

"It's easy money."

"I don't like it." Cat returned to her chair. "My family has honored a code for generations. We don't hurt people who aren't in the game. I understand killing Deondre after he stole your car. And I appreciate your killing one of the creeps who shot at our house. But Debra Grant was innocent, and you participated in her murder. That's not what we do. Honestly, there's a terrible part of me that doesn't mind your college girlfriend being dead, but you crossed a line."

"I broker deals. Tug was going to kill her regardless. I stepped in and collected some cash to make the connection. Believe me, I in no way supported this. I even tried to warn her."

"But you brokered the deal. And now you're trying to drive Tug's ex crazy. What did she do? What did Melanie do to us that's worth tearing her apart over? We're not thirteen years old. We don't destroy people over broken hearts." She seethed for a moment and said, "I got a call from Barney's consigliere today."

"*The* Barney?" Librio Barney Bellomo is the head of the Genovese crime family in New York—the most powerful crime family in the US.

"Yes. The Wizard wants to get made, so he's got a job in Minneapolis. He needs your connections to make it happen. We're talking molto denaro. The job only involves you. We can't take the leap if you're gonna keep dickin' around with Tug."

Enzo Angelini is known as the Wizard of Odds because of his work in sports betting. I never liked the guy, but he knows how to make money. If the Wizard's involved, it's a big payday, and I could use a bigger boat.

"If you go to prison for Tug again, I won't be here waiting," Catania warned. She was about to leave the room when she turned back. "And please don't tell me this is why we have a cat now."

Chapter 16

JON FREDERICK

5:00 P.M. MONDAY, APRIL 3, 2023
CARAWAY WEST APARTMENTS, BLACKSTONE, ST. LOUIS PARK

After Ricky Day told me about Melanie Pearson's bizarre predicament, I had her mark the days she noticed changes in her apartment. After work, I stopped at her five-story apartment complex near the bustling Blackstone neighborhood in St. Louis Park. Melanie's apartment had lots of white furniture and glass, which reflected a lack of children.

Melanie walked me through the apartment, adorned in an ivory blouse with a red dahlia flower design and jeans. The color in her blouse accented her thick ginger hair. She said, "I went through my calendar, like you asked, and realized I've always noticed the changes on Tuesdays. But I've asked a neighbor, who is home on Tuesdays, to keep an eye on the apartment, and she's never seen anyone around."

I stopped at a three-foot square framed print on the wall. It was gold in color and divided into rectangles. It looked like grimy blinds from the 1960s era. I knew it was a famous painting, but the artist's name escaped me. Not being a fan of paintings that are one solid color, I teased, "Did you hang this to cover graffiti on the wall?"

"This is a print of an Agnes Martin painting titled *Friendship*," Melanie explained. "Friendship is everything. After a close friend died, Martin abandoned the art world for a while and returned with this captivating inspiration. It's powerful."

"Was her friend a pharaoh? It looks like the dust from a pyramid."

"You need to almost step into it to truly appreciate her work. Martin was a genius. She once said, 'Art is the concrete representation of our most subtle feelings.'"

She must have been feeling dirty. Enough about art. I asked, "What do you do on Monday nights, like tonight?"

"Sophie and I have a cooking class at the Cooks of Crocus Hills we attend, and then we stop at Billy's on Grand for a nightcap after." A realization washed over her face.

"Do you have class tonight?" Serena and I had done a couple of classes as a date night event at the Cooks of Crocus Hill. I loved learning to cook something new with Serena and enjoying the meal when we were done without having to clean up.

"Yeah."

"Go to the class as usual tonight. I'll wait in your apartment while you're gone and see if you have company. Call before you come home."

"All right." Melanie nodded. "By the way, the original painting of *Friendship* is worth about fifteen million dollars."

"If Martin can sell that painting for a million, she is a genius."

6:00 P.M.

AFTER WAITING AN hour with the lights off, I heard someone approach the door. I could see the shadow of a man's shoes above the sill at the base of the door. He knocked, and I waited. Finally, I heard a key turn, and the door opened. The stranger turned on the light. There stood Roan Caruso, holding a cat.

I entered the room from the shadows, holding a gun and, trying to lighten the mood, commented, "What's the saying? Don't bring a gun to a catfight."

Catching a glimpse of a smile, I ordered, "Put the cat on the floor. Put your hands in the air and turn and face the door."

Roan was frustrated but followed my directions. "I found her cat. I'm just returning it."

"Good, then this should go nice and smooth."

Once he faced the door, I patted him down. "No gun?"

"On probation. Can't be caught with one," Roan responded.

"I'm going to cuff you at the beginning here, but I'll take them off if this is all peaceful."

He dropped his hands behind his back, and I cuffed him. I texted Melanie and told her I had her stalker in cuffs. I didn't know what to expect from Roan. I know he's killed before. I told Roan, "I'm aware of what you've been doing. We knew you'd be coming tonight because it's your pattern. You're on supervised release. What the hell are you thinking?"

"Yeah, I know," Roan nodded. "I'll be honest with you if you let me walk on this."

"Why are you torturing Melanie?" I asked.

"This wasn't my idea, and I had enough. Tonight, I'm returning everything. I've got a carload of clothing outside—Melanie's wardrobe, plus sizes bigger and smaller. I've got the receipts for all of it if she wants to take the extras back. We replaced her lip balm with different flavors and changed her shoes. I'm returning everything."

I looked at him in disbelief.

"I'm serious. I know you have no reason to believe me. But you know my daughter, Halle, and she told me that if I don't stop being a dirtball, she isn't going to talk to me anymore."

"Okay, Take me to your car. If the items are there, I'll remove the cuffs."

When we arrived at the car, I saw the back seat was loaded with clothes. I removed the cuffs and said, "Pop the trunk."

The trunk was also loaded with clothing. Roan asked, "Are you going to help me haul this shit up?"

"No. But I will keep holding my gun for the time being. Grab an armful and start returning it." Roan did just that.

After two trips, Roan with clothes, me still holding the gun on him, Melanie arrived at the apartment. Simba immediately ran into her arms. Interestingly, Simba's replacement wandered into the kitchen and seemed to study the scenario with envy. The impostor cat rubbed against Melanie's leg, gently massaging her. Melanie looked down at the impostor cat and said, "Sure, now you want me." She reached down and picked up Simba Two. "I have enough love for you, too." We sat at the kitchen table with Melanie's two Simbas resting on her lap. "Why?" She asked Roan, "What did I ever do to you?"

"I know, I know, I know." Roan raised his hand as if to suggest she could back off. "I made sure your cat had the best food and care. I can't give up who I work for, but I can tell you it was someone who was angry that you testified in court. Tonight, I decided, 'enough.' I came here to return everything and hope for your forgiveness. You did nothing to hurt me, and you don't deserve this."

"But why? I'm working for Tug now."

"You don't understand him," Roan said. "He's got to get his pound of flesh before he's satisfied. Why do you think Deb's dead?"

"Ten million dollars," Melanie suggested.

"At some point, Deb threatened to leave him. The insurance policies came after."

I interjected, "Tug can't stand the thought of being abandoned. It connects too strongly with painful memories of his childhood and creates narcissistic injury."

Roan admitted, "This went too far, and I'm sorry. I can't say it enough. I was stupid. Immature. Honestly, I hadn't even considered the pain you'd feel. I thought it would just be an annoying inconvenience. I truly am sorry. If you report this, the person I'm working for will know I was caught, and he'll look for another way to get even with you. If you don't report, I'll tell him I'm still doing this, but I promise I won't bother you anymore."

Melanie sighed and looked at me. "Well, he did return Simba."

"He also stole your clothes," I pointed out. "I think he should give us something that helps convict the man who initiated the harassment."

"I can't," Roan said. "I'm sorry, but I can't snitch. It's an occupational hazard."

"Get the rest of my stuff," Melanie directed.

Roan left. This time, I didn't follow him. If he didn't return, this would be enough for Melanie to press charges.

But Roan returned again and again.

Melanie called Ricky Day and then stepped into the bedroom to speak for twenty minutes as Roan continued his work. Roan appeared genuinely remorseful. He removed a piece of plastic he had inserted into the showerhead to reduce the water flow. He checked to make sure the blocks were removed from the couch legs and wrote a note apologizing for dousing her food with cinnamon.

When Melanie returned, she told Roan, "Okay, I'm not going to report this, but you need to let me know every time Tug asks you to do anything."

"Okay." Roan nodded. "Everything has been returned."

"Remember the first time we met at Hoppy Girl?" Melanie asked. "You insulted me."

"I don't remember," Roan chuckled. "But don't take it personally. Tug's always braggin' to me about the next girl he's going to bang. I'm not a cheater, so I insult them to try and get them to leave."

"I hadn't even spoken to Tug yet," Melanie clarified.

"Tug researched you," Roan explained. "He pointed you out when you came struttin' in. Tug knew you were single, struggling financially, and had no mom to support you. Tug told me to meet him there to work out a deal for his Mustang, but when he made me the same offer I declined earlier, I realized he just wanted me to see the next bunny in his mansion."

"I don't strut." Clearly bothered, Melanie asked, "Did everyone at Hoppy Girl know Tug was married?"

"Sorry, it's just how I talk. Yeah, Deb loved Hoppy Girl, and they had stayed at the bed and breakfast."

Melanie took a deep, painful breath and told him, "Ricky Day told me I shouldn't press charges but instead give you a chance to change."

"You tell Ricky I owe you both," Roan replied.

Chapter 17

MELANIE PEARSON

4:00 P.M. FRIDAY, APRIL 7, 2023
EAST FRANKLIN AVENUE, VENTURA VILLAGE, MINNEAPOLIS

I didn't dare tell Serena, but my dissociative episodes are becoming more frequent. The moments seem to be triggered when Tug comes near me, particularly when he's behind me. I must have lost a couple of minutes the other day. I came back to consciousness with Tug standing in front of my desk, asking, "What's wrong with you?"

Today, I was overwhelmed by filling out new bank forms. I was stressed, and I needed to be careful. I was still wearing ridiculously tight clothes to work for now so Tug wouldn't realize I was on to him. He was trying to get reinstated as an attorney, and I had just finished typing a letter for him to present to the bar. When I carefully checked the letter for mistakes, I felt Tug's breath on my neck. I hadn't seen him step behind my desk. I felt a pinch in my buttocks and asked, "Did you just stick a needle in me?"

5:00 P.M.

WHEN I CAME to, I was lying naked on Tug's couch.
Tug was fully dressed and adjusting his tie as he said, "I need to go. Make sure the door is locked when you leave."

I could feel I'd had sex but had no memory of it. None. I testified in court I couldn't remember every time we had sex, but no one seemed to think it was significant. Before today, I'd only lost minutes here and there. I thought back to Sebastian teasing that I must have dissociative amnesia because I was always forgetting things. I thought Sebastian had taken advantage of me, but maybe he hadn't. *What the hell is wrong with me? Who forgets having sex?*

Suddenly, I was immersed in sadness. I had to break up with Ricky. I was engaged to Darius when I testified at Tug's murder trial. I watched Darius deteriorate into rageful jealousy as Tug made me recall the details of our sexual encounters on the stand. I would be testifying against Tug again, and I was not going to put another lover through that. I called Serena, and she agreed to meet with me. I needed a hidden camera to see exactly how much of every day I was losing.

10:00 A.M., SATURDAY, APRIL 8, 2023
BARNES AND NOBLE, RAINBOW VILLAGE, 3940 DIVISION,
ST. CLOUD

THE SUNSHINE THROUGH the floor-to-ceiling glass windows at the Barnes and Noble Starbucks gave the dining area a warm glow. I ordered a brown sugar shaken espresso with oat milk, and Serena had an unsweetened iced tea. Bookstores are the place where I've historically found peace of mind. The only negative was the weird green and orange Sound and The Fury poster on the wall featuring a topless and breastless woman who appeared to have lost the arms race. Still, the sunlight created a warm, friendly environment. I sat back and asked Serena about her kids.

Serena quickly turned the conversation back to me. "What's bothering you, Melanie?"

"I need a camera for the office." I nervously scratched my arm. I stopped after noticing the intensity with which she observed my behavior.

"Why?"

"I've lost some seconds here and there." I took a sip of my brew.

"I'm so sorry to hear that." Serena reached and squeezed my hand. "Okay, you need to step out of this. I'll try to think of another way. It's not safe for you to be around Tug if you're losing time."

"I'm not quitting," I insisted. "Get me a camera. I need to see exactly how much time I'm losing." I didn't dare tell her Tug had sex with me and I didn't remember it.

"Please, Melanie, it's not worth losing your sanity. Tug is a killer. I'm more worried about your safety than about nailing Tug."

"I'm so close. Another day or two, and I'll locate the hidden files. I'm not walking away from this." *Serena still doesn't get it. I may be working covertly, but this is a war. If I don't get Tug back behind bars, he will kill me.*

"Then I need you to be honest with me, Melanie. Dissociation occurs after someone has experienced severe trauma. You asked me to help you, and I have. If we're in this together, you have to tell me what you're running away from."

"That's the thing—there's nothing there." I could tell she didn't believe me.

"Okay," she replied casually. "Tell me about your greatest shame."

"My mom died by suicide. I've always felt like I didn't do enough to help her."

Serena studied my eyes as she sipped on her iced tea. Finally, she looked over at the shelves of books for a second and turned back and said, "That isn't it."

"Don't you think that's enough?" When she didn't respond, I looked at the tables around us to ensure no one was within hearing distance. "I always say I had nothing to be ashamed of before I met Tug. That isn't true." I suddenly felt so weak, but I told her. "I was fourteen and dating a boy—Cade—the same age as me. Nice guy. Wouldn't hurt a flea. He was the only one who knew how bad it was with my mom. I'd find her passed out on the floor from pills. She was always criticizing me, but I knew it was the depression. Cade's dad had abandoned him and his mom. It would have been easier if Mom had just left. A neighbor named Del took Cade under his wing and got him work. His mom loved Del for it. Cade got me through junior high. I mattered. I could have become anything back then."

"What did he do to you?" Serena softly asked as she reached forward and took my hand.

"Huh? It's what *I* did to *him*." I pulled my hand free, stood up, and wiped my tears away. I left my latte and quickly headed to the nook in the far corner of the store where the mysteries were housed. I sat on the floor against the bookshelf and held my head in my hands. I couldn't stop crying.

A woman approached and asked kindly, "Can I help?"

I glanced up for a second and could see *Melissa* on her nametag. I shook my head. There was no helping me.

Serena came over and asked, "Could you give us a minute?"

Melissa nodded and stepped away.

Serena sat beside me, put her arm around me, and patiently waited for me to continue.

"I can still picture the two of us sitting at the top of Redwood Falls waterfall, holding hands," I told her. "And then Cade told me that Del was molesting him. He told me everything. It started when Cade was twelve. And it was bad."

"What did you tell him?"

"Nothing. I was so overwhelmed. I didn't know what to do. I could hear Dad's voice in my head screaming, 'Don't embarrass me!' Dad would go ballistic if it were all over the community that I was dating a boy who had been sodomized over and over again. Without a word being said, I got up and stepped away, and I never spoke to Cade again. I ghosted him. I was waiting for it to be all over the news, but it never was. The last time I saw Cade, he was riding as a passenger in Del's truck a week later.

The sadness in his eyes was devastating. But I didn't say anything. A month after that, Cade was gone, and I never saw him again."

"Do you think harm came to him?" Serena asked.

"I know harm came to him, but he wasn't reported missing or anything. I went by his house a month after, and he and his mom didn't live there anymore."

"What was his last name?" Serena asked.

"Bennett. Cade Anthony Bennett. Named after a great singer." I continued, "I hate myself for that. Some nights, when Mom started to whine, my misery was so intense that I'd allow myself to check out of life for a minute or two. The guilt was overwhelming. I couldn't deal with any more stress, so I shut everything out. Eventually, when I was super anxious, it occurred on its own."

"Does that ever happen during sex?"

I curiously looked Serena over. "Why would you even say that?"

"Cade was being sexually abused, and your trauma is over not saving him. Trauma can get woven into our lives in weird ways."

"No," I lied. "Never."

Serena studied me. "Are you sure nothing's happened at work?"

"Yes," I insisted.

"Okay, I'll get you a camera under the condition that we both have access to it. I don't feel good about you being in Tug's office. I need to know you're okay. Do you still have that roommate?"

"No," I sighed. "Sophie bailed after I told her Roan was messing with our apartment. I don't blame her. It was crazy."

"Okay, then we need to find you a place to stay. It has to be with someone who would immediately contact me if Tug visited." A smile crept across Serena's face. "Agnes Schraut."

Chapter 18

MELANIE PEARSON

7:30 P.M., SATURDAY, APRIL 8, 2023
ZELO, 831 NICOLLET MALL, MINNEAPOLIS

Roan Caruso gave me a voucher to eat at Zelo, an Italian restaurant in Minneapolis. It was better than a gift certificate because Roan offered to pick up the tab for anything we ate or drank and pay the tip. Ricky could only have water because he was on probation, but I enjoyed a glass of Whispering Angel Rosé. It was a little too dry, but the food was terrific, and Ricky was so humbly appreciative that it made up for it. I had the tortiglioni rossa, a savory sausage meal with sweet peas and roasted peppers in a Romana rossa sauce. Ricky's linguini di mare was even better. The seafood was served in saffron-tomato broth on pasta. I have never seen anyone so delighted to eat. I continually pushed back the thought that I was planning to break up with him tonight when we returned home. Ricky was the only one I wanted to share this dinner with.

Ricky repeated several times, "This is the best meal I've ever eaten. Thank you!"

Bless that boy for his gratefulness! I wanted to hug him and kiss him.

Catania Turrisi was in the place tonight. During my time with Tug, we periodically ran into Catania and Roan. Not even

"Cat the moonbat plutocrat," as Tug called her behind her back, could spoil this night. And then I saw Trey—Darius's obnoxious best friend. Trey never liked me. He complained that my style of dress was intended to steal Darius away from his time with the boys. I never dressed slutty, but I did wear bright colors to highlight my red hair. It was one feature I was always proud of. That pig Trey had the gall to come to our table and take a picture.

I tried to ignore him, but my heart sank in anticipation of impending doom.

Ricky assumed someone was going to post something derogatory about him, and he apologized for the intrusion. Accustomed to the criticism, he kept eating. I was sure Trey would immediately send the photo to Darius.

After I finished my limonetta bella lemon pie and Ricky finished his crème brûlée, we walked hand in hand to the metro parking ramp by Hell's Kitchen. Unfortunately, Darius was waiting for us by my car. When I tried to hold Ricky back, I realized we were surrounded by four of Darius's friends. Ricky was strong, but Darius's posse worked out regularly, and they were in great shape.

"We don't want any trouble," I pleaded. Accepting my soft request as an order, Ricky immediately quit resisting. In that fraction of a second, I realized I loved Ricky more than anyone I'd ever met. No one had ever stopped in their tracks for me. My paranoia, now in high gear, played with the notion, *Roan set us up.*

Darius arrogantly retorted, "If the correctional system isn't going to teach this child-killer a lesson, we will."

Ricky looked over the group of men and said quietly to me, "The strong do what they want, and the weak suffer what they must." He announced to Darius, "All right, but let Melanie go. She has nothing to do with my sins."

Trey said, "I think if you are going to take a killer out for a gourmet meal, you have something to do with it. Knowing

Melanie, you were probably the third wheel when she was in rut with Darius and Tug."

"That's not true," I interjected.

Ricky said, "Be kind and compassionate to one another, forgiving each other, just as Christ forgave you. Ephesians." Uninterested in scripture, Darius took a swing at Ricky.

Ricky blocked it with his forearm and stepped back. "This is going to end badly for all of us."

And then we heard a gunshot.

We all turned to see Catania standing by a black Lexus. I was glad the damn bullet didn't ricochet off something and kill somebody. Cat didn't appear concerned. She watched an Escalade pull into the parking ramp and quickly brake to a stop close to us. The doors opened in unison, and four large Italian men, including Roan Caruso, exited. Cat got into her car and drove off.

Roan walked directly at us, gave us a once-over, and then confronted Darius. "Do you have any idea who we are, boy?"

"I'm not sure," he responded.

"Look up 'Minneapolis Combination.' If any harm comes to Melanie or Ricky, they will never find your body. The ball's in your court. You have a decision to make. What are you going to do?"

Darius's friends cautiously took a step back. Trey yelled at Roan from behind us, "Do you know the dirtbag you're protecting?"

Roan slowly turned toward him and said, "You and I are having a communication problem. Are you a little slow? Let me say it again, in case you're hard of hearing. I said, you leave them alone, or you cease to exist. I did not ask for your opinion."

One of Roan's large friends walked directly at Trey and told him, "If you are incapable of understanding, our options are limited."

Darius rescued his friend. "We're going to get in our cars and never bother them again."

"Now that seems like an intelligent choice." Roan smiled. "What are you waiting for?"

Darius and his friends quickly scattered and departed.

"Are you good?" Roan asked us.

"Yes, thank you!" I responded with sincere appreciation.

"Sir, you are very kind," Ricky added.

I was so glad I didn't press charges against Roan, even if he almost drove me over the edge. I needed someone who could make Darius back off. Roan was better than the police because Darius believed the cops were under so much scrutiny that they couldn't hold him accountable. But Roan wouldn't think twice about beating the hell out of him.

Roan offered, "I think you're going to be okay, but we'll escort you home tonight just to make sure."

Chapter 19

SERENA FREDERICK

3:30 P.M., MONDAY, APRIL 10, 2023
51ST STREET & WASHBURN AVENUE SOUTH, FULTON, MINNEAPOLIS

We had hidden a miniature camera lens in a seashell-decorated frame I had Nora make for Melanie. It was strategically placed on the corner of her work desk so I could view Melanie completely. Mel thought she'd finish the hack today. She'd load the files on a flash drive, take it to the Minneapolis Electronic Crimes Unit, and report concerns that her boss was committing fraud.

With relief, Melanie turned and gave the camera a sad smile. She was heartbroken over ending her relationship with Ricky. Melanie told me she couldn't resume dating until this investigation was over. She picked up her phone and texted me. *I'm downloading the files. I'll be out of here in a few minutes.*

My anxiety over Melanie's safety escalated every day. Today, I was at Agnes Schraut's house so I could get to the office quickly if needed. Agnes did whatever she wanted, which earned my admiration. While she enjoyed my presence, she wasn't in the mood for conversation at the moment. When I tried making small talk, Agnes cranked up the volume on her Hallmark movie to the point where I would have to holler and do jumping jacks to get her attention. I laughed in response, and she patted my arm in appreciation for understanding. So, I sat in the living room with her, watching Melanie on my phone as she worked at her desk.

"Is Tug there?" I texted back.

Melanie nodded affirmatively. I watched her as she appeared to be scrolling on her computer screen. Seemingly perplexed, she suddenly stopped and scratched her head.

Melanie gazed at the flash drive and then texted, *Done.* But she didn't remove it.

C'mon Melanie, leave.

Instead, she remained sitting at her desk.

Melanie looked fine, but I stepped out of the living room and called her to make sure. "Melanie, what are you thinking?"

She whispered, "I came across something I missed the first time through his computer. I think Tug sent Blair a falsified bank notice. I need to load this, too."

Bank fraud can carry a thirty-year sentence. I found myself whispering, "Okay, but make it quick."

"Downloading." Melanie whispered, "I'm turning your volume off."

I tensed as I saw Tug enter the screen. He set an old-fashioned whiskey glass in front of her and said, "Time for a break. Take a sip."

Trying to ignore him, Melanie remained focused on her laptop screen as she responded, "I'm meeting up with a friend." She mindlessly brushed the glass away, and gold fluid splashed out as it slid.

"Is this the same friend who you once said would do a threesome with us?" Tug stepped around her desk, and I could now see him on the screen rubbing her shoulders. Primarily focused on ogling her cleavage, he didn't appear concerned over what she was doing. He suggested to her, "That's $30 worth of Blue Label spilled on your desk. Lick it up."

"Don't be ridiculous," Melanie responded.

"I have a surprise for you, too." Tug undid the top button of her blouse, leaned down, and kissed her neck.

"I have to go." Melanie swatted his hand away.

Tug's hands dropped down, and Melanie twitched. "Ouch. You pinched me! I have a friend waiting for me."

"If I remember my college lit class correctly, I believe it was Romeo who said, 'Love is rough, rude, and pricks like a thorn,' Tug said. He stepped away, and Melanie gradually seemed to lose focus.

"C'mon, Mel," I cheered, knowing full well I was still muted.

Melanie glanced up and said, "Last time..." The sentence trailed off as her eyes lost focus.

I watched helplessly as Tug stepped behind her and groped her breasts. He kissed her neck and cajoled, "If she's a friend of yours, she's likely been stood up before. Relax, babe. Let's get you out of those tight clothes."

"Melanie!" I yelled. "Crap!"

Tug pushed her head toward the spilled liquor. "Lick it up," he repeated.

Like an obedient dog, Melanie licked the amber scotch off her desk.

I was furious. Tug was such a pig. I grabbed my car keys and was out the door in seconds.

With the phone still connected, I could hear Tug say, "You can undress in my office."

I immediately ended the connection and called Melanie back, hoping the buzzing would bring her to reality.

No answer.

I tried contacting Jon, but he didn't answer. He was in Morrison County working a case for the BCA. I left a message: *I'm headed over to Tug's office. Melanie has the information we need, but she's dissociating. I need to help her.*

4:00 P.M.
EAST FRANKLIN AVENUE, VENTURA VILLAGE, MINNEAPOLIS

I SPRINTED TO Tug's office door only to find it locked. I pounded on it to no avail. I yanked on the handle, but the solid oak door wasn't budging. I returned to my SUV and dug out the tire iron. Determined to rescue Melanie, I beat on the office door as hard as I could.

After several minutes, Tug opened it, a crack.

I stuck the tool in the opening so he couldn't close it again.

As he opened it further, I could see he was wearing slacks but was bare-chested and barefoot. Tug shouted, "What the hell are you doing?" He glanced at the marks I'd left. "Do you want to pay for that?"

I pushed my way past him and ran to his office. Melanie was lying naked on the couch, as motionless as a mannequin. Noticing Tug had a large cup of iced coffee on his desk, I set the tire iron down, grabbed the java, and threw it into Melanie's face.

Startled, Melanie looked around as if she'd woken from a deep slumber. Once she realized where she was, she quickly scrambled for her clothes and dressed.

Tug had snuck up on me from behind and grabbed a fistful of my hair. He yelled, "You crazy bitch! Do you have any idea how much that couch is worth? You just broke into my office. Get your ass out."

Letting my hair rip, I pivoted and punched him in the face.

Tug returned an equally harsh punch to my jaw, followed by a slug to my stomach.

My body heaved forward as I stepped back to catch my breath.

Melanie squatted behind Tug's desk and opened the bottom drawer.

"It's not there," Tug guffawed. "I'm on probation. Can't have a gun. There are condoms if that's what you're looking for."

Melanie stood with a bottle of Johnnie Walker and struck it hard on the corner of his desk, busting off the bottom. The jagged, broken glass presented a serious weapon.

I quickly grabbed my tire iron and faced Tug.

"What the hell is going on?" Tug raised his hands in retreat.

"You're done raping my friend, creep," I shouted.

"Wait a minute. You have this all wrong." He fearfully backed up, "I ask her to take her clothes off, she does, and we get to it. That's it. She's never said no. Tell her, Melanie, you never ask me to stop." He turned to me. "Melanie loves it when I do all the work, and she can lay back and enjoy it."

Melanie silently searched her memory but was drawing a blank.

Trying to lighten the mood, Tug said, "Honestly, Melanie's kind of like fucking a sack of flour—not the liveliest soul."

"She's dissociating. Melanie's not even conscious." I was doing all I could to hold back from striking Tug. I absolutely hated that he took advantage of Melanie's semi-conscious state. Trying to calm my rage, I patted my free hand with the tire iron.

My hesitation created a sudden change in Tug. He relaxed, dropped his hands, and started laughing. "Wait a minute. How dull am I? You were the surprise Mel was talking about. This is one of those role-playing sex games you like to play. That's what you were doing in Alloy that night. I'm so damn stupid. I could have had you *and* Melanie, but I just ignored you. If I would have known a ménage à trois was on the table today, I wouldn't have—" He stopped.

"You wouldn't have what Tug?" *He drugged her.* I couldn't believe what I was witnessing. Tug's perverted brain assumed I was there because I desired him.

"You're Melanie's friend—the one she said would blow my gaskets," Tug said eagerly. "You take this roleplay shit seriously."

He was defenseless, but I seriously thought about hitting him anyway. Playing along with this self-absorbed freak, I suggested,

"We're going to have to call it off. I don't know what's going on with Melanie, but I need to get her home."

Melanie stepped around the desk toward him. Seeing how close she was to cutting him put it all back in perspective again. We couldn't be killing anybody here. I needed to get Melanie back to where she could regulate her emotions.

Playing along with Tug, I said, "I'm sorry, this went a little too far. Melanie's in a bad place." I turned to her. "Melanie, set the bottle down. Let's step outside and get some fresh air."

Recognizing the fierce intensity in Melanie's glare, Tug said, "Hey, come on. We were just having a little fun."

I took Melanie's free arm and began pulling her out of the office. She kept the broken glass aimed at Tug while we stepped away.

Disappointed that he had just lost the opportunity for a ménage à trois, Tug begged, "What can I do to fix this?"

"I need to grab Melanie's stuff and get her a breath of fresh air."

When Tug approached, Melanie swung the broken bottle at him. I had to yank her back to keep her from cutting him. I didn't want to end up at the police station trying to explain an assault charge.

Tug retreated.

"C'mon, Melanie," I gasped.

Realizing she still presented a threat, he pleaded, "Melanie, it's me, Tug. I'd never hurt you."

She raised the glass toward Tug's head, but this time didn't lunge.

While Tug focused on Melanie, I inconspicuously pocketed the flash drive. *What else do I need?* I grabbed the seashell picture frame so Tug couldn't argue we illegally recorded him. We didn't. It was for Melanie's safety, but Tug has a way of twisting things in court, so why have the argument if it could be avoided?

"Grab my purse," Melanie finally spoke.

I was pleased to hear this. It meant Melanie had some awareness of what she was doing.

Still keeping his distance, Tug gave me a lecherous grin as he offered, "If you want to stop back after you drop her off, I'll be here."

"Not tonight," I forced a smile. "I need to make sure she's okay." I led her out the door. She kept the broken bottle aimed at Tug as we left. Melanie was not okay.

Once outside, I walked Melanie to a garbage can and told her, "We're safe now. Please drop the bottle."

Fortunately, even in her semi-dissociative state, she trusted me, and as directed, she dropped the bottle in the container. Melanie was coming around but still had an odd emptiness in her eyes. I'd need to rehearse the statement she'd give the police. On the positive side, it could be brief, as the evidence was all on the flash drive.

Once in the car, my phone buzzed. After I told Jon we had the evidence we needed, he said, "Head to the BCA office in St. Paul. I'll call the Minneapolis Electronic Crimes Unit and have someone waiting for you in the parking lot."

I felt relief when BCA Director Sean Reynolds met us at the door and took over escorting Melanie. I explained what Tug was doing and how he had directly defied a court order to release all financial information in his divorce.

Melanie became more coherent as our time at the BCA progressed. When we were finished, I drove Melanie directly to the hospital. Her comment about being pinched bothered me. I requested they test her for the presence of a sedative.

Chapter 20

TUG GRANT

3:30 P.M., WEDNESDAY, APRIL 12, 2023
WABASHA STREET BRIDGE, I-77, WABASHA STREET SOUTH, WEST SIDE, ST. PAUL

I demanded that Roan Caruso meet me on the Wabasha Street Bridge over the Mississippi River. The mighty Mississippi is over a football field wide here. There was a cool breeze and whitecaps on the river. A cement barrier and a long metal rail buffered the sidewalks from traffic. I could safely see strangers approaching from a good distance. It irked me that Roan was reluctant to talk to me. *Had he forgotten who I am?*

Roan was on an overlook, alone, leaning on the railing, gazing at the rough river. "Always loved walking the Wabasha bridge," he remarked.

I glanced back to make sure no one was around before I began. "Life gets so damn complicated." I leaned on the rail next to him, and we stood silent, watching white caps roll over on the turbulent river. I couldn't help thinking back to a decade ago when my wife and I partied with Roan and Cat. We were on top of the world. I need to get back there again.

"What kind of trouble are you in now?" Roan scowled.

"My secretary accused me of drugging her."

"Did you?"

"There were no drugs found in my office. If it was just that, I'd be okay. She's not the most stable character. She turned over some files to the BCA. I need her eliminated. If she's gone, I can argue she knew more about my financial state than I did and was stealing money from me—to support her drug habit."

"I'm not going back to prison."

"One last favor, and I swear we're done."

Roan scratched his chin and thought about the possibilities. "No, I don't think so."

"I'm offering good money for it. You can subcontract if you can find someone who can deliver. It won't bother me in the least if someone beats her to death."

Roan gave me an evil glare. "You wouldn't be setting me up, would you?"

"Why the hell would I set you up? I'm free. I'm a millionaire. I want to stay both. Remember when we used to party together as couples? Let's get those days back."

"Deb's dead." Roan silently stared at the rough waters before finally asking, "What's her name?"

"Melanie Pearson. She's on a seventy-two-hour mental health hold right now but will be released tomorrow."

"Melanie? *She's* your secretary?" Roan shook his head in disbelief. "The gaslighting worked. She's over the edge." Roan questioned, "Why isn't that enough?"

"If you just would have pushed the gaslighting harder, she would have killed herself." My freedom is at stake. I can't take the chance that a jury would believe her. I pointed out, "You could have projected pictures of her dead mom in the window at night or faked messages from her mom asking Melanie to join her."

"You referred to Melanie as a whore in court in front of every major news network! Of course, she's bitter. If you hadn't hired her back, you wouldn't be in this mess!"

"Okay, we both could have done better." Melanie served my

needs in other ways. She's attractive and intelligent enough—just crazy. I recycled her. Now she's just trash."

Roan gave me a wary look. "What are you thinking?"

"Melanie has been staying with an old bat in Minneapolis. I don't care if you kill them both. I just need Melanie gone. And it can't be traced back to me."

"It'll cost you $200,000," Roan said.

"I think $100,000 should suffice."

"I won't do it for less than $200,000. I'll get a gang involved and make it look like she was killed by a stray bullet."

"Fine." Tug smiled. "It will take me a bit because I have to pull the money out of twenty accounts."

"That's fine." Roan turned to me, "But nothing happens until I walk away with $200,000 cash in a duffel bag. No more transferring funds. I'll let you know where Melanie's at when the hit is made, and you let me know where you're at so we can guarantee the two of you aren't anywhere near each other."

"All right." I shook his hand.

As we walked back to the parking lot, we talked about old times. I walked Roan to his black Caddy. He opened the trunk, and I headed to my new cherry red Tesla Roadster.

When Roan saw my Roadster parked beside him, he approached enviously. "What does one of these cost?"

"250K. This is the fastest car ever made in production."

I laughed as Roan got down on his hands and knees and then crawled partially beneath the car. The old Teslas had batteries under them. His muffled voice asked, "Where is the battery?"

"Behind the seats. This car goes from 0 to 60 in 1.1 seconds."

Roan got back to his feet. "Hell of a car, Tug."

"We'll be back on top once again." I grinned. "You'll hear from me soon."

Chapter 21

ROAN CARUSO

THURSDAY, APRIL 13, 2023
I-35 WEST BRIDGE, BOHEMIAN FLATS, MINNEAPOLIS

I strolled across the walking path on the St. Anthony Falls Bridge, glancing at the powerful Mississippi. We are small and weak compared to the forces of nature. Every Midwesterner who was driving in 2007 remembers this stretch of I-35 collapsing and pouring rush-hour traffic into the Mississippi River. In the end, thirteen were dead and 145 injured. Tug suggested the two of us "get back on top" once again. He thinks it's a pedestal. I see it more accurately as a manure pile.

My somber mood reminded me that if I didn't end my feud with the Disciples, my kids' lives were at stake. Lorenzo or Halle would be murdered in the crossfire. It was just a matter of time. I watched the Disciples' leader, the Fox, walk with two large men toward me. Fox stood about five and a half feet tall, but you could add another six inches for the afro. I approached from the east while Fox and his entourage approached from the west. My life will end violently. It's just a matter of when. I'm hoping it isn't soon.

I stopped about a hundred feet away. I raised my right hand, and he ordered his men to stay.

Fox casually strolled to me. "They say you're dead, Caruso; you just don't know it yet."

"Moribund. Near death, but you're about to resurrect me."

"No harm in listenin'. But why would I resurrect you? The brotherhood wants you gone."

"Deondre wasn't the snitch?" I asked.

"No. It turns out he was a loyal brother. And when I mentioned we had a problem, I told you I'd address it."

"We both need a resolution to our feud. You know, if something happens to me or Cat, the family is going to bring an army of major hitters in, and it will be an all-out war. I don't want that. You don't need that. We've always stayed out of your business, and you've stayed out of ours. I can't have any more drive-bys."

"This one's going to cost you. You got your car and your million-dollar signature back, and that was supposed to be enough. Done deal. Instead, you took out one of our best brothers in the struggle. We haven't been paid back for Deondre."

"You killed my daughter-in-law and grandchild—in my home!" I feel like we're even. But if he doesn't feel that way, my life is in danger.

"That wasn't ordered. Just a couple of rogue brothers."

"It was your guys. Can't you control your men?"

Fox responded angrily, "You killed Montrel Johnson and put two soldiers out of commission. Jam can hardly walk, and Ahmad's in juvie. And I didn't order the hit." Fox eyeballed me, "I'm supposed to tell the brotherhood I just let you walk?"

"Think of it like Critical Race Theory. We rewrite history and change the direction of the anger."

Wearily, Fox said, "You don't get Critical Race Theory. CRT is about understanding how racism is embedded in policy. Don't insult me."

"Okay, I'm not here to argue CRT." Tired of it all, I tried again. "I meant, let's just give them a different story. I'm offering an olive branch here."

"You've got to translate that Italian shit. I don't even eat olives."

"How can you not eat olives? They have heart-healthy monounsaturated fat. Hell, they even help you heal from sunburn. They're a fruit."

"How can olives be a fruit? They come in a can," Fox countered.

"So do peaches."

Fox gave me a side-eye. "If olives are a fruit, where's the juice?"

"Ever heard of olive oil?" When he rolled his eyes, I added, "Where's the peach juice? Did you know peaches are canned in pear juice?"

"I really don't give a shit. Cut to the chase."

I suggested, "If I can offer another explanation for Deondre's murder, what would it take to settle?"

"Honestly" —Fox looked out over the river— "$100,000 and a body. You've got to give me a scapegoat. Latrice Johnson lost her baby daddy and a brother. I've got to go back to the Disciples with something. If I'm not givin' 'em you, I need a damn good story about how you're givin' me the man who ordered the hit. They need closure."

"You'll have the true story. It's your job to convince them I was just a soldier. And then we're even, all right?"

Fox studied me skeptically. "Awright."

We shook hands and went our separate ways.

Chapter 22

JON FREDERICK

3:45 P.M., FRIDAY, APRIL 14, 2023
BUREAU OF CRIMINAL APPREHENSION,
1430 MARYLAND AVENUE EAST
GREATER EAST SIDE, ST. PAUL

My supervisor, Sean Reynolds, told us not to bring Melanie to the meeting we had scheduled with the county attorney. I didn't tell Melanie this suggested a reluctance to prosecute. Instead, I told her this occasionally happens with the first meeting. It does, but it's always a bad sign.

Hennepin County Prosecutor Bridget Bare sat at the head of the conference table. She was flanked by Sean on her right and Serena and me on her left. Bridget scanned through our written summary of Tug's offenses and said, "You honestly want me to go to court and say, 'This crazy woman said Tug stole some money, so send him to prison for the rest of his life?'" She pushed the report aside. "I can't prosecute Tug Grant on this. As much as I dislike Tug, he knows his way around the law, and his attorney, Taytum Hanson, is even better."

I pointed out, "We don't need to rely on Melanie's testimony. We have the files. We have a falsified letter from a bank to his spouse."

Bridget casually picked up her pen and then tapped it hard on the table as she drove home each point. "Melanie Pearson has been diagnosed with dissociative disorder. In other words, multiple personalities. How do I know which personality I'm going to get on the stand? And you know as well as I do that Taytum's going to drive home the fact that Melanie set Tug up. She had an axe to grind and access to his files."

"First of all, dissociation means a break from reality," Serena interjected. "It doesn't mean she has multiple personalities. And second, what motive would Melanie have?"

"Her craziness is her motive." Bridget cocked her head. "Taytum's going to say, 'Who the hell knows why Melanie does what she does?' Taytum will argue that the setup was vengeance from a scorned woman. Tug had humiliated her in court."

"Tug drugged her," Serena pleaded. "Melanie's blood test proved it."

"We found Valium in Melanie's purse," Bridget replied. "Not only is Melanie mentally ill, she's abusing benzos. Even more reason not to depend on her."

It was clear Bridget didn't want Melanie Pearson to be her star witness. When Melanie crumbled, Bridget would look incompetent.

Bridget said, "Look, I don't want to rain on your parade, but this isn't a criminal case. It's a civil case. Hand the files over to the family and let them take him to court over the money. They have a good case."

Serena argued, "Tug Grant testified under oath that he had turned over all his financial records to Blair. The falsified bank statement proves he's guilty of perjury."

Bridget turned to Sean, "The statement was typed on Melanie's computer, correct?"

"Yes, it was," Sean reluctantly agreed. "I believe Melanie, but Tug could easily blame this all on her. Tug always makes sure he has a parachute when the plane's about to crash."

"He doesn't this time," I interjected. All eyes focused on me. "Let's eliminate Melanie as a witness and instead use Blair Parker. Tug lied to Blair Parker." People weren't considering what was missing.

Sean questioned, "How do we prove Tug falsified the bank statement?"

"Tug never sent a falsified bank statement to himself." I smiled, "This means that Tug was receiving statements from the bank that tens of thousands of dollars were being removed from the accounts, and he never mentioned this to Blair. The disposition said he needed to be honest about all financial transactions. How is he going to explain that this didn't concern him? We can get the records of all the communication between Blair and Tug since the disposition to support Blair's testimony that Tug never expressed concerns that money was disappearing."

Serena squeezed my wrist as if to say, *well done*.

Sean supported me. "We certainly have enough for a search warrant. I'd bet in all their messages Tug doesn't express any concerns. It's all we need to get a conviction."

Bridget smiled. "All right. I'm fine going to battle with Blair Parker on my side. With all her charity work, she is very well respected."

I smiled at Bridget's panegyric to Blair. The fact that Blair contributed heavily to campaigns and that county attorney was an elected position may have factored in Bridget's decision to buttress Blair's case against Tug.

4:00 P.M.
51ST STREET & WASHBURN AVENUE SOUTH, FULTON,
MINNEAPOLIS

SERENA WAS A little frustrated as we began the trek north to our home. She grumped, "It ticks me off that Bridget wasn't going to prosecute based on Melanie's evidence. She tracked down his illegal accounts and was abused in the process. It feels like there is no justice for the downtrodden. We shouldn't be afraid of prosecuting someone just because he's a good attorney."

"I agree. Bridget doesn't want to lose to Tug, and she thinks we can't win with Melanie. That's why I suggested she use Blair." Bridget's argument wasn't ridiculous. Tug would attack Melanie, and in her current state, Melanie couldn't stand up to it.

"That was genius, by the way." She leaned over the console and gave me a peck on the cheek. "Melanie doesn't use drugs. It's how her mom committed suicide. Mel's told me she would never use. Her sanity hangs by a thread. She won't risk anything that would push her over the edge."

"I called Dr. Ho about the drug testing. She gave me the name of a scary drug that looks identical on drug tests to Valium. Only doctors can access it. This drug is metabolized within a couple of days and is untestable."

"So much for that," Serena sighed.

"Not true. Valium shows up on drug tests four weeks later. We can test Melanie again and prove the drug in her system wasn't Valium."

4:15 P.M.

FIFTEEN MINUTES INTO the drive, I got a call from Minneapolis Police Officer Zave Williams. Zave was an officer in his late twenties who had worked with me on the Black and Blue case. He was straightforward but still caring and respectful. Zave was dating Lauren Herald, a sketch artist who was raised near my hometown. I put him on speaker, and he said, "We've got an informant in the Disciples who suggested there's a hit out on Melanie Pearson, and it's happening tonight. I was told you might be able to help me locate her."

"What do we have for backup?'

"None," Zave responded. "Too much going on."

"She's at Agnes Schraut's house—51st and Washburn Avenue, South Minneapolis."

"I'll meet you there." Zave ended the call.

"How are we going to protect her from automatic weapons?" Serena asked. "The bullets will go right through Agnes's house."

I thought out loud, "And the Disciples are very comfortable executing people on the freeway. They just pull up alongside and open fire." I turned to Serena, "Dial Joe Hoffman for me." Joe was a friend who owned Hoffman Weber Construction.

When Joe answered, I asked, "I need an empty cement truck. Could you put me in contact with someone who has one?"

"Is this about construction or an investigation?" Joe asked.

"It's about getting a potential victim out of a house in a bulletproof container."

"I think I can do that. I'll call you right back."

Chapter 23

ROAN CARUSO

3:45 P.M. FRIDAY, APRIL 14, 2023
51ST STREET & WASHBURN AVENUE SOUTH, FULTON, MINNEAPOLIS

I sat in my car and watched Melanie Pearson enter Agnes Schraut's house. I immediately called Tug. "I have Melanie at home with the old jaguar."

"Jaguar?" Tug questioned.

"Cougar over fifty."

"You're a sick man, Roan."

"Do you still want the deed done?" I needed to be utterly certain he wanted Melanie dead. There was no going back after tonight.

"Are you on a burner phone?"

"Of course."

"Yes. What's the plan?"

"The Disciples will be here shortly. I just wanted to make sure you weren't having second thoughts."

"None. If the old hag dies, I'll throw in a bonus. No more calls. I'll wait to hear about it on the news tonight. You asked if I was setting you up. You wouldn't be setting me up, would you?"

"Tug, I went to prison for four years for you. Have I ever snitched on anyone?"

"No. Sorry. I just need her gone."

"It will be over tonight. Where are you at? We can't have her killed anywhere close to your location."

"I'm at home."

"Your neighbor's got a security camera now, right?"

"Yeah?" Tug responded curiously.

"Walk out in the yard, so you're on his video for an alibi."

"Great idea. Just get it done."

Chapter 24

JON FREDERICK

4:15 P.M., FRIDAY, APRIL 14, 2023
51ST STREET & WASHBURN AVENUE SOUTH, FULTON,
MINNEAPOLIS

Serena and I pulled up in front of Agnes's house in my Taurus. I popped the trunk, and we grabbed the two bulletproof vests. We entered the house through the unlocked door.

Agnes was already in her pajamas in the living room. She immediately confronted me. "You don't knock anymore. If I wanted people running in and out, I'd have a cave opening instead of a door."

Melanie stepped out of the bedroom to see what was happening.

"There is a gang headed here to kill Melanie," I said. "We need to get both of you out of here. Get what you need for the night. You have two minutes."

Serena told me, "I'll grab a pile of blankets and two pairs of thick gloves."

"Gimme a gun," Agnes demanded and then, with her walker, headed to her bedroom.

Serena commented sarcastically, "Do you have an automatic with a light trigger for her?" Before I could respond, she followed Agnes. "I'll help her pack."

Zave had pulled up in front. I yelled to the ladies, "Wait inside until I'm back." I left to meet my friend.

Zave was putting on his bulletproof vest as I stepped out. He said, "I spotted Roan Caruso down the block. They're going to follow our vehicle out of here. We might be better off staying put."

"We can't match their firepower. My guess is Roan's executing another contract for Tug."

At that moment, a cement truck pulled up in front of the house. I told Zave, "I have a plan." When the driver stepped out, I showed him my badge. "I'm BCA investigator Jon Frederick."

"Terry Brink." He shook my hand.

"I want you to take my car and meet me at the 3rd precinct. I'll drive the truck and meet you there."

"Yeah, that's not happening," Terry dismissed me. "I'm responsible for it, and I'm driving it."

"The Disciples are coming to kill a witness. I don't have an armored truck handy, so my plan was to transport her to the precinct in the tank."

"It'll be a rough ride in the mixing tank," Terry said. "It might be safer if we had a little cement in the back. A hell of a lot more entertaining. But if she's got gloves, she can hang on to the mixing blades inside."

"That's the plan," I responded.

"Okay, get her out here. But I'm driving."

I slipped off my vest, handed it to him, and said, "Back as close as you can to the front door. I don't care what you run over."

Terry hopped into the truck and backed it to the door, crushing the flowers Agnes had planted along the sidewalk.

Serena crawled up the thin metal ladder on the back and tossed the blankets in the mixing tank. She put on leather gloves and told me, "This opening is smaller than I thought."

"It makes it safer," I said.

She sighed and crawled inside. I did not envy her sliding into the dark, damp tank.

Melanie got on the ladder and asked, "Are you sure this will work?"

"No, but it's the best I can do at the moment. And we may only have a moment."

"If you start this spinning, you'll be cleaning vomit off your wife."

"I promise we won't spin the drum."

Melanie followed Serena into the dark tank.

Agnes stood on the porch in her pajamas, screaming, "Tell your herbicidal driver he can come back and help me replant!"

"I told him to get as close as he could. I don't have time to argue with you. We'll deal with this later."

"Now what?" Agnes brushed her pajamas. "Serena said I didn't have time to change. I'm not getting in that tank. I'd rather die. If you're going to ask that, you might as well shoot me now. You can bury me right below my decapitated flowers." Zave approached, and Agnes said, "I'll just ride with him."

Zave shook his head, "Absolutely not. I'm following so I can call for help if we pick up a tail."

"You got something against white women?" Agnes argued.

"My partner is white," Zave responded.

"She the jealous type?" Agnes continued.

I told Agnes, "You can sit between me and Terry." I guided her to the cab and helped her in."

Once the door was closed, Terry pulled away. Using the mirror, I carefully searched for followers.

Agnes bantered, "We used to say, 'dumb as a block of cement.' What does that say about a cement truck driver?"

"First of all, it's not cement; it's concrete. Cement is one of the ingredients." Terry grinned. "Viktor Frankl once said that everyone must carry out a concrete assignment that demands fulfillment. That's why I got this job."

I had yet to see any gang-like followers, but I was wary of every car.

Agnes continued, "I don't get it. So, what's your claim to fame, concrete guy?"

"I teach school and drive truck in the summer for extra cash. I tried out for the Olympic Nordic ski jumping team. I played in the national soccer tournament for St. Scholastica in college."

"Not that impressive," she remarked.

"And your claim to fame is?" Terry asked.

Agnes groaned, "You're a teacher, so I can't talk to you about history or race or sex. It kind of limits it."

"I spend the day sitting in the eagle's nest, picking off guys before they enter the school with their automatic weapons," Terry teased.

"Really?"

"No. It's more of a lair. I teach at Pine-River Backus. We're the Tigers. Perhaps you know them by their Latin name, *Panthera tigris*. What do you call a group of tigers?"

"I never thought of calling one," Agnes remarked.

"A streak," Terry replied.

"I suppose because they run around naked," Agnes commented. I opted not to interrupt the raillery as it seemed to be reducing their tension. "So, what's it like being married to a concrete guy?" Agnes asked.

"My wife tells her friends, 'Yes, he works cement. No, he's not home. No, I don't know when he'll be home. No, he's not imaginary.'"

Agnes laughed. "Okay, my claim to fame is I once caught a killer and got a large reward."

Terry glanced at her pajamas. "I was wondering how you could afford the designer clothes."

Agnes's body was close to mine, and I could feel her shaking with laughter. "I like you, concrete guy."

Before long, we arrived at the police station. Several officers met us outside and, with a mixture of curiosity and disbelief, pulled Melanie and Serena out of the back of the mixer as I helped Agnes out of the truck cab.

Serena approached and whispered, "It is creepy, dark, and humid in there. I could feel Melanie's body trembling the whole time." When Agnes stepped closer to listen, Serena took her arm and led her to the precinct. Melanie was escorted by a police officer. Serena said over her shoulder, "I'll meet you inside."

Zave pulled in next to the cement truck.

I gave Terry my number and email and told him to send me the bill. He smiled and said, "All in a day's work."

Zave and I stood in the parking lot. He said, "Maybe they saw my squad car and backed off."

"Maybe." The moon was now visible, and I wondered if Nora was pointing this out to Serena's parents. Nora and Jackson take pride in being moon-finders. I told Zave, "I didn't see anyone I'd consider a gang member on the way over."

"Neither did I."

"Maybe it was bad information."

"I don't think so," Zave said, "This guy has been dead on."

"Who knows?" I considered. "The shooters could have been picked up on an outstanding warrant before they arrived. What do we do with Melanie now?"

"Sean hasn't called you?" Zave questioned.

"No."

"Melanie is spending the night under an anonymous name at Fairview. They're going to do a mental health status evaluation, and then my girlfriend's picking her up to go stay at my future in-laws' place for a few days until it's safe for Melanie to return.

"The Disciples would quickly be noticed in Hillman, and there is no shortage of armed protection," I responded. "There are more weapons per person where Lauren grew up than on a military base."

"No doubt," Zave laughed.

Chapter 25

TAYTUM HANSON

6:15 P.M., FRIDAY, APRIL 14, 2023
400th AVENUE, ZUMBRO FALLS

Tug had rented us a cabin for the weekend. I needed to return to Roseville tonight as I promised my mother I'd make breakfast for Dad on "Husband Appreciation Day." After breakfast with my parents, I am returning to Tug for the rest of the weekend. I tried to explain to Mom that "Husband and Wife Appreciation Days" were created for married couples without children to replace "Mother's and Father's Day," and I should, therefore, be exempt from Saturday breakfast. My argument didn't take, so tomorrow morning, Dad would have what he wanted most—me standing in the kitchen next to Mom.

Mom's efforts to convince me the rumors of Dad's philandering were unfounded were pathetic. If she had just said, 'I can't live with half his money; I want all of it,' I could have respected that. Trying to get me to be her coconspirator in accepting Dad's lies diminished her in my eyes. I sometimes wonder how Dad's infidelity impacted me. He asked me once if I forgave him, and I honestly told him, "I don't think so, but I'm not going to stop having a relationship with you. I can't change you, and I'm not responsible for you, so I'm going to live my life without devoting any energy to thinking about it." At the same time, I'm their only child, and I refused to give them what they wanted most—a grandchild. Having a baby would be a reward to parents who gave no consideration to how their behavior impacted their daughter and a punishment to me. It's not happening.

When I entered the cabin, Tug was standing in his untucked dress shirt with the top three buttons already undone. He handed me a bottle of Patrimony cabernet sauvignon. By the grin on his face, I could tell it was expensive. I kissed him and asked, "How much?"

"Six hundred dollars. It's from Daou Vineyards in Paso Robles."

"I hope you've got a corkscrew. If you don't, I'm pushing the cork in and committing to the entire bottle."

He smiled and held up a glossy black rabbit wing corkscrew.

"You think of everything." I handed him the bottle. His bottle of Blue Label scotch sat handy on the kitchen counter, already open. "Where did you eat?"

"The Buck Wild Bar and Grill. It was the first time I've had a California burger since I was a kid."

"That sounds good. When I drove through town, I saw the Neptune Bar is having a meat raffle." I mentioned it in jest, as I could never picture Tug attending one.

"All bars are a bit of a meat raffle," Tug said.

I clamped my hands behind his neck and pulled him close for a passionate kiss. When finished, I slowly stepped back and told him, "I need to head back to Minneapolis tonight, but I have a couple hours."

"What do you have in mind?" Tug grinned as he uncorked the wine and poured me a glass.

In my most seductive tone, I said, "I'm going to have a sip of wine. You can gently undress me. I'll lay back on the bed while you pleasure me. Things progress from there."

"I could bind you to the headboard with my ties."

"We're mustangs. No master. No ties." Bondage is for the weak at heart. It's total submission to helplessness. Why would I surrender my power to anyone? I said, "Every mustang herd is led by a mare, so follow." The bedroom door was partially open. I held my glass of wine like the Olympic torch and led the way.

When we stepped into the bedroom, Tug asked, "When does this stallion get the favor returned?" His cool blue eyes stared into mine as he unbuttoned my blouse.

"When I'm finally over what you did in prison," I said. He set my blouse over the back of a chair. I turned my back to him, and he undid my bra. His warm body hugged my bare back, and his hands caressed my breasts.

"You're no less passionate than I am," Tug responded. "I have to believe you would have done the same if you were looking at years in lock-up."

I removed his hands and turned to him. "I would have selected a handsome guard who could protect me, used him, and then sued the state once I was released, piggybacking on the Chino and Chowchilla lawsuits, which asserted a prisoner can't legally consent to a sexual relationship with a guard." I kissed him. "Kidding. I'm not going to prison."

"I'm going to retrieve my scotch, and I'll be right back."

"I'll be in bed, waiting." My heart was softening for Tug, and it was scary. When he returned, I watched him place a tan handgun into the drawer of the nightstand. I sipped my wine and said, "If you're caught with that, you go back to prison."

"It's a Sig Sauer P365 handgun. The color is coyote tan. I love this gun—unique, like me. It's not registered. I'll just say it was in the cabin. You're not turning me in, are you?"

"Why would you even say that? I got you out of prison so we could have weekends like this."

"I'm sorry." He took my wine glass from me, set it on the stand, and kissed me. "You're the only one who will never betray me."

There was sadness in his eyes. "What's going on with you and Roan? I thought you were like besties."

"Besties? I don't have a bestie."

"What am I?"

"You're my muse."

"I'll accept that." I ran my hand through his thick white hair. Prison had aged him. My beau was worried, maybe even afraid. I tried to soothe his troubled mind. "You and I can get through anything. What's Roan up to?"

"He hasn't been the same since doing time for Deb's murder," Tug said. "He blames me for it. I could envision him setting me up for something."

"Roan should be kissing my feet for getting him out of prison. Instead, he hasn't said one word to me since his release hearing." I considered, "Did you pay him to have Deb killed?"

Agitated, he responded, "No, okay?"

There was that damned word. Instead of confronting him, I simply repeated, "Okay," and considered this our codeword for lying to each other. I picked up my glass of wine and took a sip.

Softening his tone, Tug said, "I'll explain tomorrow. I don't want to waste time on Roan if we only have a couple of hours. I will share a teaser. In a month, I'll be exactly where I want to be. Better than ever. And I'll never forget you were with me the entire journey."

"That's the difference between you and me, Tug. I'm exactly where I want to be right now."

He carefully perused my naked body and asked softly, "How's the wine?"

"Wonderful tannins." I swirled the glass beneath my nose and took one more sip. "Vanilla, licorice, and dark fruit. Love it."

"I'm going to buy a lake house on Lake of the Isles or somewhere peaceful close to the metro. I'd like you to look at houses with me. I know you love your freedom, so I don't expect you to live there, but I want you to have your own closet, dresser, and bathroom."

"You're asking me to be your primary," I teased.

"You've basically been my exclusive lover since prison."

"You married another woman." I giggled at the absurdity of his claim.

"I said 'lover.' My time with Blair was charity sex—helping her grieve."

They say we all grieve in our own way. Blair apparently grieved by screwing her husband's best friend. The idea of having more time with Tug intrigued me, and I particularly liked the idea of not having to pack or leave when I wanted to change clothes. "Okay," I said. Honestly, it excited me. "I want a beach I can walk along. This body wasn't designed for running."

"Too top-heavy," Tug agreed.

"The only appeal running has to me is hearing the heavy breathing." It wasn't that funny, but he smiled anyway. That's love. "Tug, you're talking about another layer of commitment. If I'm going to have property in your house, you can't be sleeping with other women there. That's a level of disrespect I won't tolerate. I'm not going to be your Blair or your Deb."

"Okay." He lustfully suggested, "Time for these bodies to create synergy."

I set my wine back on the nightstand. "First, you need to get the engine warmed up."

Chapter 26

TUG GRANT

8:25 P.M., FRIDAY, APRIL 14, 2023
400th AVENUE, ZUMBRO FALLS

I watched Taytum's taillights disappear into the darkness. Lightning lit up the sky in the distance. I gave the yard a cursory glance. All quiet on the western front.

I retrieved my handgun and slipped the Sig into the crease by the edge of the cushion in the leather recliner, just in case. I turned the TV on and browsed the local stations, looking for breaking news on the bottom of the screen indicating a woman had been killed in the Fulton neighborhood of Minneapolis. I took a pull of scotch and felt for my Sig. I adjusted it a little for easy retrieval. *There—perfect.*

My phone buzzed. "Hey, it's Taytum. I just want to make sure you're good. You seemed a little restless tonight."

"I'm fantastic. I just made love to the most beautiful woman on earth, and I'm sitting in my recliner with a glass of scotch."

"We can fight anything together. I hope you understand that. And I'm loving the idea of sharing a house with you. We need to have a fireplace."

"It will be essential." I was proud of how I turned my desire for freedom on her by suggesting she could "preserve her independence" by not moving in permanently. I'm a multi-millionaire.

Why would I tie myself to anyone? Taytum is the best lover I have—right now. But I'm about to be bigger than ever. *Who knows what the future holds for me?* I have more money than I'll ever spend. As mentally tough as Taytum was, she still believed in justice. It was her weakness. There is no justice. There's just power—the ability to make people do things they wouldn't otherwise do. Taytum's obsession with justice kept her from seeing that a promise from me is simply a lie that has yet to reach fruition. I've made it clear from the onset that I'm not about truth. I'm about creating a story that places the attorney in the best light. I'm the premier attorney, and I deserve the spotlight.

Still blissful, Taytum said, "I'm looking forward to having another glass of Patrimony tomorrow. It's so good I might even finish the bottle. I think I love you, Tug." She stopped herself. "I'm not begging for a response. I'm in a great mood and looking forward to tomorrow, and tomorrow, and tomorrow. Good night, love." She hung up.

Taytum needs to learn her Shakespeare references. Macbeth made the statement about one meaningless day after another. I know she loves me. They all do. I had the sense that someone was going to betray me, and she was clever enough to pick up on it. But as usual, I had planned meticulously. Only Taytum knew I was here, and Taytum was the one person I could trust.

In the past, I've trusted Roan with my life, and he's always delivered. Still, something told me it was best to lie to him about my whereabouts tonight. It bothered me that Roan insisted on knowing my exact location. Roan told me he had an IT specialist who could clear the traces of the money I had confiscated from Blair. After tonight, Melanie will be as gone as that trail of evidence. Once Melanie was gone, there was no way of proving Melanie hadn't stolen the money herself.

A pleasant gratification settled in as I thought about the five women I've slept with in the last five years. (Prostitutes don't count. You don't "sleep" with hookers.) I had Deb killed. Lily bolted after I was convicted of murder. I'm divorcing Blair. I am working on killing Melanie, but she's a space cadet with no resources. No one is going to seriously care about her death. Her only source of support is a mass killer. The easiest route will be to write off Melanie's death as another tragedy of stray bullets from a gang shooting, and law enforcement will take it. And that leaves Taytum, who has been wonderful to me for years, so who says I can't make a relationship work?

Chapter 27

MELANIE PEARSON

8:30 P.M., FRIDAY, APRIL 14, 2023
FAIRVIEW PSYCHIATRIC CLINIC, 2312 SOUTH 6TH STREET,
BOHEMIAN FLATS, MINNEAPOLIS

I finished meeting with the psychiatrist and was moved into a single room for the night. Lauren will pick me up in the morning. I stood in my blue hospital gown, gazing out the window at the city below. Riding in that dark cement tank was hell. Clinging to Serena is the only thing that kept me from having a panic attack. Serena's become the concerned older sister I never had. I sighed. My life is insane. I can't imagine sleeping tonight. The best man I ever dated was a mass killer—no wonder I'm crazy. I heard a movement behind me and turned toward the door. When I saw who stood in front of me, I thought I was going to have a heart attack.

All six feet six of Roan Caruso hovered in the doorway. He wore a black button-down shirt, black jeans, and black cowboy boots. Roan whispered as best he could with his gruff voice, "Don't scream."

"How did you know I was here?"

"You think I don't have a connection in law enforcement?" Roan laughed. "This was no easy task. I had to use up a favor with hospital security and promise no harm would be done to you—all just to be as good as my word."

I was speechless.

Roan continued, "You're not as crazy as you think. Did you know Tug was drugging and raping you?"

"Serena suspected that. I thought it was just my memory stuff." His presence was confusing. "Why are you here?"

"I promised I'd tell you if Tug wanted something done to you, so here I am. Tug Grant put out a hit on you, but I'm taking care of it. After tonight, he's not going to bother you again. You're safe here, all right? I'm going to go now." He turned to leave.

I'm not sure if it was Tug's belittling in court or the drugged rapes, but I responded, "Take me with you. I want to see him dead."

"I'm not killing Tug." Roan turned back. "He's going to die, but I'm not going to be anywhere close."

"Tell me where. I need to know it's over. It's the only thing that will bring me any relief. Please. You can't imagine everything he's done to me."

"I can." He thought for a minute and told me, "I can't take you there, but my son will. You sure you want to do this?"

"Yes. One hundred percent sure."

"Get dressed." Roan walked over to the window and looked out at the hospital grounds. "My son will pick you up on the first floor of the red ramp in thirty minutes." Roan exited.

I dug my clothes out of the cabinet in my hospital room. I had started to slip my gown off when the door opened again. I quickly pulled the gown tight over my body.

Roan re-entered the room and tossed latex gloves and paper slippers on my bed. "Wear these when you enter the dwelling, and don't touch anything. If you fail to heed my advice, you'll be the one going to prison."

"Thank you, Roan."

"You never spoke to me, all right?"

"Yeah."

He left without saying another word.

Chapter 28

JON FREDERICK

9:45 P.M., FRIDAY, APRIL 14, 2023
HOME 2 SUITES HILTON, 2270 WEST 80TH ½ STREET,
BLOOMINGTON

We took Agnes Schraut to a hotel. I didn't want her to be home alone tonight, so we got her a room that connected to ours. After Serena showered and we all enjoyed dinner together, Serena escorted Agnes safely to her room for the night.

When Serena returned to our room, I asked, "Agnes all right?"

"As all right as she ever is. She couldn't stop talking about the truck driver."

"She still mad about the flowers?"

"Agnes is over that." Serena laughed. "She thought Terry was the funniest guy on earth." Serena gave me a hug. "I'm ready to call it a night." She slipped out of her clothes and into an oversized, worn T-shirt.

I kissed Serena and swept a strand of hair out of her face. "Thanks for making the trip in the back of a cement truck with Melanie. I wanted to keep her safe. I guess my hypervigilance wasn't warranted."

"We don't really know. Roan was in the area. Maybe he backed off when he saw the truck." Serena sat on the edge of the bed. "That was about my limit, though. If it had been much longer, claustrophobia would have gotten to me. Melanie was right against me in that dark, damp tank."

My phone buzzed, and I put it on speaker. "This is Jon Frederick."

"Hi Jon, it's Taytum Hanson. Would you do me a favor and check on Tug Grant? Something's not right. I was with him in Zumbro Falls. I'm almost in Minneapolis, but I'm heading back. He's not answering his phone. I'd feel much better if you would meet me there. I heard him on the phone telling Roan he was at home in Minnetonka. He doesn't typically lie to Roan, and Tug hasn't carried a gun since he's been on probation. Tonight, he had it out of the holster, close, all night. Something bad is going to happen."

"Do you have the address?" Taytum was seriously concerned if she was willing to give up that Tug was carrying. It was a violation of his probation.

"Yes, it's a large log cabin on Zumbro Lake—400th Avenue. It looks like a ranch house. Dark wood. Triangular window above the front entry."

"I'm in Minneapolis with Serena, but I'll be on my way shortly."

Serena was redressing before I ended the call. I told her, "I need to go, and that means I need you to drive me to the BCA office so I can pick up a work car."

Serena embraced me, and as I focused on her glossy emerald eyes, she said, "So much for a nice, relaxing rest. Love you."

"Love you, too." I pulled her tight.

10:20 P.M.

HIGHWAY 52, INVER GROVE HEIGHTS

I CALLED ZAVE Williams on the way to Zumbro Falls and updated him.

"I could stop at Agnes Schraut's to see if anyone tried to break into her house," Zave offered. "I checked ShotSpotter, and there have been no gunshots in the area tonight."

The Minneapolis Police Department has placed a series of twenty to twenty-five microphones per square mile twenty feet above the ground in Minneapolis. This allows them to know the location of gunshots before they're reported. While I like the idea, there are ethical debates about the use of Artificial Intelligence in criminal cases. For example, a firecracker or a helicopter can occasionally be interpreted by AI as gunshots, so the American Civil Liberties Union argues that AI shouldn't be used. Personally, I think we need trustworthy investigators who acknowledge the limits of the technology rather than dismissing it. The technology allows officers to be aware if they're driving into a scene where automatic weapons are being fired. I told Zave, "I turned Agnes's security system on before we left."

I gave Zave the security code and continued on my way.

Chapter 29

TUG GRANT

10:30 P.M., FRIDAY, APRIL 14, 2023
400th AVENUE, ZUMBRO FALLS

I had fallen asleep in the recliner. *Had I missed the breaking news of Melanie's murder?* I looked at the nightstand, and there was less than a finger of Johnnie Walker left in my glass. I suddenly realized there was another person in the room.

An adolescent male stood in front of me in baggy pants and a black T-shirt with a gold crown on it. His most concerning accessory was the M-16 automatic weapon he was holding. He crossed his left arm over his body to reveal a tattoo of the Star of David on his bicep. The six-pointed star had a "G" on one side, a "D" on the other, and "360" in the middle. The tattoo was the symbol of the Gangster Disciples. The 360 stands for "complete knowledge."

I slowly slid my hand to my side. I've never directly killed a person. "Who are you?" My hands were sweating. *When do I draw my gun?* It was a life-and-death decision. I couldn't afford to miss.

"Jamarcus—but my friends call me Jam." He had a nervous smile, but he confidently waved the automatic weapon like a toy.

"How old are you?" He looked like he was about fifteen.

"Nineteen."

"What do you want?"

"I'm here to kill you, Tug Grant."

"I don't even know you, boy."

"Don't call me 'boy.'" Jam aimed the gun at my head. "And you don't need to know me. I know you."

I considered the possibilities that led to a hitman standing in front of me. "Don't tell me Taytum arranged this."

"I won't," Jam said. "She didn't. When I told Fox the bitch was here, he said wait 'til she's gone. We're makin' peace. Don't need complications."

"Peace with who? She's the only one who knew I was here. Why would anyone want me dead?"

"You ordered the hit on Deondre Johnson. And now my friend Montrel's dead too. Can't blame Roan for defending his home."

"That was all Roan Caruso," I argued. *How would Roan know I was here?* I thought back to Roan sliding under the Tesla to look for its battery. Roan put a tracking device on my car. He knew where I was this entire time. He's damn good. Roan kept asking me my address to keep me from even considering I was being tracked.

"Wait—" I pointed to the end table where my phone and billfold rested. "I've got money."

I had him thinking. He directed, "Empty your pockets."

"It's all right there." I needed him to turn away for just a second.

With eyes focused on me, Jam pocketed my billfold and phone. He marched over to me and pulled my pockets out. His damn gun was pointed right into my groin.

I slid my hand into the crease of my chair and gripped my gun. I couldn't afford to shoot him until he moved his automatic.

"What do we have here?" Jam grinned as he took the car keys from my pants. "That Tesla Roadster has got to be six figures."

"There's been less than a dozen Roadsters sold in Minnesota. The dealer in Eden Prairie knows exactly who owns them. You won't be able to move it."

"If you think we're selling that car in Minnesota, you're a damn fool," Jam laughed.

"Okay, take the car," I reluctantly told him. "But think about it. If you take my car, you're leaving yours here."

"I'm not here for the car," the cocky kid retorted. "And you're assuming I came alone. I asked my brothers to leave. This is my score to settle."

I heard a car pulling away outside.

Jam lowered the automatic for a moment, and I seized the opportunity. I drew my gun and fired. *Bang!*

As Jam fell back, he squeezed the trigger. *RAT-A-TAT-TAT.* A flurry of bullets flew my way.

Son of a bitch! He had fired at least two shots into my groin. As I writhed in pain, I fell forward onto the floor. The Sig slipped out of my hand.

"Fuck!" Jam shouted. I'd hit him. He picked up my gun and, with blood staining the shoulder of his shirt, scrambled out the door.

"Roan said you'd try to blame him. It was you who got Deondre's shooter off scot-free. You started all this by requesting the hit on Deondre. I'm ending it." Jam was about to pull the trigger.

The pain was unbearable. It was like being stabbed in the groin over and over with a red-hot metal poker. I needed to get to a hospital. Jam now had my phone and my car, and this damn cabin doesn't have a landline. *Think!* If I could get to my briefcase, I could use my laptop. With both hands, I dragged myself across the floor toward the kitchen. I could see my briefcase sitting open on the table.

I forced out shallow breaths to stay focused. I'd been attacked before, and I always got through it. I'd survive this. Suddenly, two slippers stood in front of me. I followed her thin legs upward. "Melanie, thank God. Call 911."

"That has to hurt like hell, Tug." With a weird calm, she asked, "Hmm, do you have an anesthetic?"

"Good idea. There's a needle in a compartment in my briefcase. It's in the kitchen. But I need to call 911 first."

"I'll call 911." Melanie left the room, but I could hear her talking.

I rolled onto my back, hoping it would somehow reduce the pain.

Melanie returned with the needle and handed it to me with her gloved hand. "I'd inject it into your inner thigh."

"Thank you. Yeah, good idea." I felt nauseous, and the pain was unbearable. Before injecting myself, I asked, "How did you know to come here?"

"A friend."

"Roan," I responded. "He didn't consider you'd save me because you still love me."

"I'm glad I wasn't too late." Her monotone was unnerving. Melanie kept her distance as she silently observed.

"Me too." I couldn't take the pain anymore and injected the entire contents of the needle into my leg. "Why are you wearing gloves?"

"I don't want to be covered in blood."

That made sense—I think. I told her, "Make sure to tell the medics I took something for the pain."

She picked up my glass of scotch and poured a puddle on the floor next to me. Darkness settled in.

Chapter 30

MELANIE PEARSON

10:30 P.M., FRIDAY, APRIL 14, 2023
400th AVENUE, ZUMBRO FALLS

I watched Tug's pants soak with scarlet. With my gloved hand, I took his scotch and poured it on the floor next to him. Serena had told me everything she witnessed the last time Tug drugged me. I watched his eyes gloss over and told him, "Lick it up."

With no questions asked, he submissively followed directions. Tug lapped the golden liquor off the floor like a thirsty dog.

After he finished, I returned the glass to the end stand. I couldn't believe how well this anesthetic worked. I could only imagine what that liar made me do during the rapes.

"You take care of me, and I'll make sure you're okay," he forced out. "Okay, Mel?" Lying had become so natural for Tug that he continued even in a semi-conscious state.

In a monotone, I asked, "How's the pain?"

"Not as bad," he forced out.

"Pull your pants down. I need to see the injury. The EMTs will need this."

Tug laid back and winced as he lowered his pants. As his pants came down, blood pooled around him.

I didn't want his clothing to clot his wounds.

His face turned ghostly white.

"Cotton top," were the last words I said to him. I crouched next to him, dipped my gloved finger in his blood, and wrote on the floor, "IM 2 M T 2 ♥ U." I watched while the spreading blood covered my letters. I stepped back and was careful to avoid the blood trail as I exited.

10:55 P.M., RYAN'S BAY, ZUMBRO LAKE

I COULD HEAR sirens in the distance, so I rushed back toward the beach. Lorenzo Caruso stood on the shore in hip waders. Lorenzo picked me up and carried me to the boat with ease.

Once seated, I slipped off my hospital slippers and latex gloves. Lorenzo took them from me and tossed them into the lake after we cruised a few hundred feet from the shore. Roan had concerns that someone might hear the gunshots and call the police, so he had Lorenzo take me to the cabin by boat. This way, we wouldn't be pulled over leaving the scene.

Lorenzo had made me surrender my phone to him earlier, so when I stepped into the kitchen at the cabin, I faked the 911 call. Lorenzo and I had a one-mile ride back to the Pondy Bar boat landing at the north end of Zumbro Lake. It was cold, and I began to shiver. I should have been depressed, but I was jittery and excited. *I won. Screw you, Tug! I won!* I shivered but smiled with glee. If I had known I was going to travel by sea, I would have worn a thicker coat.

Lorenzo glanced my way and said, "Come here." He opened his parka and invited me to sit on his lap.

I didn't hesitate. I knew this young, handsome Italian man was a wolf, but he couldn't be any worse than Tug. His coat was heated, and I snuggled against his warm body. I thought Tug was a great guy, and he turned out to be a wolf. Maybe if I started out with a guy I thought was a wolf, he'd turn out to be great. Lorenzo was almost a decade younger than me. I could feel his virile body responding to mine.

Chapter 31

JON FREDERICK

**10:55 P.M., FRIDAY, APRIL 14, 2023
400th AVENUE ZUMBRO FALLS**

With the siren on, I cruised by Taytum's BMW on Highway 52, turned on Laura Ingalls Wilder Historic Highway, and headed to Zumbro Falls. I met a Tesla Roadster in the oncoming lane. It could have been a Corvette, but it had to be electric because it didn't make any noise.

As a result of the dragon shape of Zumbro Lake, the city is trickier to drive in than Minneapolis. In Minneapolis, the streets generally run north and south, and the avenues are east and west. In Zumbro Falls, being labeled a street or an avenue is worthless, as avenues and streets run in all directions. Part of the problem is that they have roads, like 400th Avenue, that are almost a complete circle. Thank God for GPS.

The wide tar driveway in front of the ranch house was empty. When I approached the house, I noticed the door was partially open. I slipped on my gloves and called, "Tug?" as I pushed the door open with a fingertip.

I drew my gun and entered. Tug was lying on his back, with his pants to his knees on the floor, his bare groin mutilated and red. I winced as I considered the pain he experienced. He was lying in a pool of blood. A syringe lay in the blood, its plunger depressed. I crouched next to him and felt for a pulse. None. The blood streak started in the recliner, and there were bullet holes in the floor next to the chair. I immediately called my boss and told Sean, "Tug Grant's been shot to death in a cabin in Zumbro Falls. I'm standing by his body now."

"Okay. Stay put. I'll send a CSI crew immediately.

I quickly made my way through the house to ensure no one else was there. Once it was clear I was alone, I returned to Tug.

As I studied the scene more closely, I realized there was also a trail of blood out the door. Tug had injured his assailant.

I stepped around the body, careful to avoid the blood. Tug's front pockets were pulled out, indicating the killer had robbed him before he left. The CSI crew might be able to pull a fingerprint off his clothing with a vacuum metal deposit chamber. The clothing is put in a chamber, and less than a dollar's worth of gold is melted into a gas inside. When gold becomes a gas, it adheres to the oils in fingerprints. Then, they melt zinc in the chamber. Once zinc becomes a gas, it turns the gold black. The fingerprints can be seen when the clothing is removed from the chamber.

I stepped outside and watched Taytum Hanson pull into the driveway. She rushed to the house, and I stopped her before she entered. "Tug's dead. He's been shot to death."

"You have to let me see him." Taytum was frantic. "It's not like I'm contaminating the crime scene. I've already admitted I was here."

"Okay. But you have to follow my trail, and you can't touch him." I would want to see my loved one, too.

I walked Taytum in, and she burst into tears upon seeing his bloodied body. She knelt in front of him. "What did they do to you, Tug?"

I helped Taytum to her feet and walked her out of the house. She said, "That fucking Roan. I never trusted him. I'm going to commit my career to ruining him."

"Why do you think it's Roan?"

"Tug told me earlier that I was the only one who would never turn on him. He suspected Roan of something but never said what it was."

"Take a couple of days and think about your strategy before you go after Roan. Tug's dead. Roan's a force to be reckoned with. If it's a good idea, it will still be a good idea in forty-eight hours. You can't recklessly go after a made man and expect to live through it." In the American and Sicilian Mafia, a "made man" is a fully initiated member, required to take the oath of omertà—the code of silence and honor. Once "made," a person is considered untouchable and going after such a man is punishable by death. I considered the empty driveway. "How did Tug get here?"

"Tug's Roadster is gone," Taytum said.

"Someone gave the shooter a ride here," I suggested. I gestured for Taytum to have a seat on the steps. "I'll stay with you until law enforcement arrives."

"Don't you want to take off after the killer?"

"I do. But I want to make sure you're okay first." I can't leave a grieving lover at this crime scene alone. I didn't like Tug, but I felt bad for Taytum. She loved him more than he deserved.

"Thank you." Taytum squeezed my hand. "I don't feel like talking." She held her head in her hands, and the tears quietly flowed.

"It's okay. I understand."

It wasn't long before blue lights lit up the night as Wabasha County squad cars pulled up in front of the house. When the deputies approached, I told them, "Tug Grant's on the floor in the living room. He's been shot to death. His car is gone. Please secure the scene."

I left Taytum behind and sped off in my work Taurus toward Minneapolis. If Roan had something to do with this, the killer was on his way back to the metro. I called the Highway Patrol.

"What is your emergency?" a woman's voice answered.

"I'm BCA agent, Jon Frederick. I'm leaving the scene of a homicide in Zumbro Falls. I believe I met the victim's Tesla Roadster on the way to the scene. I don't know the killer, but I would guess the car is headed back to Minneapolis. It's cherry red."

"I'll have troopers on the road immediately."

11:15 P.M.
LAURA INGALLS WILDER HISTORIC HIGHWAY
(HIGHWAY 63)

RETRACING MY PATH, I headed back to Highway 63. To my surprise, it wasn't long before I came up on the round taillights of a Roadster. The driver must have pulled over to wrap his wound. The new Teslas went to a Corvette-looking taillight rather than their old trapezoid design. Now that the driver had a flashing light on his tail, he gunned it. I had never seen anything like it. The car was cruising at a speed well over one hundred miles an hour, leaving me in the dust. I shut my flashing lights off and slowed down.

People don't realize how fast a hundred miles an hour is. When I played baseball, I cranked up the pitching machine and tried to hit balls at that speed. I could barely see them. Being the curious person I am, I wheeled the machine outside and shot the ball straight up in the air at one hundred miles an hour. The ball ascended so high it disappeared. Now, imagine a ton of metal coming down the road at that speed. While the Roadster can reach speeds of 250 miles per hour, no roads outside of a racetrack are designed to allow a car to travel at that velocity. The Roadster was going to kill somebody.

My phone buzzed. "This is Doris Shileto. I've received a call saying you were in pursuit."

"Jon Frederick. I'm headed north on Highway 63. I've just shut my flashers off. The Tesla Roadster rocketed out of my reach. The car should be arriving in Lake City soon."

"I'm headed south on Highway 61 from Frontenac. I should be in Lake City in about five minutes. Do you think we should put down a spike strip?"

"I don't know. The car had to be approaching two hundred miles per hour when it left my sight. I'm hoping it slows down when it sees I'm not pursuing. If that car hits the spikes at that speed, the driver's dead."

"My concern is that the driver's going to kill someone else."

"Your call." The Highway Patrol has jurisdiction over the BCA on that decision. We are instructed to advise law enforcement but not make decisions for them.

When she fell silent, I asked, "Doris? The once married to Tony Shileto, Doris?"

"Yes. My last name isn't Shileto anymore, but I assumed it's how you'd know me."

"I thought you left law enforcement."

"I did. But after my son moved out, I wanted to come back and help. A lot of officers have left the field in the last few years." She paused and then said, "I made my decision. I'm dropping the spikes in Lake City. I'd prefer to drop them before he gets that far, but it's the best I can do at his speed."

"Make sure you get the traffic headed into the city blocked off. When that Roadster hits the spikes, it's going airborne."

"Okay. Thanks. I need to end the call and get ahold of some people. Come and visit me in prison when they arrest me for killing this guy." She hung up.

Sometimes, in law enforcement, you only have bad choices, and you're left making the best bad choice. If the driver slowed down, he should be fine when he hits the spikes. Either way, we needed to stop the car. I sped up so I could get back to help with the crime scene as soon as possible.

I've driven into Lake City in daylight, and it's beautiful. Lake Pepin, which is part of the Mississippi River, is to the east. On sunny days, sailboats glide across the lake. I slowed on Highway

63 as I prepared to turn onto Highway 61. I spotted the Roadster parked in the Rather Bee Quilting parking lot a block ahead. It made me wonder how badly the driver was injured. The good news was the rocket wasn't moving. The bad news was there was still a killer in the area.

When I was half a block away, the Roadster slowly pulled out of the parking lot and onto Highway 61, heading north. I floored the gas pedal to cut him off, but the driver gunned it, and the Roadster shot down the main drag like a rocket.

His decision to delay gave Doris and the Lake City police a chance to get traffic off the street. I watched the taillights head down the road, knowing there was nothing I could do. I had no way of stopping him. My Taurus following this Roadster was like a man running after a motorcycle.

Within three seconds, I heard screeching tires and watched the Roadster fishtail and crash into the guard rail. The rocketing Roadster flipped in a full circle in the air and nosedived as it bounced on the beach. The car's momentum sent it hydroplaning on its roof into Lake Pepin.

The streets lit up as squad car lights pulled out from the side roads.

11:55 P.M.

HIGHWAY 61, SOUTH OF STAEHLI PARK ROAD

(This beautiful stretch of Highway 61 has attracted excessive naming. It is also known as: Blues Highway, Hiawatha Pioneer Trail, Disabled Americans Highway, Great River Road & South Lakeshore Drive)

I PULLED OVER on the shoulder east of Lake Pepin Winery and walked across the road to the lakeside. The lake was only twenty feet from the highway here.

A black rubber skid marked the road for sixty feet after the car hit the spikes. I gazed into the lake and watched the taillights and the undercarriage of the car sinking below the surface. An officer stripped down to his boxers and swam out toward it.

Doris approached in her maroon state patrol uniform.

After I glanced at the imprint of the Roadster's front end on the beach, I told Doris, "He's dead."

She nodded in agreement. "There is no point in rushing to the car."

The car was fully submerged by the time the swimming officer reached the site. He dove and soon resurfaced, yelling, "I can't see anything."

"Come back!" Doris shouted. She turned to me. "That officer's going to end up with hypothermia."

"He gave it a valiant effort," I responded. "You simply can't hit anything solid at that speed and survive."

"I know." Doris said, "I called for divers and a wrecker with a winch. I hated to put the spikes out, but I couldn't live with an innocent family getting killed by this idiot. My radar gun clocked him at 183 miles an hour." When she saw the officer treading water, she yelled, "We have floodlights coming. Come in!"

He started swimming back.

I resigned myself to waiting patiently for the divers, the tow truck, and the CSI team. It would be a long night.

Chapter 32

MELANIE PEARSON

11:55 P.M., FRIDAY, APRIL 14, 2023
BEAR VALLEY CEMETARY, WABASHA COUNTY ROAD 3,
NORTH OF MAZEPPA

Lorenzo flirted with me as we drove on back roads to Minneapolis in his GMC Hummer. He took my hand and declared, "We have to celebrate." "I've been instructed not to leave a trail, so we can't stop in a bar, but I've got some coke."

"I like the idea of celebrating, but I for damn sure don't need drugs." I felt giddy and jittery. My heart was racing. I placed my hand on his leg. "I'm not sure where we can inconspicuously hide, towing a boat."

"What do we have here?" Lorenzo slowed the Hummer. He pulled down a dirt road into the Bear Valley Cemetery. We were in a graveyard in the middle of nowhere.

He leaned over the large console and kissed me, and I eagerly participated. I didn't want to think. Too much had happened in the last twenty-four hours. I wanted to mindlessly enjoy this beautiful man. "How do we do this?"

"We slide onto the bench seat behind us, and you straddle me." Lorenzo's dark eyes glistened—obviously, not his first rodeo.

"Okay." We shed our clothes like they were on fire and slid into the back.

THE SUN

12:15 A.M.

MY BODY GLISTENED with sweat. I laughed at myself, realizing I had made awkward chirping wails during sex. I crawled off Lorenzo, grabbed my clothes, and started dressing.

"Shit," Lorenzo swore. A squad car pulled into the cemetery behind us.

We dressed at light speed and crawled into the front seats.

The officer knocked at the driver's side window. Lorenzo lowered it and said, "We stopped for a bit. I was having car trouble, but it seems to be running fine again."

"Let me see your driver's license."

Lorenzo dug it out of his billfold and handed it to him.

The officer turned to me, "You okay, ma'am?"

"Like he said, just some engine trouble."

"What was it?" he pressed.

"Overheated," I answered.

"The engine?" the officer questioned.

"No, me," I quipped.

The officer started laughing and slapped the door. "I appreciate your honesty. Be on your way." He handed Lorenzo back his license.

"Yes, sir," Lorenzo responded. "We will do so immediately." Lorenzo raised the window and turned to me. "That was good."

"Thank you." I patted his leg. "Do you want to exchange numbers?"

"I'll take yours," he grinned. Lorenzo picked up his phone.

I gave him my number. "651-869-1313."

"That's a great number. Thirteen is a lucky number for Italians for a couple of reasons."

"Like?" I wondered.

"Jesus had thirteen apostles."

"I thought he had twelve."

"Not true," Lorenzo corrected me. "After Judas bit the dust,

St. Matthias joined the crew. And there are fourteen weeks in a quarter, so thirteen is the week before it ends."

"That doesn't make any sense." I furrowed my brow. "Why would that be lucky?"

"Thirteen is associated with finishing the job before the quarter ends."

"And your phone number is?" I questioned as I took my phone out.

"Not yet." He started the truck and pulled out of the cemetery.

That stung, but I simply said, "Okay." *Well, I got my one-night stand.* I thought out loud, "Are you seeing someone?"

"Sort of."

Of course, he is.

"But you'd do in a pinch." He grabbed my knee.

Boy, do I know how to pick 'em. I brushed his hand away.

"Don't tell Dad what we did. And for damn sure, don't tell him a cop checked in on us. He'd kick my ass."

"Is Roan abusive?" His dad was as intimidating as hell.

"Hell no," Lorenzo laughed. "But if he's torqued with me, he doesn't include me in deals, and I have bills to pay. They don't give these Hummers away."

I stared at the headlights shining down the road into the night. I could only see so far. What lay in the darkness beyond the beams was anybody's guess.

Lorenzo chuckled. "But go ahead and tell your buddy Ricky I made you squeal like a pig tonight."

At this moment, any attraction I had to Lorenzo was gone. "How do you know Ricky?"

"He went to prison for shooting my sister Halle, so I keep an eye on the boy." With a smug grin, he said, "I'm the one that put him in the hospital. If he wants to take on the mob, he knows where I'm at. I'll be waiting."

Now I felt ill. Ricky had gone to Roan's house to speak to him about Halle—a child Roan had out of wedlock with Ricky's sister.

Lorenzo was home, and he beat Ricky senselessly and dumped his badly bruised body in a homeless encampment. I could never tell Ricky about this. Lorenzo was a first-class prick—exactly what my initial reaction had told me. I hadn't spoken to Ricky since we broke up. I missed him, which was a hell of a thing to think right after I'd had sex with someone else.

Lorenzo continued, "You have to admit, you kind of owed me for driving you all the way out here."

"Just shut up," was my last response.

Chapter 33

JON FREDERICK

6:30 A.M. SATURDAY, APRIL 15, 2023
HIGHWAY 61, SOUTH OF STAEHLI PARK ROAD, LAKE CITY

A tow truck now sat on the shoreline, and its long cable winch slowly pulled the totaled car out of the lake. I stepped into the muddy sand to get a look at the driver as the car was pulled onto the shore. The Roadster and its driver were melded into one solid piece. It would take the jaws of life to separate the body from the wreck. He had no face, just a mess of blood. When I looked in the smashed driver's side window, I could see he had a Disciple's Star of David on his arm.

I patiently waited as the crime scene techs pulled out items. We analyzed them one by one: a billfold belonging to Tug Grant, a handgun registered to Tug Grant, and finally, the driver's billfold. Jamarcus Smith was nineteen years old.

One of the techs said, "Jamarcus is wearing a Rolex. Did Tug have his watch on?"

"No."

"Any idea why the Disciples would have a hit on Tug Grant?" Doris asked.

"No." I couldn't help but wonder how the Disciples found Tug. This wasn't a chance meeting. "Check to see if you can find a tracker on the car."

"We will, but remember this Roadster has rolled and sunk to the bottom of Lake Pepin. Even if it was there, it might be gone now. Sean will be here in a minute. I've filled him in on our findings."

Sean Reynolds was the BCA Superintendent. He arrived in his typical black suit, white dress shirt, and black tie and approached me. "Sounds like a pretty open and shut case of a homicide during the course of a robbery."

"I think there's a good possibility Roan Caruso set this up."

Sean glanced out at Lake Pepin. "Let's not confront Roan until we have evidence to support this. The police busted into his house and arrested him on the night of the drive-by without a warrant. Catania Turrisi feels we've been harassing her husband, and she wants it to end."

"When did we start letting an angry partner stop an investigation?"

"You need to consider that other agencies may be looking at Roan, and perhaps they want us to back off. Leave him alone."

"What agency?"

"Not your concern. Go home and get some sleep. It's been a long night."

"Taytum Hanson came to the scene, and she felt very strongly that Roan arranged Tug's murder. We know Roan murdered Deondre. We know he set up Deb's murder. It doesn't seem like we should be walking away from him."

"And still, we are." Sean abandoned our conversation and strolled over to Doris. After they exchanged a few words, he got into his silver Chevy Chevelle SS and cruised away. He drove seventy-four miles to tell me to leave Roan Caruso alone. I didn't like the smell of it. It's what he didn't say that bothered me the most. I felt that if an investigation were occurring, he would have given me the name of the entity involved.

Tormented, I walked to my car and called Zave. "Did you find anything at Agnes's house?"

"There was no attempted break-in," Zave responded. "The security system was still on."

"It appears that Disciples member Jamarcus Smith shot Tug Grant to death in a cabin by Zumbro Falls. He took Tug's Tesla Roadster, Rolex, and gun. When he was winding out the Roadster on the way back to Minneapolis, he rolled it and ended up dead in the Mississippi."

"Jam was just another lost kid. He had chronic pain after being shot at the Caruso drive-by. And he was still facing charges for aiding and abetting the murder at the Caruso home. Jam was recently released from juvie after being certified to stand trial as an adult."

"The patrol officer at the scene clocked the Roadster at 183 miles per hour." I paused. "Are you sure you saw Roan Caruso by Agnes's house?"

"No doubt. He wasn't hiding."

"That is very curious, isn't it?" It was as if he wanted us to see he was nowhere close to Tug Grant. Sean just directed me to leave Roan alone, but I'm going to talk to him anyway."

"Confront him?" Zave asked.

"No. I imagine Roan is well-protected on this one. I need a question answered."

"Ask him to leave Ahmad alone. He was the driver in the shooting at Caruso's house. He was the only one of the three who didn't have gun residue on his hands. Ahmad said he chickened out on the way to the house that night, so they made him drive. He was just a kid, and I'm tryin' to take him on another track."

The sun was up, so I headed back to Minneapolis. I tiredly processed what I knew. A legitimate source said a hit had been requested on Melanie Pearson. Tug was the one who benefited the most from a hit on Melanie, and it's likely he would turn to Roan to fulfill that request. Roan had a feud with the Disciples, and the Disciples killed Tug Grant. Even if I couldn't take it any further, I wanted answers.

7:30 A.M.
PIERCE STREET NORTHEAST, BELTRAMI, MINNEAPOLIS

ROAN SAT ON the front porch of his rose brick house, casually enjoying a cigar. This alone gave me one more piece to the puzzle. He wore a Hawaiian shirt, and his jovial mood would have fit in at Mardi Gras. I said as I approached, "Apparently, it's safe to sit on the porch now."

His self-assured look made me realize he knew exactly what I was talking about. His feud with the Disciples was over. Roan smiled, saying, "I don't know what you're talking about."

"Tug Grant was found dead in Zumbro Falls."

Emotionless, Roan responded, "The chickens came home to roost."

"I'm not here to interrogate you. I just want to know if Melanie Pearson is safe." I needed to handle this conversation in a manner that would keep him from complaining to my supervisor. I pointed to the open chair a couple of feet from him. "Do you mind if I have a seat?"

He gestured for me to sit.

I told him, "Melanie is a decent person. She made some bad choices, but she's trying to turn it around. You've met her. She has a kind heart."

"Melanie is safe—now. I stopped at the Schraut home yesterday to warn her; word on the street was that Tug had a hit out on her. I figured she was fine when I saw you and the squad car there."

"Where did you hear about the hit?"

I waited, but when he failed to continue, I said, "I know how Fox settles debts. Money and a body. How did you convince them to accept Tug as payment?"

"I'm not saying I did. But wasn't Tug the one who got me out of the murder charge on the Disciple Deondre?"

"And maybe Tug was involved in the sale of that signature?"

Roan didn't respond. Instead, he looked out at the neatly groomed neighborhood. His failure to deny it was an affirmation. I added, "Deondre saw the signature." I hadn't considered that neither Tug nor Roan wanted anyone to know the signature stolen from a house in Texas was now in Minneapolis. Deondre's murder was about keeping people from tracing the path of the Button Gwinnett signature. If Deondre said a word about that signature, an investigator could trace the sale back to Roan and eventually to Tug. I continued, "Tug's death sure cleans house for you. The man who paid you for a hit on Deb Grant is gone."

"I would never kill Deb." Eyes welling, he said, "The Deb I knew would have kicked Doden's ass. She was a Scout leader. She hiked and camped with her kids. Somehow, during that fight, she realized Tug had arranged the hit, and she lost her edge. Deb fought because she was tough, but it must have broken her heart. You can't afford to be depressed when your life is at stake. You need to be angry."

His remorse surprised me. I waited, but when he failed to say more, I realized I'd never have the full truth about Deb's death. I said, "You can't be retried for Deb's murder, so it doesn't make sense that you'd kill Tug over her. Was he hitting on your daughter, Halle?"

Roan furiously tapped on the table with his pointer finger as he said, "We agreed to stay away from each other. That should include family." As quick as he was to anger, he calmed down. "Don't you get it? Tug would never be done. It was Melanie. Then it would be Halle. Who knows, maybe even Serena."

I nodded and said nothing for a moment. "Could you do me a favor and leave Ahmad alone? He was the kid driving for the shooting here. Ahmad tried to back out, so they made him drive. A friend of mine thinks he can turn him around."

Anger flashed across Roan's face, and he looked away. "That marker will not be collected." He glared at me. "Ahmad is lucky. I know you guys believe in rehabilitating people. That's why you call it 'corrections,' right? I don't see people changin'. Don't ever mention Ahmad around here again."

"Thank you. You don't believe Ricky Day's changed?"

"Not really. I think Ricky was a decent kid who got squeezed to the point of exploding. His dad pushed him over the edge, but because he was sixteen, he couldn't rein it in, and the whole family paid the price."

Catania stepped out onto the porch and confronted me. "Investigator Frederick, can I see your warrant?"

"We were just talking."

Roan stood up and gave Catania a peck on the cheek. "We're good, amore mio."

Serena had taught me that *amore mio* means *my love* in Italian.

Roan turned to me. "Let me just say this. Today is a good day. There—I'm done." Humming Dean Martin's hit, *That's Amore*, Roan strolled into the house.

With cat eyes, Catania stared at me and waited for me to leave.

I stood. "Nice seeing you again, Ms. Turrisi." I had my answer. Roan Caruso was antisocial, but he wasn't a psychopath like Tug. Tug's crimes were not consistent with the work done by "the family." Tug Grant became a liability, and they ended him. My boss, Sean, instructed me to let the investigation end here. I didn't like it, but there was nothing more I could do at this point, and if I pressed it further, I'd lose my job. The wiser path would be to let it go and live to fight another day.

Chapter 34

JON FREDERICK

4:30 P.M. FRIDAY, APRIL 21, 2023
BUREAU OF CRIMINAL APPREHENSION,
1430 MARYLAND AVENUE EAST
GREATER EAST SIDE, ST. PAUL

Jamarcus Smith's fingerprints were pulled off the inside of Tug Grant's pockets, and Tug's billfold was in Jamarcus's possession. The Wabasha County Sheriff's office closed the murder of Tug Grant with the statement:

> *Tilmore "Tug" Grant was murdered during the course of a robbery at a cabin on Zumbro Lake. The suspect, Jamarcus Smith, drove Grant's stolen car at speeds approaching 200 miles an hour, lost control of the Tesla Roadster, and died leaving the scene. We are thankful no one else was injured.*

It was all true. As an investigator, I knew the situation was much more complicated, but that was the simple resolution. No charges were brought against Doris for using the spikes, and no charges were made against Roan. The piece of evidence related to Tug's death I couldn't reconcile was the presence of the needle. It didn't make sense that Tug would have an anesthetic handy in anticipation of being shot, and he clearly didn't get far from his chair. Still, Tug's fingerprints were the only prints on the needle. From the point of entry, it was most likely self-injected. It would quietly end as a simple robbery.

I spent the day trying to track down Cade Anthony Bennett. Melanie's story of the disappearance of her adolescent friend bothered me. I needed to find out what happened to him. By tracking his mother's social security number and credit card applications, I managed to trace Mary Bennett to Madison, Wisconsin.

I called the number. "Mary, I'm Jon Frederick from the Bureau of Criminal Apprehension. I am looking for your son, Cade. This is a wellness check."

"Has something happened?" her worried voice responded.

"I have a report made by a woman named Melanie Pearson that Cade had disappeared from her Gladstone neighborhood in St. Paul fourteen years ago. I want to make sure he's okay."

"Oh, thank God," she said with relief. "I think that girl turned him gay…"

After the call ended, I called Cade.

"This is Actuary Cade Bennett. What can I help you with?"

Impressive. Actuaries are employed by insurance companies, helping businesses develop policies that minimize the cost of risk. They take in a six-figure salary. "This is Investigator Jon Frederick from the Bureau of Criminal Apprehension. I had a young woman named Melanie Pearson request that we check into your disappearance fourteen years ago."

"Let me step into a private area." I could hear a door close. "Wow. Melanie Pearson. That girl broke my heart. Whatever happened to Melanie?"

"She's been struggling a little." That was a story we didn't have time for. "Melanie has a great deal of shame for walking out on you." Trying to lighten the mood, I added, "Your mom claims Melanie turned you gay."

Cade busted out laughing. That was a good sign. "Yeah, Mom wants to have a reason. She constantly tells me it isn't my fault.

I point out to her that, of course, it isn't. Just like being hetero isn't her fault."

"Melanie shared how your friendship ended, and she's incredibly sorry for not standing up for you."

"You can tell her I'm happily married and living a comfortable life."

"Whatever happened to Del?"

"It turns out that Del wasn't his real name. He went to prison for abusing another boy and is now doing life at MSOP in Moose Lake. A month after I opened my heart to Melanie, I told Mom, and she got us the hell out of there. I got help. And you can tell Melanie she didn't turn me gay. Del targeted me because he sensed I was gay. He knew I was full of shame and vulnerable. I loved Melanie. Not in a sexual way. She was such a caring soul. I don't blame her. My therapist pointed out that *I* didn't know what to do. Why would another fourteen-year-old have the answers? You can't expect a kid to resolve a problem most adults don't know how to handle. Please tell Melanie I wish the best for her, and she can call me if she'd like."

5:30 P.M.
51ST STREET & WASHBURN AVENUE SOUTH, FULTON,
MINNEAPOLIS

SERENA AND I were visiting Agnes Schraut, waiting for Melanie to return from the mental health unit. Now that Tug was dead, it was decided Melanie no longer needed to hide out at Lauren's parents' house.

Serena told Agnes, "It's nice of you to let Melanie stay with you. She's struggling to pull herself back together." Agnes appreciated having someone in the house with her, and Melanie had been waiting on Agnes hand and foot since she moved in.

Agnes spewed, "Is Melanie crazy, or does she just seem crazy because she's always dating assholes?"

"It can make you unstable." Serena countered, "I think it's best not to use the word 'crazy' with her."

"She's not as psycho as everyone thinks," Agnes said. "She was tryin' to catch a rat. You should see how frantic I get when I'm tryin' to catch a rat. I came into this world kicking, screaming, and covered with someone else's blood. That's how I plan on leaving it."

I opted not to respond. Melanie was the one person Agnes was consistently nice to. I think that when Agnes knows she could easily destroy someone, bantering is no fun.

Agnes announced, "I'm taking a nap," and headed to her bedroom.

I told Serena about my conversation with Cade Bennett.

After I had finished, Serena breathed a sigh of relief and said, "That warms my heart. If I had known how badly Melanie would be damaged, I would never have involved her in this."

"Melanie was involved before she invited you in," I reminded her. "You're not responsible for Melanie's choices. If the legal system had delivered justice to Tug, none of this would have happened. But I can't do anything about it, so I need to let it go."

"Do you think my work with Melanie was worth it?" Serena asked.

"Investigators don't get to ask that question. You get a case, and you finish it. Blair Parker's family managed to get five million dollars back from the accounts you and Melanie discovered, but there were still four million dollars unaccounted for that managed to show up in Tug's will."

"That had to come from Blair," Serena exclaimed. "There must be a way for Blair's family to recapture it."

"Recovering money from the person who stole it is easy. It's complicated to try and take it back from relatives and friends after the criminal dies. None of the people receiving the inheritance were complicit in the crime. The Department of Justice is going to try, but my guess is they'll end up settling for a fraction of what was lost. For the time being, Tug's daughters and Taytum enjoy the spoils. Tug wrote his son, Lincoln, out of his will, but he is doing okay. Tug gave his older daughters, Rebecca and Mary, four hundred thousand dollars each, and the littlest girl, Audrey, got two hundred thousand dollars. Audrey never spoke to Tug again after Deb's death. She might end up being the healthiest."

"What happened to the other three million dollars?"

"It went to Taytum Hanson, which brought to mind something Melanie told me when I was helping her and Ricky. Taytum had told her, 'When this all ends, I'll be the one left standing.'"

"I don't know if I should be disgusted or if I should admire her," Serena said. "Taytum sure played Tug right."

"Yes, she did. It helps that she never believed Tug killed Deb. That delusion made it easier for her to rationalize staying by his side. Honestly, I think Lincoln's better off without Tug's money. He's a good kid, and he'll make the world better. Deb had a lasting influence on him."

Serena put her hand on mine. "You haven't said much about Camille lately."

"I'm all right. I've thought a lot about her. I loved Mom. I still do. Mom's attitude was: it happened; it was bad; move on. She never wanted to talk about the past because if you have the opportunity to be happy right now, you shouldn't waste it." Mom died four years ago. I'm grateful to have had her guidance. My tribute to her is to be more loving to Serena and the kids every day. That's what she would have wanted.

"What is it that you say? The good guys win just often enough." Serena respected that I would talk about Mom when I needed to. As an afterthought, she added, "I feel bad for Ricky Day. He still loves Melanie."

"I have to give Ricky credit. Despite the heartbreak, he's still walking the righteous path." Serena had helped Ricky begin the process of buying a home, which is not easy to do with today's economy.

THE SUN

"He's miserably alone. Melanie's miserably alone. It's not right." Serena paused before optimistically offering, "I need to find a way to get them back together. To quote Emily Dickinson: 'If I can stop one heart from breaking, I shall not live in vain.'"

Serena's phone buzzed, and she answered. I couldn't hear what was said on the other end.

After a pause, she asked, "What kind of mood was she in?" Another pause. "Thank you." When she hung up, Serena turned to me. "Melanie insisted that the driver take her to the Mall of America. He said she was crying when she got out."

"We need to go." I stood. "The Mall of America is the number one place people commit suicide in Minnesota. Where else does the public have easy access to a seven-story ramp?"

I put the portable siren on my car, and we raced to Bloomington. We were only eight miles away.

"Let me talk to her," Serena said.

"I should go to her. It would be far easier for her to pull your body over the edge than mine."

"If you grab her and pull her off the edge, you may only save her for the moment. It doesn't stop her from killing herself as soon as we leave."

I pondered this. "Okay, but you have to agree to wear a wire."

"It's a deal. But I don't know how it's going to help. It's not like we're trying to get a confession."

"Not that kind of wire."

5:45 P.M., MALL OF AMERICA
60 EAST BROADWAY, BLOOMINGTON

I PULLED INTO the upper level of the parking ramp and popped the trunk.

We could see Melanie sitting on the exterior wall of the ramp, lost in her own world. She didn't even look back when we drove in.

I removed a fifty-foot roll of one-quarter-inch diameter cable wire from my trunk. I have kept cable handy since working the Haunted House of Hillman case. I felt I'd eventually have a use for a thin cable that could safely hold eleven hundred pounds. Serena stuck out her leg, and I tied the cable securely around the thinnest part of her ankle.

"Does it have to be so tight?" Serena asked.

"Yes. If you get pulled over the side, it will be holding all your weight." I finished and said, "Good luck. Give me a minute to tie it around one of these cement posts."

Serena pulled on the cable. "Make sure to give me some slack so I can relax and talk to her."

I checked the distance to Melanie. "You should have about twelve feet extra once I get it tied."

Serena stepped away, saying, "I need to make a quick phone call."

I imagined she felt the need to leave the kids a last *I love you* message. If I thought she was going to die, I'd never let her do this.

An older man parked close to us and carefully watched me from his truck as I tied the cable around the post. I had an eerie feeling about the way he observed me. I flashed my badge and continued working.

When Serena returned, she was off the phone. "Am I good to go?"

"Yes."

She nodded and strolled to Melanie. Serena glanced back, and for a second, I saw fear in her eyes. Before I could tell her to trust her instincts, she approached Melanie and asked, "Mind if I have a seat?"

"How did you know I was here?"

"The driver called. I asked him to make sure you were delivered to Agnes. He thought he should let me know you chose to go to the Mall of America instead." Serena climbed up on the wall and sat next to her. "What are you doing, Melanie?"

Melanie finally looked back and noticed I was only fifteen feet away. "No closer," she insisted. I could see a tear slipping down her cheek.

Serena waved me back.

I stopped in my tracks. I would silently observe until I was called in. Even though the cable was anchored, I kept it in my hands. A twelve-foot fall, tied by the ankle, is still a hard fall. I wanted to slow her descent if I needed to.

"I'm not dissociating anymore," Melanie told Serena. "I never had multiple personalities. I just blacked out. But I did learn a little about it in treatment. You know in the shows where they name all the personalities? Therapists don't actually do that. Instead, they pull you back to understanding it was all you. It wasn't Melanie Two or Three or Blackout Melanie. It was just me. I get it, but that doesn't make it any better. I let down my first love—Cade. I slept with Tug when he was married. I slept with Tug when I was engaged. I had sex with Tug when I was dating Ricky—the gentlest man I've ever met—and then I dumped poor Ricky. Three strikes, you're out, right?"

"You are so brave, Melanie," Serena pointed out. "You're the one who did the work to send Tug back to prison."

I wished we could prove Tug had injected her with a sedative, but in truth, we couldn't. We could only prove that Melanie hadn't taken Valium.

Melanie was despondent. "But ultimately, he wasn't going to be prosecuted on any information that came from me."

"That's not true," Serena interjected. "You found the falsified bank statement. Tug was being charged with perjury for lying to Blair about their financial status. Tug's decision to come after you for finding that evidence got him killed."

"He still avoided prison," Melanie muttered.

"He's dead." Serena took her hand, "The world's done with him. Tug was like a prickly weed that kept coming back. 'Gone forever' works for me."

"I guess he's not going to be coming after me anymore. I have to be okay with that," Melanie acquiesced. "But is it going to get any better? It doesn't seem like it. My dad abandoned me when I returned to Ricky. Sophie bailed when I went back to work for Tug. And I dumped Ricky when I realized I was having sex with Tug. I'm more alone than ever."

"It's going to get better. I promise you. Jon says that no situation is so bad that you can't make it worse. Don't make it worse. I'd love to be your friend. And I need to tell you something about Cade Bennett."

"I feel like I've been alone since I abandoned Cade. Del killed that poor boy."

"Well, I have good news on that front. Jon tracked Cade down. He's alive and happily married, working as an actuary in Wisconsin Dells. And Cade has no ill feelings for you. You were just a kid, and he dumped a lot on you. Cade left his number, so you can call him if you wish."

"Are you kidding?" Melanie smiled tearfully. She gazed at the sky and softly said, "Thank you."

"I am not kidding, girl." Serena put her arm around Melanie, and they sat looking down together. "People are starting to gather."

"One more group of people I'm going to disappoint." Melanie emitted a sad laugh.

"I don't care about them. I care about you. I have a friend who works at Carlson Capital Partners. Once I tell her about your great work investigating Tug, I know she'll give you an interview. She owes me a solid, and I would love to have a friend to enjoy a coffee with when I'm in the metro. Unless you're too busy."

Serena glanced back at me briefly. The satisfaction in her eyes warmed my heart. I loved the way Serena connected with people. I felt I could finally relax.

"I am definitely not too busy," Melanie said as she wiped away tears. She turned to hug Serena. The spontaneous movement caused her to lose track of where she was, and she slipped off the edge.

My arms shot out as if I could magically traverse the fifteen feet between us and grab hold.

Serena lunged and bear-hugged her.

I was hoping it wouldn't come to this. As they plunged over the side, the cable went flying through my hands. I squeezed tight and was able to slow it down, but it still slipped through. Too much cable had passed through my hands. I turned back and saw the old man had untied the knot I had around the post.

I quickly pumped my fists in a circle, tightly looping the cable around my hands. I now had a firm grasp, but I had thrown myself off balance in the process. The combined weight of the women yanked me toward the edge of the ramp. I was seconds from being pulled over the edge, so I fell to my back on the concrete and let my body slide forward until I slid into the wall. I braced my feet and carefully stepped my feet up the wall to give me a stable angle. I hung on with all my might. It stopped any further descent, but I wasn't going anywhere.

"Pull us up," Serena yelled.

"I can't!" I yelled back. "Someone untied the cable. It's all I can do to hang on. I can't even stand up to look at you. I'm lying on the concrete, feet braced against the wall."

"I feel like my ankle's being torn off my body," Serena yelled. "I've got Melanie in a hug, but I don't know how long we can hang on. If this slips off my ankle—" She didn't finish.

I could probably pull them up if I could get to my feet. It would require me to turn sideways, and once I did that, I was in trouble. All the weight would go to my highest leg and pull me over the side. My only hope of saving them was to stay put. I yelled, "Is there any way one of you can grab the cable to take some of the weight off your ankle?"

"No," Serena said. "It's all we can do to hang on."

Chapter 35

SERENA FREDERICK

6:10 P.M., FRIDAY, APRIL 21, 2023
MALL OF AMERICA, 60 EAST BROADWAY, BLOOMINGTON

When Melanie slipped off the edge, I immediately lunged and grabbed her around the shoulders. We fell past twelve feet and were still falling. We were going to die. Somehow, the wire had come loose. Our descent started to slow and then stopped. Melanie and I were in a precarious position. I was hanging upside down by my left leg. While I had squeezed Melanie into a hug around her shoulders, I didn't have a firm grip. Out of self-preservation, Melanie wrapped her legs around my left leg, which kept her upside down, facing me.

"It's all we can do to hang on," I implored.

Now, face-to-face, Melanie solemnly said, "Let go of me."

"No. Absolutely not." I gasped.

"Please. This is too much weight." Tears rolled from Mel's eyes across her forehead. I could feel her loosen her grip.

"Dammit, Melanie! Hang on! I swear if you let go—" Once again, I didn't finish. It's hard to threaten someone who wants to die.

"This wire will never hold both of us."

"Yes, it will. The cable will hold over a thousand pounds. Melanie, I lost a baby. I can't afford to lose a friend, too. Please, do this for me. If you let go, my ankle still might slip through the wire. If you let go, you seal my fate." Melanie might not fight to save her life, but she might fight to save mine. I glanced down. I could die here. Nora and Jackson would be motherless. I shook away the thought. Okay—I couldn't think about that. I needed to find a way to survive with a friend who wanted to die. Trying to sound optimistic, I said, "People are looking up. Maybe if we just hang on for a bit." She didn't respond, so I continued babbling. "There's a crowd down there. I'll be puking on them in a minute. Sorry, Mel, but I'll probably catch your hair, too."

Realizing I was losing hope, Melanie's mood changed. "I will save you if it's the last thing I do. I need you to trust me here. Loosen your grip. I'll loosen mine, too, but I can still hold my weight with my legs."

My arms were weakening. I reluctantly loosened my grip. Her loose shirt slid down under her arms, and her partially bare breasts were uncomfortably close to my face. Irritated, I asked, "What are you doing?"

She was grunting as she jerked her torso upward. "I thought I could swing my body up, but I can't. If I could grab your leg, I could work my way up to the wire and take some of the weight off your leg."

I sadly laughed at the absurdity of our situation. "You could've worn a bra." I glanced down at people looking up at us.

"I was going to kill myself. What's the point?"

"We're going to be on somebody's Snapchat video." I quickly refocused, "Okay, use your legs to pull your body up like an inchworm. I'll try to push you up with my arms."

I wasn't much help, but Melanie was able to pull her body halfway up mine by progressively clamping and unclamping her arms around me. When she squeezed right beneath my ribcage, a jolt of excruciating pain fired through my body, and I winced.

"Are you all right?" Mel asked.

"Yeah." I blew out a breath. I had to encourage her to keep trying. "You're strong."

"For the wrong reasons. I used to work out with Tug because he didn't want me to put on any extra weight like Deb apparently had." Mel sighed. "I don't know if I can hunch my body up anymore."

"Okay. Put your hand into my pants pocket. Use your thumb to grip around the top of my jeans. You can use that as a handle to pull yourself up."

"It would be easier if you wore a belt," she complained.

"If you snack enough, you don't need one." On the upside, my shirt was snug and wasn't going anywhere.

Melanie dug her hand into my front pocket and her thumb into the inside of my jeans to get a grip. She then pulled her torso over and gripped the same pocket with her other hand, enabling her to raise one arm around my leg. Mel pulled herself up until we were intersected in opposite directions at the groin. Gravity brought her shirt back down again, but I would bet someone below was still making a video. She gripped my bound leg with one arm and undid her belt with the other.

"No bra, but a belt?" I was hanging upside down, observing at this point.

"I wanted to be comfortable at inpatient, so I brought my loose clothes, with the plan of donating them all to Goodwill when I was done."

Once Mel had the belt out, she reached up and swung it around the wire right above where Jon had secured it to my foot. I realized part of her ease resulted from not being afraid of dying. She pulled the strap through the buckle and tightened it. She then wrapped the strap around her hands, looked down, and said, "Okay, now grab my leg."

"I'll never be able to pull myself up."

"I know, but it will take weight off your ankle."

I followed her direction.

Mel pulled up hard on the belt.

It was a tremendous relief to have the brunt of the weight lifted off my ankle.

Mel smiled at my reaction.

"Is there any chance you can hook my free leg?" My dangling leg was causing extreme back pain. It would be easier to keep pulling myself up if it was stabilized.

Mel hooked my leg with her hand and pulled it between her arms.

My pain was instantly lessened. Now, we needed Jon to keep hanging on. I yelled to him, "Are you okay?"

Chapter 36

JON FREDERICK

6:30 P.M., FRIDAY, APRIL 21, 2023
MALL OF AMERICA, 60 EAST BROADWAY, BLOOMINGTON

The initial adrenaline kick was fading, and I was feeling the two hundred-plus pounds I was holding. With their weight hanging so far below me, I couldn't move them. I needed help. I'd hang on until my hands were bloody, and they pulled me over the side.

The old man approached, so I told him, "Help me pull."

"Can't. Got a bad hip, bad ticker, bad back," he responded. "I thought you were going to hang yourself, so I untied it. I was going to try to talk you out of it. That badge doesn't protect you from depression."

I thought about asking him to pull his truck closer, but I was concerned he'd run me over. Most of the cable was wrapped around my left hand, steadily compressing the muscles and tendons around my bones. My body felt like it was being pulled up, and I was concerned the weight would crush Serena's foot and pull it through the cable loop.

Serena yelled, "Are you okay?"

"Yes!" I asked the old man, "Do you have a ball hitch on that truck?"

"Yeah." He looked back at the truck as if he was ready to take off.

"Get your truck."

"I'm not very good at backing up. I park in places where I can drive out. That's why I'm up here."

"You've got to help me out. I can't hold on much longer." It was dangerous, but if I could get that hitch close enough, I'd wrap this cable around it. Then I'd have him drive ahead. "Drive your truck past my body. Perpendicular to it. T-shape. Drive past me about ten feet and stop. I'll have you turn the wheel and back up slowly. I'll yell when you need to stop."

A voice thundered, "Not necessary." Ricky Day stood over me. I realized that Serena had called Ricky when she stepped away from me earlier. With mad energy, he gripped the cable and pulled. The two of us now had the weight and power to make progress. I was soon back on my feet and pulling hand over hand, cable pooling behind us.

Ricky grabbed Melanie's arms and, with one quick swoop, pulled her over the wall.

I reached down and grabbed Serena's leg. She grimaced with pain as I gripped her tight, and she swung the other foot to me so I could take hold of both.

Once over the wall, I helped Serena stand. On one foot, Serena hugged me close as she said, "Jon, that was so scary. When I realized the cable wasn't anchored, I thought we were goners." She winced in pain, so I helped her sit on the cement. "It felt like my foot was being ripped from my body. I might have done something to my hip."

I knelt and undid the cable around her leg. I was pleased to see the knot would have held. Still, I opted to keep this to myself when Serena told Melanie, "You saved my life."

Melanie clung to Ricky, and he patiently allowed the embrace to linger until Melanie was finally able to let go.

Ricky told her, "You gave me a chance to rescue you. I dreamed of getting the chance to save someone. It felt good, but it doesn't really change anything, does it?"

"It does," Melanie gasped. "It changes everything because it brought you to me." Melanie kissed him. "I love you, Ricky. I am so sorry."

"I love you, Melanie," he told her, "I've known I loved you since the first night we spoke. But don't ever do this again. It's going to be okay. I'm here. You're here. This moment is all we have. I don't care what you did. I don't even care why. I just want you to be okay. That's how much I love you."

"I don't want to die," Melanie pled. "I swear, one more chance. Is there a saying about fourth chances?"

Ricky told her, "In the Bible, 'four winds' refers to the Holy Spirit waiting to be sent forth on errands, like the call that brought me here today. I never go back to my work locker during my shift, but I did today. When I opened it, I heard my phone buzzing. Serena called and told me you were here. Chance or divine intervention?"

"I'm nauseous and dizzy," Serena interrupted. "Let's get out of this damn ramp." She gingerly accepted my help and leaned on me. I helped her to our car while Ricky and Melanie followed.

Melanie asked, "Can Ricky give me a ride to Agnes's? We have a lot to talk about."

"Sure." Once Serena was seated in the car, I told her, "I'll be right back."

I returned to the wall and wrapped the cable in loops around my arm.

The old man approached. "I didn't want to see you die. I thought maybe if you saw it was untied, you wouldn't jump." For the first time, I realized his nonchalance was an effort to mask the guilt he had for almost costing two people their lives.

"Thanks for caring." I smiled, "It all worked out." My left wrist was severely strained, but the relief I felt overcame the pain.

The man glanced at the grooves that had been molded into my skin by the cable tourniquet. "If they would have started pulling you up, I would have jumped on you for extra weight. I could do that." The man felt sheepish over his behavior.

"I'm glad it didn't come to that. You did what you thought was right. Next time, you might want to ask first. But I have great respect for people who are willing to get involved. Thank you for that."

He clearly felt better. He smiled and waved as I left.

Chapter 37

TAYTUM HANSON

4:00 P.M., SATURDAY, APRIL 22, 2023
CREMATION SOCIETY OF MINNESOTA
7110 FRANCE AVENUE SOUTH, EDINA

A celebration of life was held for Tilmore "Tug" Grant today in Edina. I had waited until the last minute at the Lunds grocery store across the street, sipping on an iced Northern Lite Latte at Caribou Coffee. The Cremation Society is a beautiful facility with wood floors and bare white walls, making it look like an art studio with ninety percent of its paintings removed.

I stood at the entry of the main room, looking at a couple of rows of relatives and lots of empty chairs. This place should be packed. It was a sad ending to a great man. There isn't anyone here who loved Tug more than I. His wife, Blair Parker, sits up front next to her son, Elon. Blair had planned on divorcing Tug. Elon hated him. Three of Tug's children were present. The youngest was absent. She hasn't forgiven Tug for Deb's death. His son, Lincoln, thinks Tug killed his mother, and the two sisters present aren't sure.

I missed the discussions Tug and I had about the law. When we worked together, we could come up with an argument to get anybody out of an indictment. I missed so many things about him.

The door opened behind me. Roan Caruso and Catania Turrisi, dressed in black, came walking in. *Are you kidding me?* I walked directly at them and screamed, "No way! Get the hell out of here!"

"Be careful, Taytum," Cat tried to shush me. "Consider who you're talking to."

"I know you murdered him." I swore to Roan, "I will ruin you!"

I'm tall, but Cat is more solid. She hammered her index finger into my chest and said, "Bitch—you just signed your own death warrant."

Roan stepped between us and told Cat, "Let's leave."

The funeral director and all attendees were now observing. Roan glanced back at me. If looks could kill, I'd be dead. This was a long way from over.

The thin mortician approached me and said, "You should leave, too."

"Huh. I should leave?" I'm the one person who *should* be here.

Chest puffed out like a rooster, Elon Parker pointed his finger at me. "You'll be returning our money. If you turn it over now, there won't be any criminal charges."

I wanted to belittle the arrogant ass, but I simply replied, "I didn't commit a crime." *Try to get it from me, dickhead.*

I decided to leave when I saw the look on Tug's children's faces. They were now parentless. Out of respect for them, I left quietly. Paying homage to Tug, I would defend his children's inheritance pro bono against the Parkers. Elon is about to learn that it's difficult to get money back given in inheritance, even if it was believed to be acquired through crime, once the criminal dies. Before leaving, I gave Blair and Elon an impish grin and reminisced about grabbing Blair's headboard in ecstasy.

Chapter 38

SERENA FREDERICK

8:30 P.M., FRIDAY JULY 28, 2023
BUREAU OF CRIMINAL APPREHENSION
1430 MARYLAND AVENUE EAST, ST. PAUL

Sean Reynolds called Jon and told him to attend a mandatory meeting in St. Paul. Jon said little about his supervisor these days, which was an indicator that they were not getting along. Sean refused to tell Jon what the meeting was about, which reflected poorly on the pending scenario. Jon and Sean had a crazy history. They respected each other as investigators, and their relationship had smoothly transitioned into Sean becoming Jon's supervisor. The dynamic became problematic when Sean fathered a child with Jon's ex, Jada Anderson. Sean felt that Jon was somehow responsible for Sean's failed relationship with Jada, even though Jon and Jada were long over when Sean dated her. Sean destroyed the relationship himself by becoming progressively more paranoid about the work-related conversations Jon and Jada had during investigations. The irony was that the whole time, Sean was cheating on Jada. Paranoia is a common characteristic of unfaithful partners.

I requested to attend the meeting, which Sean didn't oppose. He likely felt Jon would be more respectful if I were present. When we walked into the BCA office, the people who normally greeted us got busy with other tasks. There was a security person in the hall, which was unusual.

"This is awkward," I said, taking Jon's hand.

Sean was waiting for us outside his office and invited us in. Once he was seated behind his desk, Sean asked me, "Did Jon tell you he visited Roan Caruso after he left the Roadster crash site?"

"He did." I squirmed a little in my seat.

Sean raised his voice and directed his anger toward Jon. "I told you to stay away from Roan."

"I wanted to make sure Melanie Pearson was safe," Jon responded. "At the request of a Minneapolis police officer, I also got Roan to stay away from Ahmed Smith. If you look at our mission statement, the vision of the BCA is to deliver exceptional law enforcement services for a safer Minnesota. I was fulfilling our role."

Once again, Sean turned to me. "Do you want your husband dead?"

"No, I don't. But I've accepted that he's an investigator, which entails confronting unsavory characters," I countered.

"We're trying to get Minneapolis settled down. We don't need to start a war with Cosa Nostra!"

Jon responded, "Sean, you were once a great detective. How would you have handled this differently?"

"I would have listened to my supervisor."

"No, you wouldn't have," Jon remarked. Jon was more angry regarding Sean's directive to back off from investigating Roan than he had shared with me. I considered the possibilities and became convinced this conversation would end badly. If Jon wasn't fired, he was going to quit.

Sean defended himself, "I'm asking you to trust me here. Maurice Strock was the boss back then. Things were different."

"I don't know that they were," Jon countered. "Tell me the name of the agency that's asking us to back off, and I'll shut up and walk away."

"I don't have to." Sean was stonewalling.

"The state pays us for protection. We don't get to say there are guys too dangerous to go after. I won't stop doing my job so you can keep Catania Turrisi happy." Jon pulled out his billfold and started taking out his badge. "Don't ask me to."

Sean stood up and yelled, "I've had it with your disrespect. You're—!"

"I'M PREGNANT!" I stood up and outshouted everybody. We couldn't afford to lose Jon's medical benefits.

Sean debated finishing his sentence, but instead, he fumed quietly as he slowly sat back down. He finally offered, "You can't fight me on this, Jon. If you're going to stay, no more contact with Roan Caruso or Catania Turrisi. If your principles are too high to respect that, leave."

If Jon quit, he wouldn't be able to claim unemployment. Law enforcement personnel put their lives on the line every day and can leave with nothing. I told myself that if Jon walked away, I would respect his decision and that we would find a way to make it work. *I love him.*

Jon held his face in his hands for a moment. When he removed them, he smiled and said, "I guess it's time for me to shut up and fall in line."

Sean still seemed to be debating firing Jon. The problem was that he needed a legitimate reason. Terminating an employee is an extensive process in the state system. Sean told Jon, "You will receive a written reprimand for violating a direct order."

Jon nodded his acceptance and said nothing.

I stood up and told Sean, "Okay. Are we good? Jon still has a job?"

"Yes, for now," Sean's tone softened as he kindly asked, "Have your leg and hip healed after taking the dive to save Melanie? That was very brave—crazy brave."

"Almost. My hip should be healed just in time to have a baby." I smiled and told Sean, "Have a nice day." I took Jon's hand, and we left the office together.

THE SUN

Jon told me, "That's great news. Family is first." He pulled me into a hug.

"I love you, Jon. You were just being the man I fell in love with—a man with principles." I kissed Jon, and we received an ovation from all the staff, including the security guard—in his case, a standing ovation. Everybody heard my announcement. I took a deep breath. Another crisis averted—the nature of being a mom.

12:05 P.M., SUNDAY, JULY 30, 2023
PIERZ

WE DECIDED TO let Jackson tell his grandfather, Bill Frederick, our news. Jackson was so excited he looked like he was about to burst. Bill was barely in the house when Jackson announced, "Mom's got a baby. In her tummy."

"That's exciting!" Bill grinned.

"And it's a human," Jackson added.

"That is a game-changer, isn't it?" Bill bent down and scooped him up.

I watched my seven-year-old daughter Nora stand by Jon like his buddy, whispering, "Of course it's a human. What did he think she was going to have—a duck?"

Jackson reveled in being the center of attention, and I felt so blessed to have my family.

With a grin, I asked Nora, "Do you want to see your baby pictures? I can try to dig out some pictures of you and Jackson. The internet's down, but we have photos in a storage bin in the basement."

"I can bring it up," Jon offered. My overprotective husband didn't want me to do any heavy lifting during my pregnancy.

Jon retrieved the container and dumped the photos on the floor. I smiled at the pictures of my friends at Sullivan Lake from a decade ago. We were in our late twenties, and only two of the six of us were married at the time. There was one of just Heather

Hilton and me. Heather's tan neckline featured a thin gold necklace with a sideways cross. An eerie feeling crept over me, and I felt a little nauseous. Heather's name was in the Haunted House of Hillman file. She had been Marshall's attorney. *Was Heather the unidentified victim from the case?*

4:00 P.M.

HEATHER HILTON SAT outside with me, enjoying a cold glass of homemade lemonade, while Jon entertained Nora and Jackson inside. Heather was petite and thin and wore her blond hair in a pixie cut. Today, she looked tired and stressed, as if she knew what was coming. I asked, "Are you okay?"

"I'm good," Heather said. "What did you need to meet with me about today?"

I slid next to her and started flipping through my old photos. There were pictures of Heather in high school and a couple of years after, wearing a thin gold chain with a diagonal cross pendant. I then leafed through pictures of Heather taken after 2014. There were no pictures of her wearing the pendant or any Christian jewelry. In seconds, the haunting of trauma was evident in her eyes.

There was no doubt in my mind that Heather was the unidentified victim in the Hillman case. All the investigators had was a necklace which her rapist had kept as a trophy.

Trying to act casually, Heather dismissed my theory. "I grew up. Decided to add a little variety to my armoire."

Her hand was shaking, so I reached out and held it. "I'm so sorry, Heather. Jon told me he should have figured this out. You told him you knew Marshall hadn't raped and killed Julia. He hadn't considered that you knew because the same man raped you."

Heather kept her face stern while her tears flowed. "I saw him. I didn't think he was from around here. I'd never seen him before. But looking back, I should have known. Why would he be in Hillman?" She leaned into me, and we hugged. After a cry, we both sat back, and Heather said, "Yeah, that sucked. I've only missed one of our Sullivan Lake gatherings. It was about fifteen years after high school. It was the day after my assault."

"I wish you would have called me," I said. "I remember you reminded me over and over to attend when I was lukewarm about it. Then you didn't show up."

"I had planned on it. The night before, I got this bright idea to drive to the Haunted House of Hillman and get some pictures. Maybe I could talk the crew into coming out for a ghostly adventure. And that fucking Reed caught me there. Remember how I always told everyone I'd fight to the death before I'd let a man rape me?"

"Yeah."

"I submitted. I just took it like a coward. I was so afraid of dying, I froze."

"I don't know what the right answer is, Heather. We do whatever we need to do to stay alive. The victims know better than anybody what's needed at that moment to survive."

"I wasn't his first victim, and I wasn't his last."

"He's locked up now. Life without parole, underground."

"Yeah, I do have to say that helped. But it wouldn't have bothered me if Jon would have just killed him."

"Did you ever tell anyone?"

Heather gave me a sad smile. "Clay."

"How did he handle it?"

"Better than you think. There were times he knew I couldn't get in the mood, and he respected it. If my mind was racing, he'd pick me up in the middle of the night, and we'd drive around in his truck listening to music with no expectations. But Clay brings his own set of problems."

"I don't doubt that. I can't imagine how angry you must have been when you saw me kiss him. That was so stupid, and

I'm sorry. I've apologized to Jon a hundred times. Never, never, never, again."

"Thank you for the apology." She tapped my hand. "Clay would treat me respectfully and stay with me until I was asleep. But then he'd go have sex with someone else. I started telling Clay I was in the mood even when I wasn't, trying to keep him for myself. It became a new form of victimization."

"That's a great description." I considered, "Do you want that necklace back from evidence?"

"No," Heather responded. "I don't ever want to see that pendant again. You know how some attorneys can be real dicks. I don't want anyone saying, 'Heather can't take this case because she's a rape victim. She's biased.' I'm not biased. I'm informed."

"Okay. I will not tell a soul other than Jon. And that boy can keep a secret."

"Thank you."

"Have you been back to church?" I wondered.

"No," she shook her head. "Wearing a blessed cross didn't protect me."

"No, it doesn't work any better than praying as a form of birth control. I'm not going to tell you what to do, but I will share that Christianity has helped me work through my own trauma. Jon has told me people with religious beliefs are more likely to recover from trauma."

"And I bet Jon can cite the studies." Heather smiled, reached over, and squeezed my hand. "Thank you for your kindness, Serena."

I sighed. "I'm hoping we can fix whatever came between us."

"We're good." Heather remarked, "But understand, as long as you're working with Jon, we'll be on opposite sides."

"I'll always be with Jon."

"Okay," she smiled. "The lines have been drawn. I do have to ask you; did you intentionally slap me on the ass at Red's? I'm not angry about it. I know I was treating all my friends crappy at that point, so I don't blame you."

"No." My face flushed. "Vicki had done the same to me. I honestly thought you were her. You had just dyed your hair red, but I didn't know that." That is the only time I've ever struck someone as a joke, and man, did it backfire.

Heather glanced at me skeptically and laughed, "Yeah, I don't know that I believe you."

Chapter 39

JON FREDERICK

SIX MONTHS LATER
12:05 P.M., SUNDAY JANUARY 21, 2024
PIERZ

Serena slipped off her pajama pants and sat back in the corner of the couch, ready for her foot and leg rub. Our fireplace gave the room a warm glow and feel. Serena rubbed her round belly and said, "I still have two months to go. If I get any bigger, I'll explode like an atomic bomb when my water breaks."

I leaned into her and kissed her. "You're beautiful."

"Would you ever consider working for Heather?" she asked.

"No." I had told Serena that Heather had hit on me when I worked the Haunted House case.

"Good." She smiled. "I've never let her know I am aware of what she did. I'm trying to attribute her bad choices to unresolved trauma."

"That's kind. But we all have trauma. Tug used to call Heather 'Mini-T.' In his exact words, a 'shorter, thinner and less womanly version of Taytum Hanson.'"

"Are you going to take the private work Taytum offered?"

"I don't think so. Here's the scenario: A colleague of Professor Randy Kimball accused him of forcing sexual intercourse on her one night when they were the only two left in their campus building. I'm not convinced of his innocence."

"If they did a rape kit, it should be obvious."

"She didn't report it until a week later. The report said that Randy admitted talking to her in the office that night but denied any sexual activity. Reading it, I got a sense that he wasn't being honest. After being paid to help Tug Grant last year, I have no desire to work for another guilty man."

"Understandable." Serena blew out a long breath and said, "I appreciate you playing outside with the kids. They have lots of energy, and I've been so tired lately." She purred as I did a deep massage of her leg. "Mmmm. Honestly, I wouldn't mind taking on a quick case with you before the baby's born."

"There's a part of me that would like to meet Randy Kimball, just to see how he was so gullible to Tug's charm. Randy supposedly wrote a book declaring Tug was an innocent martyr convicted by a corrupt system."

"Comparing Tug to a suffering saint is pretty creepy." Serena leaned her head back as she asked, "Do you think Taytum's still going after Roan Caruso?"

"I do."

"I'm not in the mood to think about it. Too relaxed." Serena closed her eyes and said, "You rub me the right way."

Chapter 40

TAYTUM HANSON

9:30 P.M., FRIDAY, JANUARY 26, 2024
WACONIA BREWING COMPANY
WACONIA SQUARE, 255 WEST MAIN STREET, WACONIA

Roan had killed my lover and mentor, Tug Grant. Tug had been the premier attorney in the state and the youngest head of the Minnesota Bar Association. I loved that man, even after he was convicted of arranging a hit on his wife. When a poor man rises to the top, there's a plethora of highbred ingrates waiting to take him down. As a woman who wants to be a judge, it hasn't been an easy rise for me either. Tug was one person who vehemently attacked my critics and swept away the slugs who got in the way of my ascension. My diligence got my lover released from prison, only to see him executed on an order issued by his best friend.

I can't stop thinking about Tug. Getting kicked out of his celebration of life didn't help. Blair Parker did it simply to assert her power. The spiteful bitch even made Tug's kids attend their dad's funeral as "guests" rather than family. Blair insisted she and her son, Elon, were the only ones who had a right to claim they were Tug's family, and they both hated Tug at the time of his passing. Tug told me one day I'd laugh about gripping Blair's gaudy headboard when we passionately made love. That day has come. *Blair—you can kick me out of his "celebration of life," but I had him when he actually* was *alive—in your bed.*

I will not get a good night's sleep until Roan Caruso is incarcerated. My efforts to investigate Roan have not been particularly productive since he keeps himself well-insulated. I could never produce the muscle to attack him physically, so I'll have to tear him down financially. Roan was part of the Minneapolis Combination, or in other words, the Minnesota mafia, which was a role he assumed by marrying mob boss Catania Turrisi. Extortion was Roan's specialty. He pressured professionals to do business with specific companies and made his money on kickbacks.

People were tight-lipped about Roan, so tonight, I decided to try another tactic. Roan's son, Lorenzo, often stopped at a taproom in Waconia on Friday nights, and I was going to casually cross his path. Lorenzo had a reputation for being an entitled twenty-four-year-old who loved talking about himself and his toys. As they say, "born on third base, and he thinks he hit a triple."

I sat at a high table by myself in my little black dress, enjoying a glass of 255 Amber Ale. It was the brewery's flagship beer for good reason—crisp and clean with a toasty hint of toffee. It was named after the street where it's brewed.

Lorenzo's strong Italian features and tanned skin were highlighted by his crisp white polo shirt and white slacks. The sleeves were so short that I imagined you could see the hair under his armpits—if it wasn't already shaved.

A petite twenty-year-old cheerleader-type gazed up at him with loving eyes. Her inky black hair formed cursive waves down her back. After several minutes, she kissed him goodbye and glared at me as she passed my table. Women have an antenna that picks up on vixens in the vicinity who might threaten their relationship.

Not long after she was gone, Lorenzo found his way to me and said, "I couldn't help noticing you glancing my way."

The hook was set, and it was simply a matter of opening the door to the livewell. "I doubt I've been the only woman who noticed you."

His grin revealed perfect white teeth. "But you're the only one with the beauty of statuesque Aphrodite."

Nice pickup line. I said, "Venus de Milo."

"You're prettier than both combined."

"Thank you." I didn't bother to explain to him that Venus di Milo is a statue of Aphrodite. "Aren't you related to the Turrisi crime family? I have to tell you, *The Godfather* was my favorite movie." I made a point to adjust the pendant on my necklace, drawing attention to my ample cleavage.

My small gesture caught his attention, and he inched closer to me. "I am Lorenzo Turrisi Caruso. And you're Taytum Hanson. You've been to my house before, back when you and Tug Grant were a thing. Sorry for your loss."

Tug's death hurt, but that's not how I was playing this. "Tug made too many stupid decisions. I think he got what he deserved."

"Yeah. Can't argue with that." Lorenzo nodded in agreement. His breathing deepened. "Would you be offended if I told you I always thought that you were hot?"

"I'd be offended if you didn't." I took his hand and placed it on my thigh. He looked like he would explode at any moment. It was nice to know I could still impact a young man so intensely. In my best sultry tone, I asked, "Are we going to waste precious time on small talk, or would you like to stop over for a nightcap?"

"Wow," was all he could say.

"Is my place acceptable?" I knew he still lived with his parents.

"Sure."

Men are so easy.

THE SUN

11:00 P.M., FOX HILL DRIVE, CHANHASSEN

STILL LYING IN bed, I observed my pretty boy as he dressed. I asked, "Who was the girl worshipping you at the bar?"

Lorenzo seemed surprised when he responded, "Eliana. She had to pick up her kid. Mom will have a cow when she hears my girl has a five-year-old child."

"How old is Eliana, sixteen?"

"She's twenty-one."

"I get it. She's pretty—if you're into the pom-pom girl type. I'd do her if I were so inclined."

"I love Eliana. She's the one." Lorenzo hesitated before buckling his belt as he curiously considered, "It doesn't bother you?"

"No. I'm just doing this to get more dirt on my Tug so I can take some pleasure in his passing."

"Then I'm your man." With a broad smile, he said, "I did Tug's secretary, Melanie, just to piss off her boyfriend, Ricky Day. He's my half-sister's uncle. You know Halle Day? Roan's her dad, too. Anyway, Ricky went Defcon 1 on his family a couple of decades ago, shooting them all, including Halle. She was the one survivor. I beat the hell out of Ricky when he was first released from prison. Ricky's girlfriend, Melanie, had the hots for me, so I did her just to humiliate him again."

"How did Ricky react?"

"He didn't. I don't think Melanie told him." Now dressed, Lorenzo stood in front of me.

"I want you to do her again," I coyly suggested. A fiery rage still burns in me over Melanie testifying against Tug. She was the one who got him convicted, and he was never the same after prison. That pathetic little ginger ruined him.

"Are you kidding? Melanie was all right, but she wasn't great." He bent down and kissed me. "Nothing like tonight."

"Do her for me. If she'll lie for you once, she'll lie for you again." If I couldn't get to Roan directly, I could ruin his son's life.

"Melanie and I didn't end on the best terms."

"Let her know you'll tell Ricky about last time if she doesn't."

"Wow. You're really a freak." He was considering it. "I wouldn't even know how to get ahold of her. I deleted her number and I never had her address."

"Leave me your number, and I'll find her for you. If you come back and tell me about it, I'll make it worth your while. You can even tell her this one was courtesy of Taytum."

"Ehhhhhh, I don't think so."

"Your loss."

Tortured with fantasies about what "worth your while" meant, he bent down, kissed me, and departed.

My doorbell rang, so I got out of bed and slid my arms into a robe. On the way to answer it, I noticed Lorenzo had left a slip of paper with his number on it on the counter. When I opened the door, there stood my client, Randy Kimball. Randy was in his forties but in good shape. He ran and went to the gym three days a week. He had a full head of hair and was handsome enough, but even with all of that, his wife still didn't have sex with him. He asked, "Can I come in?"

"What do you have that you can't tell me at the office?" I had made the mistake of first meeting Randy and his wife, Juliet, at my house. They were successful professionals with no criminal history, but I didn't make it a practice to invite guys accused of sexual assault into my home.

He said anxiously, "I thought you should know Jon Frederick told me he wasn't interested in investigating my case. Basically, he didn't believe me."

"Well, I shouldn't have believed you either. The District Attorney told me today that they have DNA evidence."

"Okay," Randy sighed, "she was sexual with me, but we didn't have intercourse, and it was consenting. I swear, she was the aggressor."

I realized my robe was opening, and he was glancing at my

bare skin. I'm not sure why I didn't shut it, but I let it torment him as I dressed him down. "If you are truly innocent, go back and be honest with Jon and talk him into taking this case. Offer more money. I've heard his wife's pregnant, so money will provide some incentive. And once that conversation has taken place, talk to me at the office."

"I'm sorry," Randy repented as he bowed his head and backed off my porch. He was humiliated over being caught trying to sneak a peek. He muttered, "Okay—at the office." The man was a nervous wreck. He looked scared to death of me.

I slammed the door and busted out laughing—*just what I needed*—another married man.

Chapter 41

MELANIE PEARSON

9:30 P.M., SATURDAY, FEBRUARY 3, 2024
HERITAGE CENTER OF BROOKLYN CENTER
6155 EARLE BROWN DRIVE, BROOKLYN CENTER

I was a bridesmaid for my friend Sophia at a beautiful rustic venue. My dark turquoise dress left one shoulder bare and perfectly complemented my long red hair. My man, Ricky Day, was a big, strong, rugged man who looked fine in his tweed blazer and jeans.

The wedding went directly from the reception to the meal to the dance. An hour into the dance, Ricky went to the adjoining hotel and got me a room. He had been so patient while I sat and socialized with old college friends. Ricky returned, handed me a room key, and asked, "Do you mind if I go home? I could gaze at you all night, but this is risky for me. I haven't had alcohol since I was sixteen, but man, I sure want a drink tonight. Everybody's happy and having a good time. I've been fighting the urge, knowing if I take a pull, I'm headed back to prison."

"That's fine." I hugged my handsome man. "I love you, Ricky. You know I have to stay."

"Yeah. I love you too." We kissed. "Call me when you get back to your room, all right?"

"Of course." We kissed again, and I watched my gentle giant walk away. I decided to have another glass of wine.

THE SUN

12:30 A.M., SUNDAY, FEBRUARY 4, 2024
EMBASSY SUITES BY HILTON
MINNEAPOLIS NORTH, 6300 EARLE BROWN DRIVE,
BROOKLYN CENTER

MAYBE IT WAS one glass of wine too many, but I had a great night with old friends. As I approached the elevator, I saw Lorenzo Turrisi Caruso dressed sharply in a crisp pink formal shirt and designer jeans. "Here for the wedding?" I slurred out.

"No, just visiting a friend." He rode the elevator to my floor and stepped out with me. "Where's your better half?"

I was nervous and tried to ignore him, but he followed me to my room door. Before I put the key in, I said, "Good night, Lorenzo."

"Aren't you inviting me in?"

"Ricky's inside," I lied.

"No, he's not. A friend called and told me Ricky left hours ago."

"Are you following me?" I wasn't entering my room until he was gone. I was safe while I was on camera in the hallway.

"It bothers me that Ricky's free. So, I have friends call me anytime they see him out. If he'd have been drinking, I would have called law enforcement." He flicked my chin with his forefinger. "You're going to invite me in and screw my brains out."

"No, I'm not. Sleeping with you was a mistake. I'm sure there are a hundred girls out there who want to sleep with you. You don't need me."

"You're right on both accounts. You're going to beg me to sleep with you when you realize the alternative is that I'll go to Ricky and tell him how you squealed like a pig last time I railed you."

Ricky and I were on a brief break from our relationship then, but sleeping with Lorenzo was still stupid. I didn't realize at the time that Lorenzo was the guy who had beaten Ricky to the point of being hospitalized. "You know what, go ahead and tell Ricky if you feel that makes you a big man, but I'm not sleeping with you. Ricky and I are solid enough where we'll work through it."

"You're letting me in, sweetheart." Lorenzo leaned against the wall by my door. "And here's why. It's not just that you cheated on Ricky" —he softened his voice and turned his back to the camera at the end of the hall— "you let a man die. You stood silent and watched Tug Grant pass away. How do you think a man who has committed his life to God will handle that? You're an accessory to a murder."

I felt myself crumbling in his presence. Damn it! I couldn't tell Ricky. It would break his heart, and I couldn't afford to lose him. In anguish, I conceded and opened the door. "Make it quick."

1:30 A.M.

LORENZO HAD LEFT, but I couldn't sleep. I felt like I'd just been beaten up. Now sober, I realized this was never going to be over. There is clarity in defeat. I needed to be honest with Ricky and accept the consequences. I slipped on my oversized nightshirt and went to the bathroom. My reflection was disturbing. My lips were swollen, and I had red streaks on my neck from being choked during sex. I took a warm washcloth and rubbed the tears from my eyes. My life was unraveling like a roll of toilet paper being spun into a heap on the floor by a toddler. Truth was the one weapon I hadn't used. I climbed back into bed, picked up my phone, and called Ricky.

"Finally, to your room?" he asked in a cheerful voice.

"Yeah." I swallowed hard.

"What's wrong?"

"I have something to tell you, Ricky. Something terrible." The tears flowed, and I struggled to speak.

"You slept with someone."

"Yeah. I had too much to drink and wasn't thinking clearly." He fell silent.

"Ricky? I love you, Ricky, and I am so sorry."

Finally, he responded with, "Who?"

I blew out a long breath. "Lorenzo Caruso."

"Are you kidding me? You know he assaulted me."

I know now, but I didn't know that the first time I slept with him. How do I explain this? "Could you please come and get me so we can discuss this?"

"Are you alone now?"

"Yes, of course. I'm in my room."

"You should have called me a couple of hours ago. I think you should stay right where you're at tonight. I loved you, Melanie."

"Ricky, I still love you. Please just come and get me." The line went dead. I tried calling back, but there was no answer. I wanted to get a ride to him, but I owed it to Ricky to respect his request. Now what? I opened the sliding glass door to the balcony and stepped out into the night. I felt like jumping. I rushed back into the room and grabbed my dress and heels off the floor. I ran back onto the balcony and threw them as far as I could into the night. "Damn it all!" I screamed. Every good thing about tonight was ruined. But I wasn't taking the coward's way out of this. I dropped to my knees and cried. I needed to work on sobering up. I decided to start with a long, hot shower.

8:00 A.M.
NORTHEAST JACKSON STREET, MINNEAPOLIS

I HAD THE TV on all night and spent most of it looking at the clock, waiting for time to pass. I made myself wait until eight in the morning before catching an Uber to Ricky's house. When he didn't answer the door, I found my key and let myself in. "Ricky?" I asked.

No answer came. I quickly went through the house. Suddenly, a chill came over me. I prayed to God that I wouldn't find him hanging. Ricky went to prison at sixteen and was released at age thirty-two, so he has no skills to deal with heartbreak. I've been his only lover. Every room was empty. I went to the basement and continued to call, "Ricky?" He wasn't in the basement. I heard someone enter the house when I was coming up the steps.

I rushed to the front door, where Ricky's older brother, Michael, stood.

Michael was a skinnier version of Ricky, lacking Ricky's muscle mass. Michael was the one person who supported Ricky throughout his sixteen years in prison. This morning, he looked defeated and tired.

"Where's Ricky?" I asked.

"Ricky's in jail." Michael plopped onto a living room chair. "Can you think of any reason Ricky would have gone out and gotten drunk last night?"

"What did he do?"

"He got drunk. Ricky doesn't need to do anything. He can't drink. Someone spotted him in a bar and called the police. Now, he's on his way back to prison. Maybe for ten years."

My heart sank. What have I done?

Michael studied me. "Did Ricky put those marks on your neck?"

"For God's sake, Michael, no. Ricky has only been kind and respectful to me." I wanted to tell him *I cheated on Ricky—this was my fault*, but I didn't. I can't go around wielding honesty like a sword. This was Ricky's family. It was his truth to tell. I didn't want to humiliate him any further.

"Is it some type of allergic reaction?" Michael questioned.

"Yeah." I guess—sensitivity to an irritant.

Chapter 42

SERENA FREDERICK

3:30 P.M., SUNDAY, FEBRUARY 4, 2024
PIERZ

Juliet Kimball left a message for me to call her back, and I felt bad for her, so I did. "This is Serena Frederick. How did you get my number?"

"Taytum Hanson gave it to me. I'm sorry for bothering you, Serena, but we need your help. My husband made a mistake, but he didn't force sex on his colleague. Certainly, you can understand a spouse making one mistake."

The comment made me feel a little paranoid.

"But there's a big difference between giving in to advances and what Fleure's claiming," Juliet continued. "She's going to ruin our life and Randy's career. Please hear us out. Taytum says you and Jon are the only ones who could save the day on this one. I can't sleep at night. I'm not asking you to do anything immoral. Just bring the truth to light. Please. We're headed back to the cities from our cabin on Battle Lake. We're willing to meet somewhere. Please just hear us out."

They were going through Pierz on their way back to the metro, so, much to Jon's chagrin, I invited Randy and Juliet to our home to discuss the case. Jon's brother Vic was visiting, but his partner, Maddie, was on her way to pick him up.

Vic struggled with schizophrenia but was a nice guy. His medication made him less paranoid, but he still occasionally fabricated stories, particularly when he thought it might impress Jon's friends. I was hoping he'd be gone before Randy and Juliet arrived. Vic had bought a pinstriped suit and stopped over to show it off. With his long, ragged blond hair, he looked like a rock star dressed for court.

We watched the Disney movie *Coco* last night, resulting in our five-year-old, Jackson, incessantly asking about ghosts. While emptying the dishwasher, I heard Jackson ask Vic, "How do you keep ghosts out of the house?"

"I find farting to be highly effective," Vic said.

Jackson giggled and asked, "Is that true?"

"Works every time," Vic remarked. "I try to fart as much as I can just to keep them away. They say the average person farts twelve times a day. Based on my contributions to the data, there must be a lot of people who never fart at all."

"Okay," I interrupted. "I think Jackson has heard enough about farting for one day. He needs to get ready to visit Grandma."

With a hangdog look, Jackson went to retrieve his backpack. He returned and patiently waited by the door, giving me a guilt-inducing stare. Jon was in the music room helping Nora put away a project. Jackson was a momma's boy, and he didn't like to go to Grandma's if he knew I was at home.

I bent down, kissed Jackson's forehead, and stepped out to greet the Kimballs. Randy and Juliet reminded me of an entwined married couple whose straight almond-colored hair had blended to be the same for both. Randy stood slightly under six feet tall with plain, solid features and a stocky build. Juliet was half a foot shorter and had the facial features of a great horned owl—high eyebrows, big caramel round eyes, and a pointed chin. Her features were pretty but not ordinary. There was an underlying sadness in her eyes.

Once in the house, Juliet offered my sad little Jackson a

piece of Doublemint gum, and he accepted. After one chew, I could tell he didn't like it. I escorted the Kimballs to our kitchen table, returned to Jackson, and whispered, "You don't have to chew it if you don't like it." I held my hand out, and he spat the gum into it.

"Grown-ups always have gum," he muttered. "They give it away because it's mint, and mint doesn't taste very good. When I get bigger, I'm going to have my own pack of gum, and you know what it's going to be?"

"What?"

"Grape. And I'm not going to share it with anybody."

I hugged him and said, "I love you, Jackson. I promise this won't be too long." Once Jackson got to my parents' house, he always had a blast, but we went through this every time.

Jon and Nora finally emerged and left with Jackson.

Back in the kitchen, I found Vic had taken on the task of entertaining our guests. I joined Vic and the Kimballs at the table as Vic asked the couple, "Are you familiar with Orfield Laboratories in Minneapolis?"

"It used to be called Sound 80," Randy said. "It's where Prince first recorded."

Vic stated, "They have an anechoic chamber that absorbs sound. It's so quiet in the room you can hear your organs functioning. I'm in the process of inventing a device that can be placed in a room hours after a crime was committed that will tell you what was said in the room earlier."

I thought dryly, *Very early in the process—at the "thinking about it" stage.*

"How does it work?" Randy asked Vic.

"Sound travels through waves. The waves continue to bounce about in the room until they fade away. Jon will have it for his next case, but I will be the only one who can interpret it. It's quite complicated, and it takes me about four months to work through all the algorithms. It will be easier after each case."

I didn't know what to say. Vic has nothing to do with Orfield Laboratories. I didn't dare tell them how "out there" my brother-in-law's stories were because I wanted to work this investigation.

Randy said, "It must be a large device with highly sensitive baffles."

"The sensor is handheld," Vic answered. "But the machine that reads it is large, so I have to keep it in the garage."

I glared at Vic. *What are you talking about?*

Fortunately, Jon pulled into the driveway, followed by Vic's partner, Maddie Dehler.

"My ride's here," Vic announced. "Need to run."

I turned to our guests. "Randy, I understand you're a Professor at Argosy. Juliet, what do you do for a living?"

"I work security at the Allina Health Clinic in Eagan. It's on Yankee Doodle Road, where it intersects with Lexington." Embarrassed, she added, "I guess you don't need to know the exact location. I'm nervous. We really need your help."

Jon entered and, after shaking hands, got right down to business. "I need to know the status of the book you were writing declaring Tug's innocence. Rumors from the galley proofs say you're claiming Tug was our next savior."

Randy looked embarrassed.

Juliet rescued him by saying, "It's been shelved."

"I see the website's been shut down," I said. "We wouldn't have given you a second interview if you were still Tug's propaganda show."

"I warned him," Juliet concurred.

"I got taken in by his charm," Randy finally admitted. "The Parkers were our friends, and they were so adamant about his innocence. The creation of that website was imprudent."

"What convinced you otherwise?" Jon asked.

"I needed to talk to Lincoln, Tug's son, before I published," Randy explained. "Lincoln knew a lot more than what was shared in court. He convinced me Tug was guilty. There will be no book. He wasted four months of my life, time I spent writing day and night that I can't get back. I wonder now how it impacted my marriage."

"What's changed that's going to entice me to take your case?" Jon questioned.

Juliet's pained glance at her husband was so heavy it seemed that if I put my hand out toward her, I'd feel its weight. She shared, "I have severe fibromyalgia, so we don't have sex very often. It might be more accurate to say we don't have sex. I don't feel good most days and have incredible pain in my pubis."

"Enough," Randy interrupted. He took her hand. "This isn't on you. You're fine. We're fine. There's been a lot of stress on both of us. I volunteered to teach a General Psychology class to help the school out. Now, the state has passed a rule that you need to have graduate coursework in the classes you teach. My graduate degrees are in Sociology, so along with working full-time, I'm back in college. The first courses were fine, but this semester, I have an instructor who wants three APA-style papers every week, along with an embedded PowerPoint video of me explaining the graphics. If that isn't enough, the college has a hard time downloading my assignments, so it takes three hours of negotiation every week to send my homework."

Jon remarked, "I've always said college is a better measure of perseverance than intelligence. Let's get to the assault."

"Dr. Fleure Duaire has the office next to mine."

"Fleure Duaire?" I asked.

"She's very proud of her name. Fleur is 'flower' in French, which is how she pronounces it. Duaire is pronounced 'Dwire' and means 'dark color.'" Randy continued, "I always worked Thursday evenings to get as much done as possible before the weekend. Nobody was in the building late at night. For a couple of weeks, Fleure started staying on Thursdays, too. She asked me what I like to sip on for a nightcap. I told her a Kentucky whiskey like Maker's Mark hit the spot. The next week, Fleure invited me into her office for a nightcap."

"What time are we talking about?" I wondered.

"10:00 P.M.," he responded. Randy looked out the window.

Jon asked, "Were you standing or sitting? And where exactly were you in her office?"

"She was behind the desk, and I was sitting in the chair in front of it. I had finished my drink and stood up to leave. She came around the desk and propositioned me."

Jon stood up with his back to our table. "Like this?"

"My butt was resting on it. Half-sitting," Randy said.

Jon followed his direction, and Randy responded, "Yeah."

"Where was Fleure when she propositioned you?" Jon asked me, "Serena, would you mind coming here?"

I wasn't sure how far he was going to take this. I stepped in front of him.

"Was she standing directly in front of you when she propositioned you?"

"No, she was standing by my side when she spoke and then stepped right in front of me."

I stepped to Jon's side and then in front of him.

"Was that accurate?" Jon asked.

"Yeah," Randy said.

"Did she speak after she stepped directly in front of you?" Jon questioned.

"No, just when she was at my side. What difference does it make?" Randy asked.

"I don't know. Maybe none," Jon responded. "I just need the truth. What did Fleure say when she was at your side?"

Randy glanced at his wife before responding. "Fleure said, 'It's always been my fantasy for a man to take me brutally. Take me right now.' She was kind of leaning into me, and I was leaning back."

Jon asked, "And then what happened?"

"I wasn't sure if it was a setup, so I didn't answer."

I glanced over at Juliet, who was painfully taking it all in.

"Why should Fleure want to set you up?" Jon questioned.

"The word on campus was I would be named head of the department. Fleure was ten years senior to me. She always had a bit of a chip on her shoulder, and the administration didn't like her. She pouted for a bit and suddenly was super nice to me."

Jon pressed on, "What happened next?"

"She stripped."

I sat down.

Jon continued to grill him. "You didn't say anything?"

"No. I wish I would have, but I stood silent. I was kind of shocked, I guess." Randy took his wife's hand. "I'm sorry."

"Does this happen a lot?" Jon questioned. "You don't say anything, and women just strip in front of you?"

"No," Randy said. "I promised Juliet I'd be honest, and I'm being honest. She undid my belt and performed oral sex on me. When it was done, I left. That's it. My shirt was still on. My slacks never came off."

"No vaginal or anal intercourse?"

"No. She performed oral on me. That's it."

"So, what did you say to her the next day?"

"Nothing. We were on break. Fleure reported that I assaulted her before we returned, and I wasn't allowed on campus again. Fleure is now head of the department and I'm out of a job."

I wondered, "Is there a big pay raise with becoming head of the department?"

"A little, but it's more about prestige. People have to come to you for approval of new offerings. You have the final say in all departmental decisions."

I could feel Juliet's devastation and fell silent.

Jon hammered at Randy, "So this is all Fleure's fault?"

"I'm not saying that," he responded. "I could have said 'no.' I could have walked away, but I didn't."

"And why should I believe you now? Last week, you didn't have sex with her at all."

Randy looked over at Juliet. "I knew this would break her heart. It meant nothing. I was hoping it would just go away."

Jon sat. "I don't know."

Juliet finally spoke. "We'll double our original offer."

"We'll take it," I responded.

Jon addressed Randy. "*If* you agree to take a polygraph examination with former BCA Investigator Dan Ahlquist and pass it."

Juliet did her best to force a smile. "Okay."

Chapter 43

SERENA FREDERICK

8:30 A.M., WEDNESDAY, FEBRUARY 14, 2024
PIERZ

Jon met me at the front door to kiss me goodbye as I prepared to leave for Eagan. I was on my way to clean out Randy Kimball's office. I reminded him, "We promised no cards, no flowers, no clothes, and no jewelry tonight for Valentine's. I don't have anything for you, so don't embarrass me."

"I followed through with my promise, but I might have bought a chocolate cake at the Black Walnut Bakery—for the family."

While the whole family liked chocolate cake, I was the biggest fan of gourmet sweets in the house, and Jon knew what was on the top of my list. I leaned to him, kissed him, and asked seductively, "And what can I get for you that wasn't on the list?"

"A kiss that starts with glossy lipstick. Red-hot seems like the right tone for Valentine's."

"All right," I said softly. "But I should get going so I can get back."

"Sounds good." We kissed, and as I slowly opened my eyes, Jon interjected, "Work question. Let's assume for a second Randy's telling the truth. If you were going to set someone up by daring him to rape you, what precautions would you take?"

"I'd be holding a loaded gun."

"I'm asking you to think like Fleure."

"If I could plan ahead, I'd want more than *my* word against his." I considered this. "I might record it."

He took his RF detector from a bag on the floor. The walkie-talkie-sized device picks up radio frequency signals from wireless cameras.

"You want me to find a way to get into Fleure's office," I suggested.

"Yes. You're a creative woman. You'll find a way. Why would she only ask questions when she was standing sideways to him?"

"You're thinking she had her back to the camera and has a video with no sound." I blew out a long breath. "I'm not sure your faith in me is warranted."

"I have no doubt that you will find a way." Jon pulled me into a hug and kissed me.

10:30 A.M.

UNIVERSITY OF ARGOSY,

1515 CENTRAL PARKWAY, EAGAN

I HAD CLEARED out Dr. Randy Kimball's office and desk at Argosy. Jon has been mindful to place me only in safe environments now that I'm so obviously pregnant. I found Randy's office to be boring. Everything in it was related to academia, and honestly, it was embarrassingly bland. In a country where there is so much controversy, Randy tiptoed the politically correct line. There was nothing of interest in his space. I was convinced he was promoted because he didn't offend anyone in the administration. Still, walking the company line would offend a colleague who resided in the Harris or Trump camp. As I pondered this, I performed my task of filling boxes. Jon would haul them away. With my pregnancy, he didn't want me to lift anything heavy. When I finished, I called Jon and told him, "There's nothing here. Any news on the homefront?"

"Good news and bad news. I just got off the phone with the Dakota County Prosecutor. The DNA was found in Fleure Duaire's underwear. It doesn't fit Randy's story."

"And what did the rape kit say?"

"The kit was taken a week later. After four days, rape DNA is uncollectable, and the examination was inconclusive for rape."

"What did Fleure say happened?"

"He threw her on the floor and raped her. Told her she needed to submit because he was now her boss."

"I was hoping for a challenging investigation," I said with disappointment.

"Is Fleure around?" he asked.

I stopped and listened. I could hear a muffled voice next door. "I think she might be in her office."

"That's where you need to be."

"I've been putting it off. Isn't recording against the law?"

"Not in Minnesota. We're one of the few states where you can record a conversation without permission if there is no criminal intent."

"And that's where you're going to get Fleure—tortious intent—the intentional infliction of emotional distress."

"It's a shot in the dark," Jon laughed. "Yes, tortious intent. If she has a recording, we still need to find a way to subpoena it. Fleure's the reported victim."

"What's the good news?"

"Randy passed the lie detector test, indicating he didn't sexually assault her."

That was all I needed to hear. Time to visit the dark flower."

I hesitated outside Dr. Fleure Duaire's office. She was now off the phone, and the door was open, so I stepped inside. "Excuse me."

Fleure waved me in. With her gray crimped hair and long bohemian-style dress in rust red, fall orange, and turquoise designs, she had the professional hippie look down pat.

"I love your office," I told her. There was a large print of Picasso's *The Dream* on the wall. I remember studying the painting in a *Cubism and Modern Art* class. At first glance, the painting looks like a simple cartoon of a woman sleeping. As you look closer, you see a nipple sticking partially out of the top of her blouse, half of her face is shaped like a phallus, and her hands seem to be touching herself. This painting sold for $145 million. Personally, I'd take a drawing by the cartoonist for Peppa Pig over this work. The layout of the office raised red flags. A glass coffee table was next to a side chair in front of her desk. There simply wasn't room to throw her on the floor and rape her without her hitting her head or another body part on something. *Maybe she's moved furniture around since the assault.* I said, "Did you drop this?" I slid to one knee and moved the table slightly. There were indentations on the carpet from the glass table legs. This table hadn't been moved recently. The same was true of the chair.

Fleure came around the desk to see what I was doing. "Dear, can I help you with something?"

"I swear I'm losing my mind. I thought I saw a hair tie on the floor." I stood back up. "I'm sorry for bothering you. I was looking for the restroom."

"Honey, let me guide you," she offered.

"Thank you. That's so kind." When she stepped in front of me, I looked into my bag. The red light was flashing on the RF detector. I was being recorded in the dark flower's office.

1:30 P.M.
DAKOTA COUNTY ADMINISTRATIVE CENTER
1590 HIGHWAY 55, HASTINGS

ASSISTANT DAKOTA COUNTY Attorney Daniel Nelson agreed to meet with Jon and me, Randy and Juliet Kimball, and their attorney, Taytum Hanson. The Dakota County Attorney, Kathryn Keena, was in court trying a case.

We met in a conference room, with Daniel at the head of the table.

Taytum began, "We will be pressing charges against Fleure Duaire for Filing a False Police Report. Fleure is claiming she was assaulted in her office at the University of Argosy. My client, Randy Kimball, has recently passed a polygraph examination indicating he never sexually assaulted her."

"Lie detector tests can't be used in court," Daniel interrupted. "My understanding is that there is DNA evidence incriminating your client."

Randy said, "The sexual contact was consensual. I now have evidence she recorded the incident. If you search her office and find the recording, you will see I am innocent, and Fleure is guilty of falsifying a report."

Daniel guffawed. "And why exactly would she do that?"

"To get me fired," Randy said. "I was supposed to be the department head. Now I'm gone, and she has assumed the position."

"Does anyone really give a damn about who the department head is?" Daniel questioned.

Juliet finally spoke. "Apparently, Fleure does."

Daniel tapped his fingers on the desk. "How do you know the incident was recorded?"

I stated, "She invited me into her office, and I happened to have an RF detector on me, so I turned it on. RF detectors work by—"

Daniel interrupted. "I know how RF detectors work. I'm just wondering why you happened to have one in her office."

Jon rescued me. "If it's legal to record someone without their consent in Minnesota, I imagine it's also legal to check for recording devices. And keep in mind, it is illegal for someone like Fleure to record someone with tortious intent."

Jon gave me a sly grin, and Daniel acknowledged, "If true, she committed a felony."

"The video will confirm Randy is telling the truth," Juliet said. "Would we be this adamant about getting the video if he was guilty?"

After tapping his fingers on the table again, Daniel said, "I don't know that we have enough for a search warrant, but we might not need one. The office is at the college, right?"

"Correct," Jon responded. "A public employer does not need a warrant to search an employee's office."

Chapter 44

TAYTUM HANSON

9:30 P.M., FRIDAY, FEBRUARY 23, 2024
BROKEN CLOCK BREWING COOPERATIVE
1712 MARSHALL STREET NORTHEAST, SUITE 100, MINNEAPOLIS

Randy Kimball, Jon and Serena Frederick, and I stopped for a drink to celebrate the dismissal of Randy's charges. Jon enjoyed the Liquid Fidelity Lager, which seemed unnecessary, judging by Serena's condition, while Serena drank hot chocolate from the Curioso Coffee bar. The Fredericks were an acquired taste that was starting to grow on me. I enjoyed our time visiting, although Jon talks too much about his kids when he's relaxed. Serena went to the restroom, and Jon went to the bar to pay the tab. Randy and I remained at our table, observing.

A young couple wearing maroon Minnesota Gophers hoodies approached Jon at the bar. The blond man of Scandinavian ancestry asked, "Did you see the U's women's basketball team wore pink tonight in their win over Northwestern?"

His partner had long black hair and brown eyes. She added, "It was in support of breast cancer awareness. Hi, I'm Marita."

Jon smiled at her, "I love the accent. Where are you from?"

"Puerto Rico. My mom and I came to Minnesota after Dad died. Mom will still only speak Spanish unless she is absolutely forced to speak English."

The blond said, "And she sounds so angry in her n

"I know," Marita laughed as she responded. " she's only angry about seventy-five percent of the and I went to Puerto Rico during break."

Jon asked the couple, "For the rum or the rainforest?"

"The rainforests," Danny said. He put his arm around Marita and said, "But the beaches were beautiful too."

Serena returned, winked at me, and approached their conversation. She studied Jon as if he was vaguely familiar. "Do I know you from somewhere?"

I smiled and nudged Randy. "Watch this." Tug had told me that Jon and Serena love to pretend they'd just met each other as if by chance encounter.

"I don't think so." Jon glanced at her pregnant belly. "How far along are you?"

"No, not from that, silly. Didn't I run into you in Racine at Chaos Costumes? You were buying their hoof-shaped shoes with fur leggings. Not puma, if I remember right, it was Clydesdales."

The two basketball fans curiously observed.

It was all Jon could do to hold back his laughter. He glanced at her belly and said, "We'd have a problem. A newborn Clydesdale weighs one hundred eighty pounds."

"It would be like me trying to give birth to you. It's bad enough when it's an eight-pounder." Serena teased in a flirty tone, "Did you need the leggings because you were feeling a little hoarse?"

In a harsh tone, John grunted, "I am the hoarse whisperer."

"When I was young, I envisioned myself riding a centaur off into the sunset," Serena replied. "Half man-half horse."

"You're not ponying me, are you? Leading me while riding another?"

"Well," Serena rubbed her belly. "I'm looking for a stable relationship."

"Horace was wrong," Jon remarked.

Puzzled, Serena asked, "Horse was wrong?"

"Horace was an Italian poet who died eight years before Christ was born. Horace said, 'Nothing is beautiful from every point of view.' He wouldn't have said that if he'd seen you."

"You *are* the horse whisperer. I think everything has beauty, but not everyone can see it." Serena leaned into Jon and kissed his cheek. "That is your gift."

Jon lovingly told her, "And sharing this moment is your gift to me."

"I've heard enough," Serena replied. She turned to the couple, "Is this bronco with you?"

"No," the woman responded.

Serena turned to Jon and jingled her keys. "I'll lay out the bedding." She took his hand, and they left.

We watched the stupefied couple at the bar whispering back and forth over what they'd just witnessed.

Randy smiled and asked me, "Do you want another? Juliet wasn't feeling well, so she called it an early night. And I don't have a job, so I'm in no hurry. I'm going with the Cat Dad Cream Ale this time."

"I want to sip slowly on a porter. I'll try the dark Espresso Scotch Rise."

Randy went to the bar and ordered.

A porter is a person who carries burdens, and it suits me well. It's what the baggage carriers were named after. I won't get a peaceful night of sleep until Roan has paid for killing Tug. But tonight, I wanted to celebrate today's win. I told Randy, "I wish you could have seen the panic on Fleure's face when the Eagan police officers confiscated her laptop. Within an hour, she was on the phone begging the prosecutor to drop all charges against you. Two hours later, the officers were at her door, arresting her for filing a false police report. The prosecutor, Fleure, and I watched the video in a conference room. I believed you didn't force her, but I was surprised it played out exactly as you said. There you were, leaning against the desk in silence while she stripped and did the deed. When you left, she wiped her sticky hand on her underwear and placed the underwear in a plastic bag. It was all premeditated. The prosecutor asked Fleure if she wanted to explain exactly when she felt she had been assaulted. She declined and told him any further questions would need to be addressed in the presence of her attorney."

"I'm just glad it's over." Randy studied my eyes. "You have been so amazing. I couldn't see a way out of this. Women are assaulted all the time by men who feign innocence. Why would anyone believe me?"

"Thank you." I put my hand on his arm. "I enjoyed working with you. How was your Valentine's Day?"

"Lots of talk about sharp pubic pain. I think I've heard every adjective to describe it—stabbing, wrenching, throbbing, agonizing—you get the picture."

"Before or after sex?"

"What sex?" Randy shrugged. "There was none of that. We've replaced romance with conversations about despair and hopelessness."

"How's that working for you?" I hated to admit it, but I was attracted to this hopeless man. He was intelligent and strong but felt defeated in his marriage to his fragile wife. He never complained about her. Instead, he quietly went to work and paid the bills day after miserable day. She should have been happy that someone finally serviced him for her. Of course, it would have been better if Fleure didn't get him fired. I said, "You seem so troubled. I can't fix what's happening between you and the iron maiden you married, but I can help you get your job back."

"Yeah. It's not just what's going on with Juliet; it's everything—being accused of sexual assault, losing my job, and even taking this damn graduate class. You'd think working in psychology wouldn't be stressful as I should have all the tools, right? The professor accused me of self-plagiarism.

"What the hell is self-plagiarism?" I scoffed. "You copied some of your own work? Is that even a thing?"

"Apparently. The school has a software program that looks for similarities to every paper turned in online. It discovered that I had written a blog making a similar statement, so they couldn't accept my paper and warned me that my grade was subject to penalty."

"This is exactly why I didn't pursue a doctorate—petty bullshit. So, you need to give yourself permission to have the same thought twice?"

"Basically," Randy remarked. "And here's the kicker: I wrote the paper *before* I wrote the blog. She didn't get around to grading it until weeks later. I should have had a prophecy that I would write a blog and footnoted it."

"You should send her an email stating, 'Professors like you are the reason people hate college,' footnote it, and write, 'this isn't the first time I've thought it.'"

"That's good. I agreed to take the blog down, and now she will grade the paper." Randy put his hand on my arm in appreciation. "I just need something in my life to work out."

As the night progressed, my chair moved from across the table to right next to his. By the end of the night, we were commiserating shoulder-to-shoulder. Randy comforted me, like Tug once had, and like Tug, he was married, so I'd always have my freedom.

With eyes full of longing, Randy told me, "I think I better go before I do something stupid."

"You didn't say something you'd regret."

"No, I guess I didn't," Randy acknowledged.

"We could stay here for last call." I stood. "Or we could catch a ride to my place and enjoy a nightcap. But understand, if you walk in my door, there's no backing out. There's no commitment, no cameras, and in return, I don't want to hear a word about your marriage." I whispered, "You just shut up and enjoy the best sex you've ever known."

He hesitated less than a second before responding, "I'm in."

Chapter 45

MELANIE PEARSON

6:30 P.M., TUESDAY, FEBRUARY 27, 2024
MINNESOTA CORRECTIONAL FACILITY - STILLWATER
970 PICKETT STREET, BAYPORT

Tuesdays were the only days visitors were allowed at Stillwater. The MCF-Stillwater was in Bayport, a city just south of Stillwater. I was only allowed two hours of visitation, between 12:30 and 4:30 or 6:30 and 9:00 p.m., and the prison needed to be notified more than twenty-four hours in advance. I generally visited in the evening, so I didn't have to leave work, but if there was an abundance of visitors requesting time, I'd take off work and visit in the afternoon rather than have my time cut short.

Ricky's general demeanor hardened with incarceration. He was less emotional and more matter-of-fact. Still, he was always respectful to me.

I sat at a computer laptop and watched Ricky on the screen. He wore a dark blue prison uniform. Ricky had killed his abusive father, enabling mother, and brother when he was sixteen years old, twenty-two years ago. He managed to escape from jail a couple of weeks after his arrest but has not exhibited any illegal behavior since. Still, drinking alcohol was a violation of probation, and cooperating with probation was a condition of his release from prison.

"I am so sorry, Ricky." I started every visit with this sentence and always felt it deep in my heart.

"I know," he nodded.

"Please let me tell your family this was my fault."

"No. I want my family to love you because I love you. At least allow me to control that. And regardless of your behavior, I'm responsible for my choices. Corinthians 13:11: 'When I was a child, I spoke like a child, I thought like a child, I reasoned like a child. When I became a man, I gave up childish ways.' I'm not sixteen anymore. I don't rationalize my behavior anymore. I can't. It's a slippery slope. Enough about that." Ricky scratched his unshaven chin. "You said you weren't attracted to Lorenzo. Just be honest. I can handle it."

"I slept with Lorenzo once when we were broken up." I leaned into the screen and wanted to hug him. "I didn't know that he had assaulted you at the time."

"And you saw him at the wedding and thought you wanted the pretty boy again. I get it."

"No. That's not it at all. He followed me into the hotel and insisted I sleep with him. I told him 'No,' and he said he would tell you about last time if I didn't. I couldn't risk losing you. I was drunk and said, 'Make it quick and get it over with.'"

"You'd rather sleep with him than be honest with me."

I wanted to tell him the entire story but couldn't. Our conversations were recorded. Plus, I had promised Roan I would never admit he spoke to me that night. Betraying Roan would not only put my life in danger, but it could also get Ricky killed in prison. It's better to have Ricky think less of me. I said, "I'm sorry. I swear, I would give my life for the opportunity to go back and change that decision."

"I know what that's like," he said, trying to lighten the mood.

"Ricky, I've committed to sobriety, and I will be faithful to you. I would like to take over your house payments so you have a place to live when you're released. And if you decide you don't want me around once you're released, I'll leave quietly. Consider the house payments as my rent. I know you think you need money for an attorney, but I'll pay for that."

"I don't need an attorney." He brushed his uncombed hair back.

"Of course you do."

He held up his hand to stop me. "There's no court case. There's no judge. A hearings and release officer listens to a couple of witnesses and decides. That's it."

"Will I be able to attend?"

"Probably not."

"It's not like you hurt anybody. They have to consider that."

"A lot of people feel I never should have been released ten years early for good behavior. They think I should have served the full time for killing my family. I don't know that they're wrong. I just know I'd like another chance."

I nodded. "So, are you okay with me paying the rent?"

"Let me think about it. If I get ten years, I don't want you tied to me."

"I want to be tied to you."

He smiled. "That's kind. But I'm trying to do what's right. Let me do that. I promise to think about it, all right?"

Chapter 46

TAYTUM HANSON

6:07 P.M., TUESDAY, MARCH 5, 2024
FOX HILL DRIVE, CHANHASSEN

My house is on Lake Lotus, and with no buildings between me and the beach, I left my curtains open for this very moment. The vibrant orange sun was setting and warmed my naked body.

After making love, I drifted off to sleep in Randy's arms. He was now wide awake and studying me. Since the end of Randy's case, he'd been over more days than not, purging his pent-up prurience. It would be perfect if he would pour me a glass of wine and leave. Unfortunately, it appeared he wanted to talk.

"I want to make this permanent," he said. "I don't want to keep sneaking out of work early and then run home after every time we make love."

This is precisely what I feared. He was falling in love with me. I pulled away, "That was never the agreement, Randy."

"I know. But I've changed. This is more than just a fling. I've shared my deepest passions with you."

"*I* haven't changed." I slid out of bed and began dressing. "I think you need to leave before you say any more."

"I love you, Taytum. I can't stop thinking of you."

"I know you love me, Randy, but I don't know if I'll ever be there." I'm a millionaire. I only work because I love showing off my skills in the justice system. Why would I commit my life to anyone? I don't have to. There will always be another Randy. The majority of judges on the Minnesota State Supreme Court are now women, and one day, I will be among them.

"I love you, Taytum. And I don't regret telling you." He got out of bed and dressed.

"Do you ever stop and think about how easy men are?" I taunted. Randy was being ridiculous.

"I'm not all men. I've proved that in my marriage. I could have run, but I didn't."

"You're running right now. And think about it. Women own you. Fleure told you, 'I want you to rape me,' and you had sex with her. If it had been the other way around, she'd have called the police. And it took about five seconds to talk you into my bed." Lorenzo had called me earlier asking if we could get together tonight. "I could have an attractive young man on your side of the bed in an hour."

He dismissed me with an arrogant grunt.

"Randy, you're not the only man I'm seeing. Watch me."

It was as if I had just knocked the wind out of him.

"For God's sake, you're married. Don't be a hypocrite."

"I'll tell Juliet tonight; I need to be with you."

"Don't." I called Lorenzo as Randy watched and said, "Yes, an hour will be fine. I will see you then."

"Please don't do this," Randy begged.

"Leave," I demanded. Randy had been reduced to a sniveling coward.

"I don't want to go back to the life I've had."

He reached out, and I swept his hand away. "I'm not giving you a choice. Get out. It's over."

"It's not over," Randy declared, but then respected my request and left.

THE SUN

8:00 P.M.

LORENZO TURRISI CARUSO arrived as planned. I made him a Moscow Mule in the traditional copper cup, and we sat together on the couch. I was reconsidering the cruel way I'd ended it with Randy. His wife, Juliet, was a workhorse just as Deb Grant had been for Tug. The women ran the homes and took care of the men. I was not stepping into that role, and I can't be responsible for the morality of my suitors.

"Where's your mind at tonight?" Lorenzo complained.

"I'm sorry, I've got a lot going on."

"I slept with Melanie, as you suggested," he teased. "She told Ricky, he got drunk, and now he's back in prison. Case closed."

Even that failed to bring me any satisfaction.

Lorenzo teased, "Do you want to hear about it? I even shared that this was courtesy of you."

When I didn't respond, he added, "Did you know Melanie was there when Tug died?"

"What?" Now, he had my attention.

"Yeah, Melanie insisted on seeing him die. I got the job of driving her out there."

"I was there that night—right after. I would have met you."

"We came across the lake by boat." He studied my face. "I got your loins in a lather now, don't I? Melanie watched him die. Didn't intervene. Just stood there and watched."

"I want you to screw her so hard she can't walk when you're done with her."

'This is the Taytum I like," Lorenzo laughed.

"And your dad, Roan, set this all up. He had to, right?"

"I'm not talking about Dad with you tonight. You're always asking about his work with Precision Lens. He doesn't really work for them, and I'm done talkin' about it." Lorenzo took my hand and led me to the bedroom. "You wanted the Italian stallion here, and I raced over. I'm done talkin' about anything tonight."

Chapter 47

MELANIE PEARSON

10:30 P.M., TUESDAY, MARCH 5, 2024
51ST STREET & WASHBURN AVENUE SOUTH,
FULTON, MINNEAPOLIS

My heart was always heavy after a visit with Ricky, and I felt incredible shame. Prior to his arrest, I'd been staying at Ricky's house most of the time. Now, I am back full-time with Agnes Schraut. I admired the irascible octogenarian for her toughness. Tonight, she insisted on showing me her medical bills. I had enough of my own crap to deal with, and her tolerance of my melancholy was growing thin. I was afraid of living alone—afraid Lorenzo would keep finding me.

Agnes studied me and finally said, "Of course, life is a bitch. If it were a slut, it would be easy." She cackled at her joke.

"I feel like when someone tells me not to do something, I do it twice, and it goes viral."

"Can't you see it?" Agnes picked up a medical bill and waved it in front of my face, Victorian-style glasses with chains hanging around her neck.

As she leaned into me, it was apparent her gray hair had a tint of blue. I didn't dare point it out. I glanced at the bill; the bottom line indicated she owed no money. "I don't see a problem."

"I didn't have these visits."

"I brought you to Precision Lens a couple of weeks ago."

"But I haven't been there three times this year."

"Agnes, I'm not going to argue with you." I had bigger fish to fry. She glared at me, so I added, "You owe no money. This is a non-issue."

"Well, deary, if you're not going to listen to me, I'm going to my room to read." Agnes was miffed and headed to her bedroom. She yelled back, "I'm expecting an Amazon delivery."

"I'm sorry," I called after her, "I just don't see a problem."

Agnes shut the door, opened it, and shut it again, as she does when she's upset. She doesn't slam it because she doesn't want to pay for repairing anything. Not long after, the doorbell rang.

I opened the door to Lorenzo, who was taunting, "Time for another episode of *The L Word* with 'L' meaning 'lust,' of course."

I tried slamming it shut, but he pushed his way in. I yelled, "Go to hell! Never again. You're just a slimeball who shames women into sex. If Ricky hadn't been worried about returning to prison, he would have wiped the floor with you."

Lorenzo punched me in the face with so much force I felt my nose shift. No doubt, it was broken. Dazed, I stepped back against the kitchen counter. He came at me and bent down to grab my knees, as he had done last time, to put me on my back.

I kicked him in the head as hard as I could.

Lorenzo stumbled back. "You fucking bitch! I will break you." Blood ran from his eyebrow, and the tissue around his eye immediately swelled.

"Just leave, Lorenzo. I will fight you to the death." I held my hand underneath my nose, trying to keep blood off Agnes's floor. He had me boxed into the corner of the kitchen. I reached my free hand into the kitchen drawer and grabbed the first large object I could get a grip on, which turned out to be a wooden rolling pin.

"What are you going to do, roll me?" Lorenzo laughed heartily. "There's no going back now. You've seen those investigative shows about guys raping. They never end good for the woman.

Drop your pants and get down on the floor, or you're going to be the next episode. You should be begging to please me. Don't forget, girl, I can get you charged with manslaughter."

"I don't care if you tell everyone in the world. NEVER again! You're going to have to kill me first."

He stepped toward me, and I raised the rolling pin. I swear, I'd crack his skull.

"BANG!" A gun blasted, and a window shattered. There stood Agnes, hands shaking, holding a gun. "Here's an episode for you, scumbag: 'Jaguar Shoots Lowlife: Agnes Special Victims Unit.'" Agnes looked like she was about to pull the trigger again.

Lorenzo ducked and ran out of the house.

Agnes held the gun as she yelled at me, "Now what? What's the story with this dirtball?"

"I slept with him." I lifted the bottom of my shirt to catch some of the blood running off my nose.

"For God's sake, girl. What the hell is wrong with you? Who is he?"

"Lorenzo Turrisi Caruso."

"Mafia Turrisi?"

"Yeah," I muttered through my shirt.

"Board up that window and get out. I don't mind chasin' your scumbag boyfriends away, but the mob could blow up my house. I want you out tonight."

I felt dazed, but I stuffed my nose with cotton and found some plywood in the garage. I cut it with an old handsaw and nailed it to the frame to cover the busted window. I filled my suitcase with clothes and promised Agnes I'd return tomorrow to get the rest.

Still angry, she ignored me.

I felt lightheaded but managed to drive to Methodist Hospital, where they reset my nose. When they released me, I realized I had nowhere to go. I drove to Ricky's empty house and let myself in. Waiting at the hospital gave me time to think about my situation. I decided to call Lorenzo's dad, Roan Caruso. He would end the assaults one way or another. My hope was that he wouldn't conclude that killing me was his best option.

12:30 A.M., WEDNESDAY, MARCH 6, 2024

ROAN CARUSO LUMBERED his big body through the door and looked at my face. "Lorenzo did this?"

"Yes."

"What the hell did you do? Lorenzo doesn't beat women."

"He wanted to have sex with me, and I told him no." I sat at the kitchen table.

Roan continued to pace. "He's got a girl. It doesn't make sense."

I decided to put it out there and let the chips fall where they may. "Lorenzo and I had sex on the way back from Tug's passing."

"I told him to drive you straight home."

"We got caught by a cop, but I talked the cop into letting us go."

Fuming, Roan stopped directly in front of me. "Are you fucking kidding me?"

"Lorenzo's been trying to blackmail me for sex ever since." I imitated Lorenzo, "'If you don't have sex, I'll tell Ricky.' I finally told Ricky about it, and he got drunk."

"And now Ricky's in prison." Roan sat.

I added, "And if that's not enough, somehow Taytum's getting off on it."

Straightening up, Roan said, "What are you talking about?"

"The last time—he had rough sex with me and told me, 'This is courtesy of Taytum.' Evidently, Lorenzo's doing the Tug tour."

Roan stood. "Okay, okay, okay. I need you to not report this."

"I won't report it if you promise Lorenzo never touches me again."

"I promise he will never touch you again. What did you tell them at the hospital?"

"That I had a one-car accident. I didn't see how being honest would serve me. I was hoping you'd come through for me."

"What do you need?"

"Lorenzo, off my back." I started crying.

My tears made him uncomfortable, so Roan turned sideways to avoid looking directly at me. "You're too damn perceptive, that's your problem."

"What?" I blubbered.

"A good woman misses a lot. Think about the angels you knew in high school. They were all naive. Your problem is that you consider every possibility and check them out—even the bad ones." He stopped behind my chair and rubbed my shoulder. "It's done. You're a tough kid. Don't sell yourself short. You survived Tug. You'll survive this. Sometimes, you just have to sit tight, do your time, and know your day will come again."

Chapter 48

ROAN CARUSO

12:45 A.M., WEDNESDAY, MARCH 6, 2024
PIERCE STREET NORTHEAST, BELTRAMI, MINNEAPOLIS

I started up my old Cadillac and sped down the road. I needed to find Lorenzo. My son assaulted a woman. We don't do that. He was sleeping with an enemy—a cardinal sin in the Cosa Nostra. The solution would be a lot easier if he weren't my son. I fished king salmon on Lake Michigan out of Kenosha with Lorenzo and attended every one of his football games. Strong kid, an underachiever in school, and perhaps a little entitled, but he can grow out of that. He didn't appreciate his blessings. Cat always made sure he had the newest and best of everything. Talk about a recipe for disaster. My daughter Halle is the best person I know. Why? Cat and I didn't raise her. I love Cat, and I don't blame her any more than I blame myself for Lorenzo. We were busy, and it was just easier to buy him shit. Halle grew up with nothing and is kind and appreciative, with my strong personality wired into her DNA.

When I walked into the house, my wife, Catania, was putting a butterfly bandage on our son's eyebrow. She said, "Lorenzo has something to tell you."

"Oh, yeah?" I sat at the kitchen table across from him.

Still standing over him, Cat said, "Yeah, he got in a car accident with his new girlfriend tonight."

"I've been dating Eliana Castillo," Lorenzo admitted. "She's twenty-one years old and has a five-year-old kid. But I love her."

I glared at him, "That's all you got to tell me?" *What am I going to do with this kid?*

"That's enough." Cat said, "She might be fine for a fling but not as part of our family. We have traditions."

I asked my son directly, "So, was the accident before or after you beat the shit out of Melanie Pearson?"

Cat stopped dabbing away at the dried blood and stood silent.

I continued, "Is that what you do now? You punch women in the face when they don't have sex with you?"

The best he could manage was, "She disrespected me."

Cat slapped the back of his head. "You lied to me!"

"I didn't lie to you," Lorenzo argued. "I just didn't get to that part yet."

"And you were screwing Taytum Hanson," I added.

"Just a couple of times."

Cat screamed, "Taytum is our sworn enemy! You know she threatened to bury us after Tug's death, right?"

"I didn't know that," Lorenzo whined.

"And you were telling Taytum about me." I wasn't sure, but I was curious how he'd respond.

"Just stuff she could find out anywhere. Like you're working for a medical company now."

"What else?"

"In the end, you had no love for Tug. That kind of stuff," Lorenzo said.

I could feel the hair stand up on the back of my neck. "You talked about Tug's murder with her?"

Cat knew the consequences of snitching in the Minneapolis Combination. "Please don't answer that, Lorenzo."

But he didn't know when to shut up. Not even with guidance. "Not about you. Just that Melanie was there when Tug died."

"And then a cop caught you screwing her not far from the murder scene."

Catania teared up and turned her back to both of us.

The ramifications of opening his big mouth finally began to register, and my son quieted.

"How long do you think it will take to connect me to Tug's murder once they figure out you were right there?" I rubbed my forehead, "When's the last time you spoke to Taytum?"

"Tonight. It was just a booty call."

"Let me get this straight. You had sex with Taytum and then went to Melanie and broke her nose because she wouldn't have sex with you? What the hell is wrong with you?"

Lorenzo was afraid to look at his mother as he continued, "Taytum wasn't into it, and she taunted me while we were making out. 'Be man enough to teach that whore a lesson.' I was pissed, and when I got to Melanie, she disrespected me. I'm a Turrisi. A slut like her oughta feel honored when I express any interest in her."

Catania was so angry she couldn't speak.

I challenged him. "So, if she's a whore, and you're hittin' on her, what are you? You're also a Caruso." I had no desire to hide my anger. "We came out of homes like Melanie's."

"What was so bad about her home?" Lorenzo quietly asked.

"Maybe before you have sex with a woman, you should find out. I didn't get to where I'm at by assuming I'm better than people. I earned it."

"I'm sorry, Dad. It just happened—one hit. I forgot my power. And I'm not cheating on Eliana ever again."

I stood up and announced, "I have some business to address, and if you're still here in two hours, we're going for a drive. That will give you time to break up with your girlfriend. Tell her you've got to help your relatives out in Boston. You're leaving tonight and not coming back."

Lorenzo stood, and his haunted eyes pleaded with his mother for salvation.

Cat hugged him, closed her eyes, and squeezed him tight.

I left to take care of business, hoping like hell he'd be gone when I returned. The Genovese family has some heavy hitters in town, and they're suggesting there's a leak in our organization.

1:45 A.M., WEDNESDAY, MARCH 6, 2024

IT WAS A relief to see Lorenzo was gone when I got home. I plopped down by the kitchen table once again. When Lorenzo was an oppositional adolescent, his therapist claimed he had "affluenza," an upper-class psychological malaise that supposedly affects wealthy adolescents. The symptoms are a lack of motivation and a feeling of isolation. What a crock of shit! He was lazy and obsessed with Instagram. I closed my eyes and relaxed for a moment, and then I heard Lorenzo's car pull up. *Damn kid. He will be the death of me.*

Catania stared out the window in disbelief. "We have to make it look like he moved out." She grabbed the extra keys to Lorenzo's car off our key rack and went to his bedroom to pack.

Lorenzo entered the house and sat across from me. "Dad, it's taken care of."

"How?"

"I can't tell you. It will all be okay. I promise. Taytum won't be bothering us again."

"You didn't do anything stupid, did you?"

Lorenzo hesitated and said, "No."

I shook my head in disbelief. "She swore she'd get revenge after Tug died. You have no idea who she's talked to."

"You should have told me, Dad."

"I assumed you would know not to talk about my involvement in a murder."

"I didn't."

"She already had suspicions, and you confirmed them. The Minneapolis Combination is going to know you snitched. Get every indication of your presence out of this house and in your vehicle. Anything left will be destroyed." I tapped the table. "I'm going to talk to your mom, and if you're still here, we're going for a ride."

Lorenzo was still sitting at the table when I returned to the kitchen. I instructed, "You're riding with me. Your mom will meet me with your car later."

As we drove north on Interstate 94, Lorenzo told me about Eliana Castillo and her eyes that lit up a room. The sweetest girl ever, according to my son. It finally registered in my brain. "You didn't break up with her, did you?"

Lorenzo didn't respond.

Stupid kid. Is it that hard to follow directions? "We didn't ask you to break up with her because we hate her. If the Wizard thinks he can use her to get to you, they'll kidnap her. Then they'll rape her to get her to talk and kill her when they're done."

He quieted as I turned north on County Road 78 toward Battle Lake. The car was dead silent when I turned onto narrow Treetop Road.

"I need her love. I couldn't let go." Tears streamed down his cheeks. "I love you, Dad."

"I know you do."

"I'm sorry."

"I know you are." I pulled up next to a cabin. I shut the car off, got out, and pulled Lorenzo out. He squeezed me into a hug. I held on for a bit and pushed him away. "Listen to me. I love you. I'm not going to kill you. But there's a lot of money and some major players working with me right now. You are not safe in Minneapolis. Nobody knows about this place. Cat's packed your clothes and some food. She'll return with a new ID tomorrow. Stay out of the bars and away from fights. You can go to ABC Brewing once you've got your ID. They've got good food and beer. Lots of people stop in on the way through, so you won't stand out. No pictures online, all right? If they find you, you're a dead man."

"Who?"

"The Genovese family has some heavy hitters in town. That's who I met tonight. I'm telling you this because they may be coming after you. They told me Taytum is telling fraud investigators that the Cosa Nostra is involved in a medical scam. And they said the source is one of my guys."

"I didn't tell her much," Lorenzo said.

"Did you ever set your phone down?"

"I imagine at some point. I always set it on the counter until I leave again."

"Assume she's gone through it. You had texted me asking if the docs were taking the concert tickets. Remember me telling you, 'Don't text—call me'? This is exactly why. Texts are readable evidence."

"You're intimidating to talk to, Dad. I'm sorry."

"You need to stop saying that and start making some better choices. The leader of the crew is known as the Wizard of Odds. Enzo Angelini is a major player in illegal sports betting. Enzo's not a made guy, but he's close. If they speak of the Wizard, that's who they're talking about. He's got a paid hitman with him they call the Assassin. Nobody knows his identity or even what he looks like 'cause the story is, everyone who's met him is dead. Enzo is also traveling with his right-hand man, Nico Larmarte, whose name literally means 'the death.' Do you get the picture? You don't go anywhere with these guys. There's lots of money at stake and they know someone leaked information to Taytum. Information that has made it to the desk of Christi Grimm."

"Okay, who is Christi Grimm?"

"The Health and Human Services Inspector General. She investigates Medicare fraud."

"Dad, how big does this go?"

"That's enough for tonight. I need you to lay low and stay safe. And if you hear the name Everest, run. The Wizard's crew are the only ones who call me that. And I swear, if they call me that again, I'll put a bullet in every one of them."

"Everest? What does that even mean?"

"To my face, Wizard says it's because I'm a mountain of a man, and it would take a team to get over me. Behind my back, he tells his buddies it's because I'm a big dumb pussy-whipped rock who was only made by marriage."

"Dad, anybody who knows you knows that isn't true."

"People who think they're better than you have no interest in knowing you."

"Are you okay?" Lorenzo studied me. "They have to know you're hiding me out."

"You're my son. My legacy." I gestured to the house. "Let's get this place opened up." *Was I going to be all right?* Probably not. If my enemies didn't punish me, my friends would.

Chapter 49

JON FREDERICK

7:25 A.M., WEDNESDAY, MARCH 6, 2024
PIERZ

My Bureau of Criminal Apprehension colleague, Paula Fineday, called. "Jon, sorry about bugging you so early in the morning, but I'm at a murder scene and need to talk to you. Your name and number are written on a calendar in her office."

"Who was murdered?" I sat on the edge of my bed.

"Taytum Hanson, Tug Grant's paramour. Randy Kimball discovered her body when he stopped over before work. Taytum was naked, lying spread eagle on the kitchen floor. No clothes in sight. Any interest in working the case with me?"

"Yes." Holding the phone in one hand, I started dressing. "I worked privately for Randy Kimball in the case where Fleure Duaire was charged with falsifying a police report. Taytum had referred Randy to me."

"And that case is resolved now, right?"

"Yes, and my involvement is done."

"Then it shouldn't be an issue," Paula responded.

"How was Taytum murdered?"

"Not sure. I can tell you she's dead, and her body was positioned like a centerfold."

Still lying in bed, Serena watched me finish dressing as she asked, "What happened?"

"Someone murdered Taytum Hanson."

"That's terrible." She sat up, and I explained the little I knew.

Serena asked, "Before you agreed, did you tell Paula your boss instructed you to stay away from Roan Caruso? I would assume he's the prime suspect."

"I did not. I'll call her on the way and explain." I kissed her goodbye. As I was leaving the bedroom, I turned back and saw Serena place her hand where I'd been lying to feel the heat of where my body once rested. It warmed my heart.

After I was on the road, I called Paula and told her, "Taytum told me she was going after Roan Caruso when Tug Grant was murdered. Sean Reynolds gave me a direct order to stay away from Roan because his wife, Catania Turrisi, complained that they were harassed during the investigation of Debra Grant's murder." Tug had contracted Roan to kill his wife, Deb. Both were found guilty but were released early due to prosecutorial errors.

"I want you working this case," Paula responded.

"I was hoping you'd say that."

"I'll handle the interviews with Roan. I've dealt with Catania before. Like most borderline personality women, she picks one person to hate in every scenario, and when she gets her claws sunk into that poor soul, she doesn't let up."

Far enough away from home to avoid waking up the kids, I put the siren on my Taurus and headed straight south on Highway 25 toward the Twin Cities.

8:45 A.M. FOX HILL DRIVE, CHANHASSEN

TAYTUM HANSON HAD a two-story Victorian-style house on Lake Riley with a corner turret room. Paula led me into the gray bridge-plank tiled entry. Crime scene techs scurried about inside, and the antique-decorated environment reminded me of a scene from an Agatha Christie mystery.

I enjoyed working with Paula. While I tended to get obsessive about details, she was better at focusing on the larger picture, which was also necessary. She walked me into a space with whitewashed oak wood flooring between the kitchen and dining area. A small black walnut table flanked by two of the thinnest antique wooden chairs I've ever seen sat by a window behind the body. This isn't where she ate meals. It was a place for a brief conversation or to rest while she waited for something to finish cooking. A wine glass holding about an inch of red wine rested on the table.

Taytum lay with her eyes open, naked, on the floor next to the table. A sheet had been draped over her. I turned to Paula, "I thought you said legs spread."

"The scene has already been contaminated. Her lover, Randy Kimball, stopped over at seven this morning and discovered her body. Randy said he didn't like the degrading manner she had been left in, so he took a sheet off the bed, covered her, and pushed her legs to the side. Rigor mortis was already setting in, so they didn't simply go together."

The scene may be contaminated. It's also possible that Randy stayed with the body after he killed her since it's a better story to say he stopped over. When people fall dead, their legs often cross or are pulled together by tightening muscles. There was no blood, no open wounds, and no ligature marks. Taytum was pale, and her lips were blue.

Carver County Medical Examiner Angelique Quinn Strobl, MD, crouched by Taytum's body and flashed a penlight into her eyes. Taytum's pinpoint pupils were something we were all familiar with as a result of the plethora of fentanyl overdoses we've seen. The medical examiner patiently stepped to the side, waiting for me to finish taking it all in. The staging of the body meant homicide.

"Poison?" Paula asked.

"It is too early to render an opinion," Dr. Quinn Strobl said. Then she turned to me, "Now that you have taken in the scene, can we move her?"

"Yes." I gave the room a last once-over while I watched Dr. Quinn, medicine woman, and her crew carefully remove Taytum's body. I appreciated that the forensic pathologist gave me the opportunity to view the scene. Paula was the primary investigator, and she'd already been on site for over an hour. Understanding the staging of a body can be crucial to solving a crime. The way the Taytum was posed suggested her sexual behavior was an issue to the killer. I looked around the room. It was spotless, as if she were about to entertain a guest. The fact that the place hadn't been ransacked was significant. The killer wanted to leave one message: *The whore was dead.*

There was a dish towel lying close to her head. Paula said, "Randy said he took a dishtowel and wiped the vomit off her face."

"Where are her clothes?" I wondered.

"Good question," Paula replied. There's a pair of silk pajamas and underwear in the washing machine with lots of bleach. I don't imagine she'd wash her delicates like that."

We may have DNA on her body. Killers sometimes know a little about DNA, but not enough to hide it all.

Paula continued, "I think the killer stripped her and left her this way with the intent of humiliating her. But from what I knew of Taytum, I don't know that it bothered her a lot to be seen naked."

"Do you have her cell phone?"

"Her cell phone is gone. I had Randy Kimball escorted to the Sheriff's Department. He wants to talk to you."

Sargent Alex Bujalski of the Carver County Sheriff's Department had secured the scene. He was a strong, fit man in his thirties who had also been raised in the Pierz area. He said, "We've already started canvassing the neighborhood. So far, nobody's seen or heard anything. There is no indication of a struggle. It's not a coincidence that her phone was taken. Her computer is gone too, so there is no way to access the security footage from the Ring Video Doorbell."

"Do you have any suspects?" I asked.

"There were never any complaints here. Taytum was a successful professional who seemed to enjoy her privacy. She has a beautiful place. Taytum never struck me as someone who abused drugs."

"I concur. We need to treat this like a homicide until we learn otherwise."

9:45 A.M.
CARVER COUNTY SHERRIF'S OFFICE
606 EAST 4ᵀᴴ STREET, CHASKA

I BROUGHT RANDY Kimball a glass of water in the interview room and sat across the table from him. He took a large sip and thanked me. Randy's paisley tie now hung loosely around his neck. With sad eyes, he ran his fingers through his hair over and over. "I can't believe it. She's dead."

"What were you doing at her house at seven in the morning?" I asked.

"We'd had an argument."

"Let me clarify this: You were romantically involved with Taytum?"

He nodded.

"Are you still married and living with your wife? I need you to respond verbally."

"Yes. We were drawn together when the case ended. Taytum invited me in, and I accepted. I loved Juliet, but Taytum was so passionate. I can't believe she's dead."

"I'm still trying to wrap my head around this because I'm having a difficult time believing you. You said after Fleure made the allegation you were never going to cheat on your wife again, right?"

"Yeah." Randy nodded affirmatively.

"And then you had an affair with the attorney who was defending you on that very allegation."

"It began when my case ended. The night it ended. And after, I couldn't stay away."

"Did you kill Taytum?"

"No." He seemed surprised. "I love her. I would never hurt her."

"Even if she threatened to tell Juliet about your affair?"

"I'm the one who wanted to tell Juliet. I wanted to move in with Taytum. She's the one who insisted I not tell. I told Taytum I loved her."

"How did she respond?"

Randy clearly regretted making that last statement.

"Before you lie to me, I want to remind you we've been through this before." I continued, "If you're innocent, you better be honest. You could get yourself convicted of murder here."

"She asked me to leave."

"When was this?"

"Yesterday evening. About seven o'clock."

"Did she say, 'I love you' back?"

"No." He glanced down briefly and added, "But I know she did. That was just Taytum being Taytum. If she was angry and felt she had the upper hand, she made you suffer. There was no point in arguing with her. If I had begged, she would have cast me aside. Taytum loathed the weak."

"It sounds like she did dump you. You said she told you to leave, right?"

"But I honestly don't believe she meant it. That's how she was. I'd return the next morning, and we'd make another date."

"Was she naked when you left?"

"Yeah." He searched his memory. "She was dressing in the bedroom when I left."

"And then Taytum's discovered naked and dead," I egged him on. "Taytum strikes me as a woman who could throw daggers when she was angry."

"I learned quickly to limit my arguments with her. You can't win. You walk away defeated and hope she comes around later.

And she typically does. Taytum would renounce me in a heartbeat. She pushed people away with ease—not a worry on her end. The ones who recognized her brilliance returned. I didn't kill her."

"I don't believe you." Honestly, I wasn't sure, but this felt like the most productive thing to say. I disagreed with his comment that Taytum wasn't afraid of losing people. I think she was so afraid of losing people that she pushed people away because it was easier if she was the one in control of the loss.

"Taytum called another man before I left." Randy was rattled. He anxiously blurted, "And she told me she was going after some mobster."

"Do you remember his name?"

"Roan. I didn't get her other lover's name."

I glanced back at the mirrored glass, knowing Paula Fineday was there. I wondered if my boss, Sean Reynolds, was there too. I turned back to Randy. "So, the two of you had sex before you left at 7:00 p.m.?"

"Yeah."

"Did Taytum undress in the bedroom?" I scratched my chin as I considered the crime scene.

"Yeah. I undressed her. She reveled in the way I lusted for her nakedness."

"What was she wearing?

"White cream-colored silk pajamas."

"Already, before seven o'clock?"

"Once she was in for the night, she got comfortable. She didn't care what time of day it was." Randy shook his head. "I know it looks bad, but this is devastating for me."

"I imagine it is." I considered everything he'd said. "You just got done having sex with her. You told her you would dump Juliet for her, but she rejected you. You declared your love for her, and she responded by telling you to leave and calling another lover. It must have made you furious. How did you kill her?"

Realizing he had painted himself into a corner, Randy sat silent.

"A successful man with a doctorate like you gets brushed off by a woman with just a law degree. Who is she to turn you away?"

"That's not what it was like. I never once felt superior to her. You have to know Taytum. She was always in control."

It was worth a shot, but I believed him. I don't think Tug ever realized it, but I felt Taytum controlled that relationship, too. After all, when Tug died, she was the one who walked away with his fortune. I think Taytum liked married men because she could always keep them at a safe distance. That worked for Tug, but it didn't work for Randy. "Do you mind if I take a look at your phone just to verify your account of events?"

Randy nervously reached for it, then said, "No, I don't think so. I called in to help you guys out. Would I have done that if I killed her?"

"Maybe. Surrender the phone so we can rule you out."

"No. You're going to have to take my word."

"We can't do that," I pointed out. "It's not how investigations work." He sat still, so I asked, "Now what, Randy? What's your next move?"

"I'm going home, and I'm going to be honest with Juliet."

"Is that safe?"

"Honestly, I don't care. When I think of her medical issues, her daily pain, and what I put her through, I wouldn't even blame her if she attacked me. I'd stand there and take it. But that's not what Juliet does. She turns on herself. If she wants me out, I'm out." Randy tapped the table. "My advice is to find out who Taytum called when I left."

"Would you mind giving a DNA sample before you leave?"

He hesitated, "I don't like where you're going with this. I think it's time for me to get an attorney."

I already had his DNA from the glass of water. I just wanted to see his response. "Would you mind turning over your phone?"

Had he returned to Taytum's house later?

"I know my rights. We're done."

Paula entered the room and handed him a piece of paper. "Here's a search warrant hot off the press. I'll be taking your phone."

Randy glared at me as he handed it to her. "I was just trying to do the right thing by coming here."

After he left, I asked Paula, "Randy told you rigor mortis was already starting to set in when you first interviewed him?"

"Yes."

"It's an odd detail to bring up if it wasn't true. It's consistent with his timeline and isn't the type of fact that would occur to someone making up a story."

11:00 A.M.

SIOUX TRAIL (HIGHWAY 13), SAVAGE

AFTER LEAVING THE interview room, I decided to return to Taytum's house. I called Serena on the way. "Would you mind calling Juliet and asking her where she and Randy were last night? Randy just lawyered up, and when he gets home, Juliet will, too. I know she trusts you."

"Okay," Serena hung up to address my request.

She called me back within five minutes. "Juliet said Randy got home at about eight o'clock and was home with her for the rest of the night."

"That's what Randy said."

11:30 A.M.

FOX HILL DRIVE, CHANHASSEN

PAULA CALLED AND told me Dr. Quinn Strobl kindly allowed Dr. Amaya Ho to perform the autopsy on Taytum Hanson. This was important to me since Dr. Ho and I had a successful history of working together on forensic cases. The two examiners had developed a good working relationship out of necessity because the city of Chanhassen is in both Carver County and Hennepin County.

When I arrived at Taytum's, crime scene techs, adorned in white jumpsuits and masks, were moving about with the smooth synchrony of a well-rehearsed dance team. I caught the attention of one of the CSI crew members and asked her, "Were there any fingerprints on the table?"

"No. It was wiped clean," she responded.

It's not likely that Taytum wiped the table before she fell dead to the floor. "Are you done with the washing machine?"

"Yeah. No fingerprints on the washing machine or the dryer either."

I had an odd thought. I wondered what cycle her silk pajamas had been washed in. I powered the machine back on as if I were going to start another load. The setting was on *delicates.* I wasn't sure what to think about that. It didn't make sense that Randy would have sex with Taytum, bleach her clothing to cover it up, and then call the police and admit it. There was a set of sheets in the dryer. The dryer had been set on *bedding*. The bedding didn't smell like bleach.

I meandered back into the living room, recalling the one wine glass on the small table. It was now at the lab, and the contents were being tested for poison. An empty bottle of Austin Hope Paso Robles Cabernet rested on the cupboard. Serena was a fan of cabs, and this was an excellent vino we would splurge for on special occasions. A bottle of Maker's Mark whiskey was opened, but mostly full, next to it. I opened the dishwasher to find another wine glass, a copper Moscow Mule cup, and an old-fashioned whiskey glass. The dishwasher had been run, so they were clean. The whiskey glass is what Randy would have had his Maker's Mark in. *Who had Taytum shared the Moscow Mule and the glass of wine with? Was there a third person? Would she have taken a new glass for her second, or just used the glass she was using?*

I stopped again and looked at the outline of Taytum's body chalked out on the floor. Not only did the time and location have to work for the killer, but so did the means. *Who had access to fentanyl? Every major suspect.* As part of the Minneapolis Combination, Roan, Catania, and Lorenzo could get their hands on fentanyl in less than thirty minutes. Juliet was a security guard, so I imagined she'd confiscated it. As a college teacher, Randy is likely aware of students who've struggled with it and may have even handed it over to him.

Taytum had a nice-sized office that was very organized. I found my name and number written in her planner. Melanie Pearson's name was written off to the side and circled. Her last note read, *Roan Caruso—Sightpath Medical? Precision Lens?* This was a significant lead. These companies weren't small potatoes. Precision Lens is Minnesota's largest eyecare company, and Sightpath Medical is the largest national provider of mobile ophthalmic services. Millions of dollars flow through these companies annually.

My phone buzzed, and I answered, "This is Jon."

"This is Alex from the Carver County Sherriff's Department. I've been asking around about Taytum. I thought you might find it interesting to know she's been recently seen in the company of one Lorenzo Turrisi Caruso."

"Thank you." Law enforcement needed to understand they were dealing with the mafia. "I should share with you that Taytum had vowed to go after Roan Caruso because she believed he was the puppet master in Tug Grant's murder."

"If I can connect Roan to this murder, I can investigate him, but I think he resides in Hennepin County, which is out of my jurisdiction," he groaned.

"That is unfortunate, as I'd appreciate your help on this. Let me know if you come across Roan or Lorenzo in your territory."

"We still have a murder to solve here, so please share any connections you have to our case," Alex requested.

"Sure. Thank you for your work on this."

I sat at Taytum's desk in her office, hoping to capture some of her thoughts. If *I* knew she intended to go after the Minneapolis Combination, how many other people knew? Randy and Juliet Kimball had lawyered up. My boss didn't want me speaking to the Turrisi Caruso family.

My phone buzzed again, and I saw I had a call coming in from State Trooper Doris Shileto. "This is Jon Frederick."

"Serena told Tony that Taytum Hanson had been murdered, and he suggested I share some information with you." Doris was once married to a friend of mine, Tony Shileto, and they obviously still spoke. It helped to have a network of resources. Doris asked, "Taytum was Tug's mistress, right?"

"Yes."

"Are you aware that Lorenzo Caruso was caught parking with a redhead only thirty miles away from Tug Grant's murder?"

"What are you talking about? Do you know the redhead's name?"

"No, the officer didn't get her name. He said pretty, with long red hair. The officer just sent them on their way. The report went to Sean at the BCA."

It bothered me that my boss hadn't shared this information with me. "Can you think of a reason Lorenzo would be in the area? Other than to verify Tug's death?"

"No, but I don't know with certainty. It's generally peaceful, rural Minnesota. Tug was shot by Jamarcus Smith, right?" Doris responded.

"I believe that Roan arranged that murder."

"And you think Lorenzo was in the area to confirm the hit?"

"Yes. The woman matches the description of Melanie Pearson. Tug's old secretary."

"Why would she want Tug dead?" Doris questioned.

"She became aware that he was drugging and raping her."

"That would do it. Okay, what does this have to do with Taytum?"

"Tug loved Taytum to the degree of leaving her three million dollars when he died. Taytum believed Roan arranged the hit, and she swore to avenge Tug's murder."

"Is it worth opening up this can of worms when you know your boss isn't sharing information with you?" Doris questioned.

"I didn't open it, but it's open now."

Chapter 50

SERENA FREDERICK

9:30 A.M., THURSDAY, MARCH 7, 2024
PIERCE STREET NORTHEAST, BELTRAMI, MINNEAPOLIS

Paula Fineday was one of my favorite people. She had a unique way of handling authority. She did it in a quiet manner by recognizing where a conversation was going, avoiding arguing about the pending issue, and departing before she was given a directive. She knew Jon was instructed he'd be fired if he spoke to Roan Caruso, so she complied, sort of. Knowing Jon consults with me on his cases, Paula invited me to go for a ride with her to Roan's house. It didn't take me long to find a babysitter and meet up with her.

When we arrived, Roan was sitting on the front porch of his large rose brick house reading the paper. He stood and invited us to sit. Paula flashed her badge, and Roan remarked, "Of course. Now that I got that Frederick off my ass, they send an Indian over. This way, if I refuse to talk, I'm a racist. You here to discuss Columbus with me?"

"No. That would be like talking about Hitler with a first grader," Paula remarked dryly. "Taytum Hanson is dead. I'd like to know where you were on the night of March 6, 2024."

"I was in a meeting," Roan said. "And by the way, Columbus is the reason we enjoy spaghetti and pizza as we do. He brought tomatoes to Italy."

Ignoring the comment, Paula asked, "You were at a meeting in the middle of the night?"

"The folks I do business with don't keep regular hours." Roan smiled.

"Can you provide some names?" Paula asked.

"Not without a subpoena. Even with a subpoena, I probably won't. Look, honestly, I had nothin' to do with that." Roan glanced at me. "You pregnant?"

"No, I'm addicted to Crystal—Crystal Farms cheese. I'm not a lightweight. Sharp cheddar is dope." He laughed, and I continued, "Yes, I'm pregnant. I appreciate that you had the guts to ask."

"If discretion is the better part of valor, I'm the worst part. So, what are you two—the replacements?" Roan asked.

"If you could let me take a look at your phone," Paula said, pointing to the camera above us, "or your surveillance footage, we could clear you and be done with it."

"I don't think so. People say nothing is impossible. Well, I did nothing, so it's possible."

Jon had asked me to find out if Roan or Catania did their laundry. I noticed a drip of coffee on his shirt and pointed to it, "You might want to rub a little laundry detergent on that stain when you wash it. Maybe I should be talking to Catania."

"Huh," Roan grunted dismissively. "Do you think we do our laundry? I will tell you this: I'd be more likely to do it than Cat, but it's been so long I wouldn't even know how to turn the machine on."

Thinking I'd lost focus, Paula glanced at me quizzically before she pressed Roan further. "Where was your son Lorenzo that night?"

This question seemed to bother Roan. "Why do you ask?"

"People have seen Taytum with Lorenzo," Paula answered.

"They must be mistaken. Lorenzo's got a girl."

"What's her name?" Paula asked.

"I think it's time for me to talk to a lawyer." Roan callously added, "I guess Taytum's out of the picture. Nothin' personal

THE SUN

ladies. You're just barkin' up the wrong tree." He turned to me. "I didn't catch your name."

I got up and said, "I thought we were done talking."

"All right. If you're gonna be like that, off with you." He waved us away.

Paula looked frustrated when we got into her car, so I told her, "Jon said he's glad to see you're in charge of this case."

"This case is a total cluster—she stopped short. The lab says we've got DNA from two different men in Taytum's bed, and she was taking on the mafia. And my partner, Jon, can't talk to Roan and Cat, two of the most pretentious assholes in the world. Only I can. The murder of a preppy millionaire is always the worst because we end up being condescendingly addressed by a bunch of yuppies. You might think I'm handling it well, but I feel like diving headfirst into a bottle of vodka, slimming down, and getting a job stripping at Fat Jack's for some easy money. It would be more manageable than all of this."

I busted out laughing and couldn't stop. Fat Jack's is a strip club in a town of eighty people.

Finally, Paula laughed with me. She added, "Okay, maybe not. This body isn't strip club material. Well, maybe the Tuesday afternoon crowd. Regardless, Taytum's case is damn frustrating."

10:40 A.M.
51ST STREET & WASHBURN AVENUE SOUTH,
FULTON, MINNEAPOLIS

I CALLED JON, and we shared information. Jon wanted to talk to Melanie Pearson, and I agreed to meet him at Agnes Schraut's house.

As we approached her house, Jon pointed out the boarded window.

Agnes answered the door and immediately began ranting, "I know why you're here. I'm not taking that cuckoo looney back into my house." We followed Agnes to the kitchen table as she ordered, "Pour me a tea, deary. There's some on the stove."

While I retrieved her tea, Jon asked, "What happened to the window?"

"I shot it out," she bragged in her raucous voice.

"Why?" Jon questioned.

"Well, I didn't want to kill him," she remarked.

I delivered her tea. "Who?"

"Melanie's new boyfriend was over here knocking her around. Don't ask me his name, I don't remember—Mafia kid. Once I started shooting, he ran like water down a mountain stream. Not much for conversation afterward. And I'm done with Felony Melanie." She cackled at her rhyme and nudged me. "Like what I did there?"

"Was the attacker's name Lorenzo Turrisi Caruso?" I asked. It had to be.

"I honestly don't recall," Agnes responded.

"Where is Melanie staying?" I asked. We were close once, but Melanie hadn't returned my last few messages.

"She's staying at Ricky's place for now." I had heard that Ricky was back in prison on a probation violation. Agnes waved me to follow her into her bedroom. "I've got something to show you." She ranted, "A professor without a penny to his name will tell you how to make a million dollars, and a woman who can't get a date will tell you how to raise a child. But would Melanie listen to someone with eighty years of life experience?" Agnes returned and plopped a medical bill on the table. "Look at it."

Jon remained in the kitchen, examining the window.

I glanced at the bill. "It doesn't look like you owe any money."

"But I never had this appointment or this appointment." She pointed to two dates on the bill.

"Do you mind if I take this and make a copy of it? I promise to return it." The letterhead read Precision Lens. "About 7% of all Medicare billing is fraudulent, which costs taxpayers millions of dollars."

"This is why I like you, deary." Agnes put her hand on my shoulder. "You understand that I'm not just some crazy old bat."

"Let me know if you get any more of these." We returned to the kitchen. "Can you fix the window?" I asked. Jon and his friends used to periodically break windows in his parents' house while playing football in the yard. Jon's dad had a shed full of old windows, so Jon would replace the glass before his dad found out. He'd even cut it to size when necessary.

"No. Our old farmhouse windows were much easier to repair."

I told Agnes, "It doesn't pay to turn it into your homeowner's insurance. The cost will be about the same as your deductible."

"Insurance is like jumping from a plane without a parachute," Agnes complained. "They won't cover the first time, but if it happens again, they promise to be there for you." She waved it off. "Don't worry about the window. Melanie is picking up the cost of repairing it. I swear that girl's a magnet for nickel and dime crooks." Agnes turned to Jon. "Catch what I did there with the pun?"

Jon laughed. "I think so. Nickel is a magnetized metal. Even dimes are made of nickel and copper. But no coins are magnetic. If they were, they'd stick together."

"Spoil sport," Agnes groaned.

11:30 A.M.
NORTHEAST JACKSON STREET, MINNEAPOLIS

ON THE WAY to Ricky Day's house, we drove by St. Clement's Catholic Church in Minneapolis. Jon grinned at me, and his unrestrained trivia followed. "St. Clement was the third successor to the Apostle Peter as Pope. As a result of his success in expanding the influence of Christianity, Roman Emperor Trajan had St. Clement banished to Crimea, which today is Southern Ukraine. Clement died a martyr's death for his faith, being thrown into the ocean with an iron anchor tied around his neck. It was reported the tide receded two miles every year following his death, and a shrine containing his bones has now been built at the site of his death."

"Useful information," I teased. "What is St. Clement the patron saint of? They're all patron saints of something, right?"

"Marble workers."

"So, who is our patron saint?"

"The patron saint of investigators is St. Columbo."

"You just made that up."

"I kid you not. He was banished from Ireland for leading battles against greedy monasteries. He is also the patron saint of bookbinders and floods."

"What an odd combination. I can understand combining investigators and bookbinders. Columbo should be the patron saint of mystery writers." I shook my head. "But floods? A librarian once told me water is the enemy of books, so maybe it works."

I gasped at Melanie's badly bruised face when she answered the door. Her nose was bandaged, and the skin around her eyes was purple. She looked miserable, and I imagined her head was throbbing.

"What happened?" I asked.

"I had an accident," Mel immediately responded.

Instead of entering the house, Jon walked over to look at her car in the driveway. He returned without a word, and Melanie invited us in.

I noticed the prayer of St. Clement framed on the wall and read it:

> We beg you, Lord, to be our help and our support. Free us from our troubles; take pity on the lowly; raise up those who have fallen; give help to the poor, health to the sick, and bring home those who have wandered away. Feed the hungry, ransom captives, give strength to the weak and courage to the faint-hearted.

THE SUN

Melanie placed her hand on my shoulder and said, "Clement means merciful. *Raise up those who have fallen* is my new mantra."

We sat at a small round kitchen table, and Jon began the conversation, "Please don't lie to us, Melanie. Serena saved your life. We know that you were parking with Lorenzo Turrisi Caruso close to Zumbro Falls on the night Tug Grant died. We also know Lorenzo attacked you at Agnes's house. We just came from there. There is no damage to your car. Your name was circled in Taytum Hanson's planner, and now she's dead. What's going on?"

"I can't talk about it." Melanie teared up.

I finally interjected, "You were having an affair with Lorenzo. Is that why Ricky went out and got drunk?"

"Sort of." She nodded. "I had sex one time with Lorenzo when Ricky and I were broken up. Lorenzo blackmailed me into having sex the second time. I told Ricky, and he got drunk. Lorenzo found me a third time at Agnes's, and when I refused his advances, he beat the shit out of me."

"Why didn't you report it?" Jon asked.

"It's taken care of," Melanie said.

"How do you know?" I wondered.

"You went to Roan," Jon said.

Melanie's silence confirmed Jon's assertion.

Jon continued, "Why is your name in Taytum's planner?"

"I don't know. After choking me, Lorenzo told me, 'This one's on Taytum,' so they had something going."

"Taytum knew you had something to do with Tug's death," Jon suggested.

"No-no," Melanie started but then rubbed her forehead.

"You're protecting Roan Caruso," Jon said.

"I can't say," Melanie said softly.

"You were caught with his son close to Zumbro Falls on the night Tug was murdered," Jon added. "Do you really think Roan's protecting you? Look in the mirror."

"I can't say," Melanie repeated through her tears.

258

Jon uttered in frustration, "No matter what Roan does, no one ever makes a statement against him."

I gave Jon a look that warned him to back off. There was no point in battering a victim of assault.

Jon stood up and walked out of the house, leaving me to care for my friend.

When I joined Jon in the car, he said, "I want you to be very careful. You went through a lot of stress to have this child." He paused, "*We* went through a lot of stress. I know I sound hypocritical because I have to keep doing my job, but you are carrying our baby everywhere you go."

I placed my hand on my stomach and massaged our baby. "What are you thinking about Taytum's murder?"

"I don't think Roan killed her."

"Why do you say that?"

"There have been a number of cases where Roan was a suspect. In every case, he shoots the victim and leaves. I don't see him staging a body."

"Then it would be a great way to throw the investigators off, wouldn't it?"

"'They muddy the waters to make it seem deep' —Frederick Nietzsche. I think the killer wants us to think there's a lot going on, but maybe it's simple. I need to step back and allow things to settle. Things will be clearer once I get the autopsy and CSI reports."

Chapter 51

LORENZO TURRISI CARUSO

7:30 P.M., THURSDAY, MARCH 7, 2024
TREETOP ROAD, NIRVANA

I was sitting outside on the porch of the old cabin, waiting for Eliana Castillo. Dad wanted me to break up with her. She wanted to break up with me. But I loved her—more than I've ever loved anyone. My time with her was like peeking through a keyhole at an entirely new life. A life where people laughed, and hugs were sincere. In my neighborhood, I'm constantly hit up for favors from my parents. In Eliana's world, nobody even knows my parents.

I watched Eliana pull up in her 2018 Ford Fusion. They don't even make the car anymore, but I respected her for earning everything she has. I gave her a hug and offered her my hand, but she refused to accept it. I led her into the cabin and said, "Seeing you just made my day."

Eliana stepped away. She was so nervous that she was shaking when she asked, "How long were you sleeping with her?"

"What are you talking about?" I swallowed hard. Her mom was an administrative staff member for Hennepin County Community Corrections. She must have seen a report. I imagine they have my DNA.

"Don't lie to me, Lorenzo. I know."

"Aren't the reports supposed to be confidential?"

Ellie poked me in the chest and raised her voice as she said, "Your mom wouldn't tell you if a report came across your desk stating I was cheating on you? You have a chance to be honest with me. That's why I drove all the way here."

"I love you, Eliana. More than I've ever loved anyone."

"You're all nice to my son and me, but you're just a player. How many times did you sleep with that cougar?"

"Three times. I'm sorry. She came on to me. It was a mistake. Taytum picked me up in Waconia when you left that night."

"Taytum? Who's Taytum?"

"Who are you talking about?"

"I'm talking about Melanie Pearson. She came into the corrections office and made a statement to Ricky Day's probation officer that Ricky got drunk because she cheated on him with you."

"I only slept with Melanie twice."

"You can go to hell, Lorenzo." She tried pushing past me to leave and screamed, "Move, dammit! Let me leave."

I stood firm and gripped her arms tight. "We can work this out."

"Whore!" The menace in her eyes rattled me.

Crack! I slapped her and knocked her to the floor.

She glared up at me. "I hate you, Lorenzo. Let me leave."

I knelt by her. "Please, I'm so sorry."

She ran out the door to her car.

"I love you, Eliana!" I yelled in her wake, "I will always love you! Please, I'm sorry." I wanted to get in my car and run her down. My Porsche would race down the Fusion in seconds. But I couldn't afford to get pulled over. *Damn it! What is wrong with me?*

I returned to the house and retrieved the growler of Runestone Man IPA that I'd bought at ABC Brewing. The bitter ale seemed well deserved.

THE SUN

2:00 A.M., FRIDAY, MARCH 8, 2024

I WOKE UP to a couple of men with Spanish accents shaking me and dragging out the 'o' in my name. "Lorenzoooo. Time to wake up, Lorenzoooo." I was met with a barrage of punches when I opened my eyes. I rolled out of bed and started swinging. I landed one solid hit on the bigger guy, but the smaller one danced around me like a featherweight and pummeled my torso. He taunted, "You think you're a big man, slapping around our cousin. You touch her again *bobo vato*, and you're dead—*muerto*."

Something struck me hard over the back of the head, and I fell to the floor.

8:00 A.M.

WHEN I CAME back to consciousness, I was being shaken again. I immediately swung out, but she caught my punch. It was Mom. I managed to sit, and she pulled me into her bosom, repeating in Italian and English, "*Povero ragazzo*. My poor boy." Catania Turrisi to the rescue.

Through bruised and swollen lips, I asked, "What are you doing here?"

"Delivering food."

"Is Dad okay?"

"No. He hasn't been beaten, but he's meeting with the Genovese family today. They know somebody broke the code of omertà. Now tell me what happened here."

9:45 A.M.

AFTER I HAD dressed, cleaned up, and explained everything to Mom, Eliana came running into the house. Catania immediately rose to protect me and stood like a statue between us. "What are you doing here? Isn't it enough you sent your thugs to beat my son to death?"

Eliana tried looking at me, but Mom purposely remained in her way. "I didn't send them. My cousin had stayed with my son, and he saw the handprint on my face when I returned home. After I fell asleep, he took my phone and found this place by looking at my last GPS setting. I'm so sorry. I never meant for this to happen."

"Eliana, I love you," I pleaded. "I'm sorry."

Giving up, Mom stepped aside and let Eliana come to me, and I held her in a loving embrace. Mom remarked, "I will give you that. You're both a sorry excuse for lovers. Lorenzo, I swear if you hit another woman, *I'll* beat the shit out of you. And you—" She pointed to Eliana. "You want your cousins dead? You don't assault Turrisis."

Eliana approached Mom. "Please leave my cousins alone. I'll do anything."

Mom rested on a chair and made Eliana wait as she considered options. "Well, Lorenzo obviously loves you, or he wouldn't have risked his life by inviting you here. We told him to break up with you. Nothing personal; we just didn't want you dragged into this. I guess if you'll call it even and forgive him, I can let this pass."

"How is it even?" Eliana asked.

Mom explained, "You had a kid at sixteen, he cheated on you, you dumped him, he hit you, and you had your cousins beat the crap out of him. I guess you're still up one, but close enough. I'm feeling generous. I need all this drama to end."

"Even?" Eliana responded, "My having a child at sixteen has nothing to do with this. Lorenzo knew I was a package deal before I accepted our first date. Lorenzo cheated on me, with at least two women, and hit me. I didn't do anything. But I will take responsibility for my cousins if you leave them out of this."

When Mom didn't respond, Eliana added, "I'm willing to forgive Lorenzo and start over. If he cheats or hits me again, I'm gone."

"Please, Mom, let it go."

Suddenly, we heard pounding on the door. Mom shouted, "For fuck's sake, now who's that? For someone who's hiding out, you're busier than a bus station." She went to the door and said, "We're not buying any raffle tickets."

The visitor responded, "I'm Paula Fineday from the Bureau of Criminal Apprehension. I'm here to talk to your son Lorenzo."

Mom waved me back, but I went to the door anyway. Mom told the investigator, "He's not speaking to you without an attorney present."

"Okay." Paula turned to me. "I expect to see you at the BCA office in St. Paul at eight a.m. tomorrow. Here's my card."

When I took it, she also handed me a piece of paper. "And here's a subpoena for your phone. Hand it over."

Mom intervened. "We'd like the subpoena looked over by an attorney first."

"It's okay." I interrupted. "I have nothing to hide," and handed my phone to her.

Noticing it was a burner phone, Mom smiled. "Okay." She turned to Paula, "Anything else?"

Paula spotted Eliana wandering too close to the door and asked, "Who gave you that handprint on your face?"

Eliana immediately stepped back and turned away as she said, "I fell, and he tried to catch me."

Glaring at Mom, Paula said, "Nice family." With feigned respect, Paula told her, "I hope you have a wonderful day. You should get out on the lake. I hear the bluegills are biting."

Mom slammed the door shut, and the investigator departed.

I said, "Dad threw my phone in the Mississippi on the way here. There's nothing on that phone but calls to you and Ellie."

Mom nodded in approval and then turned to Eliana. "Law

enforcement followed you here. Roan and I no longer can say we don't know where Lorenzo is. Now they have evidence we're hiding him out. If that doesn't even the score, I don't know what does."

I hugged Ellie tightly and told her, "This is my fault. I'm just glad you're here with me and that we're okay again. I love you."

She kissed me passionately.

Mom declared in her miserable tone, "Mom's still here. In the room."

Chapter 52

JON FREDERICK

10:45 P.M., SATURDAY, MARCH 9, 2024
PIERZ

I poured the warm lotion into my hand and began rubbing Serena's legs.

"Mmmmm," she purred in response. "You have this perfect way of torturing information out of me." I massaged deeper, and she said, "Okay, I'll give it up. I've checked with medical companies in the Bloomington area." Serena worked in medical billing in the Minneapolis/St. Paul area prior to our marriage and still had friends at several agencies in the metro area. She told me, "Roan Caruso and a couple of guys connected to the Genovese family have been directing ophthalmologists and optometrists to purchase from specific medical supply companies."

"Strong-arming them?"

"No, offering bribes with big ticket items. Taylor Swift concerts, Vikings/Packers box seats, and front row seats at the NCAA women's basketball tourney at the Target Center."

Iowa's star has created the "Caitlin Clark phenomenon," selling out women's basketball tickets nationwide. I said, "Giving away these items must mean the contracts are lucrative."

"Millions of dollars," Serena confirmed as she pulled her right leg back and offered her left leg for a rub. "Looking at Agnes's medical bills suggests to me that Precision Lens may be making false claims to Medicare."

"I want you to share this with the US Department of Human Services, Fraud Division. Open the door and let them take over the investigation, but don't go on record. Insist they keep your name off any documents, emails, texts—anything. The Genovese crime family may be involved, and they're the strongest organized crime enterprise in the United States."

"My clairvoyance radar is sensing some trivia on the horizon," Serena teased.

"Vincente Gigante was the former Genovese mob boss. Members were never allowed to mention his name in public. They would tap their chin or make a 'C' with their fingers if they had to reference him. Vincent kept someone in his house when he was gone to prevent the FBI from sneaking in and planting a 'bug.'"

Serena scrunched her eyebrows. "Why a 'C'?"

"He had a prominent chin as a child, and his mother affectionately called him 'Chinzeeno' rather than 'Vincenzo.' His later nickname is far better. To give you an idea of how disciplined this family can be, Vincent pretended he was crazy for twenty years so he could avoid prosecution if caught. He walked around New York City in a bathrobe and checked himself into mental health units multiple times. Subsequently, he earned the nickname 'The Oddfather.' But the FBI had him in secret recordings, and the Oddfather was always coherent during mob meetings. Omertà, or the code of secrecy, is powerful with the Genovese. In the entire history of this family, only five members have turned state's evidence."

"Message delivered. They're dangerous, and if they associate my name with this, I'm dead."

"Yes."

THE SUN

9:45 A.M., MONDAY, MARCH 11, 2024
HENNEPIN COUNTY MEDICAL EXAMINER'S OFFICE
14250 COUNTY ROAD 62, MINNETONKA

I MET WITH Dr. Amaya Ho in a conference room at her office to discuss some of the forensic evidence from the murders of Tug Grant and Taytum Hanson. Amaya sat back in her white lab coat with the files in front of her. I sat next to her so I could view the files.

Confused, she said, "All of this has already been shared with the BCA."

"After Tug Grant was murdered, I transferred from the metro back to northern Minnesota, so I wasn't in the office when your reports were returned." I didn't bother to share that I had concerns my supervisor, Sean Reynolds, might have diverted some of the evidence from me. I started by paging through Tug Grant's file. There were no real surprises. Tug was killed by bullets fired from an automatic weapon. I pointed to the needle by his body in one of the pictures. "The presence of this syringe has never made sense to me. Tug didn't get far from his chair. How does he end up having an anesthetic available?"

"It was self-injected," Amaya said. "You can tell by both the angle and his prints on the syringe. I would guess that someone other than the shooter was in that cabin before he died. Maybe she retrieved it for him."

"What makes you say that?"

Amaya slid out a picture from the bottom of the file, showing smeared blood. Barely visible, written on the floor was: IM2MT2 U. "Someone wrote this on the floor and then allowed the blood to pool over it. The CSI crew carefully cleaned up the blood and noticed the slight markings beneath. Whoever wrote it probably didn't realize that when you write on a dirty surface, you leave enough of a scratch to save the message. I don't imagine it was written by the shooter, but that's your call."

"I have a pretty good idea who wrote it. Can I get a copy of this picture?"

"Sure."

I asked, "What was in the syringe?"

"It was an anesthetic. The same drug that Dr. Ashton Heaps used in his rapes of his clients."

"Heaps was Tug's prison cellmate."

Clearly angry, Amaya asked, "Any way to convict Heaps of selling it to him?"

"Probably not, now that Tug's dead. I will share my concerns with the prison in case they come across any messages or evidence." I closed Tug's file, pushed it aside, and opened the file on Taytum.

Amaya explained as I paged through, "Taytum died of a fentanyl overdose, and her wine tested positive for fentanyl. It was a high dose, but it's tasteless, so Taytum likely never knew. She fell off her chair to her death on the floor. By the manner of blood pooling after her heart stopped, it's clear she died exactly where she was found."

"Can you tell if she was dressed when she died?"

"No. I can tell you she'd had sex with two different men in the twenty-four hours before she died by the live sperm in her. Neither DNA sample had a match in CODIS. But one sample did match the DNA we got off Randy Kimball's glass. Oddly enough, his sperm wasn't on the sheet covering Taytum. Did they have sex somewhere other than the bed?"

I thought about the bedding in the dryer. "Taytum changed the sheets before her second lover arrived." The killer moved the sheets into the dryer to make room for Taytum's silk pajamas."

"We don't have a DNA match for the second lover," Amaya reiterated.

"I want you to compare Roan Caruso's DNA to the samples. Roan's is in the system, and one of the men might have been Roan's son, Lorenzo."

Amaya smiled. "I can do that."

THE SUN

11:00 A.M.
NORTHEAST JACKSON STREET, MINNEAPOLIS

I PICKED UP Serena at Agnes's house, and we headed over to speak to Melanie again. Melanie hadn't returned to work at Target Headquarters since getting her nose broken. I knew Melanie's mental health was in a precarious state, and she was always better off after speaking to Serena, so I wanted Serena with me.

On the way over, Serena said, "Agnes was showing me bills she received from Precision Lens, and she was billed for several dates of service that she didn't attend. Medicare paid for those visits. She told me about a friend who had the same experience with Sightpath Medical."

"Please keep checking into that. A note in Taytum's planner suggested that Roan Caruso has something to do with both agencies."

"But wouldn't it be a big coincidence that Roan would be involved in false billing for Agnes?"

"Not at all. I'm thinking he generated a list of older adults he knew to bill falsely. He knew of Agnes through Tug. Remember how Agnes used to jack up Tug whenever he picked up Melanie?"

Serena grinned. "I think he was afraid of her." We pulled up to Ricky Day's house, now inhabited by Melanie. She invited us inside, and we sat in the living room.

Not one to waste time, I said, "Melanie, I now have evidence you were with Tug when he died." I set the picture of the etched letters on the coffee table and said out loud, "I am too empty to love you. And you were caught parking with Lorenzo on the way back."

Serena gasped, "Mel, you were in on Tug's murder?"

"I didn't kill Tug. I was contacted on the night of our cement truck ride and told that Tug was dead. I wanted proof. That's it."

"Tug was alive when you arrived," Jon continued. "You brought Tug the syringe."

"He was dying," Melanie pleaded. "Honestly, I was told he was already dead. I went there to see the body. There was no saving him. I brought him the syringe, at his request, to reduce his suffering."

"Taytum found out you were there when Tug died," I suggested.

"How?" Confused, Melanie finally said, "Crap. She found out from Lorenzo."

"Did you kill Taytum?" Serena asked.

"No! There was no love lost between Taytum and me, but we never had a violent conversation. We'd talk in a nonchalant tone and give each other dismissive glances and then walk away saying to ourselves, 'that bitch.' It was painful to be around Taytum, so I had no desire to have any contact with her. The way she stood by Tug was pathological."

"Not even after she sicced Lorenzo on you?" Serena questioned.

"No. My goal was to place Taytum in the land of total obscurity. I wanted to be done with her. I thought by turning to—" Melanie stopped. "I'm sorry, but I can't give up his name. Look, I couldn't even tell you where Taytum lived. Search my phone. I was right here."

"Do you ever think about the consequences of protecting Roan?" I asked.

"All the time." Melanie teared up. "If I don't, Ricky could get beaten to death in prison. Lorenzo would have free rein to torment me again. I can't," she repeated through her tears.

Chapter 53

SERENA FREDERICK

9:45 A.M., TUESDAY, MARCH 12, 2024
PIERZ

After Nora and Jackson were off to school, I called Maddie Dehler to see how she and Vic were doing. After pleasantries, Maddie told me, "Vic had a broken copier delivered to our house. Not the small table type. It's one of those massive school-sized copiers. I assume he expressed interest, and they gave it away so they didn't have to pay to dispose of it."

"What does Vic plan on doing with a broken copier?" I asked this question, realizing that often, there is no logical explanation for Vic's adventures.

"Well, you know how bright copier lights are. Vic wanted to see if he could send the Batman signal into the sky with it."

"Now he has my interest." I laughed. "Can you?"

"We tried, but it didn't work. It was a clear night. We're going to try again when it's overcast."

"So, where do you store it?"

"We wheeled it into the garage," Maddie said. "A sheet barely covers the monstrosity."

"How are you doing?"

"Great! Despite his eccentricities, maybe even because of them, I love Vic. We bought tickets to see Allison Eide at the Prince of Peace Lutheran Church in Burnsville…"

After the call ended, Juliet Kimball called and said, "I wanted to see how you're doing with your pregnancy. I worry about you, Serena. I shouldn't have asked you to take on this case."

"I'm okay." I rubbed my hand over my belly. "Jon keeps me away from the worst of it. This is my last investigation for a while, so my mom takes the kids for a couple of days during the week, and I stay in the metro to help Jon."

"I hope they find Taytum's killer. It's creepy to think that Randy was there shortly after she was killed. Especially when you hear about possible mob involvement." When I didn't respond, Juliet added, "I know you can't talk about the case." She paused and waited for me to speak. When I didn't offer anything, she said, "You were so nice to me. I just wanted to check in."

"Are you okay?" I asked.

"Yeah, I think Randy finally got it all out of his system. He found this place by Brainerd that does couples massage therapy, so we're planning a weekend getaway."

Chapter 54

JON FREDERICK

4:00 P.M., WEDNESDAY, MARCH 13, 2024
BUREAU OF CRIMINAL APPREHENSION
1430 MARYLAND AVENUE EAST, ST. PAUL

Paula and I sat in a conference room at the BCA office, sharing information. Paula said, "The Carusos are Teflon. Nothing sticks. Lorenzo's burner phone has only been active since Taytum's death, so it's useless. He's called his mother and his twenty-one-year-old lover, Eliana Castillo. I saw Eliana when I confiscated the phone. She had a handprint on her face, which I imagine is Lorenzo's doing. He's hiding something. That boy looked guilty as sin."

"Lorenzo beat the crap out of Melanie Pearson, but she's refusing to press charges. Roan got to her."

"We don't know what the Carusos were up to, but we now know Randy Kimball wasn't home with his wife all night." Paula smiled. "His cell phone was bouncing off a tower in Taytum's neighborhood for an hour after he said he left, and then he shut it off. His cell phone records don't show his phone turning on again until six the next morning."

"Randy's not going to talk to us unless we haul him in and make him sit for a night in jail."

"I agree," Paula concurred. He thinks he's smarter than us. Do you want to pick him up?"

"Yes."

"I'll canvas for security cameras near Taytum's place. Lake Lotus is a nice neighborhood. Somebody has a video of the cars that were around that night."

5:30 P.M.

GALAXIE AVENUE, APPLE VALLEY

JULIET KIMBALL ANSWERED the door, holding it only partially open. "Jon, we're not talking without our lawyer present."

"That's fine. I have a warrant for Randy's arrest." I handed her the form.

"I've already told you Randy was home all night with me."

"But that isn't true, is it? If you'd share your security footage, we could clarify when Randy came home."

"Our security system wasn't working that night."

"You're a security guard. You should have the best system," I remarked.

"It's like mechanics always driving junk cars," Juliet responded. "Who breaks into the house of a security guard? Our home's never been broken into." She glanced back at Randy. "He's not your killer. He's the one who called the police. What evidence do you have?"

"DNA. Phone records." I wondered if they erased the footage.

"Randy already told you he was there."

When Randy approached the door, I announced, "Randy Kimball, you're under arrest for the murder of Taytum Hanson. You have the right to remain silent. Anything you say can and will be used against you in a court of law."

Randy interrupted, "Is this necessary?"

"Yes. You have the right to have an attorney present for questioning. If you can't afford an attorney, one will be provided at public expense to represent you before and during questioning."

"Where were you on the night Taytum was killed?" I asked.

"Right here." He put his arm around Juliet. "All night. Well, all night, after I left Taytum's."

"That's not true."

"I'm not saying anything more without my attorney present, and she's out of town today."

"Okay. Turn around and put your hands behind your back."

Juliet pleaded, "Didn't you hear him?"

"I did. Hopefully, for Randy's sake, she'll be back in town this week."

"Are you kidding?" Randy snarled. He snatched the warrant from Juliet. "It's not signed by a judge. I know my rights. You can't hold me without formally charging me."

"Well, that's sort of true. We can have you sit in jail for forty-eight hours before we need to get a judge to sign it, and then we can hold you until court is over."

"You know I didn't do it," Randy argued.

"When you say 'it,' Randy, what are you referring to?" I taunted.

"You're punishing me just to satisfy your own moralistic bullshit about infidelity," Randy added.

If looks could kill, Juliet's sneer would have left nothing of Randy but his chalk outline on the floor.

He might be right, but I was hauling him to jail anyway.

7:00 P.M.
BUREAU OF CRIMINAL APPREHENSION
1430 MARYLAND AVENUE EAST, ST. PAUL

AFTER DROPPING RANDY off at the Hennepin County Jail, I returned a call to Dr. Amaya Ho. Amaya works late on Wednesday nights. She told me, "The DNA of one man matches Randy Kimball, and the other is the son of Roan Caruso. He has half of Roan's DNA. Good call."

"Is there any indication Taytum was sexually assaulted?"

"No."

"Any luck determining time of death?"

"I would estimate Taytum died at 11:00 p.m., based on the temperature of the body and the state of rigor mortis. Bodies lose a degree and a half an hour from the time of death until they reach room temperature, and at 8:00 a.m., Taytum's temp was eighty-five degrees."

"Her body was lying in the morning sunlight. Would that have made a difference?"

"At eight in April, the sun had been up for just over an hour. At most, she may have died an hour earlier, depending on the tree line in the yard."

"Thank you, Amaya. You have been incredibly helpful, as always."

"You are welcome, Jon. Good luck."

I smiled. This might have been the warmest conversation I've had with Amaya.

Chapter 55

JON FREDERICK

9:00 A.M., THURSDAY, MARCH 14, 2024
BUREAU OF CRIMINAL APPREHENSION
1430 MARYLAND AVENUE EAST, ST. PAUL

Paula and I sat in front of a large-screen television, watching footage from Taytum's neighbor's door camera. We found a neighbor who had a camera that filmed continuously. This was a break since most security cameras are triggered by movement, so it's challenging to get discernible information by the time a car appears on the recording.

We watched Dr. Randy Kimball's Daytona Gray Audi approaching Taytum's house at 4:30 p.m. It drove by again shortly after 7:00 p.m., leaving. The Audi returned at 7:50 p.m. We watched a couple of cars drive by before a Porsche with the number 63 painted in a circle on the side sped by. I remarked, "Why couldn't Randy drive a nice, obvious car like that?"

"Do you know whose car that is?" Paula grinned.

"Lorenzo Caruso?" I questioned.

"Yes, it is. 2024 Porsche 911 S/T. It sells for about $300,000. Nice to be rich."

We both laughed as we continued to speed through the recordings. The Porsche cruised back in the other direction a little after ten. I said, "Now we're in the range of potential time of death."

As we sped through the recording, we watched Lorenzo's Porsche return at about midnight. It was headed back the other way again within fifteen minutes, at least thirty miles an hour faster.

Paula asked, "Do you think he killed her the first time or the second time?"

"Lorenzo didn't have a lot of time the second time."

"Maybe he forgot something at the house," Paula suggested.

"Where's Randy's Audi? It never came back this way. Do you think he stayed with her until morning?"

Paula fast-forwarded through cars going by until 6:35 a.m. She played the recording again, and we watched the Audi approaching Taytum's house from the same direction. Paula explained, "The road horseshoes toward Taytum's house, so he must have left the other way. Fox Hill Drive becomes Lotus Trail when it heads north. I wonder if Randy had his escape all planned out. None of the houses on Lotus Trail have cameras that show the road, so we don't know when he left Taytum's."

"It's best if we don't share that detail with Randy," I said.

"Yeah," Paula agreed. "Let's hear what Randy has to say, and if that doesn't lead to a confession, we'll run down Lorenzo. My pretty boy never showed up for his interview. I haven't issued a warrant because I'm sure Catania has an emergency identified that will excuse his absence. I want Lorenzo to relax a little and assume we're not looking for him. It will draw him out of hiding so we can pull his chain when we need him."

11:30 A.M.
HENNEPIN COUNTY PUBLIC SAFETY FACILITY
401 SOUTH 4TH AVENUE, MINNEAPOLIS

PAULA AND I sat with Randy Kimball and his petite blond attorney in a conference room at the Hennepin County Jail. Serena and I grew up with Heather Hilton, who reminded me of a smaller version of Taytum. Juliet must have sought Serena's advice for a litigator, and Serena, who was nice to everybody, gave the Kimballs the name of the best attorney she knew. I minimized my interactions with Heather because I felt she was always searching for something to gossip about. Still, I've heard she does good work.

"Why are you holding my client?" Heather asked, her pixie cut bouncing as she turned from Randy to us.

"He's lying," I said. "Randy claims he went home after leaving Taytum's at seven, but his cell phone and security tapes in the neighborhood tell us otherwise."

Heather continued, "Randy didn't kill Taytum. He put his marriage and his reputation at risk by calling the police when he discovered her body. He should be thanked for his citizenship."

Paula interjected, "Time to hear from you, Randy."

"I left Taytum's at seven, just as I said. I drove for a bit and returned. I had to see who she called. I watched some young guy enter, and I just sat there. I finally realized there was nothing I could do, so I drove home."

Paula said, "We have your car on camera, returning to Taytum's but not leaving again."

Randy looked confused. "I don't know what to say."

"And you shut your phone off in front of Taytum's."

"I did. I wanted to call her and finally decided to shut it off to remove the temptation. I loved Taytum. But I was tired of hurting Juliet. I couldn't talk to Taytum, and I didn't want to go home, so I just drove. I realized that I'd become a joke in a matter of months. I've been accused of raping a colleague, lost my job, accused of self-plagiarism in the one class I'm taking, fell in love with my attorney, and broke my wife's heart—twice. The sad part is it wasn't truly love. Looking back, it was lust. Juliet was better than Taytum in every way but one—her feral, lascivious passion."

Paula remarked, "You mean like the overt sexual message you sent when you positioned her body?"

Randy turned to me. "I understand if you both hate me. I hate me." He suddenly realized. "Wait—I have the Find My Phone app." Randy drew with his finger on the table as he retraced his route. "I took a different way back. I took Lotus Trail along the lakeshore and eventually ended up on Powers Boulevard. I remember driving through Excelsior. I drove along Lake Minnetonka and Lake Waconia before I finally started home. I honestly don't know what time I got home. I didn't bother Juliet. I just slept on the couch."

"But wasn't your phone already shut off at that time?" I asked.

"Yeah." Randy nodded.

"The Find My Phone app doesn't track your route or locations when the phone's off," I told him.

"So, you don't have an alibi," Paula sneered. "But you're a smart man. I imagine you already had that figured out when you planned your escape."

"Wait a minute," Heather interjected. "Was the camera that caught Randy's Audi right in front of Taytum's house?"

"No," Paula said.

"Well, that explains why he wasn't on camera when he left. He admits that he took a different way home." Heather added, "The bottom line is he doesn't need to prove he's innocent. You must prove he's guilty beyond a reasonable doubt. You don't even have a reason to hold him."

"Did you wash Taytum's clothes?" I asked.

"No," Randy harumphed. "That would have been a death wish."

12:30 P.M.

I CONTACTED POLICE departments around the metro and asked them to put Lorenzo's vanity plate, TURRISI (likely bought by his mother), in the license plate reader (LPR) system. Squad cars throughout the metro now had LPRs mounted on them, which recorded passing license plates. If he was anywhere close to Minneapolis or St. Paul, it wouldn't be long before we had the location of his car.

4:00 P.M.
CURIOSO COFFEE BAR, BROKEN CLOCK BREWING COOPERATIVE
1712 MARSHALL STREET NORTHEAST, SUITE 100, MINNEAPOLIS

SERENA ORDERED A hot chocolate, and I ordered a mocha. She smiled, "I don't care if you have a beer."

"My workday's not done. This is going to be a quick case."

"Then mine isn't done either." She grinned. "You already know who did it."

"I do."

"Well, don't tell me. I want to figure it out. So, what are you calling this case?"

"The Sun."

Serena carefully studied me for a moment before asking, "S-O-N?"

"No. S-U-N."

"Hmm, okay. Profile it for me without making it obvious."

"It was someone Taytum had met before. Taytum let the killer into her house. The killer will contact investigators again at some point to see how the investigation is going. This type of killer often reacts with a paranoid response to cover up something. The response ultimately draws the killer into the open."

"Why haven't you charged anyone?"

"I don't have enough evidence."

"Does the killer have any habits?" I considered. Jon has something he's not telling me.

"That's a great question. I don't know." Jon pulled open the map app on his phone and zoomed in around Taytum's house. "Would you do me a favor and walk around the Carver Beach parking area and see if you find anything interesting?"

"What are you looking for?"

"The killer came to the house to kill Taytum. It's possible that instead of parking in front of the house, they parked here, two hundred feet away, off camera."

"Has the killer been by Taytum's house before the day of the murder?"

"Great question. Yes." Jon leaned back and gave me his boyish smile.

"Can I go to Taytum's and take a look around?"

"Yes. You might not be able to enter the house, but you can look around the yard, neighborhood, and lake. Let me know if you find anything interesting."

"All right."

A call from Paula came in, so I put it on speaker. "We've located Lorenzo's car in District Del Sol in St. Paul. It's parked by Eliana Castillo's house."

"Text me the address, and I'll be there in twenty-five minutes."

I ended the call and kissed Serena. "Got to go."

"Eliana means 'sun,'" she said.

"I didn't know that."

"Juliet works at Allina, and Allina means 'sunray' in Greek."

"Closer," I commented.

"Not helpful!" she said as I walked away.

5:00 P.M.
CESAR CHAVEZ STREET, DISTRICT DEL SOL,
WEST SIDE, ST. PAUL

PAULA MET ME in Eliana's front yard and told me, "At first, her cousin played dumb, but after I made it clear we were only interested in Lorenzo, he told me the two had walked to Wabasha Brewing. It's a couple blocks from here."

I followed Paula's SUV up Caesar Chavez Street to Isabel Street West. I'd been to the taproom before and enjoyed their

Altbier Amber. We both parked in front of Wabasha Brewing. Before we entered, I slipped on my Kevlar vest.

Suddenly, Lorenzo and Eliana walked out the door.

Lorenzo looked at us and bolted north on Wabasha Street.

I raced in pursuit while Paula retrieved her SUV.

Lorenzo was in good shape, but he wasn't gaining ground on me. The problem was that I wasn't gaining ground on him either, and I had to worry about the possibility that he would turn and fire at me. Finally, Paula picked me up in her SUV, and we closed the distance.

5:20 P.M.
WABASHA STREET CAVES, 215 WABASHA STREET SOUTH, ST. PAUL

LORENZO TOOK A hard left, and Paula followed, tearing into a parking lot. We were by the Wabasha Caves.

Lorenzo stood about forty feet away in front of the cave entrance. He smiled at us, pulled the entry door open, and disappeared.

I'm not going in there," Paula remarked. "It's a death trap."

The half-mile of caves had been carved into the hillside through silica mining ventures back in the 1800s. A French immigrant, Albert Mouchnotte, began growing mushrooms in the caves, and they eventually became known as "Mushroom Valley." During Prohibition, the caves were converted to a speakeasy visited by gangsters such as John Dillinger, "Baby Face" Nelson, Ma Barker, and Alvin "Creepy" Karpis. St. Paul Police Chief John O'Connor made St. Paul a safe haven for gangsters, with the agreement they wouldn't kill people in city limits. It was referred to as the O'Connor System. Of course, you can't have gangsters congregate for long before things go bad. In 1934, a waitress in the kitchen heard the popping of a Tommy gun and, when she returned to the dining area, saw three bullet-ridden bodies with their gambling chips still sitting on the table. She ran outside and called the police. The police arrived, and after a couple of hours on the scene, she was verbally reprimanded for making a false report. The bodies were gone, and the scene had been cleaned. However, the bullet holes in the fireplace are still visible to this day. It was a time when the St. Paul police were known to carry an extra cop uniform to scenes in case a gangster needed to be snuck out. The bodies are believed to be buried in the back caves.

I turned to Paula. "I'm going in. If the entrance is open, they're either giving a tour or showing someone the place as a possible wedding venue. Either way, I can't just leave innocent people to deal with him."

She nodded and handed me some gum. "Chew this."

Confused, I responded, "I'm not much of a gum guy."

"Bats don't like mint."

Paula took out a bottle of Eucalyptus Aloe Vera lotion. "They don't like Eucalyptus either. I'm putting this on, too. Not my first cave."

"It's fine if you don't go in," I told her. "We're probably not going to have cell phone coverage inside, and we may soon have a hostage situation."

"Okay, I'll get backup here." Paula set the bottle back down. "Be careful."

I ran to the caves. The initial tunnel where guests enter was clean and well-lit. As I ran deeper into the caverns, I caught a distinguished gray-haired woman talking to a couple about using the caves as a wedding venue.

The woman pulled me aside and said, "I believe the man you're looking for just walked through."

"Get the couple out of here," I warned. "In a manner of minutes, there will be police surrounding this place."

Worried, she nodded. "Okay." She turned to the couple with a smile. "I know a great place where I can finish answering all your questions. Follow me."

I continued to walk deeper into the caves, stopping periodically and listening carefully. I thought I heard breathing behind me and realized I might have walked past Lorenzo as he hid in the darkness. Before I turned back, I heard distant footsteps deep in the cavern. I rushed toward them. The caves became progressively darker until the opening before me was utterly black.

"Lorenzo!" I yelled. "It's Investigator Frederick. I just want to talk. I'm not arresting you. I have questions you can help me with."

I waited until a voice finally responded, "I screwed everything up." I could have sworn it echoed from behind me. "Tell Mom and Dad I'm sorry."

I heard the footsteps again, ahead of me, walking on. I flashed the light from my phone into the darkness and saw nothing. I yelled, "Eliana is pretty. She didn't want to see you run. At this moment, you're not in trouble for anything. You must have something you still want to say to Eliana. I promise I'll let you talk to her first thing. We just have to get out of here."

The footsteps continued deeper into the cave. I ran toward them and realized I was a clear target, running into the darkness with my phone light on. I shut the light off and slowly started back. "Lorenzo!" I yelled. There was no answer.

A cauldron of bats fluttered off the wall and flew inches over my head. Then I heard footsteps approaching.

Chapter 56

SERENA FREDERICK

5:25 P.M. THURSDAY, MARCH 14, 2024
FOX HILL DRIVE, CHANHASSEN

I walked toward the beach on Lotus Lake in front of Taytum Hanson's house. It was blustery, and white caps rolled across the lake. Lotus means purity, rebirth, and strength. A grove of trees buttressed the opposite shore, but even the forest of maples and oaks couldn't protect the Lotus on a stormy day. I put my hand over my stomach and massaged my baby. *Child, you make me nervous, but happy.* I can't believe how uncomfortably big I've gotten with this pregnancy. My body is a triangle. I whispered, "I love you, baby," and said a quick prayer for a safe delivery.

Looking back at Taytum's house, I realized she had a beautiful view of the setting sun from her bedroom. It also meant that if she didn't close the shades, someone on the beach would have a clear view of her bedroom. Jon's title of the case tormented me—*The Sun*. There has to be something here. I scoured the shore.

On my way back to Taytum's house, I noticed a small piece of light green paper on the ground. I bent down and carefully picked up the Doublemint gum wrapper and pocketed it. Paula Fineday carried Doublemint gum. So did the Kimballs.

As Jackson suggested, maybe all adults do. I looked up popular gums online so I'd have this knowledge before I presented my evidence to Jon. Wrigley's Doublemint is the number one selling gum in the United States. *Maybe we could get a fingerprint.* Jon has told me that a fingerprint can stay on paper for years. However, if exposed to the weather, it can quickly be washed away by the elements.

Chapter 57

CATANIA TURRISI

5:30 P.M., THURSDAY, MARCH 14, 2024
WABASHA STREET CAVES, 215 WABASHA STREET SOUTH, ST. PAUL

I was pleased Eliana called me immediately when Lorenzo bolted. There might be hope for that born-again *putana* yet. I, in turn, called Roan and updated him. I sat in my Lexus, smoking and worrying about my dear boy. *Roan should be here by now.* Lorenzo's life has tanked ever since he started dating that little tramp. I've always told him to be careful who he hangs around with. If those cops kill him, there will be hell to pay—mark my words. For now, I was stuck on the perimeter, waiting. My phone buzzed, and in my agitated state, I responded, "What do you want?"

"Cat, it's the Wizard. We need to talk."

"Okay, when?"

"Now."

"I'm kind of —"

He cut me off. "Genovese family requests supersede everything. If you were dying, we'd expect you to stop and meet our demands first. I'm at 303 Thomas Avenue North, Minneapolis. I'll see you in ten minutes. Don't tell anyone. This isn't negotiable."

I found a pen and a notepad in the console and wrote the address down. I knew the Wizard gets testy when he's nervous, and his right-hand man, Nico, typically solved problems by R & T (Rape and Terminate), but the Wizard was working for a powerful family, and I needed to respond.

I made a couple of phone calls, got a phone number, and dialed it. "Hi, this is Catania Turrisi."

"How did you get my number?" Serena asked.

"Have you heard from Jon recently?"

"No. I just tried calling him, but there was no answer. Do you know where he is?"

"I haven't heard from Roan either. They met about a half hour ago over on Thomas Avenue. Are you in the metro?"

"I am," Serena confirmed.

"Do you want to meet me there? I'd feel better if it was the two of us. I'm worried about Roan."

"All right." She hesitated a moment and said, "Give me the address."

"303 Thomas Avenue North, Minneapolis. It's the old Fruen Mill."

Chapter 58

SERENA FREDERICK

5:40 P.M. THURSDAY, MARCH 14, 2024
FOX HILL DRIVE, CHANHASSEN

I tried calling Jon one last time. No answer. *Where are you, Jon?* I called Paula twice to see if she knew where Jon was, but her phone went straight to voicemail. I will never forget the sense of loneliness and dread I had in our Last Call investigation when I thought he was dead. I couldn't live with myself if something happened to Jon and I didn't show up to help. I don't care if others see it as codependent. We need each other.

6:05 P.M.
FRUEN MILL 303 THOMAS AVENUE NORTH,
MINNEAPOLIS

THE FRUEN MILL was a creepy five-story abandoned building with graffiti painted all over the bottom level. A black Bentley Continental, a steel gray Maserati, and a selenite gray Mercedes Benz were parked outside the building. It's safe to say there weren't people experiencing homelessness inside, though these guys could afford to get a little color in their lives. I sat in my Ford Explorer and waited for Cat. I finally called her. "Catania, where are you?"

Suddenly, an unshaven man with curly black hair was at my window. His most distinguishing feature was the gun he had pressed against the window aimed at my head. I told Cat, "He's got a gun."

"Pretend you're me, and they won't hurt you," Cat advised. "Tell them the cops have Lorenzo surrounded in the Wabasha Caves, and you don't know if he's going to get out of there alive."

"Get out of the car!" the man hollered.

I did as I was told.

He took my phone and shut it off.

Chapter 59

JON FREDERICK

6:07 P.M., THURSDAY, MARCH 14, 2024
WABASHA STREET CAVES, 215 WABASHA STREET SOUTH, ST. PAUL

The footsteps continued to approach me. "Please identify yourself. I don't want anybody to get hurt here." I quickly moved along after I spoke to keep someone from firing toward my voice.

The footsteps stopped for a moment and then continued. They were closer than ever. I didn't like the feel of this at all. I was done speaking; it made me an easy target. I felt along the cave walls with my hands toward daylight.

And the footsteps kept coming.

I stumbled over something on the ground. It wasn't a stalagmite. It wasn't hard, and it didn't crumble. It was cold and stiff and gave way a little, like a body might.

Finally, in dim light, I sprinted until I was through the entry and out the cave door.

Once outside in the light, I stopped to catch my breath. Officers were loading Lorenzo into the back of a squad car.

"Good work!" Paula said as she jogged to me. "I don't know what you said to Lorenzo, but you spooked the hell out of him. He dove out the door and seemed relieved to surrender." Paula gave me a quick once-over and asked, "Are you okay?"

"There's somebody still in there." I didn't want to tell her I was also terrified.

"Okay." She waved a team over and ordered them into the caves. Paula returned to me, "You look like you've seen a ghost."

"I heard footsteps, but they wouldn't respond. They just kept coming." I took a deep breath and told her, "I'm going in with the crew. I have to see what's there."

I followed the officers with their Maglites into the cave. About a quarter of a mile into the cavern, I noticed a rolled canvas tarp lying on the ground, which was likely what I had tripped over. I unraveled it, half expecting to find bones inside, but it was empty. Our search yielded no one. The Minneapolis Tribune listed the Wabasha Caves as "the most haunted place in Minnesota." I wondered if having read stories about people hearing voices and footsteps in the caves had impacted my perception. It felt real—but so had the body.

Once outside, I told Paula, "We didn't find anyone." I anticipated she would tell me to get my head examined.

Instead, she compassionately told me, "I'll do the paperwork. Let me handle the interview with Lorenzo. You can watch the recording when it's done." She seemed to have more to share but held back. Finally, she said, "I believe in spirits. Go home."

Chapter 60

ROAN CARUSO

6:20 P.M., THURSDAY, MARCH 14, 2024
WABASHA STREET CAVES, 215 WABASHA STREET SOUTH, ST. PAUL

I had a call coming in from the Wizard. As far as I was concerned, he was a hyped-up sleazeball salesman. Anybody can get people to gamble. They volunteer for it. In his raspy smoker's voice, he spat out, "Everest, I got your woman."

"What are you talking about?"

"You should have given me Lorenzo. Now I got Cat, and I'm holdin' her until you take care of business for me. You didn't give me a choice. Any luck, the police will take care of him for you. If so, Catania walks free. Everest, we need you to make sure Lorenzo can't talk."

"You understand we're made, right?" Going after made folks, like Cat and me, is punishable by death, even if you're a member of the mafia.

"Yeah, she's being handled with kid gloves. Just get the job done." He hung up.

"Asshole!" I yelled. Kid gloves? Comparing my wife to gloves made from goat leather. I ought to wring his neck. I never liked that son of a bitch. I don't have a problem with people thinking they're better than everyone else. Everybody should. But it shouldn't be part of every conversation. The Wiz needs to understand his place. I'm made. He isn't. I walked into the parking lot by the Wabasha Caves and saw Cat sitting in her black Lexus.

I opened the passenger door and sat by her. "Thank God! The Wiz just called and said he's holding you hostage."

"He is—sort of." Cat took a long drag from her cigarette and blew the smoke out her window. "I gave up Serena Frederick."

"Cat, are you nuts? She's the wife of a BCA investigator." I rubbed my forehead with both hands. "The BCA will never let this go."

"Serena's a snitch. You're getting soft, Roan. A decade ago, you wouldn't have thought twice about killing a rat. Serena's the one who directed Mother Grimm from Health and Human Services to the eye companies. The Grim Reaper is on you. What are you going to do?" When I didn't respond, she continued, "Would you rather they'd kidnapped me?"

"No. You're the most important person to me. I love you, Cat." Relieved Cat was safe, I squeezed her hand.

Cat smiled and said, "They think they have me, and I told Serena don't tell them otherwise. You decide how to play it."

"Thank God Lorenzo got out of there alive."

Cat put my hand to her lips and kissed my wedding ring.

I needed to talk to the Wizard and get this resolved, one way or another. My rage was on the verge of boiling over. I couldn't let go of the fact that he tried to kidnap my wife.

Chapter 61

JON FREDERICK

6:30 P.M., THURSDAY, MARCH 14, 2024
WABASHA BREWING COMPANY, 429 WABASHA STREET SOUTH,
ST. PAUL

Shortly after Paula dropped me off, Roan Caruso pulled up in his black '59 Cadillac Eldorado, rolled down the passenger window, and said, "Get in."

"I'm not supposed to talk to you, Roan."

"Look, Serena's in trouble, and I'm offering help. Get in."

I stepped out of my car and stood by his passenger window, peering in. "What are you talking about?"

"Try calling Serena. My bet is that it immediately goes to voicemail."

I did, and it went to voicemail. I had to quickly pull my brain out of "worst fear mode" and focus. I used my Find My iPhone app and saw Serena's phone was off. It was located near the Fruen Mill in Minneapolis. Our Find My apps allow us to locate each other's phones even when they're off. Serena was in trouble. The abandoned mill had a reputation for being the most dangerous place in Minnesota.

"You could have killed Lorenzo, but you got him out alive, so I'm going to help you here. I can take you to her." Roan continued, "Look, they know Serena gave information to the

THE SUN

fraud department. Someone from the Office of the Inspector General got careless and discarded a note with Serena's name on it."

"Okay." If Roan knew this, Serena was in serious trouble. I asked, "What am I going to need?"

"Anything that could lure the Assassin from guarding the entrance would help." Roan popped his trunk.

I opened mine and grabbed a wire spool, diagonal pliers, a red flare, and a rifle. I tossed them in Roan's trunk and sat on the passenger side of his Cadillac.

"What's the wire for?" he asked.

"I'm not sure. I've used it more than my gun in the last couple of cases, so I thought I'd grab it." We pulled away.

"No flares. We need to do this as quietly as possible. I'm helping you under one condition: You and Serena destroy everything you have on me, and you stop investigating me. Plus, you stop looking into Lorenzo regarding Taytum's murder."

"Who has Serena?"

"The Wizard, the Assassin, and Wizard's buddy, Nico. Right now, they think they kidnapped Cat. Once they realize they have Serena, they're going to kill her, or worse."

I couldn't think of a more dire scenario. "Who are these people?"

"The Wizard of Odds is Enzo Angelini, Nico Lamarta is Enzo's cleaner, and no one knows the identity of the Assassin."

"Where are they holding her?"

"Fruen Mill ruins."

"I should call for backup."

"Absolutely not! If they have any inkling there's law enforcement around, they're killing her and running. You know it as well as I do."

"How deep into the organization do they have Serena's name?"

"As far as I know, it's just those three who know. The Wiz is trying to be a made guy, so he won't want any hitches in his plan. If they knew they had Serena, she'd already be dead. They thought she was Cat."

"How did this happen?"

"It's irrelevant now. We just need to find a way to get Serena out of there. I'm not pulling into the location until you agree to my terms."

"Okay."

"What do you know about the setup?" I asked.

"The Assassin is on the first floor. Wizard's on the second floor, running his gambling operation on the phone and a laptop. I imagine Nico is on the third floor with the hostage. When they do business in a city they sit in an abandoned building and have beds and desks delivered and set up. Nothing fancy—just functional. When they're done, they pile it up, burn it, and disappear."

They avoid leaving a trail by staying away from the cameras of hotels. I realized, "You've already been there."

"I set up a meeting with the Wizard, so they're expecting my car. The last time I was there, the Assassin followed me up to the second floor and stood outside the door while I met with the Wiz. Your job is to get the Assassin to leave his post so I can get up to the next level and rescue Serena."

"How are you going to do that?" I asked.

"By any means necessary. Understand, they're going to kill her. They know it was Serena who gave fraud investigators information that could lead to their prosecution. They don't realize yet it's Serena they're holding." He hesitated momentarily and said, "I'm risking my life here, Jon, so you need to give me a break. I could walk away, but then Serena's dead. Maybe with this good deed, God will leave the back door of heaven open for me. But you've got to promise to drop the investigation of me and my son. One thing we have in common is we're good for our word."

"Okay. Everything we have is dropped. I honestly don't believe Lorenzo killed Taytum, so you're going to want to keep me and Serena alive. Otherwise, you lose an ally in that investigation. But no favors in the future. I can't owe you."

"Out of curiosity, what convinced you Lorenzo was innocent?" It was clear Roan still wasn't certain. "Lorenzo would have beat the hell out of her. It's what he does."

With a sardonic grin, Roan said, "Good point. Okay, why haven't you come after me? I didn't do it, but I had to be a suspect."

"Taytum invited her killer into her house for a drink. She would never have invited you in. And I don't think you would have stripped her and posed her body."

"Hell, no. Get the job done and get out. You're pretty damn good, Frederick."

"I'd appreciate it if you make that son of yours complete a domestic abuse program," I added.

"Tryin' to fix people up to the very end." Roan smiled. He reached across, and we shook hands. "All right." He held on a second too long and said, "You know we're probably not going to live through this, right?"

I blew out a long breath. "I do." But I didn't have a better option.

"I got one more thing to tell you that's going to piss you off until you reason through it. Cat sent Serena here."

"What?" I fumed.

"Cat is a master at reading the writing on the wall. Think about it. If Cat did nothing, Serena was dead. They had her name. By forcing you to come here and rescue her, Cat gave you the option of fighting for her life rather than simply coming home and finding her body. Or hearing she was shot to death driving your daughter to school."

I was angry, but he was right. *Why would Roan help me?* I thought out loud. "If they knew Serena was a source for the Feds, they must know Lorenzo was also a source." Roan wanted me here to fight this battle with him.

He pulled into a long driveway. "Here we are. Get down."

I slouched out of sight as he drove the mill's entrance road. "Give me a minute after I enter," Roan said. "All eyes will be focused on me. Once I'm inside, take whatever you need from the trunk. You can't get into a face-to-face shootout with the Assassin. The Assassin can remove a sliver with a bullet at two hundred yards." He reached over, opened the glove compartment, and pushed a button. "My trunk has a false bottom. There's a cache of weapons underneath. You're going to need more than wire and pliers. Take what you need."

6:40 P.M.
FRUEN MILL 303 THOMAS AVENUE NORTH,
MINNEAPOLIS

I GAVE ROAN one minute after he entered the ground floor of the mill. I opened the trunk and grabbed my wire and cutter. I put the spool around my arm and the pliers in my pocket. I took my rifle out, set it on the ground, and opened the false bottom. He had a stockpile of weapons and ammo. Roan had a Valken M-17 assault rifle with clips of rubber bullets. I imagined his assaults weren't always lethal. Sometimes, he just needed to torture people. I loaded a clip in the M-17 and grabbed it. Roan had a sand-colored Barrett Multi-Role Adaptive Design (MRAD) rifle, or as laymen call it, a sniper rifle. *Better than my rifle.* I took the MRAD. With my hands full, I ran back to the building and quietly stepped inside.

I took in the layout. I was standing on a dirty cement floor. The steps to the second floor were encased in a wall and faced the corner of the building. I wouldn't be able to shoot anyone coming down the steps. Time for plan B. The M-17 with rubber ammo would serve as a distraction. I thought about ricocheting balls off the basement corner to Nora. *Could I ricochet rubber bullets off the corner walls up the steps?* I'd soon find out. Rubber bullets aren't lethal, but they still hurt like hell.

With the wire, I tied the Valken M-17 low on a cement post and aimed it up at a slight angle into the cement corner by the steps. I tied the wire around the trigger and carefully wrapped it around the pole fifteen feet behind the gun. I then stepped off to the left with the sniper rifle so I'd have a clear shot of someone exiting the steps. The rubber bullets fired from the resting M-17 would have to distract the Assassin long enough so that he wouldn't immediately notice me. I dragged the wire to my new spot and set up my sniper rifle on the ground next to a pole. One hard pull of the wire and the M-17 would fire until the clip was empty.

I tried to be quiet, but I had made enough noise to attract attention. Someone was slowly descending the wooden steps. I would soon be face-to-face with the Assassin. I waited a second and pulled the wire. The M-17 began firing into the corner, and I watched the old concrete chip away as the bullets ricocheted up the steps.

I heard a pained groan, and like a flash, the Assassin slid halfway around the corner wearing a Kevlar helmet and a bulletproof vest. As anticipated, the Assassin fired directly at the M-17, assuming this was where the shooter was located.

I laid on the floor with my sniper rifle and fired at the Assassin's side, into his unprotected hip and legs.

The speed with which the Assassin turned and fired in my direction was remarkable. Before I could get back behind the post, I'd been grazed once and hit twice. A bullet had grazed my head, and my left arm felt like it was on fire. Of most significant concern was the incredible pain in my chest. The Assassin had ricocheted a shot off the floor into my chest. Now, behind the post, I assessed the damage. When I touched the area of severe pain in my chest, I realized the bullet hadn't penetrated my Kevlar vest. I'd been so amped up since my cave adventure I had forgotten I was still wearing it. I reached down and pocketed one of the shell casings from the sniper rifle I fired. At some point,

Roan would use this weapon in another crime, and the casing for the M118LR bullet could come in handy. Of course, that was all based on the theory that I survived this.

Was the Assassin losing more blood than me? I hope so. I had to stop the bleeding in my arm. I pulled my shirt off and tied it tightly around my bicep. *Now what?* The sniper rifle was still on its stand to the right of me, but I couldn't afford to leave the protection of my concrete post and go to it. I noticed a chip on the barrel. The Assassin would have hit me directly in the head if the bullet hadn't first nicked the barrel of my rifle. I was damn lucky to be alive. I took my handgun out of my shoulder holster. It was the only weapon I had left. *I was in trouble.*

Chapter 62

SERENA FREDERICK

(1 hour and 10 minutes earlier)
5:30 P.M., THURSDAY, MARCH 14, 2024
FRUEN MILL 303 THOMAS AVENUE NORTH, MINNEAPOLIS

My ankle was tightly cuffed to the frame of a bed on the third floor. I could hear the incessant muffled voice of a man on the phone one floor below me. It had to be Enzo Angelini, the Wizard, setting up his sports bets. I never saw or heard the owner of the third car. I'm assuming it was the Assassin. Nico Larmarte was guarding me. He hadn't hurt me. It helped that I knew his name, as he assumed Catania would. I prayed that Jon was okay and he'd come looking for me.

Nico asked, "Do you want to play cards?"

"I want to think about the trouble you'll be in if anything happens to me." I did my best to emulate Catania Turrisi."

"Nothing personal, Ms. Turrisi. It's just business. You know that better than anyone."

After considering how Cat might respond, I rudely said, "Stop talking." It was in my best interest to say as little as possible, as conversation could get me in trouble.

"As you wish." He turned his back to me and sat at his desk, playing Mortal Combat on his laptop screen while I sat on the edge of the bed, waiting.

After watching Nico's playable character, Liu Kang, kicking to death one opponent after another, Nico finally stopped and sipped his energy drink. "Time to fight Shao Kahn." Nico unplugged the laptop and set the cord on the desk. He placed the laptop on his lap and said, "He's a beast, so wish me luck!" His character, Liu, was quickly defeated, and the bloodbath finally ended. Nico swore and then turned to me. "When I heard the stories of Cat kickin' ass, I pictured this big Italian woman. Not some five-foot woman with a paunch. I honestly thought you'd be bigger."

"I thought the same about you," I said with Catania-like sneer. Even though Nico had stopped playing, the game screen replayed one character after another, being beaten to death. Having seen enough, I told him, "I have to go to the bathroom."

Nico made two quick phone calls to warn that I was coming down. Nico's friends didn't want to be seen, which I considered a good sign for my survival.

On the way down, the Wiz opened his door slightly to peek at me as I passed. I purposely avoided looking his way. I hoped to hell he didn't get a good look.

A green Porta Potty sat outside the building we all occupied. In the Potty, I noticed some feminine products, and I wondered if there were other kidnapping victims who hadn't survived.

After I was escorted back up and cuffed to the bed again, Nico stepped away to take a call. I couldn't hear what was said, but Nico's glare suggested he wasn't happy. Nico approached me, backhanded me hard, and said, "You're not Catania Turrisi. Give me a reason to keep you alive."

"I'm pregnant and have two children at home." I swallowed hard.

"That's *your* reason, but it means nothing to me. You have no value to me, and you're fat."

"There are people who are going to miss me." I decided I was better off not revealing I'm married to a BCA investigator since

Nico lived a life that placed him at odds with law enforcement. "I swear, I'll never speak of this." I glanced around the room for something I could use as a weapon. The room was barren except for the desk, laptop, desk chair, and bed.

Lowering his voice, Nico said, "While I'm making up my mind, you're going to give me the best sex you're capable of giving a man. I'd prefer not to beat the shit out of you. I could, but it's not my preference. I'm going to uncuff you because if you leave this floor without me at your side, the Assassin will end your life. If you want to have a knock-down-drag-out battle with me, we can do that, but you'll lose the baby." He taunted, "How are you going to play it, mama?"

"Gentle." There was no way out. I needed to buy time. I would do whatever I had to do to be there for Nora and Jackson. They needed me as much as I needed them.

"I can do gentle. Lose the clothes," Nico directed.

"It's kind of hard with my foot cuffed to the bed."

He came closer, unlocked the cuffs, and yanked me to my feet. When I turned my back to him, he brushed against me from behind and kissed my neck. A cold, repulsed shudder ran down my spine. I didn't dare share what I was feeling. I pulled my blouse over my head to get his lips off me. He undid my bra.

I gestured to his laptop. "Do you mind if I put something else on?"

"What do you have in mind?"

"Porn would be better than watching blood shoot out of people's heads."

"Sounds good to me," he laughed.

With my back blocking his line of vision, I stepped toward the laptop and keyed in "porn." I moved just far enough to the side so he could view the screen. I needed to distract his attention for just a moment. I looked at my belly. *I'm sorry, baby. Please hang in there.* I grabbed the power cord off the desk and squeezed it into my hand.

Nico approached me from behind and resumed kissing my neck.

"Mmm, that's very erotic," I murmured as I rotated to face him. "Let me return the gesture." I turned to him. "Let me give your senses a taste of what I feel."

Nico slipped his shirt off. He pulled his gun from his jeans and tossed it on his shirt. With all the confidence a loaded gun can offer, he undid his jeans and said, "Work your way down. Then I'm bending you over the bed so I don't have to see your belly."

That was how Jack the Ripper killed his victims. He bent them over for sex and cut their throats from behind. I wasn't getting into that position. I stepped into him and offered, "Let me kiss the back of your neck first. Gentle," I reminded him.

He slowly turned his back to me, extending his arms straight out with the grace of the *port de bras* second movement in ballet. I quickly pulled the cord over his head, crossed my hands, and dropped with all my weight to tighten the noose.

Nico's immediate reaction was to pull against it, bending forward. Jon told me this was the mistake people commonly make. When Nico couldn't pull me over his head, he backed up as fast as he could to ram me into the wall.

As we approached it, I bucked my feet into the air and jumped forward off the wall, knocking him off balance, face first to the floor. I quickly knelt up and dug my knee into his back. I pulled with all my strength. He continued trying to grab at the cord as I relentlessly pulled as hard as I could, choking him.

It may have only been minutes, but it felt like an hour before he finally passed out. I pulled his hands behind his back and tied them tightly with the cord. I felt a sharp pain in my abdomen. *I'm sorry, baby. Please be okay.* When I looked up, there stood Roan Caruso. He looked at me curiously as he picked Nico's gun up off the floor.

I grabbed my bra and shirt and turned my back to him as I dressed. When done, I noticed Nico was coming back to consciousness.

THE SUN

Roan asked, "If I get you out of here alive, will you swear I was never here?'

"Yes, absolutely," I responded.

He looked down at Nico, who was awake and trying to work his hands out of his ties. Roan questioned, "Was this consenting?"

"No, not at all," I answered.

Nico rolled to his side and said, "Everest, all they've got is her word against mine."

"*BANG! BANG!*" I jumped back as Roan fired two bullets into Nico's chest. "Problem solved," Roan remarked.

"I wasn't going to kill him."

"I know. Our odds of getting out of here alive are less than fifty percent, but they just improved a little."

I took a deep breath. "One down, two to go."

"Two down. I strangled the Wizard with his tie. That piece of shit was going to kidnap my wife. And by the way, if we survive this, you can tell Jon I discovered that people *can* change. I said I'd put a bullet in the Wizard if he called me Everest again, and I strangled him instead."

I for damn sure wasn't ever going to say the word "Everest." I pointed out, "You did shoot this guy."

"Baby steps, right? We're a long way from out of the woods. The odds are better that the Assassin will kill all three of us than we will kill him. Jon took on the task of distracting him so I could get up here."

RAT-A-TAT-TAT. BANG! BANG! RAT-A-TAT-TAT. BANG! BANG! BANG! My heart raced as the spray of an automatic weapon, in combination with the exchange of gunfire, echoed below us.

Roan warned, "Be ready. You have a baby to save here, so you can't afford to spend a second grieving. You do what you must to survive. There's no shame in it."

"What are you talking about?" I asked nervously.

"Jon's not going to win a shootout with the Assassin. If he's dead, we're in trouble."

I was on Roan's heels as he hurried down the stairs to the second floor. He motioned for me to stay back as we approached the last set of steps above the ground floor. Over his shoulder, I could see that the Assassin was a woman. She had her helmet off and was sitting on the steps, wrapping tape tightly around her bleeding leg. She looked up and went for her gun.

Roan descended toward her as he fired *BANG! BANG! BANG! BANG! BANG! BANG! BANG! BANG! BANG! BANG!* until she finally slouched over. Now next to her, he put his gun to her forehead and fired a kill shot. *BANG!*

I wanted to throw up. *How could he kill people so callously?*

"They're all down!" Roan yelled.

As I rushed past him, I slipped on rubber bullets but managed to catch my balance. I felt tremendous relief when I saw Jon walking toward us, his bloody shirt wrapped around his arm. I ran to him and wrapped my arms around his chest.

"Are you okay?" Jon asked me.

"Yeah. I'll explain later." Honestly, I still can't believe I almost killed a mobster.

Roan laughed as he looked at the wire running to the M-17. "This is some MythBusters shit." He asked Jon, "Anybody back home who can fix your arm?"

"I'm stopping at a hospital. I need the wound cleaned out," Jon responded. "I'm not sure if it went straight into my arm or ricocheted off this dirty floor. I'll tell them I was at a shooting range, and a bullet I fired ricocheted back into me."

"Okay," Roan responded. "We good? Can you erase all of this?"

"Yes. You and I have a clean slate. Serena and I are not touching anything here. We're just leaving."

"That's my preference. Need any cash?" Roan asked.

"No," Jon said. "We're good. How does this end?"

"Do you really want to know?" Roan asked.

I shook my head "no," while Jon responded, "Yes. I want to know if people are going to figure out we were here."

"No." Roan shook his head. I'll make a call, and the Genovese family will have cleaners here in three hours. I'll tell them they kidnapped Cat, and the consigliere will respect that this shouldn't have happened with a made couple. The bodies will be discovered in a warehouse in New York so the families can bury them. And understand, if all three weren't dead, Serena would never be safe."

"Either would Lorenzo," Jon said.

"Or maybe I just helped you out of the goodness of my heart." Roan's smirk confirmed he needed the three dead, and my abduction allowed him to get help from Jon.

"I imagine the Disciples will take the cars off your hands," Jon said.

"Do business locally. That's our motto," Roan replied.

"We're done. No favors owed, all right?" Jon needed resolution.

"All good," Roan nodded. "*Arrivederci.*"

"For God's sake." Jon's shirt was soaking in blood. I took his good arm. "I need to get you to a hospital."

Chapter 63

JON FREDERICK

10:00 P.M.
ABBOTT NORTHWESTERN HOSPITAL, WOUND CARE CLINIC,
FOURTH FLOOR
800 EAST 28TH STREET, MINNEAPOLIS

The wound had been cleansed, and I was lying in my room. As an investigator, I know Abbott has one of the best gunshot wound clinics in the nation. My pain medicine left me feeling woozy. I hated being less stable and aware. Everything had slowed down—my thinking, movement, and responses.

Serena sat by me on the bed and explained the ordeal she'd been through.

It took me about ten seconds to get my response from my brain to my mouth. I told her, "You're amazing," but I could tell my expression had been dampened, and my words came out flat and unemotional.

Serena laughed and said, "Little slow with the return, honey, but that's to be expected. I would like to know if the baby's okay, but I can't afford to tell anyone. It would generate a mandated report."

I hit the nurse button on my bed and focused as best I could as I told her, "I love you. You're okay. That's a big improvement from where we were a couple of hours ago. We'll deal with it."

A nurse arrived in my room and asked, "Can I help you?"

THE SUN

"Yes," I responded. "We have a situation worse than mine. Before I was sighting my rifle by the rock pile, we had a cow go into labor. Serena helped. After the calf was born, the cow went nuts, and Serena had to hold the calf down to keep it from being hurt. It was a rigorous ordeal, and she's worried she might have hurt our baby."

Shocked, the nurse told Serena, "Come with me."

Serena shook her head at me and mouthed as she departed, "Holding down a cow?"

It was the best I could do in my drug-induced state.

The nurse commented, "Your clothes are pretty clean."

"I never leave home with afterbirth on my clothing," Serena responded.

10:45 P.M.

WHILE WAITING FOR her return, I drifted off into a lucid dream. I was back in the cave, terrified. The footsteps kept approaching, but it was pitch black, and I couldn't find my way out. I stumbled over bodies. No matter how fast I ran, the killer closed the distance between us until he was right behind me. I turned and saw him. It was Roan Caruso. And then I woke up.

At first, I dismissed the dream as a crazy byproduct of the oxys they'd given me. But logically, I realized Roan could have created the footsteps in the tunnel. I saw him outside the caves shortly after I exited. There had to be several secret entrances into the half-mile of caverns. Maybe I was trying to feel better about something I couldn't understand. I guess it doesn't make any difference now. I closed my eyes and drifted back to sleep.

When I woke, Serena was lying in my hospital bed, cuddled beside me. I brushed the hair out of her face and asked, "Are you okay?"

"Yeah." She placed her hand on my chest and guided mine to her stomach. "We're all okay."

"I love you, Serena. I would have died to let you live."

"I know. I'd like to say the same, but I'm carrying our baby, so it's a little more complicated. Nobody's dying, okay? That can't be an option."

"I'm thinking of quitting, Serena. I'm covering up three killings for a mobster. We can't have law enforcement doing that."

"You did it to save my life."

"And I'd do it again. But I don't feel like a legitimate officer of the law now. I'd find a way to keep our insurance as long as possible for the kids' sake."

"For the kids' sake?" Serena teased. "You're the one who needs insurance." She kissed me and said, "Okay. But you need to solve Taytum's murder first. If you still feel the same way once her killer is behind bars, I'll support you."

Serena was the sun in my life.

Her phone buzzed, and Serena got out of bed and stepped into the hall to take it. When she returned to the room, she said, "Someone burned down Vic and Maddie's garage. Now I know who killed Taytum Hanson." She crawled back in bed with me. "If you weren't in pain, I'd tickle you for using the clue, 'the sun.' Very clever."

Chapter 64

SERENA FREDERICK

9:30 A.M., MONDAY, MARCH 18, 2024
CARVER COUNTY JAIL, 606 EAST 4TH STREET, CHASKA

"Arise, fair sun, and kill the envious moon, who is already sick and pale with grief."
—WILLIAM SHAKESPEARE, *Romeo and Juliet*

Jon and I sat in a conference room at Carver County Jail, watching Paula Fineday's interview with Lorenzo Turrisi Caruso. I had done some work for the BCA in the past, and Paula had talked her supervisor into giving me a temporary assignment so I could participate in this interview with Jon. Paula has a manner of patiently weaving interviews until, eventually, even the most oppositional criminals reveal something unintended. An untrained viewer would assume nothing was accomplished during the first twenty minutes. While Lorenzo hadn't given anything up, he was becoming progressively more agitated and impatient. Twice during the interview, Paula intentionally referred to him as "Loren," and you could sense his smoldering anger at being disrespected when he corrected her. The beauty was that Lorenzo was too narcissistic to lawyer up. That would be accepting defeat.

Lorenzo finally yelled, "I didn't kill Taytum! She made the booty call, and I delivered!"

Paula sat back and waited for him to continue.

He managed to rein it in as he said, "Something was bothering Taytum. She didn't have her usual mojo. Looking back, it was like she had a sense of impending doom. But I didn't listen to her problems, and she didn't listen to mine. That's not what we were about. She told me Melanie was up for another round with me, so I went to the address Taytum gave me. But that vajajay wasn't interested, so I went home."

Jon glanced at me, and I explained, "Vajajay was *Grey's Anatomy*'s term for a woman's genitals back when you couldn't say 'vagina' on TV." We continued studying the video.

"You broke Melanie's nose," Paula interjected.

Lorenzo avoided eye contact with Paula as he responded, "My understanding is that it happened in a car accident."

"Let me know when you're ready to be honest. You returned to Taytum's. We have your Porsche on security camera footage." Paula tapped the table. "It's nice that you drive a car with a number circled in white on the side, so it stands out clearly on camera, even at night."

Gripping his fingers into a fist, Lorenzo clenched and stretched out his fingers repeatedly. "Is it a crime to *want* to kill someone if you don't actually kill them?"

"Sometimes. Tug Grant didn't *actually* kill his wife," Paula responded. "But we both know he arranged it."

"I had nothing to do with Taytum's murder."

"No one had more motive than you." Paula rubbed her forehead. "Taytum used you. She told the Inspector General about your dad's involvement in Medicare fraud based on information she received directly from you. You let your family down."

Jon and I knew that Taytum suspected Roan had something going on with medical companies, but she hadn't made the connection with Medicare. I had done that. Like Paula, we anxiously awaited Lorenzo's response.

"I knew Taytum was pumping information out of me and

THE SUN

turning it over to fraud investigators." Lorenzo quickly realized the next question would be *How did you know?* so he added, "Melanie told me that. But what I was telling Taytum wasn't true. Haven't you ever lied to someone to get a piece of ass?"

"I did tell someone he seemed like a nice guy," Paula said.

Jon and I smiled at Paula's remark.

"Don't put this on Melanie," Paula scolded him. "We've spoken to Melanie. She didn't have a clue about what you told Taytum. You heard from your dad that Taytum was talking to the Inspector General. Roan was the only one who had the inside information. If you didn't kill Taytum, it had to be Roan."

"Dad would never have killed Taytum that night. He's smarter than that."

"Why not *that night?*" Paula questioned.

"Because I told him I had sex with her. My DNA was at the scene. The killer set me up. It's my understanding that she had sex with two guys, but only my DNA was on the sheet,"

"So, it comes back to you, Lorenzo. Poor pitiful you," Paula taunted.

"After I heard Taytum was ratting me out—I was angry. I admit that," Lorenzo recklessly rattled off. "I drove back to confront her, but she was dead when I got there. So, I shot out of there like a bat out of hell."

"Where was Taytum when you entered?" Paula pondered. "What was she wearing?"

"Nothing." Lorenzo thought for a moment. "She was laying on the floor naked, spread eagle. Whoever nailed her after me must have killed her." He muttered under his breath, "Fucking whore."

"Let me get this straight. You left Taytum to have sex with another woman. But she's a whore for having another man over?" Paula questioned.

"It's different," Lorenzo responded.

"Is it? I guess it is. You were *her* sloppy second, and she didn't have to punch you to make you have sex."

"I'm done," Lorenzo growled as she stood.

"Were her clothes by her?" Paula rushed to squeeze in a couple more questions. Lorenzo could leave whenever he wanted.

"No. I don't think so. She was gross. Vomit on her face. It was obvious she'd OD'd. I just split."

"Why didn't you call the police?"

Lorenzo nervously looked down.

"You weren't 100% sure your dad hadn't killed her. It was only later you realized he hadn't." Paula suggested.

Remaining silent, he nodded in agreement as he exited.

As the video wrapped up, I asked Jon, "Do you think he's being honest?"

"Not about everything, but yes, regarding how he found her. He didn't kill Taytum."

We stepped into an interview room. An empty chair sat at the table across from us, waiting for the interviewee. I asked Jon, "Were there any fingerprints on the Doublemint wrapper?"

"No. Honestly, we don't have enough to get a conviction. I'm planning to overwhelm her with circumstantial evidence and pray we can get a confession. This is a one-shot endeavor, and it will only work if we convince her we have the case sewed up. I know this is a bit of a contradiction since we need to deceive her, but don't get caught in a lie."

"Okay." I shook my head and muttered, "The sun."

Paula escorted Juliet Kimball into the room and said, "I've already gone over the Miranda warning with her." Paula then stepped out to observe the interview from behind the mirrored glass.

I planned on letting Jon control the interview. Jon and I were very aware of each other's strengths. While I was better at connecting emotionally, he was skilled at eliciting confessions.

Juliet shrugged her shoulders and sat down. "You read my husband his rights, too, and he was home two days later." There was a sadness in her owlish eyes.

Jon said, "It must have been hard, after finally getting your husband back, to discover he was having a passionate affair with his attorney."

"Standing on the beach, watching," I added. Jon gave me a subtle glance, urging me to be careful. His words, *don't get caught in a lie*, echoed in my head. While I believed she followed Randy and watched him enter Taytum's house, I didn't know with certainty.

Juliet looked bothered, but she didn't deny it.

Jon pointed out, "You might have thought it was clever of you to take her phone and laptop to ensure the security recordings were gone. But that made it clear that the killer knew about security systems, much like a security officer would."

"If that's all you have, it's not much of a case," Juliet responded casually. She wasn't close to breaking.

Jon reached into his pocket and laid a plastic bag containing the Doublemint wrapper on the table. He said, "Too many mistakes, Juliet. First of all, poison is a woman's weapon. Give me the name of another woman who would have killed Taytum."

"Catania Turrisi," Juliet answered.

"True." Jon smiled, "But we both know Cat is one woman who would have beaten her to death. Taytum had taken on a new married lover, and you were the scorned wife. That's serious motive. Some would even argue—justified homicide. Second, because of your physical ailments, you couldn't move her body. A man would have thrown her in bed or buried her in the woods. But you didn't have the strength. You had to strip her exactly where she fell."

I interjected, "And the message you sent to the world was, 'Here lies a dead whore.' No clothes in sight."

Juliet's eyes glinted at receiving recognition for her positioning of the body. She was proud of having demeaned Taytum.

Jon added, "You did exactly what you would have done at home. Put your dishes in the dishwasher. Threw her silk pajamas in the washing machine. Do you remember what setting?"

"Delicates," she said softly.

It still wasn't a confession, but it was something.

Jon asked, "How many men would have thought of that? Taytum had changed the bedding before her next lover arrived, so you needed to take the bedding out of the washing machine to make room for her pajamas. You placed it in the dryer, appropriately on the bedding setting. And, by the way, Cat doesn't do laundry or dishes."

Juliet sighed heavily.

Trying to show some compassion, I finally spoke. "What Randy did would have infuriated any woman. This isn't a first-degree murder charge. It was a crime of passion." We needed more, so I decided to take a shot. I hoped to hell it didn't backfire. Jon and I had a friend in law enforcement in Morrison County, so I thought I'd use his name to pretend we knew something specific. "Juliet, Officer Tschida identified you in Little Falls at the time Vic's garage burned down. At one point, he was in an unmarked car next to you and recognized you from the news clips about Randy's sexual harassment case. You were at Randy's side." I avoided looking at Jon and prayed this lie wouldn't sink our case.

Juliet gave us a hard look and was silent for a full minute before she spoke. "Absolutely ridiculous—isn't it? I end up being caught by a man who invented a device that can recall old conversations from a room. At first, I thought Vic's story was crazy, but after hearing some of Jon's obsessive conversations, I realized he could have a brother who invented that kind of technology. Then when I saw the machine in the garage, I thought, 'Holy crap!' I needed to destroy it."

"You must have been so hurt," I added.

"It wasn't just that he was having an affair. Randy fell in love with her." Juliet spoke in the matter-of-fact tone of a woman who was all cried out. "Taytum didn't give a damn about destroying me or my marriage. She did the same to Debra Grant. Taytum was the one who destroyed Deb's marriage. At some point, a woman has to stand up and say, 'Enough.' I was that woman. I would call it justified femicide." She turned to the gum wrapper. "It's weird how habits are. I don't even remember taking out a piece of gum, but obviously I did. And it's going to get me convicted, isn't it?"

"You got the fentanyl from work," Jon added as if it were an established fact.

"Fantasies of killing Taytum gave me a reason to live. Then, a guy stumbles into the clinic who had taken a lethal dose of fentanyl. He was dying and at a point where it couldn't be stopped. He still had a couple of packets of the drug in his pocket. It was fate. I was weaponized. Even then, I gave Taytum one more chance. I asked her to stay away from him, and she acted like I was crazy—told me I had nothing to worry about. She was right. I was done worrying. It was time to act. On our Find My iPhone app, I watched Randy leave work early to go to Taytum's, and I followed. I stood on the beach while she screwed my husband. I thought about intervening but was afraid Randy would choose Taytum over me. And then I watched Randy agonizing as he paced up and down the sidewalk while her next lover took his turn. I couldn't help thinking that this young man was probably married too, and eventually, his wife would be me—miserable—destroyed. But I could save her."

"Did Randy ever figure out that you killed Taytum?" I asked.

"No," she said with a sardonic smile. "As smart as he is, he's always been as gullible as a child. That's why he drives that overpriced Audi." She looked up and, without emotion, said, "I'm not sorry. I don't regret killing Taytum."

We finally had the statement we needed for her conviction. "The sun" was what Romeo called Juliet. Jon knew I'd read the play. The killer wasn't clear to me until Juliet's paranoia led her to burn up Vic's old copy machine. Looking back, Jon had told me the killer would call and ask about the investigation, as Juliet had called me. My pregnancy brain hadn't put it together.

Chapter 65

JON FREDERICK

6:00 A.M., TUESDAY, MARCH 19, 2024
PIERZ

Serena and the kids were still sleeping when I got up for work. I kissed Serena and dressed in the dark to avoid waking her. It was early, and I had a stop to make before heading to my meeting in St. Paul. I walked the river on my parents' farm until I reached the bank where I used to sit and enjoy William Shakespeare, Charles Dickens, Charlotte Brontë, and Kurt Vonnegut twenty years ago. It was as if their ghosts inhabited this wilderness while I read. They weren't better days, but they were still meaningful.

The bright yellow sun was starting to rise on this cool morning. When we were teens and Serena broke up with me, I was convinced our desires and fate traveled parallel tracks. While we own our choices, our fate is determined by forces beyond our control—forces merciless to emotion, as painful as they were pleasurable.

But I don't see it that way anymore. Understanding that desires and fate aren't the same is important, but they're not entirely parallel. They wind and intersect like the famous photo Dr. Rosalind Franklin took of the double helix structure of DNA back in 1951. You love, you lose, get your heart broken, recover, and love again—rinse and repeat. But once you take control of your life, you hold the ends of the helices of desire and fate with the potential to pull the strands into a tight cable. Serena and I are solid and stronger together than we ever were alone. I'm a loving husband and father and an advocate of justice. Those values are unshakable. But am I an honest public servant? Not anymore.

I removed my badge from my billfold and studied it. It meant a lot to me, but I resented being asked to look the other way by my supervisor regarding Roan and felt guilty about ultimately agreeing to do so on my own. I did what I had to do to save Serena and my family, but I violated the public's trust in me. I've become exactly what I've criticized. It's only fitting that my decision to walk away from my work as a BCA investigator is finalized here. I loved this farm, and we lost it to bankruptcy when I was a teen. I tossed my badge into the river and walked back to my car. I loved my job, and I lost it, too.

8:30 A.M., BUREAU OF CRIMINAL APPREHENSION
1430 MARYLAND AVENUE EAST, ST. PAUL

PAULA FINEDAY AND I sat in front of Sean Reynolds's desk. Sean asked, "Where's Serena? I assumed she'd be here."

"Serena doesn't work for the BCA." She didn't have to abide by any of Sean's directions.

"A fact that only seems to come up when it's convenient for you." Sean sat back. "Before you say anything, I'd like to know how a BCA investigator ends up being treated for a gunshot wound when I haven't seen any incident reports."

"I wasn't injured at work," I stated. I was sighting in my rifle when a bullet ricocheted and went into my arm."

Sean turned to Paula. "Were you with him?"

"No. He'd just chased Lorenzo Turrisi Caruso out of the Wabasha Caves. It was impressive work. Jon looked exhausted, so I sent him home."

Sean studied me for a moment. "Okay, why did you need to meet?"

"I'm quitting."

Sean didn't respond. I imagined he felt a sense of relief.

Shocked, Paula asked, "What? Why?"

"It's just time for me to be done."

Paula gave me a careful once-over and then suggested, "Serena's having a baby. The state has to give you twelve weeks of paternity time. You have more than that in sick and vacation leave. Take the time off and decide after."

I considered her suggestion. If I burned up that time, I wouldn't have to start paying for my family's insurance until it ended. That might be the more prudent choice.

While I was pondering this, Sean commented, "I can finally come clean with you about Roan Caruso. The Department of Health and Human Services asked us to back off Roan until they close their case against Precision Lens. Precision Lens is getting fined $485 million for fraudulently billing Medicare. Serena had reported that Roan Caruso was giving physicians tickets to sporting events and concerts for making commitments to long-term orders from specific companies. Now, you can turn in all you have on Roan Caruso without consequences. We'd appreciate it if Serena would turn in her paperwork."

"We have no paperwork on Roan. Serena was asked by one of their investigators to hypothesize what Roan was doing, and she did. We haven't checked into Roan. That would be against the direct order you gave me. I have nothing on Roan. Serena has nothing on Roan."

Sean blew out a long breath before uttering, "All right." He clearly didn't believe me but said, "Heal that arm."

Paula walked with me out of the building. "I don't know what happened, but I'm guessing it was bad. Did you kill anybody?"

"No."

"You became one more person who can't make a statement against Roan Caruso. The man is a master."

"I don't owe Roan any favors. I just need out."

Paula looked at me in disbelief.

Chapter 66

JON FREDERICK

8:00 P.M., THURSDAY, MARCH 21, 2024
ESSENTIA HEALTH, ST. JOSEPH'S MEDICAL CENTER
523 NORTH 3RD STREET, BRAINERD

The degree to which mothers love their children cannot be overstated. Serena gave birth to our daughter, Cami Jane Frederick, today. Cami is named after my mother, Camille. Cami can mean either "broken nose" or "a force of nature." We're going with the latter. After witnessing the pain Serena went through in labor and knowing the period of depression she endured after each pregnancy, it makes one wonder why she ever does it. Her experience is not unlike that of many mothers. She does it because she's an altruistic and loving woman who wants to guide another person into becoming an empathic and vital member of humanity, someday guiding Cami more than she desires. At six pounds, Cami is a little bald peanut. Beautiful. Both Serena and the baby are doing well. While my brain races with thoughts of how we're going to make all this work, my heart is filled with joy. Thank you, God! The good guys win just often enough.

Cami was in the room, napping in her crib. Serena had slept briefly, and after awakening, we spoke briefly about the birth. At the foot of the bed, a mirror was sitting up on a chair facing

Serena. It must have been brought in when I briefly stepped out. I asked, "Why did they bring the mirror in?"

"The pain was killing me, and I couldn't get comfortable. A nurse suggested that it would help to see the progress I was making. She set up the mirror. Honestly, all I could see in the reflection was her ass."

"Did it help?" I teased.

She winced in pain as she giggled. "No, it didn't, but the epidural helped. What do you think Cami will be like?"

"I'd be okay if she turns out to be the Jane Eyre type. I loved Charlotte Brontë's line about Jane. 'I am no bird; and no net ensnares me; I am a free human being with an independent will.'"

"When we read classic literature to each other as teens, you never read Jane Eyre with me," Serena said.

"I was a teen smitten by the most beautiful girl in the world. Shakespeare and Dickens were safer. Do you realize how often people ejaculate in Brontë's book?"

"In the early 1800s, 'ejaculate' was a reference to something said quickly."

"I know," I grinned. "But it wasn't something I wanted to say in front of you. And there were sentences like, 'he uncrossed his legs and sat erect.' It wasn't sexual, but it was still awkward as a teen boy to read seriously in front of someone I was enamored with."

Serena smiled at me. "Jane Eyre is a great story about a strong woman."

"I agree, and Charlotte Brontë was incredibly insightful. After Jane dresses down a man, she contemplates that he could legally thrash her, but as a Christian, he doesn't. Brontë had the courage to consider the cleavage between what was legal and moral in the 1800s."

"Cleavage?" Serena raised an eyebrow.

"What?" I asked innocently. "In the 1800s, cleavage, created by cleavers, simply meant a divide. It wasn't until a century later that cleavage was used in reference to breasts." Cleavers have gone extinct, but cleavage remains rampant.

Serena closed her eyes and, with a tired smile, asked, "Do you remember any of the superfluous lines?"

"I particularly liked where the guy walks in with dirt on his shoes and warns, 'I shall sully the purity of your floor.' And when Jane is worried she can't finish her meal, she says, 'I'm a woman of average gastronomical features placed at a feast for one hundred.'"

Serena's tired eyes opened, "We *have* to play the chance meeting game using some of this old-school dialogue. I want to wear one of those Jane Austin Regency dresses with the puffy shoulders."

"And about four layers," I reminded her.

"My undergarments will be comfort-based. I could make declarations, like Jane told the Parson, 'I am not an angel, and I will not be one till I die: I will be myself. You must neither expect nor exact anything celestial of me.'"

"You are a star to me." I bent down and kissed her.

"For the last two months, I've been the shape of a planet," Serena remarked.

"And as far as celestial behavior from me, I did moon you once."

"I'm still in too much pain to laugh," Serena winced and smirked simultaneously. "I've seen more moons from you than Saturn has."

"Saturn has 146 moons."

"That's all? Then it's not even close." Cami started to stir, and Serena gestured for me to deliver our beautiful baby daughter to her.

Chapter 67

SERENA FREDERICK

7:00 P.M., SATURDAY, MARCH 30, 2024
PIERZ

Bundled up in parkas and mittens, Heather Hilton and I sat by a blazing fire, enjoying hot cocoa. Jon was busy entertaining baby Cami, Jackson, and Nora inside. After a mostly snowless winter, we got ten inches of snow less than a week ago. Now, it was forty-five degrees, and the snow was all melting.

Juliet Kimball was in Carver County Jail, charged with first-degree murder and arson. Heather was defending her. She told me, "We've already got a plea deal in place. Juliet pleaded down to second-degree murder and will be sentenced to twelve years in Shakopee State Prison, which is the recommended sentencing guideline. She'll serve eight."

"Wow," I responded. Second-degree murder is intentional but not premeditated. It's used in "heat of the moment" homicides. "That's a pretty good deal."

"She's got a great attorney," Heather gloated.

"As long as you don't become the next attorney involved with Randy."

"Not my type. He did flirt with me. I told him, 'Randy, if I had been in Juliet's shoes, I would have killed *you*.' That pretty much extinguished the fire."

"I enjoy your directness."

"I think 'abrasiveness' is the word you're looking for. Thank you for the referral," Heather said with genuine sincerity.

Chapter 68

MELANIE PEARSON

7:30 A.M., FRIDAY, MAY 3, 2024
NORTHEAST JACKSON STREET, MINNEAPOLIS

Ricky has taught me about making amends. We can't fix what we damage, but we can help mend broken people. I wrote a long letter to Sophie apologizing for my behavior. I should have told her I was returning to work for Tug to prosecute him. I didn't want her to talk me out of it. When everyone else abandoned me, Sophie was the one friend who stood by me, and I had lied to her. I told her I understood her need to walk away and even respected her for it. She responded by getting me my job back at Target and picking me up to ride with her to work every morning. Ricky's house is only three miles from work. Sophie's friendship is everything to me at this moment.

My therapist told me my "comeback story" started when I was honest with Ricky about my night with Lorenzo. Looking back, I know my self-confidence took a nosedive when I didn't stand up for Cade at age fourteen. Sebastian was kind, but there was a distance between us, which was, at least partially, on me. I was afraid to let someone know me. And then Tug, Darius, and Lorenzo saw my vulnerability and jumped all over it. I thought I needed a strong man to build me up. Instead, they tore me down further. I was initially attracted to Ricky because I thought he

THE SUN

was cut from the same cloth, but luckily, he wasn't. So, I tested him again and again. Instead of exploding, he stepped back and asked how he could raise me up. While I was looking for a way to die, Ricky was begging for an opportunity to live—to prove himself worth loving. My dependent personality had placed my morality in the hands of ruthless men. I'm proud that I stood up to Lorenzo, even if he broke my nose. The permanent bump I see in the mirror from the fracture reminds me that I am resilient. I won that fight. I haven't heard a word from him since I reported Lorenzo's behavior to Roan.

I heard a car pull up. I grabbed my tumbler of tea and headed to the door. I watched, frozen, as the lock slowly turned. My first thought was, *Lorenzo is back. How did he get a key?*

The door opened. It wasn't Sophie, and it wasn't Lorenzo.

Ricky Day stood in all his glory directly in front of me. I pinched myself to make sure it wasn't a dream. I rushed into his arms and squeezed him tight. Finally, I asked, "What are you doing here?"

"I live here," he said with a grin. "I agreed to ninety days for the violation. It's now been ninety days."

"Why didn't you tell me?"

He closed the door and led me by the hand to his couch. "You made me realize my loving you can't fix you. That's something you have to do. So, I thought I'd see what you do in those ninety days and then decide if I can afford to be with you. You got sober, got into therapy, found full-time work, made amends with Sophie, paid my rent, and visited me at every available opportunity. That's pretty perfect."

Part of it was because I have a dependent personality disorder, but that wasn't essential to share at this moment. At this moment, I'm happier than I've ever been in my life. "I'm taking a sick day—lovesick."

"I'm taking a shower," Ricky said. "Do what you need to do. I'll be here."

"I should call Sophie."

"Sophie knows I'm here. I asked for her permission to date you again. I didn't want to if I'm bad for you, and I thought Sophie is the closest thing you have to family."

"What did she say?"

"She gave me permission but said it's your call. Sophie said she won't be stopping this morning. Call her later."

"That's a little presumptuous." Sophie knew me well. I grinned. "I think I need a shower, too."

Chapter 69

SERENA FREDERICK

9:40 P.M., SATURDAY, MAY 18, 2024
BLUE LINE SPORTS BAR & GRILL
1101 2ND STREET SOUTH, SARTELL

I talked Jon into playing our chance meeting game tonight at the Blue Line in Sartell. Jon wore a long-sleeved waffle pattern sand-colored shirt and faded jeans. Looking as strong and fit as ever, he sipped a glass of Fat Tire amber ale. His left bicep was still bandaged underneath his sleeve, so it puffed out a little. Jackson was a little jealous of the new baby, and Jon had re-opened the bullet wound by scooping Jackson up before he had permission from the doctor to lift that amount of weight, but Jon's arm was finally healing. He was talking to some young men at the bar about the Vikings' need to sign Justin Jefferson.

I wore a faded seafoam-green blouse with an embroidered floral design. It was cut lower than I typically wear, but I wouldn't say it was quite "low cut." Motherhood has been kind to my breasts. I stepped between Jon and the men and ordered a Buffalo Chicken Sandwich, a Redline burger, and sweet potato fries to go.

Jon asked, "Hungry?"

"Do you have a problem with it?"

"No," he replied. "I like a woman with an appetite for life."

I gently touched his padded bicep. "Stuffing your shirt?"

"No. Dating injury. My ex is a martial arts specialist. She saw me put my arm around another woman and broke it."

"It sounds like the two of you had a very caring relationship."

"She was just using me. Made me dance for her wearing nothing but thick winter socks."

We had the undivided attention of the men Jon had been conversing with. Wide-eyed, they sipped their beers, saying nothing.

"What type of design?" I asked.

"Mostly choreographed musical numbers," Jon responded.

I couldn't hold back my laughter. "I meant on the socks."

"Snowflakes."

"Hmm." In my sultriest voice, I said, "I like that. Was she a podophobe? One of those people who fears bare feet? Avoids beaches and pools?"

"Maybe," Jon casually responded. "And now I'm a man deathly afraid of socks." He raised his pant leg to reveal no stockings beneath his Hey Dude slip-ons.

"Kaltsaphobia is the term for fear of stockings. Lucky for you, I have a minor in psychology, and I can help you. But first, I'd like to know what else you have going on. Where do you work?"

"I don't. Quit my job."

"Why? Conscientious objector to the work?"

"No. Didn't like my boss."

"Bad dude?"

"Not really."

"Sounds like a well-thought-out decision," I teased. "What can you do with one arm?"

"I can still dance. And surprisingly, I'm quite good at holding and changing a baby."

"Now you're speaking my language. Can you sing to a baby?"

"Yes. I'm actually quite terrible. It's so bad the moms cry, but it seems to have a calming effect on babies. Infants must be capable of experiencing pity quite young."

"How does it work with colicky babies?"

THE SUN

"Calms them down like that." Jon snapped his fingers.

"You might be the man I've been looking for." I smiled. "And I can help you. Phobias are maintained by avoidance. If you're up to it, I will work you through your fear. It will only cost you the tab on my takeout order."

"What are you thinking?" Jon asked. "Systematic desensitization or exposure therapy? First, showing me a picture of socks. Then, bringing socks into the room. Gradually moving them closer…"

"No. I was thinking of a combination of flooding and indecent exposure therapy. I'll have you strip and put five pairs of socks on. You'll probably have a panic attack and pass out, but once you come to, you'll realize you won't die from a panic attack, and you'll be on the road to recovery. I'll strip, too, as a form of counterconditioning. To get you to think about something incongruent with fear."

"That will work!" Jon eagerly responded.

Penny handed me my order.

Jon left cash and a generous tip on the bar for the excellent service.

I pulled Jon close, and we kissed.

The men next to Jon stood dumbfounded.

Jon turned to them and said, "I need to go. I have a mental health emergency to address."

I took his hand and escorted him out of the bar.

8:40 P.M., MONDAY, MAY 20, 2024
PIERZ

MY LOVE FOR Jon started decades ago when, as teens, we sat on the banks of a lazy country river reading *Great Expectations*. When he gazed into my eyes and with innocent honesty recited, *I loved her against reason, against promise, against peace, against hope, against happiness, against all discouragement that could be,* I knew that I loved him with every ounce of my being.

But life is never a smooth, simple road, and we separated and reunited. Through mindful listening and forgiveness, here we are, more solid than ever. Maturity and love have given me tranquility in my home. There is something about raising children together that deepened my love and appreciation for him. Jon is my man forever. My lover, my best friend, and someone who would search the ends of the earth for me or our children if needed. Perhaps save me one more time with some weird wire trick.

Our involvement in the Minneapolis Combination saga began with our desire to have extra money for another child. The peacefulness of our home is such a contrast to the end of that case. I had this baby with me while I strangled a mafia killer. I can never put a child at such risk again. I kissed Cami's head. *I'm sorry, honey.* The top of a baby's head is what heaven smells like. From the moment that fight ended until Cami's birth, I thought for sure I'd lose my baby. Suffering is a hard teacher.

It's hard for me to read an Anne Frank quote without becoming teary-eyed, but this particular quote has always stuck with me: "I've found that there is always some beauty left—in nature, sunshine, freedom, in yourself... No one has ever become poor by giving. I don't think of all the misery, but of the beauty that still remains." God bless you, Anne!

Cami had just finished breastfeeding and drifted off into a peaceful slumber as I gently rocked her. The sun was setting in hues of red and orange through the nursery window in our country home. Cami took a deep breath and twitched her nose but remained sleeping. As the sun set, I envisioned walking with my husband out of the ruins of the Fruen Mill—my man shirtless and wounded—into the broad expanse of the tranquil sunlight that warmed our home at this moment. We were healing, tenderly in love, and more devoted than ever. Our family was gratifying, whimsical, and content. There would be no shadow over Jon and me again—just sun.

The End

ABOUT THE AUTHOR

Frank F. Weber is a forensic psychologist specializing in homicide, sexual assault and domestic abuse cases. He uses his unique understanding of how predators think, knowledge of victim trauma, and expert testimony in writing his true crime thrillers. Frank has been interviewed on investigative shows and profiled cold case homicides. His novels have earned numerous awards. Frank is the 2024 recipient of the Outstanding Achievement Award from MN Psychological Association and received the President's Award from the MN Correctional Association for his forensic work.

Frank, and Brenda (his wife/life partner/love) started CORE Professional Services in 1995 and have worked with the some of the greatest professionals on earth. They are both thankful for every person at CORE who has assisted with creating a program that helped thousands of former offenders transition back into the community after incarceration. We help people who struggle develop healthy happy lives, as do so many of you by daily acts of kindness.